ROSAMUNDE PILCHER

**A WRITER WHOSE BOOKS ARE CHERISHED
BY READERS TODAY AND DESTINED TO BE
CLASSICS TOMORROW**

"Pilcher's stories feature genuine characters whose conflicts are resolved in conclusive, satisfying ways."
—*Booklist*

"Descriptions of people, places, and things have a definite charm and fascination. [She] adds touches of eccentricity and individuality to houses and rooms as well as to their occupants. By the time her stories are finished, you have found there's a touch of drama in everyone."
—*WEBR newsradio*

"Pilcher conveys relationships and landscapes with understated poignancy."
—*San Francisco Examiner-Chronicle*

"Pilcher has a gift for creating warm and appealing characters."
—*Library Journal*

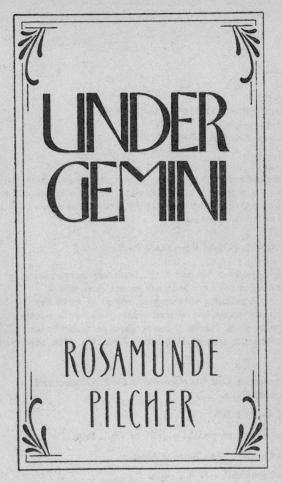

UNDER GEMINI

ROSAMUNDE PILCHER

A DELL BOOK

Published by
Dell Publishing
a division of
Bantam Doubleday Dell Publishing Group, Inc.
666 Fifth Avenue
New York, New York 10103

ISBN: 0-440-20249-3

Reprinted by arrangement with St. Martin's Press, Inc.

Printed in the United States of America

Printed simultaneously in Canada

April 1989

20

RAD

I

ISOBEL

He stood at the window, with his back to her, framed by the faded curtains which she had chosen forty years before. The sun had bleached their bright roses to a faded pink, and the linings were so threadbare that they could no longer be sent to the cleaners for fear of total disintegration. But she loved their familiarity like that of old friends. For years her daughter Isobel had been trying to persuade her to buy new ones, but "They'll see me out," Tuppy had said, without thinking very much about it. "They'll see me out."

And now it seemed that they were going to do just that. She was seventy-seven and, after a lifetime of unblemished health, had gardened too late and too long, and had caught a chill which turned into pneumonia. She didn't remember very much about the pneumonia—only that when she emerged from what felt like a long dark tunnel of sheer discomfort, the doctor was calling three times a day and there was a nurse installed to take care of Tuppy. The nurse, a widow from Fort William, was

called Mrs. McLeod. She was tall and thin, with a face like a
reliable horse, and wore navy blue uniforms with a starched bib
to her apron that made her flat chest look like a slab, and shoes
that went on forever. Her unprepossessing appearance notwith-
standing, she was very kind.

So now the business of dying was no longer a remote and
unconsidered possibility, but a cold and immediate fact.

It did not frighten her in the very least, but it was inconve-
nient. Her thoughts slid, as they so easily did these days, back
into the past, and she remembered herself as a young wife,
twenty years old, realizing that for the first time she was pregnant. And she had been annoyed and frustrated because it
meant that by December she would be round and large as the
Albert Hall and unable to go to any of the Christmas dances,
and her mother-in-law had comforted her briskly by saying,
"There is never a convenient time to have a baby." Perhaps
dying was like that, too. You just had to take it when it came.

It had been a brilliant morning, but now the sun had gone
in and a cold light filled the window beyond the doctor's bulk.
"Is it going to rain?" Tuppy asked.

"More like a sea mist," he told her. "You can't see the
Islands. Eigg disappeared about half an hour ago."

She looked at him, a big man, solid as a rock, comforting
in his well-worn tweeds, standing there with his hands in his
pockets as though he had nothing more urgent to do. He was a
good doctor, as good as his father had been, though at first it
was disconcerting to be taken care of and ordered about by
someone you had known as a small sturdy boy in shorts, with
his knees covered with grazes and sand in his hair.

Now, as he stood in the light she noticed with a pang that
that hair was beginning to gray, just at the temples. This made
her feel older than anything, even the thought of dying.

"You're going gray," she told him with some asperity, as
though he had no right to take such liberties.

He turned, smiling ruefully, putting up a hand to his head.

"I know. The barber pointed it out the other day."

"How old are you?"

"Thirty-six."

"Just a boy. You shouldn't be going gray."

"Perhaps it's the wear and tear of looking after you."

He wore, beneath the tweed jacket of his suit, a knitted pullover. It was becoming unraveled at the neck, and there was a hole in the front in need of mending. Tuppy's heart bled for him. He was uncared-for, unloved. And he shouldn't be here at all, buried in the West Highlands, tending to the day-to-day ailments of a community of herring fishers and a handful of scattered crofters. He should be in London or Edinburgh, with a tall important house and a Bentley at the pavement, and a specialist's plate on the door. He should be teaching or doing research—writing papers and making medical history.

He had been a brilliant student, marvelously enthusiastic and ambitious, and they had all known that ahead of him lay a glittering career. But then he had met that silly girl in London; Tuppy could scarcely remember her name. Diana. He had brought her back to Tarbole and nobody could stand her, but all the objections his father had raised merely stiffened his determination to marry her. (That was in character. Hugh had always been stubborn as a mule and opposition only made him more so. His parent should have recognized this. He handled it all wrong, thought Tuppy, and if old Dr. Kyle had been alive now and available, she would have told him so, mincing no words.)

The misalliance had finally culminated in tragedy, and when it was all over, he had picked up the pieces of his shattered life and come home to Tarbole to take over from his father.

Now he lived alone, like any cheerless, aging bachelor. He was working too hard, and Tuppy knew that he took a good deal less care of himself than he did of his patients, and that more often than not, his supper was a glass of whisky and a pie from the local pub.

She said, "Why doesn't Jessie MacKenzie mend that jersey for you?"

"I don't know. Perhaps I forgot to ask her."

"You should get married again."

As though deliberately changing the subject, he came back to her bedside. At once the small curled-up ball of fur at the end of Tuppy's bed resolved itself into an elderly Yorkshire terrier, rearing up from the eiderdown like a cobra and growling ferociously with a great show of teeth sadly depleted by age.

"Sukey!" Tuppy reproved, but the doctor was undismayed.

"It wouldn't be Sukey if she didn't threaten to tear my throat out every time I came near you." He put out a friendly hand, and the growls rose in a tremendous crescendo. He stooped to pick up his bag. "I must go."

"Who are you going to see now?"

"Mrs. Cooper. And then Anna Stoddart."

"Anna? What's wrong with Anna?"

"Nothing's wrong with Anna. In fact, all is right with Anna. To break a professional confidence, she's going to have a baby."

"*Anna* is? After all this time?" Tuppy was delighted.

"I thought that would cheer you up. But don't say anything about it. She wants to keep it a secret, for the time being at any rate."

"I won't breathe a word. How is she?"

"Fine so far. Not even sick in the mornings."

"I'll keep my fingers crossed for her. Oh, she must keep this child. You'll take good care of her, won't you? What a silly question, of course you will. Oh, I *am* pleased."

"Now. Is there anything else you want?"

She eyed him and the hole in his sweater, and her thoughts moved naturally from babies to weddings, and so, inevitably, to her grandson Antony. She said, "I'll tell you what I want. I want Antony to bring Rose to see me."

". . . Is there any reason why he shouldn't?"

His hesitation in replying was so slight that Tuppy told herself she had imagined it. She sent him a sharp glance, but he did not meet it, being occupied with the balky fastening of his bag.

"It's a month now since they got engaged," she went on.

"And I want to see her again. It's five years since she and her mother stayed at the Beach House, and you know, I can scarcely remember what she looks like."

"I thought she was in America."

"Oh, she was. She went out after they got engaged. But Antony led me to believe that she'd be back in this country by now. He said he'd bring her up to Scotland, but that's about as far as it's got. And I want to know when they intend getting married, and where. There's such a lot to discuss and settle, and every time I ring Antony up he just sits there in Edinburgh and makes soothing noises. I hate being soothed. I find it very irritating."

He smiled. "I'll speak to Isobel about it," he promised.

"Get her to give you a glass of sherry."

"I told you, I have to go and see Mrs. Cooper." Mrs. Cooper was the Tarbole postmistress and a strict teetotaler. "She's got a low enough opinion of me anyway, without my breathing alcoholic fumes all over her."

"Stupid woman," said Tuppy. They smiled, in complete accord, and he went away and left her, closing the door behind him. Sukey crept up the bed and curled herself into the curve of Tuppy's arm. The window sash rattled slightly as, outside, a wind got up. She looked at the window and saw the misting of rain on the pane. It would soon be lunchtime. She slipped down on the pillows and drifted, as she so easily did these days, back into the past.

Seventy-seven. What had happened to the years? Old age seemed to have taken her unaware and totally unprepared. Tuppy Armstrong was not old. Other people were old, like one's own grandmother, or characters in books. She thought of Lucilla Eliot, in *The Herb of Grace*. The epitome, one would have thought, of a perfect matriarch.

But Tuppy had never liked Lucilla. She thought her possessive and domineering. And she abhorred the snobbery of Lucilla's beautifully cut black frocks. Tuppy had not owned a beautifully cut black frock in the whole of her life. A lot of pretty dresses, certainly, but never a beautifully cut black frock.

Most of the time she existed contentedly in antique tweed skirts
and cardigans with darns in the elbows: sturdy, indestructible
clothes which did not object to a spot of rose pruning or a
sudden shower of rain.

And yet, on the appropriate occasion there was nothing
like the old blue velvet dinner dress for making one feel rich
and feminine. Especially if you splashed some eau de cologne
around and jammed the old-fashioned diamond rings over the
arthriticky joints of your fingers. Perhaps when Antony
brought Rose they would have a dinner party. Nothing elaborate. Just a few friends. She imagined the white Irish linen mats
and the silver candlesticks and a centerpiece of creamy Peace
roses.

An enthusiastic hostess, she began to plan. And if Antony
and Rose were to be formally married, then a list must be made
of guests to be asked on the Armstrong side of the family.
Perhaps Tuppy should do that now and give it to Isobel, so that
Isobel should know who to ask. Just in case . . .

Suddenly, it didn't bear thinking about. She drew Sukey's
little body tightly to hers and kissed the top of the bedraggled,
slightly smelly head. Sukey aimed a cursory lick in her direction and went back to sleep. Tuppy closed her eyes.

Descending, Dr. Hugh Kyle reached the turn of the stairs
and there stopped, his hand on the banister. He was troubled.
Not solely for Tuppy, but also on account of the conversation
he had just had with her. As he stood there, a preoccupied,
solitary figure neither upstairs nor down, his anxieties and responsibilities were mirrored on his frowning face.

Below him the big hall stood empty. At the far side, glass
doors gave onto the terrace, the sloping garden, and the sea, all
drowned now in mist. He saw the polished floors, the worn
rugs, the old chest with its copper bowl of dahlias, the slowly
ticking grandfather clock. There were as well other, less pictur-
esque bits of evidence of Armstrong family life: Jason's battered
tricycle, pulled in out of the rain; the dogs' baskets and their
drinking bowls; a pair of muddy gumboots, abandoned until

such time as their owner remembered to put them away in the cloakroom. To Hugh, it was all familiar from the beginning of time, for he had known Fernrigg all his life. But now it seemed as though the very house was waiting and watching for news of Tuppy.

There did not seem to be anybody about, although this was not surprising. Jason was at school; Mrs. Watty would be in the kitchen, busy with lunch. Isobel—he wondered where he would find Isobel.

Just as the question entered his mind, he heard her footsteps coming across the drawing room floor, and the scratch of Plummer's paws on the patches of parquet between the rugs. The next moment she appeared through the open door, with the fat old spaniel hard on her heels.

She saw Hugh at once, and stopped dead, tilting back her head to look up at him. They stared at each other and then, recognizing his own anxieties reflected in her eyes, he hastily pulled himself together, rearranging his features into an expression of robust cheerfulness.

"Isobel, I was wondering where I'd find you."

She said, in no more than a whisper, "Tuppy?"

"Not too bad." Swinging his bag, his other hand in his trouser packet, he came downstairs.

"I thought . . . When I saw you standing there . . . I thought . . ."

"I'm sorry, I was thinking about something else. I didn't mean to give you a fright. . . ."

She was unconvinced, but she tried to smile. She was fifty-four, the gawky stay-at-home daughter who had never married, instead spilling the intensity of her affection onto her mother, the house, the garden, her friends, her dog, her nephews, and now Jason, the little great-nephew who had come to live at Fernrigg House while his parents were abroad. Her hair, which had been flaming red when she was a girl, was now sandy and streaked with white, but the style had not changed as long as Hugh could remember. Nor had the expression on her face, still child-like and innocent, perhaps on account of the sheltered life she had led. Her eyes were blue as a child's and sensitive as the sky on a squally day, reflecting every emotion like a mirror: shining with pleasure, or brimming with the tears over which she had never had any control.

Now, looking up at him, they were filled with anguish, and it was obvious that Hugh's hearty manner had done nothing to reassure her.

"Is she . . . is she going to . . . ?" Her lips could not, would not, frame the dreaded word. He put a hand beneath her elbow and ushered her firmly back into the drawing room and shut the door behind them.

"She may die, yes," he told her. "She's not a young woman and she's taken a battering. But she's tough. Like an old heather root. She has a good chance of pulling through."

"I can't bear the thought of her being an invalid—not being able to get about and do all the things she wants to do. She would hate it so much."

"Yes, I know. I do know."

"What can we do?"

"Well . . ." He cleared his throat, running a hand down the back of his neck. "There is one thing which I think would cheer her up, and that would be for Antony to come over and perhaps bring that girl he's engaged to . . ."

Isobel rounded on him. She, too, could remember him as a little boy, and sometimes a very tiresome one. "Hugh, don't call her 'that girl' in that horrid way. She's Rose Schuster and you know her as well as we all do. Not that that's very well, I admit, but at least you do know her."

"I'm sorry." Isobel was always fiercely protective of any person even remotely connected with the family. "Rose, then. I think Tuppy's longing to see her again."

"We all are, but she's been with her mother in America. The trip was all planned before she and Antony got engaged."

"Yes, I know, but she may be back by now. And Tuppy's fretting about it. Perhaps Antony could be nudged a little, persuaded to get Rose north and bring her over, even if it's only for a weekend."

"He always seems to be so *busy*."

"I'm sure if you explained the situation. . . . Tell him that perhaps it would be better not to put it off too long."

As he feared, Isobel's eyes became instantly bright with tears. "You *do* think she's going to die." Already she was fumbling up her sleeve for a handkerchief.

"Isobel, I didn't say that. But you know how Tuppy is about Antony. He's more of a son than a grandchild. You can see how much it means to her."

"Yes. Yes, I do see." Bravely Isobel blew her nose and stowed away her handkerchief. Searching for some diversion, her eyes alighted on the sherry decanter. "Have a drink."

He laughed, easing the tension. "No, I won't, thank you. I'm going to see Mrs. Cooper. She's got palpitations again, and they'll worsen if she thinks I've been drinking."

Isobel smiled, too, despite herself. Mrs. Cooper had always been something of a family joke. Together they went out of the room and across the hall. Isobel opened the front door onto the chill of the damp, mist-shrouded morning. The doctor's car, parked at the foot of the steps, was wet with rain.

He said, "And promise to ring me if you're the least bit worried."

"I will. But with Nurse here, I know I won't worry so much."

It was Hugh who had insisted that they get a nurse. Otherwise, he said, Tuppy must go into a hospital. On being faced with the daunting prospect of a resident nurse, Isobel's mind had shot off at panicky tangents. Tuppy must be very ill; and where would they find a nurse? And would Mrs. Watty raise objections? And would there be umbrage taken and bad feeling in the kitchen?

But Hugh had seen to it all. Mrs. Watty and Nurse had made friends, and Isobel was able to sleep at nights. He was, in truth, a tower of strength. Seeing him off Isobel asked herself, perhaps for the hundredth time, what they would all do without him. She watched him get into his car and drive away, down the short drive between the sodden rhododendrons, past the lodge where the Wattys lived, and through the white gates which were never closed. She waited until he had gone. The tide was at the flood, and she could hear the gray waves breaking against the rocks below the garden.

She shivered, and returned indoors to phone Antony.

The telephone in the old-fashioned house stood in the hall. Isobel sat on the chest, and looked up the number of Antony's office in Edinburgh. She could never remember telephone numbers and had to look up even the most day-to-day people, like the grocer, and the man at the railway station. With one eye on the book, she dialed carefully and sat waiting for someone to reply. Her thoughts, anxious, darted in all directions: the dahlias would be dead tomorrow; she must pick some more; would Antony have already gone out for lunch? She mustn't be selfish about Tuppy. There was a time for everybody to die. If she could no longer work in her precious garden nor take Sukey for little walks, then she would not want to live. But what an unbearable void she would leave in all their lives! Despite herself, Isobel prayed wildly. *Don't let her die. Don't let us lose her just yet. Oh, God, be merciful unto us . . .*

"McKinnon, Carstairs, and Robb. Can I help you?"

She was jerked back to reality by the bright young voice. Feeling for her handkerchief again, she wiped her eyes and composed herself. "Oh, I am sorry, I wondered if it would be possible to speak to Mr. Armstrong. Mr. Antony Armstrong."

"Who's speaking, please?"

"Miss Armstrong. His aunt."

"Just a moment."

There came a couple of clicks, a pause, and then, wonderfully, Antony's voice. "Aunt Isobel."

"Oh, Antony . . ."

He was immediately alert. "Is anything wrong?"

"No. No, not wrong." She mustn't give a false impression. She must pull herself together. "Hugh Kyle's been. He's just left."

"Is Tuppy worse?" Antony asked bluntly.

"He . . . he says she's holding her own wonderfully. He

says she's as strong as an old heather root." She tried to make it light-hearted, but her voice let her down woefully. She could not get out of her mind that deeply grave expression that she had caught on Hugh's face. Had he really been telling her the truth? Had he been trying to spare her in some way? "He . . . he had a few words with Tuppy, though, and it seems that all she wants is to see you, and for you to bring Rose over. And I wondered if you'd heard from Rose—if she was back from America?"

There was only silence from the other end of the line, and trying to fill it, Isobel rattled on.

"I know how busy you always are, and I don't want to worry you. . . ."

"That's all right." Antony spoke at last. "Yes. Yes, she is back in London. I had a letter from her this morning."

"It means so much to Tuppy."

Another pause, and then steadily, Antony asked, "Is she going to die?"

Isobel couldn't help it. She dissolved into tears, furious with herself, but unable to check them. "I . . . I don't know. Hugh tried to reassure me, but I've never seen him look so concerned. And it would be so dreadful, unthinkable really, if anything should happen to Tuppy and she had never seen you and Rose together. It meant so much to her, your getting engaged. If you could bring Rose, perhaps it would make all the difference. It would give her a reason . . ."

She couldn't go on. She hadn't meant to say so much, and she could see nothing through the tears. She felt defeated, at the end of her tether, and as though she had been alone for too long. She blew her nose again and finished helplessly. "Do try, Antony."

It was a cry from the heart. He said, sounding almost as shaken as she did, "I didn't realize . . ."

"I think I've only just realized myself."

"I'll get hold of Rose. Somehow, I'll fix it. We'll be over next weekend. I promise."

"Oh, Antony." Relief washed over her. They would come.

If Antony said he would do something, he always kept his word, come hell or high water.

"And don't be too worried about Tuppy. If Hugh says she's as tough as a heather root, she probably is. She'll run rings round the lot of us, and most likely outlive us all."

Immensely comforted, Isobel raised a little laugh. "Well, it's not beyond the bounds of possibility."

"Nothing is," said Antony. "Anything can happen. See you next weekend."

"Bless you."

"Think nothing of it. And my love to Tuppy."

2

MARCIA

Ronald Waring said, perhaps for the fifth time, "We should go home."

His daughter Flora, bemused with sun and sleepy from swimming, said, "I know," also for the fifth time, and neither of them moved. She sat perched on a sloping face of granite, staring down into the jewel-blue depths of the immense rock pool in which they had had their evening swim. The sun, sliding down out of the sky, poured the last of its warmth onto her face. Her cheeks were still salty from the sea; wet hair clung to her neck. She sat with her arms wrapped around her legs, her chin on her knees, her eyes narrowed against the dazzle of the sea.

It was a Wednesday, and the last of a perfect summer's day. Or was September officially autumn? Flora couldn't remember. She only knew that in Cornwall, the summer had a charming way of spinning itself out beyond the end of the season. Down here, sheltered by the cliffs, there was no breath of wind, and the rocks, soaked by a day's sunshine, were still warm to the touch.

The tide was coming in. The first trickle of water had slid between two limpet-encrusted rocks and emptied itself into the pool. Soon the trickle would swell to a flood, and the mirror surface of the water be shattered by the vanguard of the long Atlantic rollers. Finally, the rocks would become engulfed, and the pool submerged and lost until the next low tide should set it free again.

She could not remember how many times they had sat together, just as they sat now, mesmerized by the fascination of a flooding September tide. But this evening it was even more difficult to drag themselves away, because it was the last time. They would go up the cliff path, pausing from time to time as they always did, to look back at the ocean. They would take the path that led across the fields to Seal Cottage, where Marcia was waiting for them, with supper in the oven and flowers on the table. And after supper Flora would wash her hair and finish her packing, because tomorrow she was going back to London.

It had all been planned, and it was something that Flora had to do, but at this moment she could scarcely bear to contemplate the idea. For one thing, she always hated leaving her father. She looked at him where he sat on the rock a little below her. She saw his leanness, the deep tan of his skin, his long bare legs. He wore a disreputable pair of shorts and an ancient shirt, much darned, with the sleeves rolled back off his forearms. She saw his thinning hair, tousled from the swim, and the jutting jawline as he turned his head to watch a cormorant skimming by just above the surface of the sea.

She said, "I don't want to go tomorrow."

He turned to smile up at her. He said. "Then don't."

"I have to. You know that. I have to go out into the world and start being independent again. I've been home too long."

"I'd like you to stay for always."

She ignored the sudden lump in her throat. "You're not meant to say things like that. You're meant to be brisk and unsentimental. You're meant to push your chick out of the nest."

"You promise me you're not going because of Marcia?"

Flora was truthful. "Yes, of course in a way I am, but that's not the point. Anyway, I adore her, you know that." When her father did not smile, she tried turning it into a joke. "All right then, she's a typical wicked stepmother, how's that for a reason? And I'm escaping before I find myself locked in a cellar with the rats."

"You can always come back. Promise me you'll come back if you can't find a job, or if things don't work out."

"I shall find a job with no difficulty whatsoever, and everything's going to work out."

"I still want the promise."

"You have it. But you'll probably regret it when I turn up on your doorstep again in a week's time. And now"—she picked up her bathing towel and a pair of threadbare espadrilles —"we should go home."

To begin with, Marcia had refused to marry Flora's father. "You can't marry me. You're the senior classics master of a reputable grammar school. You ought to marry some quiet, respectable female with a felt hat and a way with boys."

"I don't like quiet, responsible females," he had told her, slightly irritated. "If I did, I'd have married Matron years ago."

"It's just that I don't see myself as Mrs. Ronald Waring. It doesn't fit, somehow. 'And here, boys, is Mrs. Waring, to present the silver cup for the High Jump.' And there is me, falling over my feet, and forgetting what I'm meant to say, and probably dropping the cup or giving it to the wrong boy."

But Ronald Waring had always been a man who knew his own mind, and he persisted, courting and finally persuading her. They were married at the beginning of the summer, in the tiny stone church which was older than time and smelled musty, like a cave. Marcia had worn a very fetching emerald green dress and a huge straw hat with a drooping brim, like

Scarlett O'Hara's. And for once Ronald Waring was coordinated and all of a piece, with matching socks and his necktie firmly knotted, not slipping down to reveal the top button of his shirt. They made, thought Flora, a wonderful couple. She had taken snapshots of them as they came beaming out of the church, the brisk sea-breeze playing havoc with the brim of the bride's hat, while causing the bridegroom's thinning hair to stand up on end like the crest of a cockatoo.

Marcia was a Londoner born and bred who had somehow reached the age of forty-two without ever having been married —most likely, decided Flora, because she had never found the time. She had started her career as a drama student, graduated to wardrobe mistress with a provincial repertory company, and from that inauspicious beginning had cheerfully barged on through life, apparently ricocheting from one unexpected occupation to another, and her final job had been sales manager in a shop in Brighton which specialized in what Marcia called Arabian Tat.

Although Flora had taken to Marcia from the very first and encouraged like mad the alliance with her father, there had been certain inevitable reservations about Marcia's housewifely capabilities. After all, no girl wants to condemn her parent to a lifetime of bought pies, frozen pizza, and soup out of cans.

But even on that score Marcia succeeded in surprising them. She proved to be an excellent cook and an enthusiastic housekeeper, and was already developing all sorts of unlikely talents in the garden. Vegetables were already coming up in neat, soldierly rows; flowers bloomed if Marcia looked at them, and the deep windowsill over the kitchen sink stood two rows deep in the earthenware pots of geranium and Busy Lizzies which she had grown herself.

That evening, as they made their way up the cliffs and across the cool, long-shadowed fields, Marcia, who had been watching from the kitchen window, came to meet them. She wore green trousers and a cotton smock, heavily embroidered by some gnarled peasant hand, and the last rays of the sun lit her bright hair to a flame.

Ronald Waring, catching sight of her, lifted his head with pleasure and his footsteps quickened. Lagging behind, Flora decided that there was something special about two middle-aged people who shared a bond, not only of affection, but passion as well, so that when they met in the middle of the field, embracing without restraint or embarrassment, it was as though they were coming together after a separation of many months. Perhaps that was how they felt. Heaven knew, they had waited long enough for each other.

It was Marcia who drove Flora to the junction the next morning to catch the London train. The fact that she was actually able to do this was a source of great pride and satisfaction to Marcia. Because in attaining her great age, she had not only missed out on matrimony, but, as well, had never learned to drive.

When quizzed about this, she had a number of reasons to explain the omission. She was unmechanically minded, she had never owned a car, and there was usually someone around who was willing to drive her. But after she married Ronald Waring and found herself marooned in a small Cornish cottage at the end of nowhere, it was obvious that the time had come.

Now or never, said Marcia, and took lessons. Then tests. Three of them. She failed the first time because she ran the front wheels of the car over the booted toes of a constable. And the second time because, while backing the car into a tricky parking place, she inadvertently knocked over a perambulator which, fortunately, did not contain a baby at the time. Neither Flora nor her father imagined that she would have the nerve to try again, but they underestimated Marcia. She did, and finally passed. So when her husband regretted that he could not drive his daughter to catch the London train, owing to some educational conference which he was bound to attend, Marcia was able to say, with casual pride, "That's no trouble. I'll take her."

In a way, Flora was relieved. She hated goodbyes, inevitably becoming emotional at the sound of a train whistle. She knew that if her father were there, she would probably weep all over him, which would make the parting all the worse for everybody.

It was another warm and cloudless day, the sky as blue as it had been all year, and the bracken gold. As well, there was a sparkle to the air which made the most mundane objects as clear-cut as crystal. Marcia, whose thought processes were comfortingly simple to follow, began to carol in her fruity contralto, "Oh, what a beautiful morning, oh, what a beautiful day . . ." and then abandoned her song and stooped down to feel for her handbag, which meant that she wanted a cigarette. The car, accordingly, weaved dangerously across the white line and over onto the wrong side of the road, so Flora said quickly, "I'll get it," and found the bag and the cigarette while Marcia got the car back on course again. Flora stuck the cigarette into Marcia's mouth, and then held the lighter so that Marcia wouldn't have to take her hands off the wheel.

The cigarette going, Marcia went on with her song.

"I've got a beautiful feeling, everything's going . . ." She stopped again, frowning. "Darling, you do promise me you're not going back to horrible London just because of me?"

This question had been asked every night at regular intervals for the last seven days. Flora took a deep breath. "No. I've told you, no. I'm simply picking up the threads of my life and carrying on where I left off a year ago."

"I can't get rid of this feeling that I'm turning you out of your own home."

"Well, you're not. And anyway, you can look at the situation from my point of view. Knowing my father has found a good woman to take care of him, I can go off and leave him with a clear conscience."

"I'd feel happier if I knew what sort of a life it was going to be. I've got a horrible preconceived pictures of you in a bedsitter, eating cold beans out of a tin."

"I've told you," said Flora robustly, "I'll find somewhere to live, and while I'm looking I'm going to stay with my friend Jane Porter. It's all been fixed. The girl who lives with her is on holiday with her boyfriend, so I can have her bed. And by the time she comes back from her holiday, I shall have found myself a flat of my own and a fabulous job and I'll be home and dry." But Marcia continued to look gloomy. "Look, I'm twenty-two, not twelve. And a terribly, terribly efficient shorthand typist. There's not a thing to worry about."

"Well, if things don't work out, *promise* to call me and I'll come and mother you."

"I've never been mothered in my life and I can manage without it." Flora added, "I'm sorry. That wasn't meant to sound quite so brusque."

"Not brusque at all, darling, just plain fact. But you know, the more I think about it, the more fantastic it becomes."

"I'm not sure what you are talking about."

"Your mother. Abandoning you and your father, and you just an infant. I mean, I can imagine a woman abandoning a *husband*. At least, I can't imagine *anybody* abandoning darling Ronald—but a *baby*! It seems so completely inhuman. You'd have thought that having gone through all the business of actually *having* a child, you'd want to keep it."

"I'm glad she didn't keep me. I wouldn't have had anything different. How Pa managed, I shall never know, but I couldn't have had a more wonderful childhood."

"You know what we are, don't you? The Founding Members of the Ronald Waring Fan Club. I wonder why she went? Your mother, I mean. Was there another man? I've never liked to ask."

"No I don't think so. They were simply incompatible. That's what Pa always told me. She didn't like him being an unambitious schoolmaster, and he wasn't interested in cocktail parties and the merry life. And she didn't like his being vague and immersed in his job, and always looking as though he'd been thrown together out of a rag bag. And he obviously was never going to earn enough money to keep her in the style she fancied. I found a photograph of her once, in the back of a drawer. Very chic and elegant, and expensive-looking. Not Pa's scene at all."

"She must have been as hard as nails. I wonder why they got married in the first place."

"I think they met on a skiing holiday in Switzerland. Pa's a super skier—perhaps you didn't know that. I imagine they were both blinded by sun and snow, and intoxicated by heady Alpine air. Or maybe she was knocked flat by the manly figure he cut as he swooped down the mountainside. All I know is that it happened, and I was born, and then it was over."

They were on the main road now, approaching the little station where Flora was to catch the London train. "I do hope," said Marcia, "that he doesn't ask me to go skiing with him."

"Why ever not?"

"I can't," said Marcia.

"That wouldn't make any difference to Pa. He adores you, just the way you are. You know that, don't you?"

"Yes," said Marcia, "and aren't I the luckiest woman alive? But you're going to be lucky, too. You were born under Gemini, and I looked you up this morning and all the planets are moving in the right direction and you've got to Take Advantage of Opportunities." Marcia was a great one for horoscopes. "That means that within a week you're going to find a super job and a super flat, and probably a super tall dark man with a Maserati. A sort of job lot."

"Within a week? That doesn't give me much time."

"Well, it's all got to happen in a week, because next Friday you get a new horoscope."

"I'll see what I can do."

It was not a prolonged goodbye. The express stopped at the junction for no more than a moment, and no sooner were Flora and her considerable luggage on board than the stationmaster was walking down the platform, slamming doors and preparing to blow his whistle. Flora leaned out of the open window to kiss Marcia's upturned face. Marcia had tears in her eyes and her mascara had run.

"Telephone; let us know what happens."

"I will. I promise."

"And write!"

There was no time for more. The train began to move, gathering speed; the platform curved away. Flora waved, and the little station and Marcia's blue-trousered form grew smaller and then slid out of sight, and Flora, with her hair all over her face, shut the window and sat with a thump in the corner seat of the empty compartment.

She looked out of the window. That was a tradition, watching everything slip away, just as it was a tradition, when traveling in the opposite direction, to start leaning out of the window at Fourbourne in order to catch the very first glimpse of one familiar landmark after another.

Now the tide was low, the sand of the estuary a sort of pearly brown, patterned in blue where pools of slack water reflected the sky. On the far side was a village with white houses gleaming through trees, and then the dunes, and for an instant one could see the ocean out beyond the distant white breakers of the bar.

The railway curved inland, and a grassy headland swung into view while the ocean was lost behind a rash of seaside bungalows. The train rattled over a viaduct and through the next town, and then there were small green valleys and white cottages, and gardens where lines of washing bellied and flapped in the brisk morning breeze. The train thundered over a level crossing and a man waited at the closed gate with a red tractor and a trailer filled with bales of straw.

They had lived in Cornwall since Flora was five years old. Before that her father had taught Latin and French at an exclusive and expensive Sussex preparatory school, but the job, though comfortable, was not much of a challenge, and he had begun to run out of the sort of conversation acceptable to the mink-coated mothers of his well-heeled charges.

He had always had a hankering to live by the sea, having spent Easter and summer holidays in Cornwall as a boy. Thus, when the post of senior classic master at the Fourbourne Grammar School came up he promptly applied for it, much to the concern of the preparatory school headmaster, who felt that the bright young man was destined for better things than pumping classics into the heads of the sons of farmers, shopkeepers, and mining engineers.

But Ronald Waring was adamant. At first he and Flora had lived in digs in Fourbourne, and her first memory of Cornwall was that small industrial town, surrounded by a bleak country of shallow hills spiked with old mine workings which stood out on the horizon like so many broken teeth.

But once they had settled down and her father had found his feet in his new job, he bought an ancient car, and on weekends father and daughter cast about for somewhere else to live.

Finally, following the directions of the estate agent's office in Penzance, they had taken the road from St. Ives out toward Lands End, and after one or two wrong turns found themselves bumping down a steep, brambly lane which led in the direction of the sea. They rounded a last corner, over a stream which ran permanently across the road, and came to Seal Cottage.

It was a bitter winter's day. The house was derelict, had no running water or sanitation and, when they finally forced the swollen old door open, appeared to have been overrun by mice. But Flora was not afraid of mice, and Ronald Waring fell in love not only with the house but also with its view. He bought it that very day, and it had been their home ever since.

At first their existence had been desperately primitive. It had been a struggle to simply keep warm and clean and fed. But Ronald Waring, besides being a classical scholar, was a gregarious man of great charm. If he went into a pub knowing nobody, he would become fast friends with at least half a dozen people by the time he left.

Thus, he found the stonemason who repaired the garden walls and rebuilt the sagging chimney. Thus, he met Mr. Pincher the carpenter, and Tom Roberts, whose nephew was a plumber with weekends to spare. Thus, he made the acquaintance of Arthur Pyper, and so of Mrs. Pyper, who bicycled in a stately fashion from the local village each day to wash the dishes, make the beds, and keep a motherly eye on Flora.

At ten years old, much to her disgust, Flora was dispatched to a boarding school in Kent where she stayed till she was sixteen. That was followed by a session learning how to be a shorthand typist, and another one learning how to be a Cordon Bleu cook.

As a cook, she took jobs in Switzerland (in the winter) and Greece (in the summer). Returning to London, she reverted to being a secretary, shared a flat with a girlfriend, waited in bus queues, shopped in her lunch hour; she went out with impoverished young men who were learning how to be chartered accountants, or slightly less impoverished young men who were opening boutiques. And in between times, she took the train up and down to Cornwall for holidays, to help with the spring cleaning, to roast the Christmas turkey.

But, at the end of last year, after a dose of flu and an unsatisfactory love affair, she had become disenchanted with the big city, homed to Cornwall for Christmas, and had needed little encouragement to stay there. It had been a wonderful, relaxed year, knowing, as the winter gave way to a particularly beautiful and early spring, and spring turned to summer, that she could stay and watch it all happening; there was no deadline; no day on the calendar when she would have to pack a suitcase and get back to the grindstone.

She did, in fact—to pass the time and earn a little money —take jobs, but they were all temporary, undemanding, and usually amusing: picking daffodils for a local market gardener; working as waitress in a coffee bar; selling caftans to summer tourists mad to spend their money.

It was in the caftan shop that she had first met Marcia and had taken her back to Seal Cottage for a drink. She had watched in delighted disbelief the instant rapport which sprang up between Marcia and her father. The rapport, it soon became obvious, was not simply a passing fancy.

Love made Marcia bloom like a rose, and Flora's father became so appearance-conscious that he actually went out and bought himself a new pair of trousers without anybody suggesting that he do so. As the relationship steadily deepened and strengthened, Flora tactfully tried to withdraw, making excuses not to accompany them on their jaunts to the pub down the road and finding reasons for going out in the evening so that they could have Seal Cottage to themselves.

When they were married, she started making noises almost at once about returning to London and to work, but Marcia had persuaded her to stay on at Seal Cottage, at least for the summer. That she had done, but time was running out. It was no longer Flora's life, just as Seal Cottage was no longer her home. In September, she promised herself, she would go back to London. In September, she told Marcia, I'm leaving you two old lovebirds to yourselves.

Now, it was all over. Already it was in the past. And the future? *You're going to be lucky,* Marcia had said. *You were born under Gemini and all the planets are moving in the right direction.*

But Flora was not so sure. She took out of her coat pocket the letter which had come that morning, which she had opened and read, and then swiftly stowed away before Marcia should ask about it. It was from Jane Porter.

8 Mansfield Mews
S.W.10

Darling Flora,

The most ghastly thing has happened and I just hope this reaches you before you start out for London. Betsy, the girl I share with, has had the most ghastly row with her boyfriend, and after two days in Spain has *come home.* She's here now in the flat, weeping all over everything, and obviously waiting for the phone to ring, which it never does. So the bed I promised you isn't available, and though you'd be more than welcome to a sleeping bag on my bedroom floor, the whole atmosphere is so fraught and Betsy is so utterly impossible that I wouldn't ask my darkest enemy to share it. I do hope you can fix something just till you find a pad of your own. Terribly sorry to let you down like this, and hope you'll understand. Be sure to ring me so

that we can get down to a proper gossip. Longing to see
you again and I'm sorry, I'm sorry, but it wasn't my fault.
Masses of love,
Jane

Flora sighed, folded the letter, and pushed it back into her
pocket. She hadn't said anything to Marcia, because Marcia in
her new role of wife and mother had developed an alarming
tendency to fuss. Had she known that Flora was going back to
London without anywhere to lay her head, she would probably
have refused to let her go. And having made up her mind,
Flora felt that she could not bear to postpone her departure for
one more day.

Now, she applied herself to the problem of what she was
going to do. There were friends of course, but after a year, she
wasn't sure what they were doing, where they were living, nor
even who with. Her previous flatmate was now married and
living in Northumberland, and there was nobody else Flora felt
she could telephone out of the blue, to plead for temporary
accommodation.

It was a vicious circle. She didn't want to take a flat until
she'd found a job, but it would be difficult to do the rounds of
the agents without some sort of a base in which to park her
belongings.

In the end she hit upon the idea of the Shelbourne, the
small, old-fashioned hotel where her father used to take her en
route to one of their rare holidays abroad (perhaps to ski in
Austria, or spend a couple of weeks with one of Ronald Waring's esoteric friends, who owned a ramshackle mill in Pro-
vence). The Shelbourne was not smart and, if her father had
stayed there, would certainly not be expensive. She would
check in there for the night, and tomorrow start jobhunting.

It wasn't a great solution, but rather a compromise. And
life, as Marcia was wont to say, tearing the brim from one hat
and stitching it to the crown of another, was made up of com-
promises.

The Shelbourne was a relic like an old barge beached in a

backwater while the river of progress flowed by. Situated at the
back of Knightsbridge in a narrow street which had once been
elegant, it was slowly being dwarfed by plush new hotels, of-
fices, and blocks of flats. Yet it clung grimly on, like an aging
actress who refuses to retire.

Outside was present-day London: traffic jams, car horns,
the roar of planes flying overhead, the vendor selling newspa-
pers on the corner, the young girls with their black-rimmed
eyes and their tottering clogs.

But entering through the slowly revolving doors of the
Shelbourne was like stepping into yesterday. Nothing had
changed—not the potted palms; not the face of the hall porter;
not even the smell, a mixture of disinfectant and floor polish
and hothouse flowers, rather like that of a hospital.

Behind the reception desk sat the same sad woman in her
drooping black dress. Could it be the *same* dress? She looked
up at Flora.

"Good evening, madam."

"Would it be possible to have a single room, just for tonight?"

"I'll just look . . ."

A clock ticked. Flora waited, her spirits sinking by the
moment; she half-hoped that the answer would be no.

". . . Yes, I can let you have a room, but it's at the back
of the hotel, and I'm afraid . . ."

"All right, I'll take it."

"If you could sign the register, and I'll ask a porter to take
you up."

But the thought of long, stuffy hallways and a gloomy
single bedroom at the end of it was too much for Flora.

"Not just now. I have to go out. Out to dinner," she improvised wildly. "I'll be back about half past nine. It doesn't
matter about my luggage. Just leave it here in the hall till I get
back. I'll take it up then."

"Just as you wish, madam. But don't you want to see your
room?"

"No. It doesn't matter. I'm sure it's very nice. . . ." She

felt as if she were suffocating. Everything looked so dreadfully old. She picked up her bag and backed away, still mumbling excuses. She nearly knocked over a potted palm, rescued it in the nick of time, and finally fled out into the fresh air.

After two or three reviving gulps, she felt better. It was a lovely evening, chilly but clear, with a pellucid blue sky arched over the rooftops and one or two pink-tinged clouds aimlessly blowing along like balloons. Flora dug her hands into her pockets and began to walk.

An hour later, she found herself deep into Chelsea, heading south towards the King's Road. The little street lined with charming houses interspersed with small shops was familiar. Unfamiliar, however, was the small Italian restaurant which now stood where before Flora remembered a cobbler's with dusty windows filled with dog leads and luggage straps and unlikely plastic handbags.

The restaurant was called Seppi's. There were bay trees in tubs out on the cobbled pavement, a cheerful red-and-white striped awning, and a great deal of fresh white paint.

Just as Flora approached the door opened and a man came out carrying a small table which he set up on the pavement and covered with a checked red-and-white cloth. He went back into the shop and returned with two small wrought iron chairs and a Chianti bottle in a straw jacket, all of which were duly set out.

The breeze caught at the tablecloth and sent it flapping. The man looked up and saw Flora. His dark eyes flashed her a Mediterranean smile.

"Ciao, signorina."

Italians were wonderful, Flora decided. The smile, the greeting, made her feel like some old friend he was enchanted to be meeting again. No wonder they made such successful restaurateurs.

She smiled. "Hello, there. How are you?"

"Fantastic. After such a day, who could feel anything else? It is like being back in Rome. And you look like an Italian girl who has been to the sea for the summer. The tan." He made an

appreciative gesture which involved a kissing sound and an airy
spread of finger tips. "Marvelous."

"Thank you." Disarmed, she stopped to talk, not unwill-
ing to continue this delightful conversation. Through the open
door of the restaurant drifted mouth-watering smells—suggestions of garlic and great red tomatoes and olive oil. Flora real-
ised that she was ravenous. She had had no lunch on the train
and since leaving the Shelbourne had walked, it seemed, for
miles. Her feet ached and she was thirsty.

She looked at her watch. It was just past seven. "Are you
open?"

"For you we are always open."

She said, accepting the compliment, "I only want an omelet or something."

"You, signorina, can have anything you want . . ." He
stood aside, a welcoming arm outflung, and thus, so charmingly invited, Flora entered. Inside there was a little bar, and
beyond this the long narrow restaurant reached back. Ban-
quettes upholstered in knobbly orange material ran down the
length of each wall, and there were scrubbed pine tables and
fresh flowers and brightly checked napkins. The walls were
mirrored, the floor scattered with straw matting. At the far
end, judging from the clatter, smells, and raised Italian voices
which emanated from that direction, was the kitchen. Everything felt cool and fresh, and after an exhausting day, Flora was
left with the pleasant sensation of being welcomed home. She
ordered a lager and then went in search of the ladies', where
she washed the train grime from her hands and face and
combed her hair. Back in the restaurant, the young Italian was
waiting for her, a table pulled away from the wall, so that she
could take her place, the tall frosted glass of lager neatly
poured, some dishes of olives and nuts set out for her pleasure.

"You are sure you want only an omelet, signorina?" he
inquired, as Flora sat down and the table was pushed in again,
over her knees. "We have very good veal this evening. My sister
Francesca will cook it for you like a dream."

"No, just an omelet. But you could put some ham in it. And perhaps a green salad."

"I will make the special dressing."

Up to now the place had been totally empty, but at this moment the door from the street opened and a few more customers drifted in, settling themselves around the bar. The young waiter excused himself to Flora and went to serve them, and she was left alone. She took an icy mouthful of lager and looked about her, wondering if any stray female who happened to wander into this delightful place was accorded the same welcome. Everybody said how grim London was becoming, how offhand were the people, how unhelpful. It was heartwarming, for once, to have everybody proved wrong.

She set down her glass, looked up, and caught sight of herself reflected in the long plate glass mirror which lined the opposite wall. The faded blue of her denim jacket and the orange of the seat behind her were the colors of Van Gogh. As for herself . . . she saw a thin girl, with strong features, dark brown eyes, and a mouth that was too big for the rest of her face. She was still tanned from the Cornwall summer, her skin shining and clean, and her hair the color of gleaming mahogany, casual, chin-length, looking like the hair of a young boy in need of a good cut. With her faded jeans and jacket she wore a white turtleneck sweater, a gold chain knotted at the neck. Her hands and wrists, emerging from the folded back cuffs, were long-boned and tanned as her face.

She thought, *I've been away from London too long. This casual image isn't going to get me any sort of a job. I ought to get my hair cut. I ought to buy . . .*

The door onto the street opened and shut again. A girl's voice called, "Hi, Pietro!" and the next instant the newcomer came right through the bar and into the restaurant, at home as a cat in familiar surroundings. Without looking in Flora's direction, she stopped at the table next to hers, pulled it out to make space for herself, and flopped down onto the banquette with her eyes shut and her legs stuck out in front of her.

So casual, almost insolent, were all these movements that

Flora decided she must be some relation to the Italian family
who owned the restaurant. A cousin from Milan, perhaps,
working in London . . .

Hi Pietro. No, of course not, not an Italian, an American.
From the New York branch of the family . . .

Diverted by that intriguing possibility, but not wanting to
stare, Flora shifted her gaze slightly and observed the other
girl's reflection in the mirror opposite. She looked away. And
then back again, so swiftly that she felt her hair swinging
against her cheek. The perfect double take, she thought. The
classic double take.

It was herself.

But it wasn't herself because there were two reflections in
the mirror.

The newcomer, unaware of Flora's mesmerized gaze,
pulled a bright silk scarf off her head, shook back her hair, and
then reached into a black crocodile bag and took out a cigarette
and lit it from a book of matches that lay in the ashtray on the
table. At once the air was filled with the smell of strong French
tobacco. She stuck out a booted foot, hooked it around the leg
of the table, and yanked the table toward her. She leaned forward, twisting her head away from Flora, and called again,
"Hi, Pietro!"

Flora could not drag her eyes from the mirror. The girl's
hair was longer than her own, but shining and the same dark
mahogany brown. She was carefully and elaborately made up,
but that only served to emphasize the strong features and the
mouth that was too big for her face. Her eyes were dark brown,
the bristly lashes sooty with mascara. She reached out to pull
the ashtray toward her, and Flora saw the dazzling, chunky
ring and the scarlet nails, but the hands were slender and long-
boned, their shape identical to Flora's own.

They were even dressed alike, in jeans and turtleneck
sweaters. But the other girl's sweater was cashmere, and her
jacket, which had been slung around her shoulders and was
now shrugged aside, was a dark, gleaming mink.

The young waiter, having dealt with the customers at the

bar, answered her summons, suddenly appearing almost at a run.

"Signorina, I am so sorry, I thought that . . ."

Slowly, he came to a standstill, his movements, his words, his very voice seemed to run down to a halt, like an old-fashioned gramophone that nobody's remembered to wind.

After a little, "O.K., so what did you think?" said the girl who sat beside Flora. "You must surely realize I'm needing a drink."

"But I thought . . . I mean, I have already . . ." He had gone quite pale. His dark eyes traveled cautiously to Flora's face. So obviously shaken was he that Flora would not have been surprised if he had crossed himself, or made that sinister Mediterranean gesture which is meant to ward off the evil eye.

"Oh, Pietro, for heaven's sake . . ."

But in the middle of that small burst of exasperation, she looked up and saw Flora watching her through the mirror.

The silence seemed to go on forever. Pietro broke it at last. "It is amazing," he said, his voice scarcely audible and full of wonder. "It is amazing."

They looked away from each other and into each other's eyes and it was still like looking into the mirror.

The other girl recovered herself first. She said, "I'll say it's amazing," and she did not sound nearly as sure of herself as she had before.

But Flora could think of nothing to say.

Pietro broke in once more. "But Signorina Schuster, when the other signorina came in, I thought it was yourself." He turned to Flora. "I am sorry. You must have thought that I was very familiar, but I naturally mistook you for Signorina Schuster, she comes often, but I have not seen her for some time, and . . ."

"I didn't think you were being familiar. I just thought you were being very kind."

The girl with long hair was still staring at Flora, her dark eyes moving over Flora's face, like an expert assessing a portrait. She said now, "You look just like me," and she even sounded a little annoyed, as though this were some sort of an affront.

Flora felt moved to defend herself. "Well, you look like me," she told her mildly. "We look like each other." Still unnerved, she swallowed. "I think we probably even sound like each other."

This was instantly confirmed by Pietro, who still stood rooted to the ground, his head going from one face to the other, like a spectator at a tennis match.

"That is so. You have the same voice, the same eyes. Even the same clothes. I would not have believed it unless I had seen it for myself. Mamma mia, you could be twins. You are . . ." He made finger-snapping motions, searching for the right word. "The same. You know?"

"Identical," said Flora, flatly.

"That's it! Identical! It's fantastic!"

"Identical twins?" said the other girl, cautiously.

Their astonishment, the way that they couldn't take their eyes off each other, finally got through to Pietro.

"You mean that you have never seen each other before?"

"Never."

"But you must be sisters."

He put his hand over his heart. Suddenly, it seemed, he could take no more. Flora wondered if he was going to faint, and hoped that he wasn't. Instead, he took more practical action. He said, "I am going to open a bottle of champagne. It is a present . . . on the house. And I am going to drink a glass, too, because a miracle like this has never happened to me before. Just wait there . . ." he added, unnecessarily straightening the tables before them, as though afraid they might escape. "Don't move. Just wait there," and he bolted back to the bar, his starched white jacket alert with importance.

They scarcely heard him, scarcely noticed his going. Sisters. A strange obstruction had suddenly manifested itself in Flora's throat. She made herself say it. "Sisters?"

"Twin sisters," the other girl amended. "What's your name?"

"Flora Waring."

The other girl closed her eyes and opened them again, so slowly that it couldn't be called a blink. She said, with studied calm, "That's my name, too. Only I'm Rose."

3

ROSE

"Rose Waring?"

"Well, not strictly speaking. Rose Schuster, really. But Waring's my middle name, because my father was called Waring, but my stepfather's called Harry Schuster. And he's been my stepfather for years and years, so I've always been called Schuster, but Waring's my middle name." She stopped, having apparently run out of breath. They continued to gaze at each other, still astonished, but with a growing sense of recognition, of realization.

"Do you know who your real father was?" Flora asked at last.

"I never knew him. He and my mother separated when I was a baby. I think he was a schoolmaster."

Flora thought of her father. Vague, loping about, maddening, but always totally honest and truthful. She thought, *He couldn't have. He couldn't have done such a thing and never told me.*

The silence between the two girls lengthened. Rose seemed to have nothing more to say. With an effort, Flora searched for words.

"Your mother. Was she called . . ." The name, scarcely ever mentioned, swam up out of her subconscious. "Pamela?"

"That's right."

"How old are you?"

"Twenty-two."

"When is your birthday?"

"The seventeenth of June."

Now, it was final. "Mine, too."

"I was born under Gemini," said Rose, and it was disconcerting to hear Marcia's words of that very morning repeated so naturally. "The sign of the twins." She smiled. "That's appropriate enough, if you like."

My twin. My sister. "But what happened?" asked Flora.

"Simple. They decided to separate, and they took one each."

"But did you ever have the slightest idea?"

"Not the slightest. Did you?"

"No. That's what shakes me."

"Why should it shake you? It's perfectly normal human behavior. Very tidy, very fair."

"I think we should have been told."

"What good would that have done? What difference would it have made?"

It was obvious that Rose was more amused than shattered by the situation. "I think it's hysterical," she went on. "And the most hysterical part of the business is that our mother and father have been found out. And what a fantastic coincidence that we should meet up like this. Out of the blue. Have you ever been to this restaurant before?"

"Never."

"You mean, you just walked in?"

"I only arrived in London this evening. I've been in Cornwall for the past year."

"That makes it more unbelievable than ever. In the whole

of this immense city . . ." She spread her hands, leaving the sentence to finish itself.

"They always say," said Flora, "that London is made up of a lot of villages. I suppose if you stick to your own village, you're bound to meet someone you know."

"That's true enough. Walk into Harrod's and you bump into acquaintances all the way through. But it still doesn't stop it being the most extraordinary thing that's even happened to me." She pushed her hair back from her forehead with her fingers, a gesture that Flora recognized, with some shock, as one of her own. "What were you doing in Cornwall?" Rose asked, as if it could make any difference.

"My father and I went to live there. He still does. He teaches there."

"You mean he's still a schoolteacher?"

"Yes, he's still a schoolmaster." It was ridiculous to continue to feel as shaken as she did. She decided to be as matter of fact about the uncanny coincidence as Rose was. "And what happened to you?" she asked, sounding unreal, like a person at a formal cocktail party.

"Mother married again when I was about two. He's called Harry Schuster and he's an American, but he's spent most of his life in Europe as representative for his firm."

"So you were brought up in Europe?"

"You could say that. If it wasn't Paris it was Rome, and if it wasn't Rome, it was Frankfurt. You know how it is. . . ."

"Is he nice? Mr. Schuster, I mean."

"Yes. Sweet."

And terribly rich, thought Flora, eyeing the mink and the cashmere and the crocodile bag. Pamela, ditching the penniless schoolmaster, had done a good deal better for herself the second time around.

She thought of something else. "Do you have any brothers or sisters?"

"No. Just me. How about you?"

"I'm an only, and likely to stay that way. Pa's just married again. She's called Marcia and she's super, but she's not exactly a chicken."

"What does your father look like?"

"Tall. Scholarly, I suppose. Very kind. He wears horn-rimmed spectacles and he forgets things. He's very . . ." She searched for some brilliant word that would describe her father, but only came up with "charming." And she added, "And very truthful. That's why I find this all so extraordinary."

"You mean, he's never palmed you off with a fib?"

Flora was a little shocked. "I never imagined he was capable of suppressing a truth, let alone telling a lie."

"He must be something." Rose stubbed out her cigarette, thoughtfully grinding it to pieces in the middle of the ashtray. "My mother is perfectly capable of suppressing the truth, or even telling a wing-ding of a lie. But she also is charming. When she wants to be!"

Despite herself, Flora smiled, because Rose's description matched so exactly what she had always imagined for herself.

"Is she pretty?" she asked.

"Very slim and young-looking. Not beautiful, but everybody thinks she is. It's a sort of confidence trick."

"Is . . . is she in London now?" Flora made herself ask, thinking, *If she is and I have to meet her, what will I say to her? What will I do?*

"No, she's in New York. Actually, she and Harry and I have been on a trip; I only flew in to Heathrow last week. She wanted me to stay, but I had to come back, because . . ." She did not finish the sentence. Her eyes slid away as she reached for another cigarette and burrowed in her bag for her lighter. ". . . Oh, various reasons," she finished unsatisfactorily.

Flora waited hopefully to be told the reasons, but they were interrupted once more by Pietro returning with the champagne bottle and three glasses. With some ceremony he drew the cork and poured the wine, passing the neck of the bottle from glass to glass without spilling a drop. He wiped the bottle clean with a starched napkin, picked up his own glass, and raised it to them.

"To the reunion. To sisters finding each other. It is, I think, an act of God."

"Thank you," said Flora. "Happy days," said Rose. Pietro departed once more, by now quite moist at the eyes, and they were left with the bottle to finish between them. "We'll probably get plastered," said Rose, "but never mind about that. Where had we got to?"

"You were saying you had to come back to London from the States."

"Oh, sure. But now, I think I am going to Greece. Perhaps tomorrow or the next day. I haven't exactly decided."

It sounded a marvelously jet-set, spur-of-the-moment existence.

"Where are you staying?" Flora asked, expecting to be told the Connaught or the Ritz. But it appeared that Harry Schuster's job carried with it a flat in London as well as the apartments in Paris, Frankfurt, and Rome. The London flat was in Cadogan Gardens. "Just round the corner," said Rose, casually. "I always walk round here when I want something to eat. How about you?"

"You mean, where do I live? Nowhere at the moment. I told you, I only came up from Cornwall today. I was going to stay with a girlfirend, only it didn't work out, so I've got to find a flat. I've got to find a job, too, only that's beside the point."

"Where are you spending tonight?"

Flora told her about the Shelbourne, the luggage dumped in the hall, the potted palms, and the suffocating atmosphere. "I'd forgotten how depressing it was. But never mind, it's only for one night."

She became aware that Rose was watching her with a cool and thoughtful expression in her dark eyes. (Do I ever look like that? thought Flora. The word *calculating* sprang to mind and had to be hastily slapped down.)

Then Rose said, "Don't go back." Flora stared. "I mean it. We'll have something to eat here, and then we'll find a taxi and go and collect your luggage, and we'll go back to Harry's flat, and you can stay there. It's vast, and there are loads of beds.

Besides, if I go to Greece tomorrow I shan't see you again, and we've got so much to talk about, we shall need an entire night to ourselves. And anyway, it's super, because you can stay in the flat after I've gone. You can stay there until you've found somewhere else to live."

"But . . ." For some reason Flora found she was searching for objections to this apparently delightful plan. "But won't anybody mind?" was all she could come up with.

"Who should mind? I'll fix it with the hall porter. Harry never minds what I do. And as for Mother . . ." Something amused her. She left the sentence unfinished and began to laugh. "What would she say if she could see us now? Getting together, making friends. What do you think your father would say?"

Flora shied from the idea. "I can't imagine."

"Will you tell him that we've found each other?"

"I don't know. Perhaps. One day."

"Was it a cruel thing to do?" asked Rose, suddenly thoughtful. "Separating identical twins. Identical twins are meant to be two halves of the same person. Separating us was perhaps like cutting that person in half."

"In that case, they may have done us a kindness."

Rose's eyes narrowed. "I wonder," she said. "why my mother chose me, and your father chose you."

"Perhaps they tossed a coin." Flora spoke lightly, because for some reason, it didn't bear thinking about.

"Would everything have been upside down if the coin had fallen the other way?"

"It would certainly have been different."

Different. She thought of her father, of Seal Cottage by winter firelight, and the tarry smell of burning driftwood. She thought of tender, early springs and summer seas dancing with sun pennies. She thought of red wine in a carafe set in the middle of the scrubbed table and the comforting sound of Beethoven's *Pastoral* thundering from the record player. And now, she remembered the warm and loving presence of Marcia.

"Would you have wanted it to be different?" asked Rose.

Flora smiled. "No."

Rose reached out for the ashtray and stubbed out her cigarette. She said, "Nor me. I wouldn't have changed a thing."

Now it was Friday.

In Edinburgh, after a morning of cloud and rain, the sun had finally struggled through the murk, the sky was clearing, and the city glittered in a brilliant autumn light. To the north, beyond the deep indigo of the Firth of Forth, the hills of Fife lay serene against a sky of palest blue. Across Princes Street the municipal flower beds of the Waverly Gardens were ablaze with fiery dahlias, and on the far side of the railway line the cliffs swept up to the theatrical bulk of the castle with its distant, fluttering flag.

Antony Armstrong, emerging from his office into Charlotte Square, was taken unaware by the beauty of the afternoon. Because he was taking a long weekend, it had been an exceptionally busy morning. He had not bothered about lunch. He had not even raised his eyes to glance out of the window, imagining that the day was continuing much as it had started.

Preoccupied and anxious, he hurried to get to his car and drive to the airport. He was to catch the London plane and go in search of Rose. In spite of all that he was brought to a standstill by the unexpectedness of the sunshine reflected in still-damp pavements, by the glittering, coppery leaves of the trees in the square, and by the smell. It was a country smell, of autumn—a suggestion of peat and heather and wild uplands. It blew in with a freshening breeze from hills not after all so very far away. Antony, standing on the pavement with his raincoat slung over his shoulder and an overnight bag in his hand, took a few deep sniffs and was reminded of Fernrigg and of Tuppy. That he found comforting. It helped him to unwind and stop feeling so anxious.

Still, there was no time to waste, so he went and retrieved his car, drove out to Turnhouse, parked the car again, and checked in at the departure desk. Then, because there was half an hour to wait before his flight, he went upstairs for a sandwich and a glass of beer.

The barman was an old acquaintance, familiar after many business trips to London.

"Haven't seen you for a while, sir."

"No. I guess it's been a month or more."

"Do you favor ham, or egg?"

"Better give me one of each."

"Going down to London?"

"That's right."

The barman assumed a knowing expression. "Nothing like a weekend off."

"It may not be a weekend. I may be back tomorrow. I don't know. It depends."

"You might as well take the weekend, and enjoy yourself." He slid the tankard of Export across the counter. "It's lovely warm weather down in London."

"It's not so bad here."

"No, it looks like a good afternoon. You'll have a pleasant flight."

He wiped down the top of the counter and went to serve another customer. Antony took his beer and his plate of sandwiches over to a table by the window, shed his raincoat and his bag, and lit a cigarette.

Beyond the window, beyond the parapet of the terrace, he saw the hills, the shredding clouds, the flying windsock. He was hungry. The beer and sandwiches waited. Sitting there, watching the cloud shadows run across the puddled runways, he forgot about being hungry and let his mind return to the problem of Rose.

That required no conscious effort at all on Antony's part. As far as Rose was concerned his thoughts seemed to have taken on a will of their own, worrying away like an old dog digging up a bone, fretting around in circles and never getting anywhere.

As though the action were in itself some answer to his dilemma, he reached into his jacket pocket and took out her

letter, although he had already read it so many times that he
knew it by heart. It was not in an envelope for the simple
reason that it had not arrived in an envelope, but rather in an
untidy parcel around a small box containing the sapphire and
diamond ring that Antony had bought her.

He had given it to her four months ago in the restaurant of
the Connaught Hotel. They had finished dinner, the waiter had
brought their coffee to the table, and somehow, quite suddenly,
the moment had arrived: the time, the place, and the woman.
Antony, like a conjurer, had produced the little box from his
pocket, flipped it open, and let the light sparkle on the jewels
within.

Rose had said, instantly, "What a pretty thing."

"It's for you," said Antony.

She looked up into his eyes, incredulous, flattered, but
something else as well. He had not been able to make up his
mind what that something else was.

"It's an engagement ring," he went on. "I bought it this
morning." For some reason, it had been important that the ring
should be in his hand when he asked her to marry him, as
though he knew that she needed this extra leverage, this material persuasion. "I think—and I'm hoping that you think so,
too—I think that we ought to get married."

"Antony."

"Don't sound so reproachful."

"I'm not sounding reproachful. I'm sounding surprised."

"You can't say, 'this is so sudden,' because we've known
each other for five years."

"But not really *known* each other."

"I feel as though we have."

And indeed, at that moment, that was just how Antony
did feel. But their relationship was unusual, and the most unusual thing about it was the way that Rose kept recurring in his
life—turning up when he least expected to meet her, as though
the whole relationship had been preordained.

And yet, the first time he had met her, she had made no
impression on him at all. But then he had been twenty-five and

in the throes of a love affair with a young actress doing a season in Edinburgh. And Rose was only seventeen. Her mother, Pamela Schuster, had taken the Beach House at Fernrigg for a summer holiday. Antony, home for a weekend, and escorting Tuppy to the beach for a picnic, had been introduced and eventually invited back to the Beach House for a drink. The mother was charming and very attractive, but for some reason Rose had been in a bad mood that afternoon. Antony had simply dismissed her leggy gawkiness along with her sulky expression and the monosyllabic replies she gave him each time he tried to talk to her. By the time he made his next weekend visit to Fernrigg, both she and her mother had gone, and he never gave the Schusters another thought.

But then, a year ago in London on business, he had come upon Rose having a drink in the Savoy bar with an earnest young American in rimless spectacles. Rose now was something quite different. Seeing her, recognizing her, Antony could scarcely believe it was the same girl. Slender, sensational-looking, she held the attention, open or otherwise, of every man in the place.

Antony moved in and introduced himself, and Rose, perhaps bored by her monumentally sincere companion, responded with flattering delight. Her parents, she told him, were on holiday in the south of France. She was flying to join them tomorrow afternoon. That had created a pleasant sense of urgency, and without much urging Rose abandoned the American and went out to dinner with Antony.

"When are you coming back from the south of France?" he wanted to know, already hating the thought of having to say goodbye to her.

"Oh, I don't know. I haven't thought."

"Don't you have a job, or anything?"

"Oh, darling, I'd be useless in a job. I'm never on time for anything and I can't type, so I'd just be the most dreadful nuisance. Besides, there's no need. And I'd just be taking bread from some deserving mouth."

Antony's Scottish conscience made him say, "You're a

drone. A disgrace to society." But he said it with a smile, because she amused him, and Rose took no sort of umbrage.

"I know." She checked her elaborate eye makeup in the little mirror she had fished out of her handbag. "Isn't it ghastly?"

"Let me know when you come back from the south of France."

"Of course." She flipped the compact shut. "Of course, darling."

But she hadn't let him know. Antony had no idea where she lived, and no address in London, so it was impossible for him to get in touch with her. He tried looking up Schuster in the telephone directory, but no number was listed. Discreetly, he made inquiries of Tuppy, but Tuppy only remembered the Schusters at the Beach House, and had no idea of their permanent address.

"Why do you want to know?" Her voice over the telephone was clearly curious.

"I met Rose again in London. I want to get in touch with her."

"Rose? That pretty child? How intriguing."

By the time Antony found her again, it was the beginning of the summer. London gardens were fragrant with lilac, and the parks veiled in the young green of newly opened leaves.

Once more Antony was south, interviewing a client for his firm. Lunching at Scott's in the Strand, he met an old school friend who asked him to a party that evening. The friend lived in Chelsea, and as Antony walked through the front door of the top-floor flat the first person he saw was Rose.

Rose. He knew after the way that she had behaved that he should be furious with her, but instead, his heart missed a beat. She wore a blue linen pantsuit and high-heeled boots, with her dark hair loose to her shoulders. She was talking to some man whom Antony did not even bother to inspect. She was here. He had found her. Fate had stepped in. Fate did not intend that they should be kept apart. Antony, brought up in a Highland household, was a great believer in fate.

He took a drink from a passing tray and went to claim her.

This time, it was perfect. He had three days in London, and she wasn't going to the south of France. As far as he could find out, she wasn't going anywhere. Her mother and father were in New York, where Rose planned to join them—sometime. Not just now. She was living in her father's flat in Cadogan Court. Antony checked out of his club and moved in too.

Everything went right. Even the weather smiled upon them. During the day the sun shone, spikes of lilac bobbed against the blue sky, windowboxes were filled with flowers, and there always seemed to be taxis and the best tables in restaurants waiting for them. At night a round, silver moon sailed up into the sky and bathed the city in its romantic light. Antony spent money like water—as though he were made of it—and the uncharacteristic orgy of extravagance culminated the morning he walked into a Regent Street jeweler's and bought the diamond and sapphire ring.

They were engaged. He could scarcely believe it. To make it true, they sent cables to New York, made telephone calls to Fernrigg. Tuppy was amazed, but delighted. She had been longing for Antony to get married and settle down.

"You must bring her up to see us. It's so long since she was here. I can scarcely remember what she looks like."

Antony, gazing at Rose, said, "She's beautiful. The most beautiful thing in the world."

"I can't wait to see her again."

He said to Rose, "She says she can't wait."

"Well, darling, I'm afraid she'll have to. I have to go to America for a moment. I promised my mother and Harry. He's made such plans, and he always gets into such a state if he has to change them. I must go. Explain to Tuppy."

Antony explained. "Later, we'll come," he promised. "Later, when Rose is back again. I'll bring her up to Fernrigg and you can get to know her all over again."

So Rose went to New York, and Antony, bemused with love and good fortune, returned to Edinburgh. "I'll write," she

had promised, but she didn't write. Antony penned long, loving
screeds which she never answered. He began to fret. He sent
cables, but there was no reply to them, either. In the end he put
through a wildly expensive telephone call to her home in West-
chester County, but Rose was away. A servant answered the
telephone in an accent so strong as to be practically incompre-
hensible. He could only gather that Rose was out of town, her
address unknown, and her return date uncertain.

He was beginning to feel desperate when the first postcard
arrived. It was a picture of the Grand Canyon with a scrawled
and affectionate message that told him nothing. A week later
came the second. Rose stayed in America the entire summer
and during that time he received five postcards from her, each
more unsatisfactory than the one before.

Plaintive queries from Fernrigg did nothing to help the
situation. Antony managed to fend them off with the same excuses that he had started making to himself. Rose was simply
not a good correspondent.

But, despite these excuses, doubts loomed and grew like
monstrous balloons, like clouds darkening his horizon. He began to lose confidence in his own solid, Scottish common sense.
Had he made a fool of himself? Had those magical days in
London with Rose simply been a blinding illusion of love and
happiness?

And then something happened to drive all thoughts of
Rose from his head. Isobel telephoned from Fernrigg to tell him
that Tuppy was ill: she had caught a chill, it had turned to
pneumonia, a nurse had been engaged to take care of her. Trying to sound calm, Isobel did her best to reassure Antony. "You
mustn't worry. I'm sure it will be all right. It's just that I had to
tell you. I hate worrying you, but I knew you'd want to know."

"I'll come home," he said instantly.

"No. Don't do that. It'll make her suspicious, make her
think something's really wrong. Perhaps later, when Rose gets
back from America. Unless . . ." Isobel hesitated hopefully.
". . . perhaps she's back already?"

"No," Antony had to tell her. "No. Not yet. But any day now, I'm sure."

"Yes," said Isobel. "I'm sure." She sounded as if she were comforting him, as she had comforted him through all the anxieties of his childhood, and Antony knew that he should be comforting her. That made him feel more miserable than ever.

It was like worrying about a grumbling appendix and suffering from acute toothache at one and the same time. Antony did not know what to do, and in the end, with a lack of decision that was quite foreign to his nature, he did nothing.

The nonaction lasted for a week, and then, simultaneously, all his problems came to a ghastly head. The morning post brought the parcel from Rose, untidily wrapped and sealed, postmarked London and containing his engagement ring along with the only letter she had ever written him. And while he was still reeling from the shock, the second telephone call came, from Isobel. That time Isobel had not been able to be brave. Her tears and her very real anguish broke through, and her shaking voice betrayed the shattering truth. Hugh Kyle was obviously worried about Tuppy. She was, Isobel suspected, much worse than any of them had guessed. She would perhaps die.

All Tuppy wanted was to see Antony and Rose. She was yearning for them, worrying, wanting to make wedding plans. And it would be so dreadful, said Isobel, if something should happen, and Tuppy was never to see Antony and Rose together.

The implication was obvious. Antony had not the heart to tell Isobel the truth, and even as he heard himself making that impossible promise, he wondered how the hell he was going to keep it. Yet he knew that he had to.

With a calmness born of desperation, he made arrangements. He spoke with his boss, and with as few explanations as possible, asked for and was granted a long weekend. In a mood of dogged hopelessness, he put through a telephone call to the Schuster flat in London; when there was no reply, he drafted a wordy telegram and sent that instead. He booked a seat on the London plane. Now, at the airport waiting for that plane to be

called, he reached into the pocket of his jacket, and took out
the letter. The writing paper was deep blue and opulent, the
address thickly embossed at the head of the page.

Eighty Two Cadogan Court
London, S.W.1

But Rose's writing, unfortunately, did not live up to the
address. Sprawling, unformed as a child's, it meandered cross
the page, with the lines trailing downward, and the punctuation
nonexistent.

Darling Antony.
        I'm terribly sorry but I'm sending your ring back be-
cause I really don't think that after all I can bear to marry
you, it's all been a horrible mistake. At least, not horrible,
because you were sweet and the days we had together were
fun, but it all seems so different now, and I realize that I'm
not ready to settle down and be a wife, especially not in
Scotland, I mean I don't have anything against Scotland, I
think it's very pretty, but it isn't really my scene. I mean,
not for ever. I flew into London last week, am here for a
day or two, not sure what happens next. My mother sent
her love, but she doesn't think I should get married yet
and when I do she doesn't think I should live in Scotland.
She doesn't think it's my scene either. So terribly sorry,
but better now than later. Divorces are such messy things
and take so long and cost such a lot of money.
                                        Love (still)
                                        Rose

Antony folded the sheet of paper and put it back into his
pocket, and felt the smooth leather of the box with the diamond
and sapphire ring inside. Then he started in on his beer and
sandwiches. There was scarcely time to finish them before his
flight was called.
        He was at Heathrow at half past three, caught the bus to

the terminal, and then took a taxi. London was noticeably warmer than Edinburgh and bright with autumn sunshine. The trees had scarcely started to turn and the grass in the park was worn and brown after the long summer. Sloane Street seemed to be filled with light-hearted children going home from school hand in hand with smartly dressed young mothers. *If Rose isn't there,* he thought, *I shall sit down and bloody well wait for her.*

The taxi rounded the corner of the square, stopping in front of the familiar red-brick building. It was a new block, very plush, with bay trees at the head of the wide flight of stone steps, and a great deal of plate glass.

Antony paid off the taxi and went up the steps and through the glass door. Inside there was dark brown wall-to-wall carpeting and palm trees in tubs and an expensive smell, mostly compounded of leather and cigars.

The porter was not behind his desk, nor anywhere to be seen. Perhaps, thought Antony, pressing the bell for the lift, he's nipped out for an evening paper. The lift silently descended. Silently the doors slid open for him. As Antony went in they slid silently shut. He pressed the button for the fourth floor and recalled standing in that very lift with Rose in his arms, kissing her every time they passed another floor. It was a poignant memory.

The lift stopped and the doors opened. Carrying his bag, he stepped out, went down the long passage, stopped at the door of number Eighty-two and without giving himself time to think about it pressed the bell. From inside came the deep note of the buzzer. Setting down his bag and putting up a hand to lean against the edge of the door, he waited, without hope. She would not be there. Already he felt exhausted by what must follow.

And then from within he heard a sound. He stiffened, becoming suddenly alert, like a dog. A door shut. Another door opened. Footsteps came down the short passage from the kitchen, and the next moment the door was flung open. There stood Rose.

Staring at her like a fool, a number of thoughts flew

through Antony's mind. She was here, he had found her. She didn't look too furious. She had cut her hair.

She said, "Yes?" which was a funny thing for her to say, but then this was a funny situation.

Antony said "Hello, Rose."

"I'm not Rose," said Rose.

4

ANTONY

That Friday was, for Flora, fogged in a curious unreality, a carryover from the events of the previous incredible day. She had intended to do so much and had ended up by achieving nothing.

Physically, she went through the motions of jobhunting and visiting various estate gents, but her mind refused to concentrate on the matters in hand.

"Do you want permanent or temporary work?" the girl at the agency had asked, but Flora simply stared at her and did not reply, obsessed as she was by images that had nothing to do with shorthand and typing. It was as if a well-ordered house had suddenly been invaded and taken over by strangers. They had caught Flora's attention to the point where she could think of nothing else.

"There's a ground-floor flat going in Fulham. It's very small, of course, but if it was just for yourself . . . ?"

"Yes." She should go and see it. It sounded perfect. "Yes.

I'll think about it." And she stepped out into the street and continued on her way, aimless and preoccupied.

Part of the trouble, of course, was that she was short of sleep and physically exhausted by the traumas of yesterday. It had been a hysterical evening. Flora and Rose had dined together at Seppi's, finished the champagne, been presented with a second bottle, and sat over coffee until Seppi, with a queue of customers waiting for tables, had reluctantly had to let them leave. Rose had settled the bill with a credit card. The dinner cost more than Flora could believe possible, but Rose dismissed it airily. She said not to worry because Harry Schuster would settle the account. He always did.

They then found a taxi and drove to the Shelbourne Hotel, where Rose made derogatory remarks about the decor and the staff and the inhabitants, while Flora, embarrassed and trying not to laugh, explained the inexplicable situation to the sad lady behind the reception desk. A porter was finally persuaded to haul all the suitcases back out into the waiting cab, and they headed for Cadogan Court.

The flat was on the fourth floor. Flora had never dreamed of such luxury—so much carpeting, concealed lighting, and space-age plumbing. Plate-glass windows slid aside to allow access to a little balcony crammed with pot plants; a button could be pressed to draw the filmy linen curtains; in the bedrooms the carpets were white and about two inches deep (maddening if you dropped a ring or a bobby pin, Rose said), and the bathrooms all smelt of the most expensive soaps and oil.

Flora was carelessly assigned a bedroom (pale blue curtains made of Thai silk and mirrors everywhere) and told to unpack, which she did, to the extent of taking out her nightgown while Rose sat on the bed.

An idea suddenly struck Flora. "Do you want to know what your father looks like?"

"Photographs!" Rose sounded as though she had only just heard of such a thing.

Flora pulled out a big leather folder and handed it over to Rose, and they sat together on the big bed, dark head against dark head, their twin reflections caught in mirrors all about the room.

There was Seal Cottage, and the garden, and the wedding shot Flora had taken of her father and Marcia coming out of the church. There was the big one of him sitting on the rocks below the cottage, with a backdrop of sea and gulls, his face very brown and the breeze blowing his hair.

Rose's reaction was gratifying. "Oh, he's great! Like some smashing film star with spectacles. I can quite see why my mother married him. And yet I can't either. I mean, I can only imagine her married to a man like Harry."

"You mean a rich man."

"Yes, I suppose I do." She peered at the photograph again. "I wonder why they got married in the first place? Do you suppose they had anything in common?"

"Perhaps a mutual infatuation. They met on a ski holiday. Did you know that?"

"No kidding."

"Ski holidays are a bit like ocean voyages, or so I've been told. Wine-like air and tanned bodies and nothing to do except physically exhaust yourself and fall in love."

"I'll remember that," promised Rose. She was suddenly bored with the photographs. She tossed them down on the silk bedcover and looked long at her sister. Without any change in the tone of her voice, she asked, "Would you like a bath?"

So they both had baths, and Rose piled records onto the recordplayer while Flora made a pot of coffee. In their dressing gowns (Flora's, her old school one, and Rose's, a miracle of drifting flower-splashed silk) they sat on the king-size velvet sofa and talked.

And talked. There were many years to cover. Rose told Flora about the house in Paris and the finishing school at Chateau d'Oex, and the winters in Kitzbühel. And Flora filled Rose in on her own history (which didn't sound nearly so exciting), making the most of the finding and buying Seal Cottage, the arrival of Marcia into their lives, the jobs she had taken in Switzerland and Greece. That reminded her of something.

"Rose, did you say *you* were going to Greece?"

"I may be. But after this summer of flying around the United States, I'm beginning to feel I never want to get into another plane. Ever."

"You mean you spent the whole summer out there?"

"Most of it. Harry's been planning this trip for years, and we did everything from shooting the rapids on the Salmon River to riding down the Grand Canyon on muleback, hung about with cameras. Typical tourists." She frowned. "When did your father get married again?"

It was hard to keep track of her thought processes. "In May."

"Do you like Marcia?"

"Yes, I told you. She's great." Flora grinned, remembering Marcia's swelling hips and straining blouse buttons. "In more ways than one."

"He's so attractive, isn't he? I wonder how he managed to stay single for so long?"

"I've no idea."

Rose tipped her head to one side and regarded Flora from beneath long, bristling black lashes. "How about you? Are you in love, engaged, thinking of getting married?"

"Not at the moment."

"Have you ever thought about getting married?"

Flora shrugged. "You know how it is. At first, you think every new man you meet is going to end up standing next to you at some altar. And then it stops being important." She looked at Rose curiously. "How about you?"

"Same with me." Rose got up and went in search of a cigarette. Lighting it, her dark hair swung forward, hiding her face. "Anyway, who wants to settle down to boring old house-work and yelling kids?"

"Perhaps it's not that bad."

"You'd probably like it. You'd probably like living in the depths of the country, in the back of beyond."

For some reason Flora felt compelled to stand up for such

an existence. "I like the country. And I'd live anywhere provided I was living with the man I wanted to live with."

"Married to him, though?"

"I'd prefer it that way."

Rose took her cigarette and turned her back on Flora. She went over to the window, drew back the curtain, and stood looking down into the lamp-lit square. After a little she said, "Talking about Greece—if I went tomorrow, and left you here alone, would you mind very much?"

It was hard not to sound taken aback. *"Tomorrow?"*

"I mean Friday. Well, that's today I suppose."

"Today?" Despite herself Flora's voice came out in a squeak of surprise.

Rose turned back. "You would mind," she told Flora. "Your feelings would be hurt."

"Don't be ridiculous. It's just that you took me by surprise. I mean, I didn't think you were serious about going to Greece. I thought you were just talking about it."

"Oh, yes. I've even got a seat booked on the plane, but I wasn't sure whether I wanted to go. But suddenly I think I will. You don't think it would be mean of me to go?"

"Of *course* not," said Flora, robustly.

Rose began to smile. She said, "You know, we're not as alike as I thought we were. You're so much more honest, transparently so. And I know what you're thinking."

"What am I thinking?"

"You're thinking I'm a bitch to leave you. You're wondering why I suddenly have to go to Greece."

"Are you going to tell me?"

"I think you've probably guessed. It's a man. You had guessed, hadn't you?"

"Perhaps."

"I met him at a party in New York, just before I flew back to London. He lives in Athens, but I got a cable from him yesterday morning, and he's in Spetsai, he's been lent a house by some friends. He wants me to join him."

"Then you must go."

"You really mean that, don't you?"

"Of course. I'm no reason for you to stay in London. Besides, I've got to get down to finding a job and somewhere to live."

"You'll stay in this flat till you do?"

"Well . . ."

"I'll fix it with the porter. Please." The tone of Rose's voice was anxious, almost pleading. "Say you will. Just for a day or two. For the weekend, anyway. It would mean so much to me if you would."

Flora was puzzled, but there was no obvious objection, nor reason to argue with such a pleasant invitation. "Well, all right. Till Monday. But only if you're sure it's all right."

"Of course it's all right." Rose's wide smile, the image of Flora's own, split her face. She came across the room to hug Flora in a great gesture of affection, only to revert almost at once to her usual disconcerting manner. "And now come and help me pack."

"But it's three o'clock in the morning!"

"That doesn't matter. You can make some more coffee."

"But . . ." Flora had been on the point of saying, "I'm exhausted," but for some reason she didn't. Rose was like that. She went so fast that you went too, caught up in the slipstream of her speed, whirled along behind her, without any clear idea of where you were headed.

Rose finally set out at eleven o'clock Friday morning on the first stage of her long journey to Spetsai. She left Flora standing on the pavement outside the block of flats.

"I'll see you," she said, hugging Flora goodbye. "Leave the key with the porter when you finally go."

"Send me a postcard."

"Of course. It's been great. I'll be in touch."

"Have fun, Rose."

Rose leapt into a waiting taxi, slammed the door, and leaned out of the open window. "Take care!" she called, and the taxi moved off with Rose still waving a mink-furred arm.

Flora stood there waving until the taxi rounded the corner of the square and disappeared into Sloane Street.

So that was it. It was over. Slowly Flora turned and went back indoors, up in the lift, and into the empty flat. She felt alien. Without Rose, everything seemed very quiet.

She went into the sitting room and began, in a desultory fashion, to plump up flattened cushions, draw back curtains, and empty ashtrays. Her attention was soon diverted, however, by Harry Schuster's bookshelves. Browsing, she forgot about housework and found that he read Hemingway and Robert Frost and Norman Mailer and Simenon (in French). There were albums of Aaron Copland in the stacks by the record player, and the Frederick Remington which hung over the fireplace bore witness to his pride in his own country and the best of its achievements.

Harry Schuster was taking shape. Flora decided that she would like him. But it was hard to feel so kindly toward a mother who had gaily abandoned you at birth and swanned off to a life of married ease, taking your twin sister with her.

From last night's session with Rose, plus photographs, Flora had built up a picture of Pamela Schuster so real that it seemed as if she had actually met her: beautiful and worldly, smelling of Patou's Joy, dressed by Dior, or slender as a boy in faded Levi's; Pamela at St. Tropez, skiing at St. Moritz, lunching at La Grenouille in New York; dark eyes bright with amusement, dark hair cut short, her smile a flash of white. She had all the charm and assurance in the world—but love, tenderness? Flora was doubtful.

The clock on the mantelpiece struck noon with silvery strokes. The morning had gone. Flora pulled herself together, made a sandwich, drank a glass of milk, picked up her handbag, and left the flat.

Without enthusiasm, she set out to look for a job. She returned to the flat at the end of the afternoon having achieved nothing except a sort of furious annoyance at her own indecision and procrastination. She was worn out from walking and climbing stairs. She went into the kitchen to put on the kettle

and make herself a cup of tea. This evening she would have a
bath, watch television, and go to bed early. Rose had insisted
she stay over the weekend. Perhaps by Monday she would feel
more energetic and businesslike. Just as the kettle boiled, the
front doorbell rang.

For some reason that was the last straw. Flora said,
"Damn," switched off the kettle, and went out of the kitchen
and down the passage to the front door.

Passing a mirror she caught a glimpse of herself looking
both tired and untidy, her face shining and the sleeves of her
white shirt rolled carelessly back from her wrists. She looked as
though she had been scrubbing a floor and didn't care. She
opened the door.

A man—tall, thin, quite young—was standing outside. He
wore a smoothly cut brown herringbone suit, and his hair was a
dark copper red, the color of an Irish setter. His face was fine
drawn, with pale and freckled skin—the sort that would burn
before it tanned. His eyes were light and clear, a sort of green-
ish gray. They stared down at Flora, as though waiting for her
to make the first move. Finally Flora said, "Yes?"

He said "Hello, Rose."

"I'm not Rose," said Flora.

There was a short pause during which the young man's
expression scarcely altered. Then he said, "Sorry?" as if he had
not heard her properly.

"I'm not Rose," Flora repeated, raising her voice slightly,
as if he were deaf, or stupid, or possibly both. "I'm Flora."

"Who's Flora?"

"Me," said Flora unhelpfully, and then instantly regretted
it. "I mean, I'm staying here for the weekend."

"You have to be joking."

"No, I'm not."

"But you're identical . . ." His voice trailed away, lost in
total confusion.

"Yes, I know."

He swallowed, and said in a voice that cracked slightly,
"Twins?"

"Yes."

He tried again. "Sisters?"

"Yes."

"But Rose doesn't have a sister."

"No, she didn't, but she does now. I mean, she has since yesterday evening."

There was another long pause, and then the young man said, "Do you think you could explain?"

"Yes, of course. You see . . ."

"Do you think, before you start explaining, that I could come in?"

Flora hesitated, her thoughts racing. Harry Schuster's flat, full of precious things; her responsibility; unknown young man, possibly with criminal intentions. . . .It was her turn to swallow the slight obstruction in her throat.

"I don't know who you are."

"I'm Antony Armstrong. I'm a friend of Rose's. I've just flown down from Edinburgh." But Flora still hesitated. With some justification, perhaps, the young man became impatient. "Look, ask Rose. If she isn't there, go and ring her up. I'll wait."

"I can't ring her up."

"Why not?"

"She's gone to Greece."

"Greece?"

The incredulous horror in his voice and the way that the color drained from his face finally convinced Flora. No man, however evil his intentions, could feign such shock. She stood aside and said, "You'd better come in."

To her relief he seemed instantly at home in the flat, dropping his overnight bag and the raincoat he carried onto the chair in the hall as though he had done so many times before. Reassured by that, Flora suggested that he might like a cup of tea. He accepted her offer in a bemused sort of way. They went into the kitchen, and Flora switched on the kettle again. She began to get cups and saucers out of the cupboard, all the time conscious of his unwinking stare as he watched her every movement.

"Do you want Indian or Chinese?" she asked him.

"Indian. Very strong." He found himself a tall kitchen stool and lankily hitched himself up onto it. "Now come along," he said, "tell."

"What do you want to know?"

"Are you really Rose's sister?"

"Yes. I really am."

"But what happened?"

In as few words as possible Flora told him: the broken marriage of Ronald and Pamela Waring; the splitting up of the twin babies; and the two sisters, each growing up in total ignorance of the other's existence until the meeting last night at Seppi's.

"You mean, this didn't happen till yesterday evening?"

"I told you that."

"I can scarcely believe it."

"We could scarcely believe it either, but it happened. Do you take milk and sugar?"

"Yes, both. So what happened then?"

"Well, we had dinner together, and then Rose invited me back here and we talked all night."

"And then this morning she went to Greece?"

"Yes."

"And what are you doing here?"

"Well, you see, I only came up from Cornwall yesterday on the train. I've been away from London for a year, living down there with my father and my stepmother. And actually, I haven't a job in London yet, nor a place to live. I meant to find something today but somehow I didn't. Anyway, Rose asked me to stay here over the weekend. She said it wouldn't matter. Nobody would mind." She turned to hand Antony his cup and was taken off guard by the expression on his face. She added, as though he needed placating, "She made it all right with the porter."

"Tell me, did she particularly ask you to stay here over the weekend?"

"Yes. Why? Shouldn't she?"

He took the cup and saucer from her and began to stir it, still not taking his pale eyes from Flora's face.

"Did she by any chance tell you that I was arriving?"

"She knew you were coming?"

"She didn't mention a telegram I sent her?"

"No." Flora, mystified, shook her head. "Nothing. She didn't say anything."

Antony Armstrong took a large mouthful of scalding tea, then laid down the cup and saucer, got off his stool, and went out of the room. A moment later he was back, a telegram in his hand.

"Where did you find that?" asked Flora.

"Where people invariably put telegrams and invitations and letters they mean to answer when they've got a moment to spare—behind the Rockingham sugar bowl at the end of the mantelpiece. Only in this flat, it happens to be a large, polished lump of alabaster." He held out the telegram to Flora. "You'd better read it."

Reluctantly, Flora took the telegram, while Antony perched himself once more on the stool and continued to drink his tea as if nothing extraordinary was happening.

"Go on, read it."

She did so.

PARCEL AND LETTER RECEIVED. VITALLY IMPORTANT I SEE YOU. TUPPY SERIOUSLY ILL. FLYING LONDON FRIDAY WILL BE WITH YOU LATE AFTERNOON. SIGNED ANTONY.

Flora's worst fears were confirmed. That was a telegraphic *cri de coeur* if ever there was one. And Rose had ignored it, never mentioning it to Flora. She had indeed run away from it.

It was hard to think of any intelligent comment to make. In the end, she said, "Who's Tuppy?"

"My grandmother. Did Rose say why she was going to Greece?"

"Yes, she . . ." Flora looked up. Antony's eyes narrowed, alert. All at once she did not want to tell him. She made an elaborately unconcerned face and tried to think up some elaborately unconcerned lie, but it wasn't any use. Like it or not, she was involved in it right up to the top of her head, and there seemed no way of getting out of it.

"Yes?" he prompted.

Flora gave in. "She's gone to see some man she met in New York. She met him at a party just before she came back to London. He's been lent a villa in Spetsai and he's invited Rose out to join him." This information was received in stony silence. "She had a seat booked on the plane. She went this morning."

After a little Antony said, "I see."

Flora held out the telegram. "I don't know what this—your grandmother—has to do with Rose."

"Rose and I were engaged to be married. But this week, she sent my ring back and broke it off. But Tuppy doesn't know that. She still thinks it's all going to happen."

"And you don't want her to know?"

"No, I don't. I'm thirty and she thinks it's high time I got married. She wants to see us both, make plans, think about the future."

"And what did you want Rose to do?"

"To come home with me. Ride along with the engagement story. Make Tuppy happy."

"Lie to her, in fact."

"Just for a single weekend." He added, his face very serious, "Tuppy's very ill. She's seventy-seven. She may be dying."

The word, final, despairing, hung in the silence between them. Flora could think of nothing to say. Awkwardly, she pulled out a chair and sat at the kitchen table, resting her elbows on its gleaming white surface. It became necessary to be very matter-of-fact. She asked, briskly, "Where's home?"

"The west of Scotland. Arisaig."

"I wouldn't know. I've never been to Scotland."

"Argyll, then."

"Do your parents live there?"

"I haven't any parents. My father's ship was lost during the war, and my mother died just after I was born. Tuppy brought me up. It's her house." He added, "It's called Fernrigg."

"Does Rose know Tuppy?"

"Yes, but not very well. Five years ago Rose and her mother took the Beach House at Fernrigg for two weeks in the summer, and we all got to know them then. Then they went away, and I never thought about them again, until about a year ago when I met up with Rose in London. But Tuppy hasn't seen her since that time."

Fernrigg. Argyll. Scotland. Rose hadn't mentioned Scotland. She had talked about Kitzbühel, St. Tropez, and the Grand Canyon, but she had not mentioned Scotland. It was all very confusing. But one thing was painfully clear. Confronted by crisis, Rose had decided to clear out.

"You . . . you said you came from Edinburgh."

"I work in Edinburgh."

"Will you go back there?"

"I don't know."

"What will you do?"

Antony shrugged and laid down his empty cup. "God knows. Go back to Fernrigg on my own, I suppose. Unless . . ." He looked at Flora, and went on, as though it were the most natural suggestion in the world. ". . . unless you'd like to come with me."

"Me?"

"Yes, You."

"What good could I do?"

"You could pretend to be Rose."

What really offended Flora was the calm way he came out with this outrageous suggestion: sitting there, cool and composed, and wearing on his face an expression of marvelous innocence. His original idea of conning Rose into pretending that she was still engaged to him, had shocked Flora to the core. But this . . .

She found that she was so dismayed that it was difficult to find anything to say. "Thank you *very* much," was all she came up with, and very feeble it sounded, too.

"Why not?"

"Why not? Because it would be the most terrible, ghastly lie. And because it would mean deceiving someone I imagine you're very fond of."

"It's because I'm so fond of her that I'm prepared to deceive her."

"Well, I'm not deceiving anybody, so you'd better start thinking of something else. Like picking up your bag and your raincoat, and getting out of this flat and leaving me alone."

"You'd like Tuppy."

"I wouldn't like anybody I was lying to. You never lie to people who make you feel guilty."

"She'd like you, too."

"I'm not coming."

"If I said please, would it help?"

"No."

"Just for the weekend. That's all. Just the weekend. I've promised. I've never broken a promise to Tuppy in all my life."

Flora found that her indignation was fading, and this was frightening. Outrage was by far her best defense against this disarming young man. It wasn't any use being touched by his sincerity. It wasn't any use allowing herself to be sorry for him.

She said, "I won't do it. I'm sorry. I can't."

"But you can. You've already told me that you haven't got a job, that you haven't even got anywhere to live, except here. And your father's in Cornwall, so he presumably won't be worrying about you." He stopped. "Unless, of course, there's someone else to worry about you."

"You mean, have I got some man who's crazy about me and telephones every five minutes? Well, I haven't."

Antony did not reply to this outburst, but she saw a gleam

of humor in his eyes. "I don't know what's so funny about that," she said.

"It's not funny, it's ludicrous. I always thought Rose was the most gorgeous thing on two legs, and you're her identical twin. Nothing personal, I promise you, just an artistic appreciation. So what's wrong with all the men down here in this mealy-mouthed country south of the border? Have they lost their sight?"

Now he was laughing, and it was the first time that Flora had seen him smile. Before, she had thought him an ordinary-looking young man, even ugly in an attractive sort of way. But when he smiled he became, all at once, quite devastating. She began to see why Rose had succumbed to his charm. She began to wonder why Rose had thrown him over.

Reluctantly, despite herself, Flora smiled too. She said, "For a man who's just been jilted by the woman he loves, you don't seem to be too broken up."

His smile died. "No," he admitted. "But then at heart I'm a pawky, hard-headed Scottish businessman and I had seen the writing on the wall. Anyway, a man who never made a mistake never made anything. And it was good while it lasted."

"I wish she hadn't run out on you. She knew you needed her."

Antony crossed his arms. "I need you too," he told Flora.

"I couldn't do it."

"You just told me you'd never been to Scotland. And here I am, handing you a free trip on a plate, and you're turning it down. You'll never get such an offer again."

"I hope I don't."

"You'd like Fernrigg. And you'd like Tuppy. In fact, the two are so bound up together that it's impossible to imagine one without the other."

"Does she live alone?"

"Heavens, no. There's a family of us. Aunt Isobel and Watty the gardener, and Mrs. Watty who does the cooking. And I've got an older brother called Torquil with a wife called Teresa. I've even got a nephew called Jason. All Armstrongs."

"Does your brother live at Fernrigg?"

"No, he and Teresa are in the Persian Gulf. He's an oil man. But Jason was left at home with Tuppy, which is why he's at Fernrigg right now. It's a sort of dream place for small boys. The house is on the shore, with the sea all around and sands to walk on, and there's a little mooring where Torquil and I used to keep our dinghy. And inland there are streams full of trout and lochs covered with water-lilies, and now, in September, all the heather will be out and the rowan berries scarlet. Like beads. You really ought to come."

It was the most invidious sort of coaxing. Flora, with her elbows on the table and her chin in her hands, eyed Antony Armstrong thoughtfully. She said, "I once read a book about a man called Brat Farrar. And he pretended to be someone else— an impostor, you'd call him—and he had to spend months learning all about himself—about the person he was going to pretend to be. The very thought of it always gave me the shivers."

"But—" Antony got off his stool and came to sit across the table from Flora, so that they faced each other like a pair of conspirators. "But you see, you wouldn't need to do that. Because nobody knows Rose. Nobody's seen her for five years. Nobody known what she's been doing, except getting engaged to me. That's all they're interested in."

"Well, I don't know anything about *you.*"

"That's easy. I'm male, single, thirty years old, and Presbyterian. Educated at Fettes, did my training in London, went back to Edinburgh to join the firm I work for now. I've been with them ever since. What else do you want to know?"

"I'd like to know what makes you think I'd do this dreadful thing."

"It's not a dreadful thing. It's a kindness. Call it a kindness."

"Call it anything you like. I still couldn't do it."

"If I ask you again. If I say please, again, would you think about it? And remember that it isn't for myself I'm asking, it's for Tuppy. And for Isobel too. For promises kept and not broken. Please, Flora."

She longed to be tough—not to be touched or sentimental. She longed for the strength to stick to her own convictions. Because she was right. She knew she was right.

She said cautiously, "If I said I'd come, when would we go?"

Antony's features took on an expression of wary excitement. "Tonight. Now, in fact. There's a plane just after seven; we ought to be able to catch it if we get our skates on. My car's at the airport in Edinburgh. We can drive to Fernrigg. We'll be there first thing in the morning."

"And when would I come back?"

"I have to be at work on Monday morning. You could catch the London plane from Edinburgh that day."

She knew instinctively that she could trust him. Antony would not break his word. "I couldn't be Rose," she warned him. "I could only be myself."

"That's all I want you to be."

She wanted to help him. She liked him, but it had, as well, obscurely, something to do with Rose. *I am my brother's keeper.*

"Rose is very naughty. She shouldn't have run out on you and left you in such a mess."

"The mess is as much my fault as hers. Rose owes me nothing. For that matter, neither do you."

The final decision, Flora knew, was hers. But it was hard not to be impressed by the lengths to which Antony Armstrong was prepared to go in order to keep his promise. Perhaps, she told herself, if a wrong thing were done for a right reason, then that made it right—at least not wholly bad.

A lie was a dangerous thing. Flora's finer instincts, painstakingly cultivated over the years by her father, reacted violently against the insane scheme. And yet, in some way, it was her father's fault. He was responsible for the dilemma in which she now found herself simply because he had never told her of the existence of Rose.

At the same time other, unsuspected reactions were manifesting themselves. They had to do with Rose, and on inspection proved to be part curiosity and part—Flora felt ashamed—envy. Rose seemed to have so much. The temptation offered by this young man to become Rose, just for a couple of days, was growing harder to resist by the minute.

He was waiting. She finally met his eyes across the table and discovered to her shame that when it came to the crunch, words were not going to be necessary. He sensed that she had fallen. A sudden smile lit up his face, and with it, the last of her defenses crumbled about her ears.

"You'll come!" It was a shout of triumph.

"I must be mad."

"You'll come. And you're not mad, you're marvelous. You're a super girl."

He remembered something, and from the pocket of his jacket took out a jeweler's box. Out of it he produced a sapphire and diamond ring. He took Flora's left hand, and pushed it on. She looked down at it, glittering on her finger and thought it looked very pretty. He closed her fingers into a fist and held it within his own two hands.

He said, "Thank you."

5

ANNA

Jason Armstrong, seven years old, sat up in the big double bed alongside his great-grandmother and listened while she read him *The Tale Of Two Bad Mice*. He was really too old for *Two Bad Mice*. He knew it, and Tuppy knew it, but her being in bed and unwell made him nostalgic for babyhood pleasures. When she sent him for a bedtime book, therefore, he had chosen *Two Bad Mice*, and she, being tactful, had not commented, but had put on her spectacles, opened the book at the front page, and started to read.

"Once upon a time there was a very beautiful doll's house."

He thought she read books very well. She read aloud to him every evening after he had had his bath and his supper, usually in the drawing room by the fire. But lately she hadn't been able to read to him at all, since she was too ill. "Now don't you go worrying your great-granny," Mrs. Watty had told him.

"I'll read to you," Aunt Isobel had promised, and had kept

her promise too, but somehow it wasn't the same as Tuppy's reading. Aunt Isobel didn't have the same voice. And she didn't smell of lavender the way Tuppy did.

But, as Mrs. Watty was apt to say, "Every cloud has its silver lining," and there was no denying that there was something pretty special about being in Tuppy's bed. It was unlike anybody else's bed. It was brass decorated with knobs; the pillows were enormous with great white monogrammed covers; and the linen sheets were hemstitched and very old and full of interesting patches and darns.

Even the furniture in Tuppy's room seemed magic and mysterious, made of carved mahogany and faded buttoned silk. The dressing-table was crowded with silver-topped jars and strange things like button hooks and hair nets which Tuppy had told him ladies used to use in the olden days, but now no longer had any need of.

"There were two red lobsters, and a ham, a fish, a pudding, and some pears and oranges."

The curtains were drawn, but outside a wind was getting up and a draft edged its way through the ill-fitting sash windows. The curtains ballooned slightly as though there were someone hidden behind them. Jason drew closer to Tuppy and was glad that she was there. These days he did not like being too far away from her in case something nameless happened and she would not be here when he got back again.

There was a nurse, a proper hospital nurse, who had come to Fernrigg to take care of Tuppy until she was better. Her name was Mrs. McLeod, and she had come all the way from Fort William to Tarbole on the train, and Watty had taken the car to Tarbole to fetch her. She and Mrs. Watty had made friends, and talked importantly in half whispers at the kitchen table over endless cups of tea. Nurse McLeod was thin and starched. She had varicose veins, too, which was perhaps one of the reasons that she and Mrs. Watty had made friends. They were always comparing their varicose veins.

"One morning Lucinda and Jane had gone out for a drive in the doll's perambulator."

Downstairs, in the cavern of the hall, the telephone started to ring. Tuppy stopped reading and looked up, taking off her spectacles.

After a little Jason said, "Go on."

"There's the telephone."

"Aunt Isobel will answer it. Go on."

Tuppy went on, but Jason could tell her mind wasn't on Lucinda and Jane. Then the ringing stopped and once more she stopped reading. Jason gave up. "Who do you think it is?" he asked.

"I don't know. But I've no doubt that in a moment or two Isobel will come upstairs and tell us."

They sat together in the big bed, the old lady and the small boy, expectant. The sound of Isobel's voice floated dimly up the staircase, but they could not hear what she said. At last there came the single ring as she put down the reciever, and then they heard her coming up the stairs and along the passage toward Tuppy's room.

The door opened and Isobel put her face around the edge of it. She was smiling, radiating suppressed excitement. Her soft grayish hair formed an untidy aureole about her beaming face. On such occasions she looked very young, not at all like a great-aunt.

"Do you two want to hear some nice happy news?" she asked, coming in and shutting the door behind her. Sukey, almost lost in the folds of the silk eiderdown, raised her head to give a cursory growl, but Isobel took no notice. She leaned on the rail at the end of Tuppy's bed and said, "That was Antony, calling from London. He's coming home for the weekend and he's bringing Rose."

"He's *coming.*" Tuppy loved Antony more than anyone else in the world, but now she sounded as though she were about to cry. Jason glanced at her anxiously but was relieved to see no sign of tears.

"Yes, they're coming. Just for a couple of days. They both have to go back on Monday. They're catching the evening flight to Edinburgh and then driving over. They'll be here first thing in the morning."

"Well, isn't that splendid?" Two patches of color glowed on Tuppy's wrinkled cheeks. "They're really coming." She smiled down at Jason. "What do you think of that?"

Jason knew all about Rose. He knew that one day Antony was going to marry her. But, "I've never met Rose," he said.

"No, of course you haven't. You weren't living here when she and her mother stayed at the Beach House."

Jason knew about the Beach House, too. It had once been a fisherman's croft, tucked into the curve of the beach which lay to the north of Fernrigg. Tuppy had converted it into a little cottage and let it out in the summer to holiday people. But now the summer was over and the Beach House was closed and shuttered. Jason sometimes thought it would be a nice place to live. It would be pleasant to step out of the front door, straight onto the sand.

"What's she like?"

"Rose? Well, she was very pretty. I can't really remember very much else about her. Where is she going to sleep?" she asked Isobel.

"I thought the little single room, since it's warmer than the great big double one, and the bed's made up. I'll do some flowers."

"And Antony's room?"

"Mrs. Watty and I will do that this evening."

Tuppy laid down *The Tale Of Two Bad Mice.* "We must ask one or two people in . . ."

"Now, mother . . ." Isobel started in a warning sort of voice, but Tuppy took no notice of her. Perhaps because she was so happy, Isobel did not seem to have the heart to persist in her objections.

". . . Just a little supper party. When do you think we should have it? Sunday night? No, that wouldn't be any use because Antony will have to start back to Edinburgh. It'll have to be tomorrow night. Tell Mrs. Watty, will you, Isobel? Perhaps Watty can lay his hands on some pigeon, or better still, some grouse. Or Mr. Reekie might be able to let us have some scampi."

"I'll see to it," promised Isobel, "on one condition—that you don't start trying to organize anything yourself."

"No, of course I won't, don't be so silly. And you must ring up Mr. and Mrs. Crowther, and we'll ask Anna and Brian Stoddart over from Ardmore; they knew Rose when she was out here before, and it'll be nice for Anna to have an evening out. You don't think it's too short notice, do you, Isobel? You'll have to explain, or they'll think we're very rude . . ."

"They'll understand. They won't think it's rude at all."

Mr. Crowther was the Presbyterian minister from Tarbole, and Mrs. Crowther taught Jason at Sunday School. He did not think it sounded a very gay party.

"Do I have to come?" he asked.

Tuppy laughed. "Not if you don't want to."

Jason sighed. "I wish you'd finish the story."

Tuppy began to read again, and Isobel went away to do her telephoning and confer with Mrs. Watty. Just as Tuppy reached the last page, with the picture of Hunca Munca with her dustpan and broom, Nurse McLeod came in. With her starchy rustle and her big red hands, she whisked Jason out of the bed and bundled him good-naturedly out of the way, scarcely giving him time to kiss his great-grandmother good-night.

"You don't want to make your great-granny tired," she told him. "And what Dr. Kyle would say to me if he were to come in the morning and find her all peely-wally, well, I wouldn't like to imagine."

Jason, who had sometimes overheard Dr. Kyle letting fly at something that had annoyed him, could imagine well, but decided to keep it to himself.

He went slowly through the door, not disliking Nurse, because it was nice that she was going to make Tuppy better, but wishing that she didn't always have to be in such a hurry. Feeling ill-used, he trailed along to the bathroom to clean his teeth. In the middle of this, he remembered that tomorrow was

Saturday, which meant that he did not have to go to school.
And Antony was coming. Perhaps he would make Jason a bow
and arrow. In good spirits, Jason finally retired to bed.

When the telephone rang at Ardmore House, Anna Stoddart was out in the garden. At that hour between daylight and
darkness, the outdoors had a special magic for her and even
more so at this time of the year, when the evenings were drawing in and the twilight was thick with nostalgia for the blue and
gold evenings of the summer that was over.

It was easy to come indoors at tea time and draw the
curtains and sit by the fire, forgetting about the scents and the
sounds of outside. But then there would be a ruffle of wind
against the windowpane or the scream of a gull or, at high tide,
the whisper of the sea, and Anna would make some excuse, put
on her jacket and gumboots, pick up her secateurs, and whistle
up the dogs and go outdoors again.

From Ardmore the views of the coastline and the Islands
were spectacular. This was why Anna's father, Archie Carstairs, had chosen the site for his pretentious granite mansion.
Indeed, if one did not mind being a mile from Ardmore Village
(where there was a general store cum post office, and the yacht
club, and little else) and six miles from the shops of Tarbole, it
was a marvelous place to live.

One of the reasons Anna usually liked this time of the
evening was the lights. Just before dark they came on, shining
out at sea, along the coast road, from the great mountains
which shouldered up inland; the riding lights of fishing boats,
and the warm yellow windows of distant crofts and farms. The
street lights of Tarbole stained the night sky with a reddish-
gold reflection, and beyond that again Fernrigg stretched like a
long finger into the sea, with at its tip, half-hidden by trees,
Fernrigg House.

But this evening there was nothing to be seen. The half-
light swirled in mist, a fog horn sounded out at sea, and Ardmore was isolated by the weather like a house forgotten at the
end of the world.

Anna shivered. Being able to see Fernrigg across the sound had always been a comfort to her. Fernrigg meant Tuppy Armstrong. Tuppy was Anna's touchstone, living proof that a person could live contentedly and usefully, surrounded by family and friends, never confused or lacking confidence, apparently totally happy. Tuppy, it always seemed to Anna, had lived her considerable life—and in many ways it had been a tragic one—in a straight line; never diverging, never faltering, never defeated.

Anna had been a shy little girl when she first remembered Tuppy, the only child of an elderly father more interested in his thriving business and his yachting ventures than his small silent daughter. Anna's mother had died soon after Anna was born, so that Anna had been cared for by a series of nannies and insulated from children her own age by her shyness and her father's considerable wealth.

But Tuppy never made Anna feel that she was either plain or stupid. She had always had time for Anna—time to talk and time to listen. "I'm just going out to plant bulbs," she would say. "Come and help me, and while we're working we can talk."

The memory made Anna want to cry. She pushed it to the back of her mind because she could not bear to think of Tuppy ill, much less imagine Tuppy dying. Tuppy Armstrong and Hugh Kyle were Anna's best friends. Brian was her husband and she loved him so much that it hurt, but he wasn't her friend and he never had been. She sometimes wondered if other married couples were friends, but she never got to know the women well enough to be able to ask them and find out.

She was picking the last of the roses, pale shapes in the gloom. She had meant to pick them that morning but had forgotten, and now was gathering a bunch before the first frost could nip them. The stems felt cold in her bare hands, and fumbling a little in the half light she pricked her thumb on a thorn. The smell of the roses was faint and somehow old as though already they had died, and all that remained of their summer glory was their scent.

She thought, *When they come again—the new buds and then the flowers—the baby will be here.*

That should have filled her with happy anticipation, but instead was more of a talisman, like touching wood. She would not think of this baby dying, of it never being born. It had taken so long to become pregnant again. After five years, she had almost given up hope. But now the living seed lay within her, growing every day. She was planning for it: knitting a tiny sweater, getting the old wicker cot down from the attic, putting her feet up in the afternoons the way Hugh had told her to do.

Next week she was going to Glasgow to buy a lot of expensive maternity clothes, and to have her hair done. A woman was at her most beautiful when she was pregnant—so the magazines proclaimed—and all at once Anna had visions of herself as a new person—someone romantic and feminine, loved and cherished.

The old-fashioned words started her. *Loved and cherished.* They seemed to reach her consciousness from some remote past. But now with the new baby coming, there was perhaps real reason to feel hopeful.

Brian had always wanted a child. Every man wanted a son. The fact that she had lost the last one had been Anna's own fault. She had worried too much and become upset too easily. But this time it was going to be different. She was older, less anxious to please, more mature. She would not lose this child.

It was nearly dark and, now, quite cold. She shivered again. Inside the house, she heard the telephone begin to ring. She thought that Brian would probably answer it, but turned toward the house anyway and began to walk up the garden, across the damp grass, up the slippery stone steps, across the crunching gravel, and through the garden door.

The telephone continued to ring. Brian had not appeared. She laid down the roses and, without bothering to remove her rubber boots, went across the hall to the corner under the stairs which, when he had built the house years ago, her father deemed a suitable place for the tiresome instrument. There were other telephones at Ardmore now—in the drawing room, the kitchen, and by Anna and Brian's bed—but this one remained in its stuffy little nook.

She picked it up. "Ardmore House."

"Anna, it's Isobel Armstrong."

Fear caught at Anna. "Tuppy's all right?"

"Yes, she really is. She's looking better and she's eating quite well. Hugh got a nurse for us, a Mrs. McLeod from Fort William, and she's settled down splendidly. I think Tuppy quite likes her."

"What a relief."

"Anna, would you both be able to come over for supper tomorrow evening? It's rather short notice, but Antony is coming home for the weekend and bringing Rose, and of course the first thing Tuppy thought of was a party."

"I think we'd love to come. But isn't it too much for Tuppy?"

"Tuppy won't be there, but she's planning the whole thing. You know what she's like. And she specially wanted you and Brian to come."

"We'd love to. What time?"

"About seven thirty. And don't dress up or anything, it's just family, and maybe the Crowthers . . ."

"That'll be fun."

They chatted for a little longer, and then rang off. Isobel had not said anything about the baby because she didn't know. Nobody knew except Brian and Hugh. Anna didn't want anybody to know. If people knew perhaps she would never have it.

She came out of the little cubbyhole and began to take off her gumboots and her coat. She remembered Rose Schuster and her mother. She remembered the summer they had taken the Beach House, because that was the summer Anna had lost her baby. Pamela Schuster and her daughter were thus part of the nightmare, though that was not their fault, but Anna's own.

She remembered now that where Mrs. Schuster had been frighteningly sophisticated, her daughter was almost indecently youthful. Their glamour had rendered the shy Anna inarticu-

late. Because of that they had had nothing to say to Anna.
Indeed after a few cursory remarks, they had taken no notice of
her at all.

But Brian they had enjoyed. In the warmth of their appreciation he had been at his best, amusing and charming, his wit a
match for anything they could offer. Anna, proud of her attractive young husband, had taken a back seat and been glad to do
so. She wondered when her Rose had changed, whether being
engaged to someone as nice as Antony had taken some of the
sharp edge from her personality.

Now she stood listening, wondering where she would find
Brian. The house was silent. She went across to the drawing-
room door, opened it, and found the room full of light and
firelight, and Brian stretched out in the armchair reading the
Scotsman. A tumbler of whisky stood close by his hand.

He lowered the paper as she appeared and eyed her over
the top of it. The telephone stood on the table by his side.

She said, "Didn't you hear the telephone ring?"

"Yes. But I guessed it would be for you."

She did not comment on this. She came over to the fire,
stretching her cold hands to the blaze, warming herself. She
said, "That was Isobel Armstrong."

"How's Tuppy?"

"She seems to be all right. They've got a nurse for her.
They want us to go over and have supper at Fernrigg tomorrow. I said that we would."

"That's all right by me."

He began to go back to his newspaper and Anna said
quickly, to keep the conversation going, "Antony's coming
home for the weekend."

"So that's the reason for the celebration."

"He's bringing Rose with him."

There was a long silence. Then Brian lowered his paper,
folded it, and laid it on his lap. He said, "Rose?"

"Rose Schuster. You remember. He's engaged to her."

"I thought someone said she was in America."

"Apparently not."

"You mean, she's coming to Fernrigg for the weekend?"

"That's what Isobel told me."

"Well, I never did," said Brian. He sat up, dropping the paper onto the hearth rug, and reached out for his drink. He tipped it back, finished it, got slowly up out of his chair and went over to the drink table to replenish his glass.

Anna said, "I've been out picking roses." The siphon swished into Brian's tumbler. "It's raining. The mist's coming in."

"It felt like that earlier on."

"I was afraid of frost."

With the glass in his hand, Brian came back to the fireside and stood looking down into the flames.

Anna straightened up. There was a mirror over the mantelpiece and their reflections stared back at them, only slightly distorted: the man, slim and dark, his eyebrows sharp-drawn as though some artist had brushed them on in India ink; and the woman, short, reaching only to his shoulder, dumpy and plain. Her eyes were close-set, her nose too big, her hair, neither brown nor fair, frizzed from the damp of the mist.

So convinced had she been by her own visions of an Anna made romantic by incipient motherhood, that her reflection came as a shock. Who was this person who stared back at her from the faded glass? Who was this person, this stranger, standing next to her handsome husband?

The answer, came, as it always came. Anna. Plain Anna. Anna Carstairs that was, Anna Stoddart that is. And nothing was ever going to change her.

Following the urgency of Antony's trip to London, the drama of their confrontation, and her eventual decision to accompany him, Flora imagined that once in Edinburgh they would get into his car and drive hotfoot or post-chaise, or whatever you wanted to call it, to Fernrigg.

But now that they were actually there, Antony's whole personality seemed to change. Like a man coming home and shrugging on an old jacket and a pair of comfortable slippers, he relaxed, slowed down, and appeared to be in no hurry to get to Fernrigg.

"We'd better get something to eat," he decided, after they had located the car, loaded Flora's suitcase into the trunk, and settled themselves in.

She looked at him in surprise. "Something to eat?"

"Yes. Aren't you hungry? I am."

"But we had a meal on the plane."

"That wasn't a meal. That was a plastic snack. And I have a horror of cold asparagus."

"But don't you want to get home as soon as possible?"

"If we start now, we'll arrive at four in the morning. The house will be locked, and we'll either have to sit outside for three hours, or wake somebody up and doubtless disrupt the entire household." He started up the engine. "We'll go into Edinburgh."

"But it's late. Will we find anything open at this hour?"

"Of course we will."

They drove to Edinburgh and Antony took her to a small club of which he was a member, where they had a drink and an excellent dinner, and then coffee. It was all very leisurely and pleasant and completely incongruous. It was nearly midnight when they finally emerged once more into the outdoors. The wind of the morning had died, and the streets of Edinburgh shone black with a thin, cold rain.

"How long will it take us?" Flora asked, as they got back into the car, fastened their seat belts and generally settled down to the long drive.

"About seven hours with this rain. The best thing you can do is go to sleep."

"I'm not very good at sleeping in cars."

"You can always try."

But Flora did not sleep. She was too excited, too apprehensive, and already suffering from a severe case of cold feet. The knowledge that she had burnt her boats, that she was on her way and there was not a mortal thing she could do now to change anything, left her feeling quite sick. If it had been a fine bright night she might have tried to still her nerves by observing the passing countryside, or even reading their route on the map. But the rain was incessant, and there was nothing to be seen but the black, wet, winding road, pierced by the headlights of Antony's car, racing up to meet them in a succession of endless curves and bends, and falling away behind into the darkness to the hiss of tires on wet tarmac.

And yet, as they drove, the countryside made itself felt, even through the darkness and the deadening murk. It became more deserted, more desolate, the small country towns fewer and farther apart. They passed the long glimmer of an inland loch, and as they left it behind them the road began to climb, winding against the slope of the incline.

Through the half-open window came the smell of peat and heather. More than once Antony, with a murmured oath, was forced to brake the car to a standstill while a stray sheep or two, caught in the headlights, made its untroubled way off the crest of the road.

Flora was aware of mountains—not the little hills of home, the familiar cairns of Cornwall, but real mountains, sheer, rearing their way up at right angles and forming deep caverns and lonely glens down which the road ribboned ahead of them. There was bracken in the ditches, shining with rain, and always, even about the sound of the car's engine, the suggestion of running water which every now and then became a torrent as a waterfall leapt from some distant unseen ledge down onto the rocks of a roadside stream.

The dawn on that wet, gray morning came so gradually that Flora scarcely noticed it. It was simply a paling of the gloom, imperceptible, so that slowly it became possible to pick up the white glimmer of a hillside croft and to see the damp shapes of flocks of sheep before one was actually in danger of hitting them.

There had been little traffic on the road all night but now they began to meet great lorries coming in the opposite direction, passing them with roaring Diesel engines and waves of muddy water washing across the windscreen.

"Where have they suddenly appeared from?" asked Flora.

"They've come from where we're going," Antony told her.

"Fernrigg?"

"No, Tarbole. Tarbole used to be an unimportant fishing village, but it's a great herring port now."

"Where are the lorries going?"

"Edinburgh, Aberdeen, Fraserburgh—anywhere they can sell the herrings. The lobsters get taken to Prestwick and flown straight to New York. The scampi goes to London. Salted herrings go to Scandinavia."

"Hasn't Scandinavia got its own herrings?"

"The North Sea's been fished out. That's why Tarbole came into its own. Very prosperous we are these days. All the fishermen have new cars and color televisions. Jason goes to school with their children, and they have a low opinion of him because we don't have color television at Fernrigg. It cramps his style a bit, poor chap."

"How far is Tarbole from Fernrigg?"

"About six miles."

"How does he get to school each day?"

"He gets taken by Watty, the gardener. He'd like to bicycle, but Tuppy won't let him. She's quite right. He's only seven, and she lives in fear that some terrible accident will befall him."

"How long has he lived with Tuppy?"

"So far, a year. I don't know how much longer he'll stay. I suppose it depends on Torquil's job."

"Does he miss his parents?"

"Yes, of course he does. But the Persian Gulf is really no place for a child his age. And Tuppy wanted him to stay. She doesn't like the house without a little boy messing the place up. There have always been little boys at Fernrigg. I think that's one of the reasons Tuppy always seems ageless. She's never had time to grow old."

"And Isobel?"

"Isobel's a saint. Isobel was the person who looked after you when you were ill, and coped when you'd been sick, and woke up in the middle of the night to get you a drink of water."

"She never married?"

"No, she never married. I think the war had something to do with that. She was too young at the beginning of the war, and by the end all she wanted was to come back to Fernrigg to live. And the West Highlands aren't exactly teeming with eligible bachelors. There was a suitor once, but he was a farmer with every intention of buying a property on the Isle of Eigg. He made the mistake of taking Isobel to see it, and she was seasick on the way over, and when she got there it rained incessantly for the entire day. The farmhouse was intensely primitive, the loo was down at the end of the garden, she was seasick all the way home again, and after that the romance died an entirely natural death. We were all delighted. We didn't like the chap at all. He had a bright red face and was always talking about going back to the simple life. A terrible bore."

"Did Tuppy like him?"

"Tuppy liked everybody."

"Will she like me?"

Antony turned his head slightly and sent Flora a smile that was both rueful and conspiratorial, and not really a smile at all.

"She'll like Rose," he said.

Flora fell silent once more.

Now it was light, and the rain had turned to a soft blowing mist which was beginning to smell of the sea. The road ran downhill through cuttings of pinkish granite along sloping hills planted with stands of larch and fir. They came through small villages slowly starting to stir for the new day and by inland lochs where the dark water shivered under the touch of the west wind. With each turn of the road a new and marvelous prospect presented itself, and when at last they came to the sea, Flora realized it only when she saw the salty waves breaking onto weeded rocks at the head of yet another loch.

For a few miles they drove by the shore. Flora saw a ruined castle, the grass about its walls cropped by sheep; a coppice of silver birches, the leaves turned the color of bright new pennies; a farm with sheep pens and a dog barking. It was all remote and very beautiful.

She said, "It's romantic. Such a corny word to use, but the only one I can think of. It's romantic country."

"That's because it's Bonnie Prince Charlie country. Steeped in tradition and nostalgia. The birthplace of a thousand lost causes, the start of long years of exile and depopulation, and all those sterling Scottish women coming into their own."

"Wouldn't you like to live here? I mean, all the time."

"I have to earn a living."

"Couldn't you earn a living here?"

"Not as a chartered accountant. I could be a fisherman. Or a doctor, like Hugh Kyle. He looks after Tuppy and he's lived here, on and off, all his life."

"He must be a happy man."

"No," said Antony. "I don't really think he is."

They were in Tarbole by half past six, driving down the steep hill to the little harbor, empty now of the huge fish lorries and enjoying a quiet soon to be shattered by the boats coming in with the night's haul.

Because they were still too early, Antony drove down to the harbor road and parked the car in front of a wooden shack which faced out over the wharves and piers and the cranes and the smokehouses.

As they got out of the car the cold struck at them, rich with the smell of sea, tarred ropes, and fish. The shack had "Sandy Soutar. Teas, Coffees, Snacks" written over the door, and a warm yellow light shone from the steamy windows.

They went in, stepping up by means of an old herring box. Inside it was very warm, and smelt of new bread and bacon frying, and from behind the counter a fat woman in a flowered overall looked up from her urn, saw Antony, and broke at once into a welcoming smile.

"Antony Armstrong. For heaven's sake! What are you doing here, turned up like a bad penny?"

"Hello, Ina. I'm home for the weekend. Could you give us some breakfast?"

"Well, of course. Sit down. Make yourselves at home." She looked past him at Flora, her eyes bright with interest. "And is this your young lady you've brought with you? We heard you were going to be married."

"Yes," said Antony, and he took Flora's hand and pulled her forward. "This is Rose."

It was the first time. The first lie. The first hurdle.

"Hello," said Flora, and somehow, as easily as that, the hurdle was behind her.

6

JASON

Tuppy had been awake since five o'clock, expecting Antony and Rose since six.

If she had been well, she would have gotten up and dressed, gone downstairs into the silent sleeping house, and engaged herself in all the familiar routine jobs which she found so comforting. She would have opened the front door and let out the dogs and then gone into the kitchen to put on the kettle, all ready for a cup of tea. Back upstairs, she would have switched on the electric fires in the two prepared bedrooms and checked that all was ready and welcoming, with the bedcovers crisp and fresh, hangers in the wardrobes, and the drawers of the dressing tables lined with clean white paper.

Then down again to let in the dogs and give them biscuits and a little petting, to draw curtains, thus letting in the morning light, to stir the embers of the hall fire and lay on some more peat. All would have been warm and welcoming.

But she was old and now ill, and had to stay in bed while

others performed those pleasurable tasks. Frustration and boredom gnawed at her. For two pins, she thought, she would get up and get dressed, and Isobel and Nurse McLeod and Hugh Kyle could all go to the devil. But behind her resentment there was a very real fear. A miserable homecoming it would be for Antony to find his grandmother prone at the foot of the stairs because she hadn't the sense to do what she was told.

She sighed, accepting the inevitable. She ate a biscuit out of the tin by her bed and drank a little tea, which Nurse left each night in a thermos. She would contain herself in patience. But being ill, she decided, was a thorough bore. She was thankful she had never tried it before.

At seven o'clock the house began to stir. She heard Isobel come out of her room and go downstairs; she heard the sounds of dogs and the opening of the big front door, the dungeon-like iron bolts being shot back, and the great key being turned.

Presently Mrs. Watty's voice joined Isobel's and before very long the faint smell of breakfast cooking drifted up from below. Next she heard Jason go to the bathroom, and then his raised voice as he called over the banister, "Aunt Isobel!"

"Yes?"

"Have Rose and Antony come?"

"Not yet. Any moment now."

Tuppy watched her door. The handle turned, and it slowly opened. "I'm awake," she said, as Jason's blond head came around the edge of it.

"They haven't got here yet," he told her.

"By the time you get dressed, they'll probably be here."

"Did you sleep well?"

"Like a top," lied Tuppy. "Did you?"

"Yes. At least, I think I did. You don't know where my Rangers T-shirt is, do you?"

"Probably in the airing cupboard."

"Oh, all right. I'll go and look."

He disappeared, leaving the door open. The next event was the arrival of Sukey who, having been let in from her morning visit to the garden, had headed straight upstairs. She pattered across the floor and leapt by means of a chair onto Tuppy's bed. With no more ado she settled herself in her usual place at the foot of the eiderdown.

"Sukey!" Tuppy reproached her, but Sukey was without conscience. She stared coldly at Tuppy for a moment, and then settled down to sleep.

Nurse was the next visitor, drawing curtains, shutting windows, turning on the fire, and making all Tuppy's ornaments rattle as she trod heavily about the room.

"We'll need to get you tidied up before your grandson and his young lady arrive," Nurse said, with a gleam in her eye. She pulled at sheets and pillows, reached into the depths of Tuppy's bed for her hot water bottle, asked her what she wanted for breakfast. "Mrs. Watty's frying bacon . . . she says Antony always looks forward to fried bacon his first morning home. Would you fancy a little yourself?"

And then, just as Tuppy was telling herself that she couldn't wait another moment, she heard the sound of Antony's car roaring up the road, through the open gates, and up the potholed driveway. The morning's calm was shattered by the double flourish of his horn, the screech of brakes, and the spatter of flying gravel. (In Tuppy's opinion, he always drove too fast.) Downstairs minor pandemonium broke out. Plummer began to bark, footsteps came up the back passage and across the hall, the door opened with a bang, and happy voices filled the house.

Here you are. Oh, how are you? How lovely to see you.

Jason said, "Hello, Antony. Did you have a good journey? Will you make me a bow and arrow?"

Tuppy heard Antony's voice. "How's Tuppy?" (Her heart melted with love for him.)

"She's *awake,*" she heard Jason telling him, his voice squeaky with excitement. "She's waiting for you."

Tuppy hugged herself in anticipation and sat watching her door and waiting for him to come, which he did almost immediately, taking the stairs two at a time as usual.

"Tuppy!"

"I'm here!"

Long strides took him down the landing and through the door. He burst into her room and stood beaming at her with a grin on his face like a Cheshire Cat.

"Tuppy." He wore Bedford cords and a thick sweater and a leather car coat, and when he came over to her bedside to give her a kiss she could feel the night's stubble on his chin scraping her cheeks. He was cold and his hair was too long and she could scarcely believe that he was really here.

They hugged enormously. He drew away from her. "But you're looking marvelous. What an old fraud you are."

"There's nothing wrong with me. You're later than usual. Did you have a horrid drive over?"

"No, a very good one. So good that we stopped for breakfast with Sandy in Tarbole. We're stuffed with sausages and strong tea."

"Is Rose with you?"

"Yes. Downstairs. Do you want to see her?"

"Of course I want to see her. Fetch her up at once."

He went out of the room, and she heard him calling down the stairs. "Rose!" There was no response. Then, louder this time, *"Rose!* Come along up. Tuppy's waiting to see you."

Tuppy watched the door. When he came back into the room, he was leading Rose by the hand.

She thought they both seemed shy, almost ill-at-ease, and she found this endearing, as though being in love had peeled away a little of Antony's bright veneer of sophistication.

She looked at Rose and remembered her, and thought that the five years between seventeen and twenty-two had transformed a pretty but sometimes sulky girl into something very special. She saw the tanned skin, clear with health and sheer cleanliness; the shining fall of brown hair; the eyes—such dark brown eyes. Tuppy had forgotten they were so dark. She wore the regular uniform of the young these days: washed-out jeans and a turtleneck sweater, and over it a navy blue coat with a tartan lining.

Rose said, shyly, "I'm afraid I don't look very tidy."

"Oh, my dear! How could you look tidy when you've been traveling all night? Anyway, I think you look charming. Now come and give me a kiss."

Rose came across and stooped to kiss Tuppy. The dark hair fell forward and touched Tuppy's cheek. Rose's own cheek was smooth and cool, reminding Tuppy of crisp, newly picked apples.

"I thought you were never coming to see me!"

Rose sat on the edge of the bed. "I'm sorry."

"You've been in America?"

"Yes."

"How's your mother?"

"Very well."

"And your father?"

"He's well too. We were on a trip." She caught sight of Sukey. "Oh, look, is this your dog?"

"You remember Sukey, Rose! She used to come on picnics on the beach with us."

"She . . . she must be getting quite old."

"She's ten. That's seventy in dog years. And even that's younger than I am. I've got more teeth than she has, but then Sukey hasn't been stupid and ill like me. Did you say you'd had breakfast?"

"Yes," said Antony. "We had it in Tarbole."

"Oh, what a shame, Mrs. Watty's frying bacon specially for you. You'll have to go and toy with it, or at least have a cup of coffee."

She smiled at Rose, feasting her eyes on the girl. She relished the thought of having her married to Antony and the pleasure of having her here, at Fernrigg.

She said, "Let me see your ring," and Rose showed it to her, the diamonds and sapphires glittering on the slender brown hand.

"What a pretty one! But then I knew it would be. Antony has very good taste."

Rose smiled. It was one of those all-embracing, lighting-up smiles that Tuppy loved . . . the teeth very white with the two front ones a little crooked, making her seem very young and vulnerable.

"How long can you stay?" asked Tuppy, not able to endure the idea that they would have to go away again, ever.

"Only till tomorrow night," said Antony. "We both have to get back."

"Two days. It's such a short time." She gave Rose's hand a little pat. "Never mind, long enough to enjoy ourselves. And we're going to have a little party tonight, just one or two people, as it's such a special occasion." She caught sight of Antony's expression. "Now, don't start fussing. I have that all the time from Isobel and Nurse. Did you know they engaged a nurse to look after me? Mrs. McLeod, and she comes from Fort William." She dropped her voice to a whisper. "She looks exactly like a horse." Rose gave a snort of laughter. "Such a lot of rubbish, but it does make things a little easier for Isobel. And of course I'm not coming to the party. I shall sit up here with a supper tray and listen to you all having a good time." She turned to Rose. "I asked Anna and Brian—you remember them, don't you? Yes, of course you do. I thought it would be fun for you to see them again."

Rose said, "I just wish you could be there too."

"How sweet you are. But if I stay in bed for just a little while longer, then I'll be on my feet for your wedding and that's the most important thing of all." She smiled again at them, her eyes moving from one face to the other. They watched her, the two pairs of eyes, one so pale and one so dark. Tuppy noticed that the dark eyes were shadowed with tiredness. She said, "Rose, have you slept at all?"

Rose shook her head. "I couldn't."

"Oh, my dear, you must be exhausted."

"I am, a little. Suddenly. Just sleepy."

"Would you like to go to bed? Sleep until lunchtime and then you'll feel better. And perhaps Antony . . ."

"I'm all right," Antony said quickly. "I'll maybe have a snooze later on in the day."

"But Rose must sleep. Mrs. Watty shall make you a hot-water bottle. And afterwards you can have a lovely bath. You'd like that, wouldn't you?"

"Yes, I would," Rose admitted.

"Then that's what you shall do. And now go down and placate Mrs. Watty by eating some bacon, and tell Nurse I'm ready for my breakfast, and," she added as they headed for the door, "thank you again, both of you, so much, for coming."

Waking was strange. The bed was strange, though marvelously soft and comfortable. The cornice of the ceiling was strange, the deep pink of the drawn curtains unfamiliar. Before she had even oriented herself, Flora drew her arm up out of the covers and looked at her watch. Eleven o'clock. She had been asleep for five hours. And here she was, at Fernrigg—Fernrigg House, in Arisaig, in Argyll, in Scotland. She was Flora, but now she was Rose, engaged to be married to Antony Armstrong.

She had met them all: Isobel; little Jason; Mrs. Watty, billowy and wholesome and floury as a newly baked scone; and Watty, her husband, tramping into the kitchen while they sat drinking coffee, with carefully doormatted boots and inquiries about vegetables. Everybody seemed delighted to see her, and it wasn't just because of Antony. Reminiscences had been the order of the day.

"And how's Mrs. Schuster?" Mrs. Watty had asked. "I remember that summer how she used to walk up to the garden every morning for fresh eggs, and Watty used to give her a head of lettuce, because she said she couldn't go a day without a fresh salad."

And Isobel remembered a certain picnic when it had been so warm that Tuppy had insisted on swimming, borrowing one of Pamela Schuster's elegant bathing suits for the purpose. "She wouldn't let any of us watch her going in. She looked indecent, she said, but actually she looked very nice, because she was always very slim."

And Antony had teased Isobel. "If Tuppy wouldn't let you

watch, how do you know she looked nice? You must have been peeping."

"Well, I just wanted to make sure she didn't get a cramp." Only Jason, much to his disgust, had nothing to remember. "I wish I'd been here when you were here," he told Flora, gazing at her in open and interested admiration. "But I wasn't. I was somewhere else."

"You were in Beirut," Isobel told him. "And even if you had been here you wouldn't remember very much, because you were only two."

"I can remember when I was two. I can remember lots of things."

"Like what?" asked Antony skeptically.

"Like . . . Christmas trees?" he tried hopefully.

Everybody smiled but nobody laughed at him, Flora noticed. Thus, although he knew that nobody quite believed him, his dignity remained unimpaired.

"Anyway," he added, "I would *certainly* have remembered Rose."

So their welcome was not just on account of the fact that Rose was meant to be marrying Antony. The Schusters had apparently made a certain impact on their own account five years ago which was still happily recalled, and that made things easier.

Flora looked at her watch again. Five past eleven now, and she was wide awake. She got out of bed, and went across to the windows and drew the curtains and looked straight out over the garden to the sea.

The rain had stopped and the mist was dissolving. Far away outlines of the distant islands were faintly beginning to take shape.

The tide was out, revealing a small jetty and a steep pebble beach, toward which the garden sloped in a series of grassy terraces. Away to one side she glimpsed the netting of a tennis court. Below her, the leaves of flowering shrubs were scarlet and gold, and a rowan tree hung heavy with the weight of its berries.

Flora withdrew from the window, closed it, and went in search of a bath. That she found to be a coffin-like Victorian structure enclosed in polished mahogany with sides so high that it took considerable effort to get into it at all. The water was boiling hot, very soft, and stained brown with peat. The rest of the bathroom and its accessories were all strictly period. The soap smelt faintly medicinal, the towels were vast and white and very fluffy, and there was a jar on the bathroom shelf labeled "bay rum." Altogether it was very old-fashioned and immensely luxurious.

Clean and dressed, having made her bed and hung up her clothes, Flora ventured out of her room. She walked to the end of the passage, to where the wide staircase led down to the big hall in a series of flights and landings. She stopped, listening for some sound of domestic activity, but heard nothing. She saw Tuppy's bedroom door, but was afraid of disturbing her in the middle of a nap, or in the midst of a session with her doctor or the brisk and businesslike nurse. She went downstairs and saw the smoldering fire in the huge hearth. She smelt the peat and thought it delicious.

Still there was no sound. Not really knowing her way around the house, Flora finally found the kitchen, where to her relief she saw Mrs. Watty standing at the table and plucking a bird. Mrs. Watty looked up through a drift of feathers.

"Hello, Rose. Have you had a nice wee rest?"

"Yes, thank you."

"Do you want a cup of coffee?"

"No, it's all right. I wondered, where is everybody?"

"Everybody's away on their own business. At least, as far as I know. Nurse is waiting for the doctor to come, and Miss Isobel's away to Tarbole for the errands for the party tonight, and Antony and Jason have gone over to Lochgarry to see if Willie Robertson can do something about patching up the potholes in the drive. Miss Isobel's been on at Antony each time he comes home to do something about those potholes, but you know how it is. There never seems to be enough time. But this morning he agreed and he and Jason went off about an hour ago. They'll be back for lunch." Mrs. Watty took up a murderous knife and severed the chicken's head from its body. "So it looks as though you've been left to your own devices."

Flora averted her eyes from the severed head. "Can't I do something to help you? I could lay a table or something. Or peel potatoes."

Mrs. Watty gave a peal of laughter. "Mercy, that's all done. There's nothing for you to worry your head about. Why don't you go out for a wee walk? The rain's stopped and a bit of fresh air won't do you any harm. You should go down to the Beach House. Have a look at it. See if it's changed after all these years."

"Yes," said Flora. It was a good idea. Then she would know about the Beach House and be able to talk about it the way Rose might. "But I can scarcely remember how to get there."

"Oh, you can't miss it. Just go away round the house and down the path to the sands. Mind, you should take a coat. I wouldn't trust the weather this morning, though the afternoon might be fine and bright."

Thus bidden, Flora fetched her coat from her room, came downstairs again and let herself out of the front door. The morning was cool and sweet and damp, smelling of dead leaves and peat smoke and, behind it all, the saltiness of the sea. She stood for a moment trying to get her bearings and then turned to the left, crossed the gravel in front of the house and so came to a path which led down between sloping lawns to a grove of rhododendrons.

When she finally emerged from the rhododendrons, she found herself in a newly planted stand of young firs. The path led on, however, through the saplings, until she came out at last by a gate in a drystone wall. Beyond and below this was heather, and then rocks, and then a beach of the whitest sand she had ever seen.

She realized that she had come out onto the southern shore of yet another sea loch. Now, at low tide, only a narrow channel of water split the two white beaches, and on the far

side the land sloped up to a pleasant prospect of shallow green
hills patchworked in sheepfolds and small fields where the new-
cut hay stood in hand-built stooks.

There was a small croft with blue smoke rising from the
chimney and a dog at the door, and sheep (as always in this
part of the world) dotted over the hillside.

Making her way down to the water's edge, Flora searched
for the Beach House. She spotted it almost instantly, unmistak-
ably tucked into the curve of the bay, and backed by a copse of
gnarled oak trees.

As she started to walk towards it, she noticed the wooden
steps which led up over the rocks from the beach, and the
closed and shuttered face of the little house. The walls were
painted white, the roof slate-blue, and the doors and shutters
green. She went up the steps and saw the flagged terrace where
a fiberglass dinghy had been pulled up, and a wooden tub stood
filled with the dying remains of the summer's geraniums.

She turned and leaned her back against the door and
looked at the view and, like an actress with a new part to play,
tried to think herself into the person of Rose. Rose at seventeen.
What had she done with herself that summer? How had she
spent her time? Had it been fine and hot so that she could
sunbathe on the terrace? Had she gone out on the loch at high
tide in the little dinghy? Had she swum and collected shells and
walked the shining sands?

Or had it bored her stiff? Had she sulked the days away,
yearning for New York or Kitzbühel or any of her other hunt-
ing grounds? Flora wished she knew and could be more sure
about Rose. She wished there had been time to get to know her
sister better.

She turned and backed away from the house, gazing at it,
trying to learn something from it. But its shuttered façade was
like a secret face, telling her nothing. She abandoned it and
went back to the beach right down to the edge of the sea, where
the glass-clear water lapped the sand, and shells lay for the
gathering, smooth and unbroken in the peaceful inlet.

She picked up one and then another, and became so absorbed in this aimless occupation that she lost all sense of time. There was therefore no way of knowing how long she had been there when, quite suddenly, Flora became aware that she was being watched. Looking up from the shells, she saw a car parked by the edge of the narrow road at the head of the loch. It had not been there before. And by it, motionless, his hands in his pockets, stood a man.

They were perhaps a hundred yards apart. But at once, realizing that Flora had seen him, he took his hands out of his pockets, made the short descent down onto the beach, and began to walk across the sands toward her.

Immediately Flora was self-conscious. She and the approaching man were the only two souls in sight (if you discounted a number of greedy sea-birds), and various fantasies flashed through her mind.

Perhaps he was lost and wanted to ask the way. Perhaps he was looking for somewhere to spend next summer's holiday with his wife and family, and Beach House had caught his eye. Perhaps he was a sex maniac out for a walk. Flora wished she had thought to bring a dog with her.

But then she told herself not to be a fool, for even at this distance, his solid respectability proclaimed itself: in his size, which was exceptional, for he was very tall and broad in proportion, wide-shouldered and long-legged; in his purposeful, unhurried stride which covered the distance between them with the easy lope of a man used to walking; in his conventional, country clothes. Perhaps he was a farmer or a neighboring landowner. She imagined a large, drafty house and shooting parties in August.

The time had come to make some sort of acknowledgment rather than just stand there with her hands full of shells, staring at him. Flora tried a faint smile, but got no response. He simply continued to approach, bearing down on her like a tank. He was perhaps between thirty and forty, with a face set in strong lines; his hair, his suit, even his shirt and tie were of no particular color and totally unobtrusive. Only his eyes broke the pattern, being so bright and deep a blue that Flora found herself

taken off guard. She had expected many things, but not this chill, this bright glare of antagonism.

He came at last to a halt, not a yard from where she stood, standing braced against the slope of the beach, with his weight on one foot. A wind stirred and blew a strand of hair across Flora's cheek. She pushed it away. He said, "Hello, Rose."

I'm not Rose.

"Hello," said Flora.

"Are you reviving happy memories?"

"Yes. I suppose I am."

"How does it feel to be back?" His voice held the soft cadence of the West Highlands. So he was a local man. And he knew Rose. But who was he?

"It feels nice," said Flora, wishing that her own voice would sound more sure of itself.

He slid his hands into his trouser pockets. "You know, I never believed that you'd actually come back."

"That's not a very kindly welcome. Or is it?"

"You were never a fool, Rose. Don't let's pretend that you ever expected anything else from me."

"Why shouldn't I come?"

He nearly smiled at that, but it did nothing to improve his expression.

"I don't think either you or I need to ask that question."

Somewhere, deep in the pit of Flora's stomach, small stirrings of annoyance began to make themselves felt. She did not like being so openly disliked.

"Did you walk all the way down the beach, just to tell me that?"

"No. I came to tell you one or two other things. To remind you that you are no longer an artless teenager. You're engaged to Antony. A grownup woman. I simply hope, for your own sake, you've learned to behave like one."

If she felt intimidated, she was determined not to show it.

"That sounds like a threat," said Flora as jauntily as she could.

"No. Not a threat. A warning. A friendly warning. And now, I'll bid you good day and leave you to your shells."

And with that he turned and left her, moving away from her as abruptly as he had come, apparently unhurried, but covering the ground with his long-legged stride and astonishing swiftness.

Flora, rooted to the ground, watched him go. In no time, it seemed, he had reached the rocks, mounted them easily, got into his car, turned it, and driven back onto the road which led to Tarbole.

Still she stood there like one punch-drunk, holding the shells, her mind seething with questions. But out of all this emerged only one possible answer. Rose, at seventeen, had had some sort of an ill-fated affair with that man. Nothing else she could think of could explain such resentment, such ill-concealed dislike.

She dropped the shells abruptly and began to walk, slowly at first and then more quickly, back towards the comfort of Fernrigg. She thought of finding Antony, of telling him, of taking him into her confidence; and then on second thought decided against it.

After all, she was not really involved. She was Flora, not Rose. She was only here at Fernrigg for two days. They would be leaving tomorrow night, and then she would never see any of them again. She would never see that man again. He had known Rose, but that did not mean he was a friend of the Armstrongs. Even if he were an acquaintance, it seemed highly unlikely that Tuppy Armstrong would ever ask such a disagreeable person to her house.

Having come to this conclusion, Flora vowed to put the entire incident out of her mind. But it was hard not to suspect that Rose had, perhaps, not behaved as well as she might.

After that it was something of a relief, as she emerged from the rhododendron grove, to see Antony and Jason walking across the grass toward her, coming to find her. They both wore disreputable jeans and large bulky sweaters. There were holes in the toes of Jason's canvas sneakers, and his shoe laces were undone. When he saw Flora, he started to run to meet her, tripped on the lace, fell flat on his face, got up immediately, and continued running. Flora caught him as he reached her, picked him up, and swung him around.

"We've been looking for you," he told her. "It's nearly lunchtime, and it's shepherd's pie."

"I'm sorry. I didn't realize it was so late." She looked up over his head at Antony.

"Good morning," he said, and unexpectedly, stooped to kiss her. "How are you?"

"Very well."

"Mrs. Watty told us you'd come out for a walk. Did you find the Beach House?"

"Yes."

"Everything all right?"

He was not asking about the Beach House, but about Flora, about how she felt, how she was coping with the situation into which he had plunged her. His concern touched her, and because she did not want him to think that anything untoward might have happened, she smiled and told him firmly that everything was perfect.

"Did you go to the Beach House?" asked Jason.

"Yes." They began to walk back to the house, Jason holding Flora's hand. "But it's all shuttered up and I couldn't see inside."

"I know. Watty goes down at the end of every summer and does that, otherwise boys come out from Tarbole and break the windows. Once somebody broke a window and got in and stole a blanket." He made it sound as criminal as murder.

"And what have you been doing this morning?" Flora asked him.

"We went to Lochgarry to see Willie Robertson about the holes in the drive, and Willie's going to come with his tar machine and fill them all up. He said he'd come next week."

Antony was not so sure. "That probably means next year," he told Flora. "This is the west of Scotland and the passage of time is of no concern. *Mañana* means yesterday."

"And Mrs. Robertson gave me some toffee and then we went to the pier at Tarbole and there's a ship in from Denmark and they're packing herrings in barrels and I saw a gull and it ate a mackerel in *one gulp.*"

"Herring gulls are always very greedy."

"And this afternoon, Antony's going to make me a bow and arrow."

"Perhaps," suggested Antony, "we should ask Rose what she wants to do."

Jason looked up at her in some anxiety. "You'd like to make a bow and arrow, wouldn't you?"

"Yes, I would. But I don't suppose it'll take very long. Perhaps there'd be time to do something else as well. Like go for a walk. Don't the dogs like being taken for walks?"

"Yes, Plummer loves it, but Sukey's lazy, she just likes sitting on Tuppy's bed," Jason answered.

"I must say, she looks very comfortable there."

"She's Tuppy's dog, you see. She's always belonged to Tuppy. Tuppy loves her. But I think Sukey's breath smells horrid."

As the dining-room table had already been laid for the supper party that evening, everyone had lunch in the kitchen, sitting around the big scrubbed table. It had been spread with a blue-and-white checked cloth and decorated with a jug of yellow chrysanthemums. Antony sat at one end of the table and Jason at the other, with Isobel, Nurse McLeod, Flora, and Mrs. Watty ranged down either side. There was the promised shepherd's pie, and then stewed apples and cream, all very simple and very hot and very delicious. When they had finished, Mrs. Watty made coffee, and they sat there discussing how they would spend the remainder of the day.

"I'm going to garden," said Isobel firmly. "It's going to be a beautiful afternoon and I've been wanting to get at that border for days."

"We thought we'd go for a walk," said Antony.

"In that case you can take Plummer with you."

Jason broke in. "But Antony, you said that . . ."

Antony interrupted him. "If you mention that bow and arrow once again, I shall make one and then shoot you with it, straight through the heart." He aimed an imaginary bow and arrow in the direction of Jason and fired it. "Twang."

With an air of righteousness, Jason said, "You mustn't ever fire things at people. Never never let your gun pointed be at anyone."

"It's a laudable stricture," said Antony, "but a useless piece of verse." He turned to Flora. "Shall we go up and see Tuppy for a moment?"

But Nurse McLeod invervened. "Mrs. Armstrong had a bad night and didn't sleep at all, so not just now, if you don't mind. I'm just away upstairs to settle her for a little nap. It doesn't do for her to get overexcited."

Antony, meekly, accepted this. "Just as you say, Nurse. You're the boss." Nurse pushed back her chair and stood up, towering over them all like some formidable nanny. "But when can we come and see her?"

"How about before dinner tonight? When you're all dressed up and ready for the party? It'll make a wee occasion for her, to see you all then."

"All right. Tell her we'll be along about seven o'clock, looking unbelievably dressy."

"I'll do that," said Nurse. "And now, if you'll all excuse me, I must see to my patient. And thank you for lunch, Mrs. Watty, it was just delicious."

"I'm glad you enjoyed it, Nurse," Mrs. Watty beamed, reaching out her huge arm to pour them all another cup of coffee.

When Nurse had left them, Antony leaned his elbows on the table and said, "She talks as though we were going to throw some great reception here, with all the men in boiled shirts and monocles, and Aunt Isobel sweeping about in the heirloom diamonds and a train. Who's actually coming?"

"Anna and Brian. And Mr. and Mrs. Crowther . . ."

"Gayer and gayer," murmured Antony. Isobel sent him a

fairly cool glance and went on, undeterred. "And, provided he isn't called out for a baby or an appendix, or some other emergency, Hugh Kyle."

"That's a bit better. Conversation will doubtless sparkle."

"Now don't try to be too clever," his aunt warned him.

"He'll not catch Mr. Crowther napping," Mrs. Watty observed. "Mr. Crowther is very quick at the repartee."

Flora asked, "Who's Mr. Crowther?"

"He's the Presbyterian meenister," Antony told her, in an accent more Highland than Mrs. Watty's own.

Jason chipped in. "And Mrs. Crowther teaches Sunday school, and she's got very big teeth."

Isobel said, "Jason!" but Antony said, "All the better to eat you with. Are you coming to the party, Jason?"

"No," said Jason. "I don't want to. I'm going to have supper here with Mrs. Watty, and Aunt Isobel's got me a bottle of Coke."

"If conversation gets too sticky in the dining room," said Antony, "I might well come and join you." Isobel said, "Antony!" again, but Flora could tell that she knew he was teasing. He had probably teased her all his life, which was one of the reasons she so missed him and looked forward to his coming home.

Making the bow and arrow took a little time. Antony's good penknife and a length of suitable string had to be found, and then the right sort and shape of branch for the bow. Antony was neat-fingered and had obviously done this thing many times before, but still indulged in a good deal of cursing and bad language before the new bow and a few arrows were finally done. Then with a piece of chalk he drew a target on the trunk of a tree, and Jason, straining every muscle of his puny arms, fired the arrows, missing with most but finally making some sort of contact with the target. The arrows, however, were not flying true.

"They need to be feathered," Antony told Jason.

"How do I feather them?"

"I'll show you tomorrow. It'll take too long now."

"I wish you'd show me now."

"No. We're going for a walk now. We're going to take Plummer. Do you want to come?"

"Yes."

"Well, put the bow and arrow away, and then we'll go."

Jason gathered up his new possessions and went back to the house to stow them inside the front door, along with a battered croquet set and a number of fraying deck chairs. Antony came over to where Flora and Plummer had been sitting patiently on the grass, waiting for the target practice to be over.

He said, "I'm sorry. It took a long time."

"That's all right. Do you know, it's like summer, sitting here. It's turned into a beautiful summer's day."

"I know. It happens in this part of the world. And tomorrow will probably be a drencher." Jason came running back up the grass toward them. Antony held out a hand to Flora. "Come along," he said.

They went down the drive, through the gate and across the road, and on up the hill that rose behind the house. They crossed fields of stubble and pastures full of sturdy cattle. They climbed a dike and jumped down into deep heather crisscrossed with sheep tracks. Plummer, nose down, tail going like a piston, startled a family of grouse which exploded out of the heather at their feet and sailed away ahead of them, calling, *Go back, go back, go back.*

The slope of the hill became steeper, sweeping on and up to the skyline. Ahead, the ruins of a croft appeared with a scarlet-berried rowan tree by the gaping doorway, and nearby a lonely Scots pine, twisted and deformed by the constant wind, stood guard.

In front of the croft was a stream, its water peat-brown, tumbling down the hill in a series of miniature waterfalls and deep pools where the dark foam gathered like lather beneath tufts of overhanging heather. Rushes grew in clumps as green as emerald. The ground was boggy and the white canna blew in the wind. They crossed the stream by means of some wobbling stepping stones and came into the shelter of the ruined walls.

They had now reached the crest of the hill. On all sides the land fell away, and suddenly unexpected breathtaking views revealed themselves. To the south, beyond the forested hills, lay the Sound of Arisaig; to the north the blue waters of an inland loch, imprisoned by massive flanks, reached deep into the hills. And to the west . . .

They sat with their shoulders against a crumbling dike and gazed at the incomparable view. The western sea, a brilliant blue now, was dancing with sun pennies. The sky was cloudless, and the visibility clear as crystal. Under those conditions, the islands lay on the water like mirages.

"Imagine living here," murmured Flora, "and looking at that every day of your life."

"Yes, except that you wouldn't see it. Most of the time you couldn't see the end of your nose for rain, and if it wasn't raining it would be blowing a force twelve gale."

"Don't spoil it."

He quoted, " 'A naked house, a naked moor, a shivering pool before the door.' Robert Louis Stevenson. Tuppy used to read him to Torquil and me when she thought we were in need of a little culture." He pointed. "The small island is Muck. And that is Eigg. The mountainous one is Rhum, and then away to your right is Sleat, and beyond Sleat the Cuillins."

The distant needle peaks glittered silver against the sky. "That looks like snow," said Flora.

"It is, too. We must be in for a hard winter."

"And the loch, the one in the mountains. What's that called?"

"That's Loch Fhada. You know the sea loch where the Beach House is? That's Fhada, too. The fresh-water loch runs out into the sea, right there, under the road bridge. There's a dam and a fish ladder for the salmon . . ."

His voice trailed away. Talking, they had forgotten about Jason. He stood beside them, listening, puzzlement in his eyes.

"Why?" he asked. "Why do you tell Rose all these things as though she'd never been here before? You make it sound as though she'd never been to Fernrigg before. As though she'd never *been* here."

Antony said "Yes . . . well . . ."

But Flora spoke quickly. "It was so long ago, and when I was seventeen, I wasn't very interested in learning the names of places. But now I am."

"I suppose that's because you're coming to live here."

"No, I won't come and live here."

"But if you marry Antony?"

"Antony lives in Edinburgh."

"But you'll come and stay here, won't you? With Tuppy?"

"Yes," Flora finally had to agree, "yes, I expect I will."

The slightly strained silence which fell upon the party was tactfully broken by Plummer who, though old enough to know better, suddenly decided to chase a rabbit. Off he went, bouncing through the heather with his ears flying, while Jason, who knew that Plummer was quite capable of chasing the rabbit to the ends of the earth and losing himself in the process, went after him.

"Plummer! Plummer, you're very naughty. Come back!" His legs were spider-like, his high voice carried away by the wind. "Plummer, come back!"

"Ought we to help?" asked Flora.

"No, he'll catch him." Antony turned to her. "We nearly messed things up there, didn't we? Jason's a bright child. I never realized he was listening."

"I forgot, too."

"Are you going to be all right tonight? Conversation-wise, I mean?"

"If you stick near me, I'll be all right."

"I was teasing Aunt Isobel at lunchtime. They're nice people."

"Yes, I'm sure." She smiled, to reassure him.

He said, slowly, "You know, I can't get used to this idea that you look like Rose, but you aren't Rose. It keeps coming back and hitting me just as hard as it did the first time."

"Do you wish I were?"

"I didn't mean that. I meant that something—perhaps the chemistry—is different."

"You mean you're not in love with me like you were with Rose."

"But if I'm not in love with you, then why aren't I?"

"Because I'm Flora."

"You're nicer than Rose. You know that, don't you? Rose would never have had any time for Jason. Rose wouldn't have known how to talk to people like Mrs. Watty and Nurse."

"No, but she would have known what to say to you, and perhaps that's more important."

"She said goodbye to me," Antony pointed out with some bitterness. "And went off to Spetsai with some bloody Greek."

"And you told me you were so hard-headed."

He grinned, ruefully. "I know. But I do want to get married, that's the funny thing. After all, I'm thirty, I can't go on being a bachelor for the rest of my days. I don't know. I suppose I just haven't met the right girl."

"Edinburgh must be running with them. Fresh-faced lassies living on their own in Georgian flats."

He laughed. "Is that how you imagine life in Edinburgh?"

"Life in Edinburgh, to me, is dinner with Antony Armstrong, on a wet, black night." She looked at her watch. "You know, when Jason and Plummer finally return, I think we should go home. If Isobel's going to wear the family diamonds, I should at least wash my hair."

"Yes, of course. And Jason and I have promised to do the hens for Watty." He looked at her and gave a snort of laughter. "Family life. So glamorous." He stooped and kissed her, a proper kiss, on her mouth. When he drew away she asked, "Is that for Rose, or for Flora?"

"It's for you," Antony told her.

That evening the sun went down behind the sea in a welter of liquid golds and reds. Flora, having washed her hair and now trying to dry it with an old-fashioned device borrowed from Isobel, left the curtains drawn back and watched the sunset with something like disbelief. Gradually, as the light altered, the colors changed, and the islands turned pink and then a dusky blue. The sea was a mirror for the sky and when the sun had finally gone, it darkened to an inky indigo starred by the riding lights of fishing boats setting out from Tarbole for the night's work.

While all that was going on, the house rang with the pleasant sounds of the preparations for the evening's festivities. People went up and down stairs, called to each other, drew curtains, built up fires. There was the clatter of pots and china from the kitchen, and delicious smells of cooking presently began to drift upstairs.

What to wear was no problem for Flora, since she had brought only one possible outfit: a long skirt of turquoise wool, a silk shirt, and a wide belt to cinch the lot together. In fact, recalling the speed with which she had packed in London, she was amazed that she had brought even these. When she had done her hair and made up her eyes, she put them on, screwed on some earrings, and squirted herself with the Chamade that Marcia had given her for her birthday. The smell of it, in the way that smells are apt to do, brought back Marcia and her father and Seal Cottage so vividly that all at once Flora felt lost.

What was she doing here? The answer to the question was outrageous. The insanity of what she was doing hit her like a kick in the stomach, and she was overwhelmed with panic. Everything turned sour. She sat at the mirror staring at her own reflection and knew that the evening lay ahead of her like a nightmare of lies. She would make a fool of herself, give herself away, let Antony down. And they would all know that she was nothing but a lie on two legs, the worst sort of cheat.

Every instinct in her being told her to get out. Now. Before anybody could find out. Before anybody could be hurt. But how could she go? And where would she go? And hadn't she given Antony a sort of promise? Antony, who had embarked on the crazy deception with the best of intentions, and all for the sake of Tuppy.

She tried to pull herself together. After all, neither of them was going to get anything out of it. Neither of them stood to gain a mortal thing, except perhaps an uneasy conscience for the rest of their lives. It wasn't really going to affect anybody else.

Or was it? All afternoon Flora had resolutely not thought about the man on the beach. But now he came back again, that big antagonistic man, with his veiled threats that he had called a warning. While he existed there was no sense in pretending that the situation was simple. She could only hope that he had nothing to do with the Armstrongs. And, when one came down to basics, Tuppy was the only person who mattered. *Perhaps if a wrong thing were done for a good reason, that made it right.* And if ever there was a good reason, then it was Tuppy, the old lady in her room down the passage, waiting now for Flora to go and say goodnight to her.

Flora? No, not Flora. Rose.

She took a deep breath, turned away from the mirror, drew the curtains, turned off the lights, went out of her room and down the passage to Tuppy's door. She knocked and Tuppy called, "Come in."

Flora had expected to find Antony there, but Tuppy was alone. The room was half-dark, lit only be the bedside lamps which cast a warm circle of light over the great bed at the end of the room. In it, supported by many pillows sat Tuppy, wearing a fresh lawn nightdress with lace at the throat and a bedjacket of palest blue Shetland wool, tied with satin ribbons.

"Rose! I've been waiting for you. Come and let me look at you."

Flora obligingly stepped forward into the light and displayed herself.

"It's not very grand, but it's all I've got with me." She went to the bedside to give Tuppy a kiss.

"I love it. So young and pretty. And you look so tall and

slim with that tiny waist. There's nothing so pretty as a tiny waist."

"You look pretty too," Flora said, settling herself on the edge of the bed.

"Nurse dressed me up."

"I love the bedjacket."

"Isobel gave it to me last Christmas. It's the first time I've worn it."

"Has Antony been to see you yet?"

"He was in about half an hour ago."

"Did you sleep this afternoon?"

"A little. And what did you do?"

Flora began to tell her, and Tuppy lay back on her pillows and listened. The light fell on her face, and Flora was suddenly afraid for her, because all at once Tuppy looked frail and exhausted. There were dark smudges of fatigue beneath her eyes, and her hands, gnarled and brown as old tree roots, fidgeted restlessly with the hem of the sheet as Flora talked.

And yet it was a wonderful face. Probably as a girl she had not been beautiful, but in old age the bone structure, the vitality, came into their own, and Flora found her fascinating. Her skin, fine and dry, tanned by a lifetime of being outdoors, was fretted by wrinkles; to touch her cheek was like touching a withered leaf. Her white hair was short and curled disarmingly about her temples. The lobes of her ears had been pierced for earrings and had stretched, deformed by the weight of the old-fashioned jewelry she had worn all her life. Her mouth was the same shape as Antony's, and they shared the same warm, sudden smile. But it was Tuppy's eyes which held your attention, deep-set eyes, shining periwinkle blue, bright with interest in everything that was going on.

". . . And then we came home, and the boys went off to feed the hens and collect the eggs and I washed my hair."

"It looks lovely. Shiny. Like well-polished furniture. Hugh's just been in to see me, and I was telling him all about you. He's downstairs now, having a drink with Antony. So nice he could come. He's such a busy man, poor pet. In a way it's his own fault, though. I'm always on at him to get a partner. The practice had grown too much for any single man over these last years. But he swears he can manage on his own. I think he prefers it that way. Then there isn't time for him to brood and be unhappy."

Flora remembered Antony talking about Hugh Kyle.

He's lived here on and off, all his life.

He must be a happy man.

No. I don't really think he is.

"Is he married?" she asked, without thinking.

Tuppy sent her a sharp look. "Don't you remember, Rose? Hugh's a widower. He was married, but his wife was killed in a car accident."

"Oh, Oh, yes, of course."

"It was all so sad. We've known Hugh all our lives. His father was the Tarbole doctor for years, and we watched Hugh growing up. He was always such a clever, bright little boy. He was working in London for his F.R.C.S., but when his wife died he threw the whole thing over and came back to Tarbole to take over from his father. He was still in his twenties then, and I could hardly bear it for him. Such a waste of all the promise, all that talent."

"Perhaps he should get married again."

"Of course he should, but he won't. He says he doesn't want to. He's got a housekeeper called Jessie McKenzie, but she's very slapdash and careless and between the two of them they manage to run a very cheerless establishment." Tuppy sighed. "But what can one do? We can't run other people's lives for them." She smiled, her eyes bright with amusement. "Even I can't run Hugh's life for him, hard though I try. You see, I've always been an impossibly bossy, interfering person. But my family and friends know this, and they've come to accept it quite graciously."

"I think they probably enjoy it."

"Yes." Tuppy became thoughtful. "You know, Rose, lying here this afternoon, I had such a good idea . . ." Her voice faltered a little, and she reached out and took Flora's hand in her own, as though the physical contact would give her some of the younger person's strength. "Do you *have* to go back with Antony?" Flora stared at her. "I mean, Antony has to get back to Edinburgh because of his job, but I thought perhaps—do you have a job in London?"

"Well, no, not exactly, but . . ."

"But you have to get back?"

"Yes, I suppose I should. I mean . . ." It was Flora's turn to falter. She found herself, horrifyingly, without words.

"Because," Tuppy went on, more forcefully now, "if you didn't have to get back, you could stay here. We all love you so much, and two days is scarcely long enough to get to know you again. And there are so many things I want to do. I really ought to do. About the wedding . . ."

"But we don't know when we're getting married!"

"Yes, but there are lists to be made of people who ought to be invited. And then there are things here that belong to Antony, that he should have when he sets up an establishment of his own. Some silver that was his father's and pictures that belong to him. And furniture, and his grandfather's desk. All those things should be arranged. It isn't good to leave everything in the air."

"But Tuppy, you're not meant to be worrying about Antony and me. That isn't why we came back to see you. You're meant to be resting, getting strong again."

"But I may not get strong. I may never get better. Now, don't put on that prissy face, one must face facts. And if I don't, then it makes everything so much easier if all these tiresome little details have already been seen to."

There was a long pause. At last Flora, hating herself, said, "I really don't think I can stay. Please forgive me. But I must go tomorrow with Antony."

Disappointment clouded Tuppy's face, but only for an instant. "In that case," she said, smiling, and giving Flora's hand a little pat, "you'll just have to come back to Fernrigg again before too long, and we'll have a little session then."

"Yes, I'll try to do that. I . . . I'm truly sorry."

"My dear child, don't look so tragic. It's not the end of the world. Just a silly idea I had. And now, perhaps you should go downstairs. Our guests will be arriving and you must be there to greet them. Off you run."

"I'll see you tomorrow."

"Of course. Goodnight, my dear."

Flora leaned forward to kiss her goodnight. As she did so, the door behind them opened and Jason appeared in his dressing gown, with his bedtime book under his arm.

"I'm just going," Flora assured him, getting up off the edge of the bed.

He closed the door. "You look nice. Hello, Tuppy, did you have a good sleep this afternoon?"

"A splendid sleep."

"I didn't bring *Peter Rabbit,* I brought *Treasure Island,* because Antony says it's time I made myself brave enough to listen to it."

"Well, if it's too frightening," said Tuppy, "we can always stop and try something else."

He handed her the book and without more ado climbed into the large soft bed beside her, arranging the sheets and blankets over his knees, and generally making himself snug.

"Did you have a good supper?" asked Flora.

"Yes, delicious. I'm all burpy with Coke." Wanting her to go away so that he and Tuppy could get on with the story, he added, "Hugh's downstairs, but not anybody else yet."

"In that case," said Flora, "I'd better go down and say good evening."

She left them, closed the door behind her, and stood there, her hands pressed to her cheeks, trying to compose herself. She felt as though she had come through some dreadful ordeal, and hated herself for feeling this way. The disappointment she had seen in Tuppy's eyes would haunt her, she felt, for the rest of her life. But what else was there to say? What else could she have done, but refuse to stay?

Why couldn't life remain simple? Why did everything have to be complicated by people, emotions, and human relationship? What had started out as well-intended and innocent deception, was turning ugly, swelling out of all proportion. How could Flora have known what she was letting herself in for? Nothing Antony had said could have prepared her for the impact that Tuppy's warm and loving personality had made upon her.

She sighed deeply, bracing herself for the next hurdle. She started downstairs. The carpet felt thick beneath the soles of her gold slippers. There was a fresh arrangement of beech leaves and chrysanthemums on the windowsill. The hall had been tidied for the expected company, the curtains drawn across the french windows, the fire made up. The drawing-room door stood half-open and from beyond it came the sound of voices.

Antony was speaking. "What you're telling, us, Hugh, is that Tuppy's going to make some sort of a recovery. Is that it?"

"Certainly. I've said so all along."

The voice was deep, the intonation dismayingly familiar. Flora stopped dead, not meaning to eavesdrop but all at once unable to move.

"But Isobel thought . . ."

"What did Isobel think?"

Isobel replied, sounding both nervous and foolish, "I thought . . . I thought you were trying to protect me. To keep it from me."

"Isobel!" The voice was filled with reproach. "You've known me all my life. I would never keep anything from you. You must realize that. Most certainly if it was to do with Tuppy."

"It . . . it was the expression on your face."

"Unfortunately"—he sounded as if he were trying to make a joke of it—"I can do nothing about the expression on my face. I was probably born with it."

"No, I remember." Isobel was being very definite. "I came out of the drawing room, and you were standing halfway up the stairs. Just standing there. And there was a look on your face that frightened me. I knew it had to be about Tuppy . . ."

"But it wasn't about Tuppy. It was something else, something that was worrying me very much, but it wasn't about Tuppy. And I told you she was going to be all right. I told you, if I remember, that she was as strong as an old heather root, and she would probably outlive us all."

There was a pause and then, Isobel admitted, "I didn't believe you," sounding as if she were about to burst into tears.

Flora could bear it no longer. She walked in through the open door.

The drawing room at Fernrigg that evening had the aspect of a stage set, lit and furnished for the opening act of some Victorian piece. The illusion was heightened by the disposal of the three people who, as Flora suddenly appeared, stopped talking and turned to look at her.

She was aware of Antony, in a dark gray suit, occupied at a table on the far side of the room, and in the process of pouring a drink; and of Isobel in a long dress of heather-colored wool, standing at one side of the fireplace.

But she had eyes only for the other man. The doctor. Hugh Kyle. He faced Isobel across the hearthrug. He was so tall that his head and shoulders were reflected in the Venetian mirror that hung above the high, marble mantelpiece.

"Rose!" said Isobel. "Come close to the fire. You remember Hugh, don't you?"

"Yes," said Flora. As soon as she had heard his voice, she had known that it would be him. The man she had met on the beach that morning. "Yes, I remember."

7

TUPPY

"Of course," he said. "We remember each other. How are you, Rose?"

She frowned. "I couldn't help hearing. You were talking about Tuppy."

Antony, without asking what she wanted, brought her over a drink. "Yes," he said. "There seems to have been some sort of a misunderstanding."

She took the tumbler which was iced and very cold to her hand. "She's going to be all right?"

"Yes. Hugh says so."

Flora felt as if she might burst into tears.

"It was my fault," Isobel explained quickly. "My silly fault. But I was so upset. I thought Hugh was trying to tell me that Tuppy was going to . . ." She couldn't manage the word *die*. "That she wasn't going to get better. And that's what I told Antony."

"But it's not true?"

"No."

Flora looked at Antony and his steady eyes met hers. The two conspirators, she thought. Hoist with their own petard. They need never have come to Fernrigg. They need never have embarked on this maniacal charade. The whole carefully manufactured deception had been for nothing.

Antony had an expressive face. It was plain that he knew what Flora was thinking. They had made fools of themselves. He was sorry. And yet there was a sort of relief there, too, a lessening of the tension in his fine-drawn face. He was inexpressibly fond of his grandmother.

He said again, with the deepest satisfaction, "She's going to get better." Flora found his hand and pressed it. He turned back to the others and went on, "The thing is, that if Rose and I hadn't believed there was a certain urgency to the situation, we probably wouldn't have come at all this weekend."

"In that case," said Isobel, sounding recovered, "I'm very glad I was so silly and misunderstood Hugh. I'm sorry if I frightened you, but at least it got you here."

"Hear, hear," said Hugh. "I couldn't have prescribed a more effective medicine. You've both done Tuppy a world of good." He turned his back to the fire and settled his wide shoulders against the mantelpiece. Across the room, Flora felt his eyes on her. "And now that you're here, Rose, how does it feel to be back in Scotland?"

His manner was pleasant, but his blue eyes no warmer, and she remained wary of him.

"Very nice."

"Is this your first visit since you were last here?"

"Yes it is."

"She's been in the States all summer." That was Antony, the alert prompter in the wings.

Hugh raised his eyebrows. "Really? Whereabouts?"

Flora tried to remember where Rose had been. "Oh . . . New York. And the Grand Canyon. And places."

He inclined his head, acknowledging her traveled state. "How is your mother?"

"She's very well, thank you."

"Is she coming back to Fernrigg, too?" He sounded patient as he persevered with the sticky conversation.

"No. I . . . I think she's going to stay in New York for a bit."

"But she'll doubtless be coming over for the wedding. Unless you plan to be married in New York?"

"Oh, don't suggest such a thing," said Isobel. "How could we all get to New York?"

Antony said quickly, "Nothing's been decided, anyway. Not even a date, let alone where it's going to take place."

"In that case," said Hugh, "it sounds a little as though we're crossing bridges before we get to them."

"Yes. It does."

There was a small pause while they all sipped their drinks. Flora cast about for some fresh topic of conversation, but before she could think of one, there came the sounds of cars arriving, the slamming of doors, and Isobel said, "There are the others."

"It seems," said Antony, "that they've all come at once." And he laid down his drink and went out to greet the new arrivals.

After a moment Isobel said, "If you'll excuse me," and to Flora's horror, she, too, put down her glass and followed Antony, doubtless to take the ladies of the party upstairs, to divest themselves of coats and perhaps comb their hair.

Thus, Flora and Hugh Kyle were left alone. The silence that lay between them was pregnant with things unsaid. She toyed with the idea of going straight into the attack—of saying, *I can see that you want to keep the good opinion of the Armstrongs, but you're being a great deal more pleasant to me now than you were this morning.* But, she told herself, this was neither the time nor the place for a showdown. Besides, it was impossible to defend herself when she had no idea what it was she was supposed to have done.

The possibilities, however, were daunting. Rose, Flora was beginning to accept, was not a woman of the highest principles.

She had ditched Antony without a qualm of conscience, swanned off to Greece with some newly met swain, and deliberately left Flora to pick up the pieces of her broken engagement.

Who could guess at the horrors that Rose, at seventeen, would have been capable of committing? Flora had imagined her as young and frustrated and bored stiff. Was it so unlikely that in order to amuse herself, she had taken up with the first eligible man who came her way?

But Hugh Kyle did not look that sort of person. Not a man that any girl would consider playing fast and loose with. He was, in fact, formidable. Flora made herself look at him, standing as before with his back to the fire, his penetrating blue eyes watching her, unblinking, over the rim of his tumbler of whisky. This evening he wore a dark suit of some distinction, a silk shirt and some sort of a club tie with emblems on it. She wished that he were not so large. It was disconcerting having to stand there, looking up at him, and the expression she found on his face caused the very last of her courage to dribble away. She was confounded. She was without anything to say.

He seemed to be aware of her discomfiture and, surprisingly, to take pity on her, for it was he who broke the silence.

"Tuppy tells me that you and Antony have to leave tomorrow."

"Yes."

"Well, you've had one lovely afternoon."

"Yes, it was lovely."

"How did you spend it?"

"We went for a walk."

At that juncture they were mercifully interrupted by Antony, ushering in the two males among the newly arrived guests.

"Everyone came at the same time," he told them. "Rose, I don't believe you've met Mr. Crowther. He came to live in Tarbole after you'd been here."

Mr. Crowther was dressed in his minister's somber best, but with his red face, thick gray hair, and well-set-up figure he looked more like a successful bookie than a man of the church.

He took Flora's hand in a hefty grip and proceeded to pump it up and down, saying, "Well, this is a pleasure. I've been looking forward to meeting Antony's young lady. How do you do?"

He sounded like a bookie as well. The very timbre of his deep voice made the crystal baubles of the chandelier knock together with a fine chiming sound. Flora imagined him preaching hellfire and brimstone from his pulpit. She was sure he had a fine reputation for meaningful sermons.

"How do you do?"

"Mrs. Armstrong's been so looking forward to a visit from you, as indeed we all have." He caught sight of Hugh Kyle, let go her hand at last, and went toward the other man. "And it's yourself, Doctor. And how's life treating you?"

"Rose," said Antony.

She had been aware of the other man, waiting for all the effusion to run its course. Now she turned toward him.

"You remember Brian Stoddart?"

She saw the brown face, the dark eyebrows, the laughter lines around his eyes and mouth. His hair was dark, too, and his eyes a very pale, clear gray. Not as tall as Antony, and older, he nevertheless radiated a sort of animal vitality which Flora recognized as being immensely attractive. Unlike the other men of the party, he had put on semiformal evening clothes—dark trousers and a blue velvet smoking jacket—and with these he wore a white turtleneck sweater.

He said, warmly, "Rose, what a long time it's been." He held out his arms and without thinking Flora moved toward him, and they kissed each other, circumspectly, on both cheeks.

He held her off. "Let me see if you've changed."

"Everybody thinks she's got prettier," said Antony.

"Impossible. She couldn't get prettier. But she's looking wonderfully happy and well. You're a lucky man, Antony."

"Yes," said Antony, not sounding particularly certain. "Well, having decided that, and kissed the poor girl silly into the bargain, come over and tell me what you want to drink."

While they were thus occupied Isobel made her entrance escorting the two wives, and the whole scene was replayed, this time with Isobel making the introductions. This was Mrs. Crowther, whom Rose had not met before. (Big teeth, as Jason had warned, but a pleasant-faced person, dressed, as if for a ceileidh, in a tartan dress pierced by a Cairngorm brooch.) Mrs. Crowther was as enthusiastic as her husband. "So lovely that you were able to come and see Mrs. Armstrong again. It's just a shame that she's not able to be with us tonight." She smiled over Flora's head. "Good evening, Dr. Kyle. Good evening, Mr. Stoddart."

". . . and Anna, Rose," said Isobel in her gentle voice. "Anna Stoddart of Ardmore."

Anna Stoddart smiled. She was obviously painfully shy and rather plain. It was hard to guess her age, and it was equally hard to guess how she had managed to collar such a devastating husband. She wore an expensive, if rather stodgy, dinner dress, but her jewelry was beautiful. Diamonds shone from her ears and her fingers, and trembled at the neck of the dull dress.

She put out her hand and then awkwardly withdrew it again, as though she had made a social gaffe. Flora, suffering for her shyness, quickly took hold of the hand before it disappeared altogether and held it firmly.

"Hello," she said, feeling for clues. "I do remember you, don't I?"

Anna gave a little laugh. "And I remember you," she said. "I certainly remember you. And your mother."

"And you've come from . . . ?"

"Ardmore. It's over the other side of Tarbole."

"It's a lovely place," Isobel told Flora. "Right out on the end of Ardmore point."

"Are you very isolated?" asked Flora.

"Yes, a little, but I've lived there all my life, so I'm quite used to it." There was a pause and then, as if encouraged by Flora's interest, she went on, in a rush of words. "You can see Ardmore from Fernrigg on a clear day. Right across the Sound."

"It was clear this afternoon, but I never thought of looking."

"Did you see the sunset?"

"Wasn't it fabulous? I watched it while I was dressing . . ."

Quite happy together, beginning to make friends, they were interrupted by Brian. "Anna, Antony wants to know what you're going to drink."

She seemed confused. ". . . I don't really want anything."

"Oh, come along," he said patiently, "you must have something."

"An orange juice, then . . ." He went away to fetch it for her.

Flora said, "Would you like a sherry?"

"No." Anna shook her head. "I don't really like it." With that the two of them were overwhelmed by Mr. Crowther's coming at them across the carpet like a ship in full sail, saying, "Now then, we can't let these two pretty girls spend their time talking together."

Somehow, the evening progressed. Flora talked and smiled until her face ached, sticking close to Antony (so devoted, everybody would be thinking), and avoiding Hugh Kyle. Anna Stoddart found a chair and sat down, and Mrs. Crowther drew up a stool and settled herself beside her. Brian Stoddart and Antony discussed some mutual friends in Edinburgh, and Mr. Crowther and Hugh Kyle gravitated back to the fireplace and appeared, from their gestures, to be swapping fishing experiences. Isobel, making sure that all her guests were happily occupied, slipped away to speak to Mrs. Watty.

Presently the gong sounded, and they all finished their drinks and trooped out of the room and across the hall to the dining room.

Even in her present state of nerves Flora could not help but notice how charming it all was: the dark walls, the old portraits, the brightly burning fire. White linen and shining silver were reflected in the gleam of the mahogany table. There was a centerpiece of late roses, and pale pink candles filled the silver candelabra.

After some confusion on the part of Isobel, who had lost her plan and forgotten where everybody was meant to be, they were all finally seated in the right places: Hugh at one end of the table and Mr. Crowther at the other, while Brian and Antony faced each other across the middle. The women were placed in the four corners, Flora between Hugh and Brian, with Mrs. Crowther opposite her.

When at last they were all settled, unfolding enormous linen napkins and placing them across their laps, and before conversation could start in earnest, Isobel said quickly, "Mr. Crowther, would you say grace?"

Mr. Crowther rose ponderously to his feet. They all bowed their heads, and Mr. Crowther, in tones that would have filled a cathedral, gave thanks to the Lord for the food which they were about to eat, asked him to bless it and also all the people in this house, especially Mrs. Armstrong who could not be with them, but who held such a special place in all their hearts. Amen.

He sat down. Flora suddenly liked him very much. Mrs. Watty then emerged from the door at the other end of the dining room and, as conversation got going, began to serve the soup.

Flora, in agony in that she might be expected to make light conversation with Hugh Kyle, was thankful when Mrs. Crowther firmly took him over. Mrs. Crowther had had two sherries, and not only was her color high, but also her voice.

"I was visiting old Mr. Sinclair the other day, Doctor, and he was saying that you'd been to see him. He's not been keeping as well as he should . . ."

Beside Flora, Brian Stoddart said, "You're going to have to talk to me."

She turned to him, smiling. "That's all right by me."

"I can't tell you how wonderful it is to see you again. Like a breath of fresh air. That's the worst of living up here in the back of beyond. Without realizing it, we're getting older and becoming very dull, and it's hard to know what to do about it. You're just in time to come and shake us all up."

"I can't believe you feel old or dull," Flora told him, partly because this was obviously what he wanted to be told, and partly because there was such a sparkle to his eyes that the temptation to flirt a little was hard to resist.

"I do hope that's a compliment."

"Not at all, it's a fact. You don't look old and you don't sound dull."

"It *is* a compliment!"

She began to eat her soup. "You've told me the worst of living up here. Now tell me the best."

"That's more difficult."

"I can't believe that. There must be a thousand advantages."

"All right. A comfortable house, good shooting, good fishing. A ketch moored in Ardmore Loch, and in the summer, time to sail her. And space on the roads to drive my car. How does that add up?"

She noticed, sadly, that he had not included his wife in this catalogue.

"Isn't it a little materialistic?"

"Now come, Rose. You didn't expect anything else."

"How about a few responsibilities?"

"You think I should have responsibilities?"

"Don't you?"

"Yes, of course I do."

"Such as . . . ?"

He seemed amused by her persistence, but remained obliging. "Running Ardmore uses up more of my time than you could possibly imagine. And then there's the 'Coonty Cooncil.' It takes many committee meetings to decide where they're going to widen the road for the fish lorries, or whether the Tarbole Primary School should have more lavatories. You know the sort of thing. Riveting stuff."

"And what else do you do?"

"What are you anyway, Rose? Because you sound like a

prospective employer." But he still looked amused, and she knew that he was enjoying himself.

"If that's all you do with your time, I'd say you were in real danger of becoming very dull indeed."

He laughed out loud. "Touché! O.K., does running the Yacht Club count as a job?"

"The Yacht Club?"

"Well, don't say, 'The Yacht Club?' in that blank voice as though you'd never heard of it before." He began to speak very clearly, as though she were both deaf and stupid. "The Ardmore Yacht Club. You Came There with Me Once."

"Oh. Did I?"

"Rose, if I didn't know you so well, I really would believe you'd forgotten. Those five years must stretch further back than I'd imagined."

"Yes, I suppose they do."

"You should renew your acquaintance with the Yacht Club. Except that it's closed for the winter right now, and there's not much going on. But you could come over to Ardmore House and see us. How long are you staying?"

"We're going tomorrow."

"Tomorrow? But you've only been here about five minutes."

"Antony has to get back to work."

"And you? Do you have to get back to work too?"

"No. But I have to get back to London."

"Why don't you stay on, for a week or so, anyway? Give us all a chance to get to know you again. Get to know you properly."

Something in his voice made Flora glance at him sharply, but his pale eyes were innocent.

"I can't stay."

"Don't you want to?"

"Yes, of course. I mean, I'd like to come over and visit you and Anna, but . . ."

Brian had taken up a roll and was crumbling it between his fingers. "Anna's going to Glasgow for a shopping spree at the beginning of the week." His profile was dark and sharply cut against the glow of the candlelight. It seemed that the remark was significant, but Flora could not imagine why.

"Does she always go to Glasgow to shop?"

It was an innocent question, but now he laid down his spoon and turned to face her once more, smiling, his eyes dancing as though they were sharing some marvelous private joke.

"Almost always," he told her.

Their conversation was interrupted by Isobel's getting to her feet and going around the table to collect the empty soup plates. Antony, excusing himself, also rose, and went to the sideboard to deal with the wine. The door from the kitchen opened, and Mrs. Watty appeared once more with a tray laden with steaming dishes and a pile of plates. Mrs. Crowther, bereft of Antony, leaned across the table to tell Flora about the Christmas church sale, and the nativity play she planned to produce.

"Is Jason going to be in it?" Flora asked.

"Yes, of course."

"Not an angel, I hope," said Hugh.

"Now why shouldn't Jason be an angel?" Mrs. Crowther was playfully indignant.

"Somehow," said Hugh, "he doesn't quite have the countenance."

"It's amazing, Doctor, how angelic the most devilish child can become once you dress him in a white nightgown and a gold paper crown. You'll have to come and watch, Rose."

"Huh?" said Flora, caught unawares.

"Won't you be coming to Fernrigg for Christmas?"

"Well . . . I hadn't really thought." She looked for support from Antony across the table, but Antony's chair was empty. Casting about for some alternative assistance she found herself, to her annoyance, gazing blankly at Hugh.

He prompted gently, "Perhaps you'll be in New York?"

"Yes. Perhaps I will."

"Or London, or Paris?"

She thought, *How well he knows Rose!* "It depends," she said.

Brian leaned forward, chipping into the discussion. "I've already suggested that Rose not go back to London tomorrow but stay on here for a few days. But my idea was turned down flat. A blank refusal."

"But that's a shame!" Mrs. Crowther sounded quite indignant. "I think Brian's is a wonderful idea. Have a little holiday, Rose. Enjoy yourself. I think we can see to it that you have a good time. What do you say, Dr. Kyle?"

"I think," said Hugh, "that Rose would have a good time wherever she was. She certainly doesn't need any help from us." His voice was dry.

"Besides, just think how pleasant it would be for Mrs. Armstrong . . ."

But, if bemused by wine and company, Mrs. Crowther had not recognized Hugh's snub for what it was, Flora had. She felt herself blushing with angry embarrassment. Her glass was full, and she took it up and drank the wine as though she were suffering from some unquenchable thirst. She saw that her hand, as she set down the glass, was shaking.

Neatly, without fuss, the next course was served. Some sort of a casserole, then creamed spinach and mashed potatoes. Flora wondered how she was going to be able to eat it. At the sideboard Isobel, who had been helping Mrs. Watty with the serving, picked up a small tray and started for the door. Mr. Crowther, with his eagle eye, spied her from the far end of the table.

"And where are you off to, Miss Armstrong?"

Isobel paused, smiling. "I'm just going to take Tuppy's tray up to her. I promised I would, and tell her how the party's going."

Hugh got up to open the door for her.

"Send her our respects," said Mr. Crowther, eliciting a murmur of assent from around the table.

"Of course I will," Isobel promised as she went out of the room. Hugh closed the door behind her and came back to his chair. As he settled himself, Antony, having returned to his own place, leaned across Mrs. Crowther and asked Hugh if he had laid up his boat yet.

"Yes," Hugh told him. "Last week. Geordie Campbell's got her in the boatyard at Tarbole. I went to see him the other day. He was asking after you, Antony, and was very interested to hear that you'd got yourself engaged to be married."

"I should try and take Rose down to see him."

Fortified by the wine she had gulped, Flora had overcome her embarrassment, but Hugh Kyle's snub still rankled. Now, she broke into the conversation coolly, as though he had never made that remark. "What kind of a boat have you got?"

He told her, in a voice that seemed to suggest that she would have no idea of what he was talking about anyway.

"A gaff-rigged seven-tonner."

"Do you keep her at the Ardmore Yacht Club?"

"No, I've just said. She's in the boatyard at Tarbole."

"She must be getting pretty elderly now," said Brian.

Hugh sent a chilly glance in his direction. "She was built in nineteen twenty-eight."

"Like I said. Elderly."

"Does everyone have a boat?" Flora asked. "I mean, do you all sail?"

Hugh laid down his knife and fork, and, sounding as though he were trying to explain something to a particularly dim-witted child, said, "The west of Scotland has some of the best sailing in the world. Unless one was totally disinterested one would be a fool to live here and not take advantage of it. But you need to know what you're doing. You need experience and some knowledge to cope with, say, a Force Twelve gale when you find yourself out beyond the end of Ardnamurchan. It's not quite the same as sitting in Monte Carlo harbor with a gin-and-tonic in one hand and a blonde in a bikini in the other."

Mrs. Crowther laughed, but "I never thought it was," Flora told him coolly. He was not going to intimidate her. "Have you sailed a lot this summer?"

He picked up his knife and fork again. "Scarcely at all," he told her, sounding sour.

"Why not?"

"A sad lack of time."

"I suppose you're very busy?"

"Busy!" Mrs. Crowther could not listen in silence. "That's the understatement of the year. No man in Tarbole works harder or longer hours than Dr. Kyle."

"Tuppy thinks you should get a partner," Flora told him, meanly. "She told me so before, when I was saying goodnight to her."

Hugh was unimpressed. "Tuppy's been trying to run my life for me since I was six years old."

"If you'll excuse my saying so," said Brian, gently, "she seems to have made a melancholy failure of it."

There followed an icy silence. Even Mrs. Crowther was bereft of words. Flora looked for help from Antony, but he had turned to talk to Anna. She laid down her knife and fork, very gently, as though it were forbidden to make a noise, and reached again for her wineglass.

Across her, forever it seemed, the eyes of the two men met and clashed. Then Hugh took a mouthful of wine, laid down his glass and said, quietly, "The failures have all been my own."

"But of course, Tuppy is quite right," Brian went on in his light voice. "You should take a partner. Some energetic, ambitious, thrusting young medico. All work and no play makes Jack a dull boy."

"Better a dull Jack than an idle one," Hugh threw back at him.

It was time to intervene before they started striking each other. "Don't you . . . don't you have anyone to help you?" Flora asked.

"I have a nurse in the surgery." His voice was brusque. "She gives injections and eyedrops and makes up prescriptions and bandages cut knees. She's a tower of strength."

Flora imagined the nurse, aproned and buxom, perhaps

young and pretty in a fresh, country way. She wondered if she
was in love with the doctor, like an old A. J. Cronin novel. It
did not seem beyond the bounds of possibility. Discounting the
fact that she heartily disliked him, he was a personable man,
even handsome in his heavy-built and distinguished way. Perhaps this was what had attracted Rose. Perhaps Rose had made
a pass at him, and he had taken it seriously, and remained
bitterly resentful ever since.

She had forgotten about Isobel. Now the door opened and
Isobel returned to the party, apologizing for having been so
long. She helped herself from the sideboard and came back to
her place beside Mr. Crowther, who got to his feet and held
Isobel's chair for her.

"How is Tuppy?" everybody wanted to know.

"She's splendid. She sends you all her love." There was
something special about Isobel this evening. "And she has a
message for Rose."

They all turned to Flora, smiling, pleased because the message was for her; then they looked back at Isobel, waiting to
hear what the message was.

"She thinks," said Isobel clearly, "that we should keep
Rose for a little. She thinks that Rose should stay on at Fernrigg and let Antony go back to Edinburgh on his own." She
beamed at Flora. "And I think it's a marvelous idea, and I do
so hope, Rose, that you will."

Oh, Tuppy, you traitor.

Flora stared at Isobel, scarcely able to believe her ears. It
was like being on stage, blinded by footlights, and with a thousand eyes looking at you. She had no notion of what she was
meant to say. She looked at Antony and recognized her own
appalled expression reflected in his face. Silently begging him to
come to her aid, she heard herself saying in a voice scarcely
recognizable as her own, "I . . . I don't think . . ."

Antony came, valiantly, to her rescue. "We told you,
Isobel, Rose has to get back . . ."

But from all sides his excuses were shouted down.

"Oh, rubbish."

"Why does she have to go?"

"So lovely for us all to have her."

"So lovely for Tuppy."

"No reason why she should go . . ."

They were all smiling, beseeching her to stay. Beside her, Brian leaned back in his chair and said in a clear voice which silenced everybody else, "I've already made that suggestion. I think it's the best idea in the world."

Even Anna, from across the table, was trying to persuade her. "Do stay. Don't go back just yet."

Everybody had spoken except Hugh. Mrs. Crowther, from the other end of the table, noticed this. "How about you, Doctor? Don't you think that Rose should spend a few more days with us?"

They were all silent, looking expectantly toward Hugh, waiting for him to fall in with their suggestions, to agree with them.

But he didn't. "No, I don't think she should stay," he pronounced, and then added, too late to take the sting from his words, "Not unless she wants to." He looked at Flora, and his cold blue stare was a challenge.

Something happened to Flora: something to do with the wine she had drunk; something to do with that encounter on the beach this morning; something that was annoyance, and a good deal that was sheer contrariness.

From across the years, from a long time ago, she heard her father's cautionary voice. *You're cutting off your nose to spite your face.*

"If Tuppy wants me to stay," she told them all, "of course I'll stay."

After the ordeal of the evening was over—after everybody had gone, the dogs had been taken out, the coffee cups had been carried into the kitchen, and Isobel had kissed them both and gone upstairs to bed—Antony and Flora faced each other across the dying fire.

"Why?" asked Antony.

"I don't know."

"I thought you'd gone out of your mind."

"Perhaps I had. But it's too late now."

"Oh, Flora!"

"I can't go back on my word. You don't mind, do you?"

"I don't mind. If you can bear it, if you can cope and Tuppy wants it, then how can I mind? But . . ." He stopped.

"But what?"

"Believe it or not, it's you I'm thinking about. You made me promise it would only be for a weekend."

"I know. But it was different then."

"You mean, we thought Tuppy was going to die, and now we know she isn't?"

"Yes. That and other things."

He sighed heavily and turned to look down at the fire and poke a dying log with the toe of his shoe. He said, "What the hell is going to happen now?"

"It depends on you. You could tell Tuppy the truth."

"You mean, tell her that you're not Rose?"

"Would that be so impossible?"

"Yes. Impossible. I've never lied to Tuppy in my life."

"Till now."

"O.K. Till now."

"I think you underestimate her. I think she'd understand."

"I don't want to tell her." He sounded like a stubborn little boy.

"To be perfectly honest," Flora admitted, "neither do I."

They stared at each other, hopeless. Then Antony grinned, but there was not much mirth behind it. "What a couple of cowards we are."

"A couple of scheming conspirators."

"And not, I'm beginning to think very successful ones."

"Oh, I don't know." She tried to turn it into a joke. "For beginners, we're not doing too badly."

He said, in an aggrieved voice, "I wonder why the hell I can't fall in love with you."

"That would solve everything, wouldn't it? Especially if I

were to fall in love with you at the same time." It was getting chilly. Flora shivered and drew closer to what remained of the fire.

He said, "You look tired. And no wonder. It was a hell of an evening, and you sailed through it with flying colors."

"I don't think I did. Antony, Hugh, and Brian—they don't like each other, do they?"

"No, I don't suppose they do. But then they're so completely different, it's not surprising. Poor old Hugh. I often wonder if he ever sits through a complete meal without the telephone ringing and calling him away."

Hugh had gone before they had even finished the second course. Summoned by Antony, who had answered the telephone, he had gone out into the hall, and minutes later, wearing his overcoat, put his head around the door to make his apologies and say goodnight. His departure had left a very empty space at the head of the table.

"Antony . . . do you like Hugh?"

"Yes, I like him enormously. When I was growing up he was the person I most wanted to be like. He played rugger for Edinburgh University and I thought he was a sort of god."

"I don't think he likes me. I mean, for some reason, he doesn't like Rose."

"You're imagining things. He can be pretty dry, I know, but . . ."

"Could he and Rose ever have had . . . some sort of an affair?"

Antony was shocked into silence by genuine astonishment. "Hugh and Rose? Whatever gave you that idea'?"

"Well, there's something."

"But not that. It could never have been that." He took her by the shoulders. "Shall I tell you something? You're tired, you're overwrought, and you're imagining things. And I'm tired, too. Do you realize that I haven't been to sleep for thirty-six hours? It's just beginning to hit me. I'm going to bed." He kissed her firmly. "Goodnight."

"Goodnight," said Flora. "Goodnight, Antony." And because by then there was nothing else to do and no more to be said, they put the guard on the fire, turned off the lights, and with their arms around each other, more for support than anything else, went slowly up the shadowed stairs.

Tuppy awoke early to the sound of a bird singing from the beech tree outside her window and to a warm sensation of happiness.

It was a long time since this had happened. In recent years, her awakenings had been deviled by forebodings—anxieties for her precious family, for her country, for the whole disastrous state of the world. She disciplined herself, each day, to read the papers, to watch the nine o'clock news on the television, but often, particularly in the early mornings, she wished that she didn't have to. Sometimes it seemed as if the cold light of dawn held no promise, no hope for any of them, and on such mornings it took a real effort on Tuppy's part to get up, put on her clothes, compose her features into their usual cheerful expression, and go downstairs to breakfast.

But this morning it was different. She seemed to be floating sweetly into consciousness from some particularly happy dream. For a second she was afraid to stir, even to open her eyes, for fear of the dream dissolving and cold reality taking its place.

But slowly it was borne upon her that it was true. It had really happened. Isobel had come upstairs at the end of dinner to say that Rose had finally been persuaded and had promised to stay on at Fernrigg after Antony had returned to Edinburgh.

She was not going away.

Tuppy opened her eyes. She saw the rail at the end of her bed, gleaming in the first place shine of light from the window. It was Sunday. Tuppy loved Sundays, which, once she had been to church, she liked to spend in celebrations of family, friends, and food. It had always been thus. At Fernrigg seldom did they sit down fewer than twelve to Sunday lunch. Afterward, according to the season, there might be tennis, or putting competitions on the bumpy lawn, or long blustery walks along Fhada sands. Later, everyone would gather for tea, perhaps on the terrace, or by the drawing-room fire. There would be hot scones dripping with butter and blueberry jelly; chocolate cake and fruit cake; and a special sort of ginger biscuit which Tuppy had had sent from London. Then perhaps there would be a card game or reading the Sunday papers, and if there were any children present, reading aloud.

The Secret Garden, The Wind in the Willows, A Little Princess—all the old-fashioned books. How many thousands of times has she read them aloud! *Once upon a time there was a very beautiful doll's house.* The other evening it had been Jason. But with his small frame tucked into the curve of her arm, the crown of his head sweet-smelling from his bath, just under her chin, he could have been any of them. The little boys. So many little boys. Sometimes when she was tired, and time and memories became confused, she forgot when they had been born and when they had died.

James and Robbie, her baby brothers, playing with their lead soldiers on the hearth rug. And Bruce, her own child, wild as a gypsy, running barefoot, and everybody shaking their heads and saying it was because he didn't have a father. And then Torquil, and Antony, and now Jason.

They had perhaps looked different, but they had all kindled the same pleasures in Tuppy's heart, as well as clouding her life with the most appalling anxieties: broken arms and bleeding knees, measles and whooping cough. Say, Thank you. Say, Please can I get down? *Tuppy, don't get into a fuss or anything, But Antony's just fallen out of the fir tree.*

And the milestones. Learning to swim, learning to ride a bicycle, being given the first air gun. That was the worst of all. *Never never let your gun pointed be at anyone.* She had made them say it every night, aloud, before they said their prayers.

And there was going away to school, and the miserable counting of days, and the hideous tear-stained goodbyes at Tarbole station, with the new trunk packed, the tuck box, the faces already grimed with railway dust.

The little boys were part of a long golden thread stretching back into the past. But the miracle was that the same thread reached steadfastly on into the future. There was Torquil—solid, capable Torquil, doing so well for himself, married to Teresa, living in Bahrein. Torquil had never caused Tuppy a mite of worry. But Antony now was a different kettle of fish. Restless, volatile, attractive, he had in his time brought dozens of girls back to Fernrigg, and yet never, it seemed, was it the right girl. Tuppy had begun to give up hope of his ever marrying and settling down. But now, out of the blue, he had met up with Rose Schuster again, and Tuppy's faith in miracles was restored once more.

Rose. Could he, she asked herself, in a thousand years, have found a more enchanting girl? As though Antony had presented Tuppy with some precious gift, her natural reaction was a desire to share her pleasure with the rest of the world. Not just the Crowthers and the Stoddarts, who were, after all, such close neighbors as to be almost family, but everybody.

The notion took seed and began to take shape in her active brain. The dinner party last night had, Isobel assured her, been a complete success. But Tuppy had had no part in it and had been frustrated beyond words by the distant hum which was all that she could glean of the dinner-table conversation. And Hugh, the overbearing brute, had forbidden visitors, so that Tuppy was denied even the pleasure of fresh faces and a little local gossip.

But by the end of the week. . . . She did a few calculations. Today was Sunday. Antony was going to leave Rose at Fernrigg and then return next weekend to spirit her away once more. They had a week. There was plenty of time.

They would have a party. A proper party. A dance. The very word conjured up the sound of music, and all at once her head was filled with the jig and beat of a Highland reel.

Diddle diddle dum dum, dum dum dum.

Her toes beneath the sheets began to beat time of their own accord. Excitement took hold of her, and as the seed of the idea exploded into inspiration, she forgot about being ill. The prospect of dying, which she had never taken seriously anyway, faded into insignificance. All at once there were a hundred more important things to think about.

It was nearly daylight. She reached out her hand to turn on her lamp and look at the time by the small gold clock which sat by her bed. Seven thirty. Cautiously, she drew herself up in her bed and pushed the pillows into shape with her elbows. She reached for her spectacles and then her bedjacket, which seemed to take rather a long time to put on. With clumsy fingers she tied the ribbon bow at the neck. Then she opened the drawer in her bedside table and found a pad of writing paper and a pencil. At the head of the clean sheet of paper she wrote:

Mrs. Clanwilliam

Her writing, which had once been so beautiful, seemed spidery, but what did that matter? She thought a little, her mind ranging round the neighborhood, and continued:

Charles and Christian Drummond

Harry and Frances McNeill

It would have to be on Friday. Friday was a good night for a dance, because Saturday was apt to slip into the small hours of the Sabbath, and that would offend people. Antony would have to get Friday afternoon off in order to be at Fernrigg in good time, but she had no doubt that he would be able to arrange this.

She wrote:

Hugh Kyle
Elizabeth McLeod
Johnny and Kirsten Grant

In the old days all the food, including the cold salmon, the great roast turkeys, the mouth-melting puddings, had all come out of the Fernrigg kitchen, but Mrs. Watty could scarcely be

expected to cope with that on her own now. Isobel must speak
to Mr. Anderson at the Station Hotel in Tarbole. He had a
perfectly adequate cellar and a capable chef. Mr. Anderson
would see to the catering.

More names went on the list. The Crowthers and of course
the Stoddarts, and that couple that had come to live in Tarbole
—he had something to do with deep-freezing.

Tommy and Angela Cockburn
Robert and Susan Hamilton

Diddle diddle dum dum, dum dum dum.
The postmistress, Mrs. Cooper, had a husband who played
the accordion and who could rustle up, if persuaded, a small
band. Just a fiddle and some drums. Isobel must arrange that.
And Jason would come to the party. Tuppy saw him dressed in
the little kilt and velvet doublet that had belonged to his grandfather.

The page was nearly full, but still she wrote:

Sheamus Lochlan,
The Crichtons
The McDonalds

She turned to a fresh page. She had not been so happy in
years.

It was Isobel who broke the news to the rest of the Fernrigg household. Isobel, who had gone upstairs to say good
morning to her mother and retrieve her breakfast tray, returned
to the kitchen in what appeared to be a state of mild shock.

She laid down the tray on the table with something approaching a thump. Violence was so out of character with
Isobel, that they all stopped what they were doing and looked
at her. Even Jason, with a mouthful of bacon, ceased to chew.
Something was obviously wrong. Isobel's wayward hair looked
as though she had lately run distracted fingers through it, and

the expression on her gentle face held part exasperation and part a sort of grudging pride.

She did not speak at once, but simply stood there, lanky in her tweed skirt and her best Sunday sweater, defeated, and apparently lost for words. Her very silence claimed instant attention. Mrs. Watty, peeling potatoes for lunch, sat, waiting with knife poised. Nurse McLeod, taking last night's glasses from the dishwasher and giving them a final and unnecessary polish, was equally attentive. Flora laid down her coffee cup with a small chiming sound.

It was Mrs. Watty who broke the silence. "What is it?"

Isobel pulled out a kitchen chair and flopped into it, long legs stretched out before her. She said, "She wants to have another party."

Tuppy's household, with the debris of last night still very much in evidence, received this information in wordless disbelief. For a moment the only sound to break the silence was the slow ticking of the old-fashioned clock.

Isobel's eyes went from one blank face to the other. "It's true," she told them. "It's to be next Friday. It's to be a dance."

"A *dance*?" Nurse McLeod, with visions of her patient dancing reels, drew herself up with all the authority of her profession behind her. "Over my dead body," she declared.

"She has decided," Isobel went on, as though Nurse had said nothing, "that Mr. Anderson from the Station Hotel shall do the catering, and she is going to get Mrs. Cooper's husband to organize a band."

"For heaven's sakes," was all Mrs. Watty could come up with.

"And she has already drawn up a long list of people who are to receive invitations."

Jason, who could not think what all the drama was about, decided to finish his bacon. "Am I being invited?" he asked, but for once he was ignored.

"You told her no?" asked Nurse, coming forward and fixing Isobel with a steely eye.

"Of course I told her no."

"And what did she say?"

"She took absolutely no notice whatsoever."

"It's out of the question," said Nurse. "Think of the upheaval, think of the noise. Mrs. Armstrong is not well. She is not up to such carryings on. And she's not by any chance imagining that she's going to come to the party?"

"No. On that score you can rest easy. At least," Isobel amended, knowing her mother, "I *think* you can."

"But why on earth?" demanded Mrs. Watty. "Why does she want another party? We haven't got the dining room straight after last night yet."

Isobel sighed. "It's for Rose. She wants everybody to meet Rose."

They all turned their eyes upon Flora. Flora, who had more reason than any of them to be completely horrorstruck by this latest bombshell, found herself blushing. "But I don't want a party. I mean, I said I'd stay on because Tuppy wanted me to, but I had no idea she had that up her sleeve."

Isobel patted her hand, comforting her. "She hadn't, last night. She thought it all up in the early hours of the morning. So it's none of it your fault. It's just Tuppy with her mania for entertaining."

Flora searched about for some practical objection. "But surely, there's not enough *time*. I mean, a dance. If you're going to send out invitations, there's not even a week . . ."

But that, too, had been thought of. "The invitations are to be by telephone," Isobel told them, and added in a resigned voice, "with me doing the telephoning."

Nurse decided that this nonsense had gone on for long enough. She drew out a chair and sat down, the starched bib of her apron puffing out in front of her, so that all at once she looked like a pouter pigeon. "She'll have to be told no," she announced again.

Mrs. Watty and Isobel, in concert, sighed. "That's not going to be so easy, Nurse," said Mrs. Watty, in the voice of a parent with a brilliant but maddening child. "You don't know Mrs. Armstrong the way Miss Isobel and I know her. Why, once she sets her mind on something, then not *wild horses* will make her see differently."

Jason took some toast and buttered it. "I've never been to a dance," he observed, but again nobody took the slightest notice of him.

"How about Antony, could he not talk to her?" Nurse suggested hopefully.

But Mrs. Watty and Isobel shook their heads. Antony would be no use at all. Besides, Antony was still in bed, catching up on his sleep, and nobody was going to disturb him.

"Well, if none of her family can make her see reason," Nurse announced, her tones indicating that she thought them a very poor lot, "then Dr. Kyle will have to."

At the mention of Hugh's name, both Mrs. Watty and Isobel brightened visibly. For some reason, they had not thought of Hugh.

"Dr. Kyle," repeated Mrs. Watty thoughtfully. "Yes. Now, that is a good idea. She'll take no notice of anything we might have to say, but she'll take a telling from the doctor. Is he coming to see her this morning?"

"Yes," said Nurse. "He mentioned some time before lunch."

Mrs. Watty leaned her massive forearms on the table, and dropped her voice, like a conspirator. "Then why don't we just humor her till then? There's no point, and I'm sure you will agree, Nurse, in upsetting Mrs. Armstrong with a lot of argument and fuss. Let's just leave it to Dr. Kyle."

And so the problem was satisfactorily shelved for the time being, and Flora had it in her heart to be sorry for Hugh Kyle.

The morning wore on. Flora helped Mrs. Watty with the breakfast dishes, vacuumed the dining-room carpet, and laid the table for lunch. Isobel put on her hat and bore Jason off to church. Mrs. Watty started cooking, whereupon Flora, primed by Nurse, went upstairs to see Tuppy.

"And mind you're noncommittal about that dance," warned Nurse. "If she starts on about it, you just change the subject."

Flora said that she would. She was just on her way out of
the kitchen when Mrs. Watty called her back, dried her hands,
opened a drawer, and took out a large paper bag containing a
number of hanks of gray with which she intended to knit a
sweater for Jason.

"This'll be a nice little occupation for you," she told Flora.
"You and Mrs. Armstrong can wind my wool for me. Why
they can't sell it rolled in those neat wee balls is beyond my
comprehension, but there it is, they don't seem to be able to."

Obediently bearing the bag of wool, Flora made her way
upstairs to Tuppy's room. As soon as she went in she saw that
Tuppy was looking better. Gone were the dark rings beneath
her eyes, the air of restlessness. She sat up in bed and held out
her arms as Flora appeared.

"I hoped it would be you. Come and give me a kiss. How
pretty you're looking." Flora, in deference to Sunday, had put
on a skirt and a Shetland sweater. "Do you know, this is the
first time I've seen your legs. With legs like that I don't know
why you have to cover them up with trousers all the time."
They kissed. Flora began to draw away, but Tuppy held her.
"Are you angry with me?"

"Angry?"

"About staying. It was very unfair of me to send you that
message by Isobel last night, but I wanted you to change your
mind, and I couldn't think of any other way of doing it."

Flora was disarmed. She smiled. "No, I'm not angry."

"It's not as though you had anything dreadfully important
to get back to. And I wanted you to stay, so badly."

She let Flora go, and Flora settled herself on the edge of
the bed. "But now you're in the doghouse," she told Tuppy,
deliberately forgetting Nurse's instructions. "You know that,
don't you?"

"I don't even know what a doghouse is."

"I mean you're in disgrace for planning another party."

"Oh, that." Tuppy chuckled, delighted with herself. "Poor
Isobel nearly fainted when I told her."

"You're very naughty."

"But why? Why shouldn't I have another party? Stuck in this silly bed, I must have something to amuse myself."

"You're meant to be getting better, not planning wild parties."

"Oh, it won't be wild. And there have been so many parties in this house that it will practically run on its own momentum. Besides, nobody has to do anything. I've organized it all."

"Isobel's got to spend an entire day at the telephone, ringing people up."

"Yes, but she won't mind that. Anyway, it'll keep her off her feet."

"But what about the house, and the flowers that will have to be done, and the furniture moved and everything?"

"Watty can move the furniture. It won't take him a moment. And . . ." Tuppy cast about for inspiration. ". . . you can do the flowers."

"Perhaps I can't do flowers."

"Then we'll have pot plants. Or get Anna to help us. Rose, it's no good trying to put obstacles in my way, because I've already thought of everything."

"Nurse says it depends on what Hugh says."

"Nurse has had a face on like the back of a bus, all morning. And if it depends on Hugh, you can set your mind at rest. Hugh will think it's a splendid idea."

"I shouldn't count on that, if I were you."

"No, I'm not counting on it. I've known Hugh all my life, and he can be as pig-headed as the next man." Tuppy's expression changed to one of amused speculation. "But I'm surprised you've found that out so quickly."

"I sat next to him last night at dinner." Flora opened the paper bag and took out the first hank of gray wheeling. "Do you feel strong enough to wind wool for Mrs. Watty?"

"Yes, of course I do, I'll hold it and you can do the winding."

Once they had organized themselves and started in on this undemanding task, Tuppy went on, as though there had been no pause in the conversation, "I want to hear about last night, all about it."

Flora told her, deliberately enthusiastic, making it all sound sheer fun from start to finish.

"And the Crowthers are so nice, aren't they?" said Tuppy, when Flora had finally run out of things to describe. "I really like him so much. He's rather overwhelming to meet for the first time, but such a really good man. And Hugh enjoyed himself?"

"Yes. At least, I think he did. But of course there was a telephone call for him halfway through the evening, and he had to go."

"The dear boy. If only he'd get someone to help him. But there it is . . ." Tuppy's hands dropped and Flora stopped winding wool and waited for her. ". . . I think that for Hugh being so busy is a sort of therapy. Isn't that what they call it nowadays? A therapy?"

"You mean, because of his wife's dying?"

"Yes. I think that's what I mean. You know, he was such a nice little boy. He used to come here quite a lot to play with Torquil. His father was our doctor—I told you that. Quite a humble man, from the Isle of Lewis, but he was a splendid doctor. And Hugh was clever, too. Hugh got a scholarship to Fettes, and then he went on to study medicine at Edinburgh University."

"He played rugger for the university, didn't he?"

"Antony must have told you that. Antony always thought the world of Hugh. Yes, he played rugger for the university, but what was more exciting was that he passed his finals with honors and he won the Cunningham Medal for Anatomy, and the whole wonderful world of medicine was open to him. Then Professor McClintock—he was professor of surgery at St. Thomas's in London—he asked Hugh to go down to London and study under him. We were all so proud. I couldn't have been more proud of Hugh if he'd been my own child."

Flora found it difficult to equate all this brilliance with the dour dinner companion of last night. "Why did it all go wrong?" she asked.

"Oh, it didn't go wrong exactly." Tuppy lifted her hands with the hank of wool looped around them, and Flora continued winding.

"He got married, though?"

"Yes. To Diana. He met her in London and they got engaged, and he brought her back to Tarbole."

"Did you meet her?"

"Yes."

"Did you like her?"

"She was very beautiful, very charming, very well turned out. I believe her father had a great deal of money. It couldn't have been easy for her, coming up here and knowing nobody. Tarbole was a very different world from the one she'd been used to, and she didn't really fit in. I think she thought we were all dreadfully dull. Poor Hugh. It must have been a desperate time for him. I didn't say anything to him, of course. It was nothing to do with me. But I believe that his old father was a little more outspoken. Too outspoken, perhaps. But by then Hugh was so besotted by her that it would have made no difference what any of us said. And although we didn't want to lose him, we *did* want him to be happy."

"And was he?"

"I don't know, Rose. We didn't see him again for two years, and when we did it was because Diana was dead—killed in a dreadful car accident—and Hugh had thrown everything up and come back to Tarbole to take over from his father. And he's been here ever since."

"How long is that?"

"Nearly eight years."

"You'd think he'd have got over it by now. Married again . . ."

"No. Not Hugh."

They fell silent, winding wool. The ball was getting quite big. Flora changed the subject. She said, "I liked Anna."

Tuppy's face lit up. "I am glad you liked Anna. I love her, but she's not easy to get to know. She's very shy."

"She told me that she's always lived here."

"Yes. Her father was a great friend of mine. He was called Archie Carstairs and he came from Glasgow. He'd made a great deal of money and everybody thought he was a very rough diamond—people were so silly and snobbish in those days—but I always liked him. He was a great sailing man—he used to cruise around in a very ostentatious ocean-going yacht. That's how he first came to Ardmore. He fell in love with the loch and the beautiful country, and indeed, who could blame him for that? There's nowhere like it in all the world. Anyway, just after the First World War, he built Ardmore House, and as the years went by he spent more and more time here, and eventually he retired to Ardmore. Anna was born there. Archie married late in life—I think he'd always been too busy making money to get married before—and so Anna was the child of quite elderly parents. In fact, her mother lived only for a few months after Anna was born. I often think, if her mother had survived, that Anna would have been a very different sort of person. But there it is, these things happen, and it's not for us to question why."

"And Brian?"

"What about Brian?"

"How did she meet Brian?"

Tuppy gave a little smile. "Brian sailed into Ardmore loch one summer, in a shabby little boat that he'd brought single-handed from the South of France. By then Archie had started the Ardmore Yacht Club. It was his toy, a hobby to keep him busy in retirement, and also to make sure that he kept in touch with all his old sailing friends. Brian tied up and came ashore for a drink, and Archie got talking to him, and he was so impressed by Brian's feat of seamanship that he asked him back to Ardmore House for dinner. For Anna it was like young Lochinvar, riding in on a white horse. She looked at Brian and lost her heart and she's been in love with him ever since."

"She married him."

"Of course."

"What did her father have to say about that?"

"He was fairly wary. He admired Brian and he even quite liked him, but he'd never intended him as his son-in-law."

"Did he try to talk Anna out of it?"

"To give him his due, yes, I think he did. But the most unexpected people can be very stubborn. Anna was a woman by then, no longer a child. She knew what she wanted and she intended having it."

"Was Brian in love with her?"

There was a long pause. Then Tuppy said, "No, I don't think so. But I do think that he was fond of her. And of course he was also fond of all the material things that being married to Anna represented."

"You're saying—in a very nice way—that he married her for her money."

"I don't want to say that, because I'm so fond of Anna."

"Does it matter anyway, provided they're happy?"

"That's what I asked myself at the time."

"Is she very rich?"

"Yes. When Archie died she inherited everything."

"And Brian?"

"Brian has nothing but the settlement Archie made on him. I happen to know it was very generous, but the capital, the bulk of the wealth, is Anna's."

"Supposing—the marriage broke up?"

"Then Brian's settlement would be dissolved. He would have nothing."

Flora thought of Anna with her diffidence and her beautiful diamonds. And she was sorry for her, all over again, because it must be a cheerless thing to have your husband tied to you by nothing but money.

"Brian's very attractive."

"Brian? Yes, of course he's attractive. Attractive and frustrated. He doesn't have nearly enough to do with himself."

"They've never had any children?"

"Anna lost a child, that summer you and your mother

were here. But I don't suppose you'd remember. You'd probably gone by then."

The ball of wool was nearly finished. The last few strands
lay across Tuppy's thin wrists. "She's pregnant again," said
Tuppy.

Flora stopped winding. "Anna? Is she? Oh, I am glad,"

Tuppy was instantly concerned. "I should never have said
anything. It just slipped out. I wasn't meant to tell anyone.
Hugh told me, just to cheer me up when I was feeling so ill.
And I promised I'd keep it a secret."

"Your secret is safe with me," Flora vowed. "In fact, I've
forgotten it already."

It was midday and they were onto the last hank of wool
before Hugh appeared. They heard his footsteps up the stairs
and along the passage. There came a cursory thump on the
door, and the next moment he was in the room with them. He
wore his workday suit. His bag swung from his hand and a
stethoscope spilled from the pocket of his jacket.

"Good morning," he said.

Tuppy eyed him. "You don't look as though anybody had
ever told you that Sunday is meant to be a day of rest."

"I forgot it was Sunday when I woke up this morning." He
came to the foot of the bed and straight to the point. "What's
all this I've been hearing?"

Tuppy made an exasperated face. "I knew they'd tell you
before I had a chance to."

He set down his bag on the floor and leaned his arms on
the brass rail at the end of her bed. "Then you tell me now."

The end of the wool slipped off Tuppy's wrists and onto
the last fat ball.

"We're going to have a little party next Friday for Rose
and Antony," Tuppy told him, as though it were the most
natural thing in the world.

"How many people does a little party consist of?"

"About . . . sixty." She met his eye. "Seventy?" she
amended hopefully.

"Seventy people bouncing about in the hall, drinking champagne and talking nineteen to the dozen. What do you think that's going to do to your state of health?"

"If anything, it will improve it."

"Who's going to organize all this?"

"It has already been organized. It took me exactly half an hour before breakfast. And now I shall wash my hands off the entire affair."

He looked, naturally, skeptical. "Tuppy, I find that hard to believe."

"Oh, don't be such an old stick-in-the-mud. Everybody's carrying on as though we were going to give a state ball."

Hugh looked at Flora. "And what does Rose think about it?"

"Me?" Flora had been gathering up the balls of wool, putting them back into the paper bag. "I . . . I think it's a lovely idea, but if you think it's going to be too much for Tuppy . . ."

"Don't be such a turncoat, Rose," Tuppy interrupted crossly. "You're just as bad as the rest of them." She turned back to Hugh. "I've told you, it's all planned. Mr. Anderson will do the catering, Rose will do the flowers, Watty will clear the hall of furniture, and Isobel will telephone everybody and ask them to come. And if you don't take that expression off your face, Hugh, *you* will not be asked."

"And what are you going to do?"

"Me? Not a thing. I shall simply sit here and stare into space."

Her blue gaze was innocent. Hugh cocked his head and watched her warily. "No visitors," he said.

"What do you mean, no visitors?"

"I mean, nobody nipping upstairs to see you and having little chats."

Tuppy looked bitterly disappointed. "Not even one or two?"

"Start with one or two, and by the end of the evening your bedroom would be like Piccadilly Underground at rush hour. No visitors. And I won't even take your word on it. I shall post

Nurse at the door as a sentry, armed with a pike or a bedpan or whatever weapon she chooses. And that, Mrs. Armstrong, is the deal." He straightened up and came around to the side of the bed. "And now, Rose, if you'd be so kind as to go and find Nurse, and tell her I'm here."

"Yes, of course." Thus dismissed, Flora kissed Tuppy quickly, got off the bed, and went out of the room. Nurse was already on her way upstairs, and they met on the landing.

Nurse's face was grim. "Is Dr. Kyle with Mrs. Armstrong?"

"Yes, he's waiting for you."

"I hope he's put an end to this scatter-brained idea of hers."

"I'm not sure. But I rather think the party is on."

"The Lord save us," said Nurse.

Mrs. Watty was more philosophical about it all. "Well, if it's a party she wants, why shouldn't she have it?" She added, "It's not as though we can't manage. Why, there've been so many parties given in this house that we could probably manage standing on our heads."

"I'm meant to be doing the flowers."

Mrs. Watty looked amused. "So you've been given your own wee job. Mrs. Armstrong's very good at giving people jobs to do."

"Yes, but I'm hopeless at flowers. I can't even put daffodils in a jug."

"Oh, you'll manage fine." She opened a cupboard and counted out a pile of plates. "Was the doctor easily persuaded?"

"Not easily, but he was persuaded. On condition that Tuppy doesn't have any visitors. Nurse is going to be put to stand guard at her door."

Mrs. Watty shook her head. "Poor Dr. Kyle, what a time he does have, to be sure. As if he didn't have enough to worry about without us unloading more trouble onto his shoulders. And, seemingly, he has no help at the moment. Jessie McKenzie—she's meant to be his housekeeper—well, two days ago I hear she took the Skye Ferry over to Portree. Her mother lives there and seemingly the old lady's poorly."

"Oh, dear."

"It's not that easy to get help in Tarbole. Most of the women are working with the fish these days, packing herrings, or in the smokehouses." She glanced at the clock, remembered her roasting joint, and forgot about Dr. Kyle's woes. Cautiously she stooped to open her oven door, and they were assailed by fragrant steam and the sizzling of fat.

"Is Antony not up yet?" Mrs. Watty drove a skewer into the flank of the roast. "I think it's time you went and gave him a call. Otherwise he'll sleep through the day, and the next thing it'll be time for him to start for home."

Flora went to do this, but as she crossed the hall, she heard Hugh come out of Tuppy's room, and start down the upstairs landing. She had reached the foot of the stairs when he appeared. When he saw her, she stopped and, without really knowing why, waited for him to descend.

He was wearing horn-rimmed spectacles, which made him look distinguished. When he had reached her side he set down his bag, took off the spectacles, towing them in a case, and slipped the case into the pocket of his jacket. He looked at Flora. "Well?" he prompted, as though she should have something to say to him. To her surprise, Flora found that she had.

"Hugh, last night . . . You didn't want me to say I'd stay on, did you?"

He seemed unprepared for such forthrightness. "No. But I have a feeling that that is what made you change your mind."

"Why didn't you want me to stay?"

"Call it premonition."

"Of trouble?"

"If you like."

"Does Tuppy's party count as trouble?"

"We could have done without it."

"But it's on?"

"At the moment it is." She waited for him to enlarge on

this, and when he didn't, she became persistent. "But it will be all right? I mean, Tuppy will be all right?"

"Yes, provided she does as she's told. Nurse McLeod is rigidly disapproving. Her opinion of me has sunk to rock bottom. But, in fact, it may prove to be the small stimulus that Tuppy needs. And if it doesn't . . ." He stopped, letting the unsaid words speak for themselves.

He looked so worn down by all this that despite herself Flora was sorry for him. "Never mind," she said, trying to sound cheerful, "at least she's doing what she most loves doing. Like the old man of ninety, being asked how he wants to die, and choosing to be shot by a jealous husband."

Hugh's face broke into a smile, spontaneous as it was unexpected. She had never seen him smile properly before and was caught unaware by its sweetness, by the way it altered his whole face. For an instant she caught a glimpse of the young, light-hearted man that he had once been.

He said, "Exactly so."

The morning had been gray and gentle, very still. But now a breeze had got up, clouds were being blown aside, as they stood there at the foot of the stairs, the sun broke through and all at once everything was bathed in its liquid, golden light. It poured into the hall through the two tall windows which stood on either side of the front door. The beams became filled with floating dustmotes and previously unnoticed details sprang into vivid clarity and importance: the texture of his suit, shabby and, in places, growing threadbare; the pockets sagging with the weight of various articles which he had stuffed into them; his pullover, which had an inept darn, right in the middle; and his hand, which he had placed over the newel post as he talked. She saw the shape of it, the long fingers, the signet ring, the scrubbed and clean look.

She saw that he was tired. He was still smiling at the small joke she had made, but he looked bone-weary. She thought of him coming out to dinner last night, getting dressed in his best, searching the cheerless house for a clean shirt, because his housekeeper had left him to go off to Portree to visit her mother.

She said, "Last night, the telephone call you had—I hope it wasn't anything serious."

"Serious enough. A very old man, getting older, and a daughter-in law at the end of her tether. He'd got out of bed to go to the lavatory and he'd fallen down the stairs."

"Did he hurt himself?"

"By a miracle, no bones were broken, but he's bruised and badly shocked. He should be in a hospital. There's a bed for him in Lochgarry Hospital, but he won't go. He was born in the house he lives in now, and that's where he wants to die."

"Where is the house?"

"Boturich."

"I don't know where Boturich is."

"Up at the far end of Loch Fhada."

"But that must be fifteen miles."

"Thereabouts."

"When did you get home?"

"About two o'clock this morning."

"And what time did you get up again?"

His eyes crinkled with amusement. "What is this? An inquisition?"

"You must be tired."

"I don't have time to be tired. And now"—he glanced at his watch and stooped to pick up his bag—"I must be on my way."

She went with him to the door to open it for him. The sunlight made a dazzle of damp grass and gravel and shining flame-colored leaves. He said, reverting to his usual manner, "I'll doubtless see you," and she watched him go down the steps, into his car, down between the rhododendrons past the lodge, and through the open gate.

In the sun, it should have been warm, but Flora shivered. She came indoors, closed the door, and started upstairs to wake Antony.

She found him already up and shaving, standing in front of

the basin dressed in a pair of scarlet leather slippers and two towels, one tied around his waist and the other slung like a muffler round his neck. As she put her head around the edge of the door he turned to look at her. His face was lopsided, one side soapy, the other clean.

She said, "I've been sent up to wake you. It's twelve thirty."

"I'm awake, and I know it is. Come on in."

He turned back to the mirror and continued his task. Flora shut the door and went to sit on the edge of the bed. She said, to his reflection, "How did you sleep?"

"Like the dead."

"How strong are you feeling?"

There was a pause and then, "For some reason," Antony told her, "that question fills me with nameless apprehensions."

"And so it should. There's going to be another party. Next Friday. A dance."

After a little, he said, "I see what you mean about feeling strong."

"Tuppy organized the whole thing before breakfast. And she seems to have steamrolled everyone, including Hugh Kyle, into letting her have her own way. The only person who's really opposed to it is Nurse, and she's going around with a face of doom."

"You mean, it's really on?"

"Yes. It's really on."

"I suppose it's for Antony and Rose."

Flora nodded.

"To celebrate the engagement."

"Right again."

He had finished shaving. Now he turned on the tap to wash his razor. "Oh, God," he said.

She was remorseful. "It's my fault. I shouldn't have said I would stay."

"How could you have known? How could any of us have guessed she'd think up something like this?"

"I don't suppose there's anything we can do about it."

He turned to face her, his copper-colored hair standing on end, and an expression of gloom on his usually cheerful face. He jerked the towel from round his neck and threw it across a chair.

"Not a bloody thing. It's like drowning in a quagmire. By the end of the week, all that will be left of us will be a couple of bubbles. And muddy ones at that."

"We could make a clean breast of it. Tell Tuppy the truth." The idea had been shadowing around at the back of Flora's mind all morning, but it was the first time she had brought it out into the open and acknowledged it, even to herself.

Antony said, "No."

"But . . ."

He turned on her. "I said no. O.K., so Tuppy's better. O.K., so Isobel got everything wrong and Tuppy's going to make a miraculous recovery. But she's old, and she's been very ill, and if anything happened just because you and I insisted on the luxury of a clean conscience, I'd never been able to forgive myself. You see that, don't you?"

Flora sighed. She said, miserably, "Yes, I suppose so."

"You are the most super girl." He stooped to give her a kiss. His cheek was smooth; he smelt clean and lemony.

"And now, if you'll excuse me, I must get some clothes on."

That afternoon, the tide was out. After lunch Flora and Antony, meanly evading Jason, who wanted to come with them, set out for a walk. They took the dogs—even Sukey, whom Antony had firmly scooped off Tuppy's eiderdown—and went down to Fhada sands, left clean and white by the ebb tide. They headed toward the distant breakers while the wind blew gusts of sunshine at them out of the west.

It was not a cheerful outing. Antony's departure for Edinburgh lay over them both like doom, and they talked scarcely at all. And yet the silence that lay between them was in its own way companionable, because Flora knew that Antony's thoughts were as troubled as her own.

At the water's edge they halted. Antony found a long rope of seaweed and flung it out into the waves for Plummer to retrieve, which he did with a great deal of splashy swimming. Moments later he was leaping back at them out of the sea with the seaweed trailing from the side of his mouth. Sukey, who did not like getting her feet wet, sat well back and observed him. Plummer laid down the seaweed, shook himself stupendously, and sat with his great wet ears pricked, waiting for Antony to throw it again. This he did, even farther out this time, and Plummer plunged once more into the breakers.

Standing in the wind, they watched him go. Flora said, "We'll have to tell them sometime, Antony. Sometime they'll have to know that I'm Flora, I'm not Rose. Perhaps a clean conscience is a luxury, but I can't live with this for the rest of my life." She looked at him. "I'm sorry, but I simply can't."

His profile was stony, his face ruddy from the wind. He dug his hands deep into his pockets and sighed.

"No, I know. I've been thinking that too." He turned his head to look down at her. "But it has to be me who does the telling. Not you."

She was a little hurt. "I'd never think of doing such a thing."

"No. But it isn't going to be easy for you these next few days. It's going to get worse, not better, and I'm not going to be here to support you. Next weekend, after the dance, if Tuppy's all right, then we'll make a clean breast of it. Confess, if you like." He looked quite drawn at the thought. "But meantime, you must promise not to say anything to any of them."

"Antony, I wouldn't."

"Promise."

She promised. The sun went behind a cloud, and it became suddenly chilly. They waited, shivering slightly, for Plummer to return to them, and then turned and started on the long trudge back to the house.

When they got home, Plummer was banished to Mrs. Watty's kitchen until he had dried off, and Sukey shot like an arrow back up the stairs to Tuppy's bedroom. Antony and Flora shed

coats and gumboots and went into the drawing room, where
they found Isobel and Jason by the fire eating tea, engrossed in
some swashbuckling adventure on television. Conversation was
obviously not expected so they joined them, in silence, eating
buttered toast, and mindlessly watching some spirited sword-
play and a great deal of running up and down flare-lit spiral
staircases. It was finished at last, with the hero clapped into a
dungeon until the following week's episode. Isobel switched off
the television, and Jason turned his attention to Antony and
Flora.

"I wanted to take a walk with you and when I looked for
you, you'd *gone.*"

"Sorry," said Antony, sounding not sorry in the least.

"Will you play cards with me?"

"No." He laid down his empty teacup. "I've got to go and
pack and then start back for Edinburgh."

"I'll come and help you."

"I don't want you to come and help me. Rose is going to
come and help me."

"But why . . ." His voice rose to what sounded perilously
like a whine. He was often in a bad humor on Sunday evenings
because he knew tomorrow morning was Monday, which
meant school again. Isobel tactfully intervened.

"Antony and Rose have got a lot of things they want to
discuss without all of us listening. And if you get the cards out
of the drawer, I'll play a game with you."

"It's not fair . . ."

"Do you want to play Beggar My Neighbor, or Pelmanism?"

They left Jason spreading the cards on the hearth rug for
Pelmanism, and went up to Antony's room, which was painfully neat, almost as though he had already gone. The curtains
had not been drawn; the center light was cheerless. He began
collecting his shaving gear and putting it into his bag, while
Flora stacked clean shirts and folded his dressing gown. It
didn't take very long. He put his silver brushes on top of the

pile, closed the lid, and snapped the locks shut. The room, stripped of his possessions, became unfriendly.

He said, "You'll be all right?"

He looked so anxious that she made herself smile. "Of course."

He felt in his pocket and took out a scrap of paper. "I wrote my telephone numbers down for you in case you want to get in touch with me. That's the office, and that's my flat. If it's something you don't want anybody to hear, you could probably borrow one of the cars and get yourself to Tarbole. There's a call box down by the harbor."

"When will you be back?"

"As early on Friday afternoon as I can manage."

"I'll be here," she told him, unnecessarily.

"You'd better be."

Carrying his suitcase, he went along to say goodbye to Tuppy, while Flora went downstairs to tell Isobel and Jason that he was just about to leave. Jason was dispatched to fetch Mrs. Watty, who appeared from the kitchen with a box of buttered scones and a bag of apples. She could not bear the thought of one of the family setting out on any sort of a journey without being well-provisioned. Antony then came downstairs, kissed them all, and told them not to work too hard. They all said, "See you on Friday," and returned to their various occupations, while Antony and Flora let themselves out into the dusky evening. His car waited on the gravel outside the front door. He flung his case into the back seat, put his arms around Flora, and gave her a hug.

She said, feebly, "I wish you didn't have to go."

"So do I. Take care of yourself. And try not to get too involved."

"I'm involved already."

"Yes." He sounded hopeless. "Yes, I know."

She watched him drive away, the taillight of his car whisking out of sight beyond the gates. She went back into the house, closed the door, and stood in the hall feeling desolate. From

behind the drawing room door came the murmur of voices as
Isobel and Jason continued their game. Flora looked at her
watch. It was nearly a quarter to six. She thought she would go
upstairs and have a bath.

Her bedroom, which she had liked so much from the beginning, seemed, in the chill half-light, unfamiliar; the room of
a stranger staying in a strange house. She drew the curtains and
turned on the bedside lamp, thus improving things, but only
slightly. She turned on the electric fire and, longing to be warm,
knelt on the hearth rug as close to the reddening bars as she
could get.

It took a few moments to realize that she was suffering
from loss of identity. Antony had known that she was Flora,
but she hadn't realized that this was so important. Now, with
him gone, it was as though he had taken Flora with him, and
left only Rose behind. She knew that she had come to distrust
Rose, almost to dislike her. She thought of Rose in Greece,
trying to imagine the sort of things Rose would be doing, like
sunbathing, and dancing under the stars to soft guitar music or
whatever it was one danced to in Spetsai. But none of those
mental pictures had any depth. They were two-dimensional,
unconvincing, like overcolored postcards. Rose, it seemed, was
not in Greece. Rose was here, at Fernrigg.

Her hands were frozen. She spread them to the warmth.
I'm Flora. I'm Flora Waring.

The promise she had made to Antony hung on her conscience like a weight. Perhaps because she had made it, she
longed passionately to be able to tell the truth. To someone. To
anyone who would listen and understand.

But who?

The answer, when it came, was so obvious that she could
not think why it had not occurred to her right away. Promise
not to say anything to any of them, Antony had insisted. And
she had given him her word. But "any of them" surely only
meant the Armstrongs, the people who lived in this house.

There was a little bureau in the corner of her bedroom,
which she had not even thought to investigate. Now she got up

and went over to it, and lowered the flap. Inside, this being the well-ordered establishment that it was, she found embossed writing paper and envelopes, a blotting pad, and a pen in a silver tray. She pulled up a chair, took up the pen, drew a sheet of paper toward her, and wrote the date.

Thus she started what was to be a very long letter to her father.

8

BRIAN

Early the next morning, as Flora came down to breakfast the telephone rang. Crossing the hall, she hesitated. When nobody appeared to answer it, she answered it herself, going to sit on the edge of the chest and pick up the receiver.

"Hello."

A woman spoke. "Is that Fernrigg?"

"Yes."

"Is that Isobel?"

"No. Do you want Isobel?"

"Is . . . is that Rose?"

Flora hesitated. "Yes."

"Oh, Rose, it's Anna Stoddart."

"Good morning, Anna. Do you want to speak to Isobel?"

"No, it doesn't matter, you'll do just as well. I only wanted to say thank you for the dinner party on Saturday. I . . . I enjoyed it so much."

"I'm glad. I'll tell Isobel."

"I'm sorry about ringing so early, but I forgot to ring yesterday, and I'm just off to Glasgow. I mean, I'm leaving any moment now. And I didn't want to go without saying thank you."

"Well, I hope you have a good trip."

"Yes, I'm sure I will. I'm only going for a couple of days. Perhaps when I get back you'd like to come over to Ardmore and see me. We could have lunch, or tea or something . . ."

Her voice trailed away uncertainly as though she felt she had already said too much. Flora could not bear her being so diffident. She said quickly, making her voice enthusiastic, "I'd love it. How kind of you. I'd love to see your house."

"Really? That would be fun. I'll maybe give you a telephone call when I get back."

"You do that." She added, "Have you heard about the dance yet?"

"Dance?"

"I thought perhaps it might have got through to you via the grapevine. There's going to be a dance here next Friday night. Tuppy thought the whole thing up by herself yesterday morning."

"*This* Friday?" Anna sounded incredulous, as well she might.

"This very Friday. Poor Isobel's got to spend the morning on the telephone, ringing people up. I'll tell her I've told you; and that'll be one less call she'll have to make."

"But how exciting. I'm so glad you told me, because now I can get a new dress when I'm in Glasgow. I need a new dress anyway . . ."

Once more her voice faded uncertainly. Anna was obviously a person who found it difficult to round off a telephone call. Flora was just about to say, in a conclusive sort of way, well, have a good time, when Anna said, "Just a minute. Don't ring off."

"I wasn't going to."

There were a few murmurs from the other end of the line,

and then Anna said, "Brian wants to talk to you. I'll say goodbye."

Brian? "Goodbye, Anna. Have a good time." Then Brian Stoddart spoke in his light, clear voice.

"Rose!"

"Good morning," said Flora warily.

"What an unearthly hour for a telephone conversation. Have you had your breakfast yet?"

"I'm just going to have it."

"Has Antony gone?"

"Yes, he went yesterday after tea."

"So you're bereft. And Anna's just on the point of abandoning me. Why don't we keep each other company tonight? I'll take you out for dinner."

A number of thoughts chased themselves through Flora's mind, the most important being that Anna was obviously aware of the conversation, so there could be nothing underhand about his invitation. But what would Tuppy think about it? And Isobel? And was it wise to spend an evening with that devious and attractive man? And even if his suggestion was innocent and harmless, did she particularly want to?

"Rose?"

"Yes, I'm still here."

"I thought you'd gone. I couldn't even hear heavy breathing. What time shall I pick you up?"

"I haven't said that I'm coming yet."

"Of course you're coming, don't be so coy. We'll go to the Fishers' Arms down in Lochgarry and I'll stuff you with scampi. Look, I've got to go. Anna's just on the point of departure, she's waiting for me to go and see her off. I'll pick you up about seven thirty, eight o'clock. That be all right? If Isobel's feeling generous, she can give me a drink. Love to Tuppy, and thank Isobel for the party the other night. We both enjoyed it enormously. See you later."

He rang off, and Flora was left holding the dead receiver. An outrageous man. Slowly, she put the receiver down. She thought, well . . . and then she began to smile, because really it was ridiculous. Brian's charm, which had come gusting down the telephone wires towards her, was too obvious to be dangerous, or even important. The whole incident was too trivial to merit a great session of soul-searching. Besides, she liked scampi.

She realized that she was hungry and went in search of breakfast.

Jason had gone, borne off to school by Mr. Watty. Isobel was still at the kitchen table, reading a letter and drinking a final cup of coffee with Nurse. Mrs. Watty, at the window, was slicing steak for a pie.

"Did I hear the telephone ring?" she asked. She liked keeping in touch with what was going on.

"Yes, I answered it." Flora sat down and filled a bowl with cornflakes. "It was Anna Stoddart, Isobel, saying thank you for the other night."

Isobel looked up from her mail. "Oh, how kind," she said vaguely.

"She's just off to Glasgow for a couple of days."

"Yes, she said something about that."

"And Brian's asked me to go out to dinner with him tonight."

She watched Isobel's face, waiting for the slightest shadow of disapproval. But Isobel only smiled. "What a nice idea. That is kind of him."

"He said as I was without Antony and he was without Anna we might as well keep each other company. And he's coming to pick me up at half past seven, and he says if you're feeling generous you can give him a drink."

Isobel laughed, but Mrs. Watty said, "He's a cheeky devil."

"Don't you like him, Mrs. Watty?"

"Oh, I like him well enough, but he's awful forward."

"What Mrs. Watty means," said Isobel, "is that he just doesn't happen to be a dour Scot. I think it's very nice of him to take pity on Rose."

"And I told them about the dance on Friday so you don't

need to ring them up. And Anna's going to buy herself a new dress."

"Oh, dear," said Isobel.

"What does that mean?"

"Anna's always buying new clothes. She spends the earth on them, and they all look exactly the same." She sighed. "I suppose we've all got to start thinking about what we're going to wear next Friday. I could bring out that blue lace thing again, but everybody must be getting very tired of it."

"You're bonny in your blue lace," Mrs. Watty assured her. "It's no matter if people have seen it before."

"And Rose. What are you going to wear, Rose?"

The question, for some reason, caught Flora quite unprepared. Perhaps because there had been so many other more important issues to worry about, the thought of what she would wear to Tuppy's party had not even entered her head. She looked around at their expectant faces. "I haven't the faintest idea," she told them.

Nurse stared at Flora in some disbelief. She still remained rigidly opposed to the very idea of Tuppy's party, but despite herself it was impossible not to be caught up in the general anticipation. She was also a great social snob, and now she could scarcely believe that a young lady would come away to stay in a house like Fernrigg without packing at least one ballgown and possibly a tiara to wear with it.

"Haven't you got anything in your suitcase?" she asked Flora.

"No. I only came for the weekend. I didn't think I'd need a dress for a dance."

There was a pregnant silence while they all digested this information.

"What about what you wore the other night?" suggested Isobel.

"That was just a woolen skirt, and a shirt."

"Oh, no," breathed Mrs. Watty. "The party's to be in your honor. You'll need something a little more dressy than that."

She felt that she was letting them all down. "Could I buy something?"

"Not in Tarbole," Isobel told her. "Not within a hundred miles could you buy something to wear."

"Perhaps I should have gone to Glasgow with Anna."

"Is there nothing in the house that we could alter?" asked Nurse. Flora had visions of herself in a dress made out of old slip-covers.

Isobel shook her head. "Even if there were, we're none of us what you'd call dressmakers."

Nurse cleared her throat. "I used to make all my own clothes when I was a girl. And perhaps I've got a little more time than the rest of you."

"You mean you'd make something for Rose?"

"If it would help . . ."

At this suggestion, Mrs. Watty turned from her meat slicing, her kindly face at variance with the murderous-looking knife in her hand. "What about the attic? Those trunks in the attic are just full of old things that once belonged to Mrs. Armstrong. And lovely materials . . ."

"Mothballs," said Isobel. "They all smell of mothballs."

"A good wash and a blow on the line would see to that." The idea took hold. Mrs. Watty laid down her knife, washed her hands, and said that she for one was going upstairs to look, and there was no time like the present. It seemed there wasn't. In no time, all four of them were trooping up to the attics.

These were huge, stretching from one end of the house to the other. They were also dimly lit, cobwebby, and smelling of camphor and old cricket boots. A number of fascinating objects which Flora would have loved to inspect stood about: a weighing machine of the old type with brass weights and a measuring stick attached to the side; a Victorian doll's pram; a dressmaker's dummy; some brass ewers once used for carrying hot water.

But Mrs. Watty snapped on a dingy light and made her way straight to the line of trunks which stood ranged along the wall. They were of immense size and weight, with rounded lids and leather handles for carrying. Together Mrs. Watty and Isobel lifted the lid of the first. It was stuffed with clothes. The smell of mothballs was indeed distressingly strong, but out came the garments, each one more ornate and impossible than the one before: black silk with jet embroidery; tea-rose satin with a fringed skirt; a drooping bouclé jacket lined with shredded chiffon, which Isobel assured Flora used to be known as a bridge coat.

"Did Tuppy really wear all these things?"

"Oh, in her day, she could be quite dressy. And of course, being such a thrifty old Scot, she's never thrown a thing away."

"Whatever's that?"

"It's an evening cape." Isobel shook out the crumpled velvet and blew on the fur collar. Out of the fur flew an intrepid moth. "I can remember Tuppy wearing this . . ." Her voice grew dreamy as she recalled far-off days.

It became more and more hopeless. Flora was on the point of suggesting that she go now to Tarbole, catch the next train to Glasgow and buy herself something there, when Mrs. Watty pulled out something that had obviously once been white, in lawn and lace. Like an old handkerchief, Flora thought, but it was a dress with a high neckband and long sleeves.

Isobel recognized it in some excitement. "But that was Tuppy's tennis dress."

"Tennis dress?" Flora was incredulous. "She surely didn't play tennis in that?"

"Yes, she did when she was a girl." Isobel took it from Mrs. Watty and held it up by the shoulders. "What do you think, Nurse? Could we do anything with that?"

Nurse handled the cobweb cotton with experienced fingers, pursing up her lips. "There's nothing wrong with it . . . and there's lovely work there."

"But it's much too short for me," objected Flora.

Nurse held it against her. It was too short, but there was, Nurse opined, *a good hem*. "I could let it down and you'd never notice."

Secretly Flora thought it was awful. But at least it wasn't

old slip-covers, and anything was better than having to make the trip to Glasgow.

"It's completely transparent. I'd have to wear something underneath."

"I could line it," said Nurse. "In some pretty shade. Perhaps pink."

Pink. Flora's heart sank, but she said nothing. Mrs. Watty and Isobel looked at each other for inspiration. Then Mrs. Watty remembered that when Isobel's bedroom curtains had been replaced they had ordered too much lining cotton. A length of it, good as new, must still be lying around somewhere. Finally, after a certain amount of pondering and poking around, Mrs. Watty, with a cry of triumph, produced it from the top drawer of a yellow-varnished dressing table.

"I knew I'd put it somewhere. I just couldn't mind where."

It was a pale eggshell blue. She shook it out of its folds and held it behind the drooping garment of yellowed lawn that was to be Flora's ball dress.

"What do you think?" she asked Flora.

The blue at least was better than pink. Perhaps when washed the dress wouldn't be too bad. She looked up and saw that they were all watching her dubious face, anxious for her approval. Like three ill-assorted fairy godmothers, they waited to turn her into the belle of the ball. Flora felt ashamed of her own lack of enthusiasm. To make up for it, she now smiled as though delighted and told them that if she had searched for a week, she couldn't have found a more perfect dress.

By afternoon the bulky letter addressed to Ronald Waring had still not been posted. For one thing, Flora had no stamp. For another, she had no idea where to find a letter box. After lunch, when Isobel asked her what she would like to do, Flora remembered the letter.

"Would you mind if I went to Tarbole? I've got a letter I want to post."

"I wouldn't mind in the least. In fact, it would be splendid because I've run out of hand cream and you can buy me some."

She added, "And you can fetch Jason from school and that will save Watty a journey." A thought occurred to her. "I suppose you *can* drive a car?"

"Yes, if nobody minds my borrowing one."

"You can take the van," Isobel told her placidly. "Then it doesn't matter if you do hit something."

The word went round that a trip was being made to Tarbole, and at once Flora was inundated with errands to be performed. Nurse needed fine sewing needles and blue silk to match the lining of the new dress. Tuppy wanted face tissues and four ounces of extra strong peppermints. Flora, with her shopping list in her hand, went into the kitchen to search out Mrs. Watty.

"I'm going to Tarbole. And I'm going to fetch Jason from school. Do you want me to get anything for you?"

"Does Watty know that he doesn't have to go to Tarbole?"

"No, I'm going to tell him on my way out. Isobel said I could take the van."

"Well, if Watty isn't going," said Mrs. Watty, heading for her fridge, "then you can deliver this for me." And she withdrew, from the fridge, a large steak pie in an enamel dish.

"Where do you want me to take that?"

"This is for Dr. Kyle." She took grease-proof paper from a drawer, tore off a generous sheet, and wrapped the pie in it. "I was making one for the dinner tonight, and I said to Miss Isobel, I might just as well make one for that poor man without his housekeeper. At least, he'll have one square meal in the day."

"But I don't know where he lives. I don't know where his house is."

"In Tarbole, up at the top of the hill. You can't miss it," Mrs. Watty added, which made Flora certain that she would, "because you'll see the new surgery tacked onto the side. And there's a brass plate on the gate."

She handed Flora the parceled pie. It was extremely heavy and should nourish Dr. Kyle, she reckoned, for at least four days.

"What shall I do with it? Leave it on the front doormat?"

"No." Mrs. Watty obviously thought Flora was being dense. "Take it inside into the kitchen and put it in the refrigerator."

"What if the door's locked?"

"Then the key will be on the ledge, inside the porch, on the righthand side."

Flora gathered up the rest of her things. She said, "Well, I just hope I leave it in the right house," and made her way out through the back door, leaving Mrs. Watty in fits of laughter, as though she had made a joke.

Watty was found in the vegetable garden. Flora gave him the message about Jason and said that Miss Armstrong had said that she could take the van. Watty told her that it was in the garage, and the key in the ignition. He added that the van had no peculiarities.

It may have been easy to drive, but for all that it was a peculiar van:—Tuppy's pride, Mrs. Watty's shame, and the joke of Tarbole. Tuppy, having decided that the old Daimler used too much petrol and that another, smaller, car was needed for day-to-day runs, had bought it secondhand off Mr. Reekie, the Tarbole fishmonger. And although Watty, bidden by his wife, had given it a coat of paint, the lettering on the side was still clearly visible:

Archibald Reekie
Fish of Quality
Freshly Smoked Kippers Delivered Daily

Flora, seeing it for the first time, thought it had great class. She got in behind the wheel, turned on the engine and, with only a small amount of gear-crashing, sped toward Tarbole.

The little town was a seething mass of activity that afternoon. The harbor was full of boats and the quays were packed with lorries. The air was full of the sounds of engines running and the churning of cranes, shouted orders, the gush of high-pressure hoses, and the endless screaming of the hungry gulls.

There were people everywhere: fishermen in yellow oilskins, lorry drivers in overalls, harbor officials in their uniforms. There were women in rubber boots and striped aprons, and all of them were involved in the complicated business of unloading the fish from the boats, gutting it, packing it, loading it into the waiting lorries, and sending it on its way.

She remembered Antony telling her about Tarbole—how only a short time ago it had been simply a small fishing village, but lately it had become the center of a vast herring industry. Inevitably, all that prosperity had left its mark. As she came down the road from Fernrigg, Flora passed the new school which had been built to accommodate the growing population of Tarbole children. Council houses spread up the hill behind the town, and not only fish lorries, but cars as well, choked the narrow streets around the harbor.

After driving Mr. Reekie's van around in circles for five minutes, Flora finally parked it in front of the bank beside a sign which said, *Parking Strictly Forbidden.* She did her shopping—which did not take long, since most of the purchases were made in the same shop—and then without much difficulty found the post office. She bought a stamp which she stuck onto the envelope addressed to her father, and then hesitated only for a moment before dropping it into the box. She heard it land with a fat thud and stood for a moment, not sure whether she felt glad or sorry that it was actually gone, out of her hands, beyond control. She thought of her father receiving it, reading it first to himself, and then perhaps aloud to Marcia. Knowing Marcia would be with him made all the difference. Everything would seem less dramatic, and he would perhaps not think too badly of Flora. More important, Marcia would not let him think badly of himself.

She made her way back to the car, but as she came around the corner was horrified to see a young constable standing waiting beside it. She began to run, meaning to apologize, beg for mercy, get into the car, and race away, but when she reached him, he only said, "You'll be a friend of Mrs. Armstrong of Fernrigg?"

Flora was taken aback. "Yes, I am."

"I thought I recognized the wee car."

"I am sorry, I thought . . ."

"Have you more errands to do?"

"Yes. I've got to deliver a pie to Dr. Kyle. And then I've got to get Jason from school."

"If you're going to Dr. Kyle's house, you'd be better to walk up the hill and leave the van here. Don't be worrying, I'll keep an eye on it."

"Oh. Thank you."

He opened the door for her, in a most courteous fashion. She tipped the parcels onto the seat and extracted the pie. The young constable smiled down at her benevolently.

"You . . . you couldn't tell me where he lives?"

"Up the hill, out of the town. It's the last house on the left, just before you get to the hotel. It has a garden in the front, and Dr. Kyle's plate on the gate."

"Thank you so much."

The young constable smiled, bashful. "You're welcome," he said.

The hill out of the town was very steep, so steep that the pavement had been graded into steps. It was a little like climbing a long, shallow flight of stairs. At first there were small terraced cottages flush with the street, and then a pub, and then more cottages. The houses became larger, each set in its own little garden. Finally, near the top of the climb Flora came to the last house of all, which was bigger than any of them, solid and unadorned, set back from the road, with a tiled path that led up from the gate to the porch. It had a white concrete building attached to its side which looked rather like an enormous shoebox. Though she did not need that last assurance, Flora inspected the wrought iron gate, and there was the brass plate with Hugh Kyle's name upon it. Thinking that it could do with a good buffing, Flora opened the gate and went up the sloping path to the front door.

She rang the bell, but as soon as she heard the mournful tinkle from the back of the house she knew that there was nobody in. The pie, after her climb up the hill, was beginning to become very heavy. She rang again for politeness' sake, and then reached up as Mrs. Watty had bid her, to feel for the front door key. It was a large one, easily found, and Flora inserted it into the keyhole, turned it, and opened the door.

Inside was a tiled hall, a staircase rising into gloom, and a smell like that of old antique shops, rather musty but quite pleasant. She went in, leaving the door open behind her. She saw the old-fashioned hatstand with a place for umbrellas, the pretty little inlaid table, the white painted wrought-iron banister. Everything was very dusty. There was a clock, but it had stopped. She wondered if it was broken or if nobody had remembered to wind it—or had the time to wind it.

There was a door on her right which she opened to find the most unlived-in-looking living room she'd ever seen, with nothing out of place, not a flower to be seen, and the blinds half-drawn. She closed that door and opened the one opposite to reveal a ponderous Victorian dining room. The table was mahogany and massive, and there was a sideboard of matching proportions ranged with decanters and silver wine-slides. All the chairs had been placed around the room against the wall, and here again the blinds were half-drawn. It had, thought Flora, all the cheer of a funeral parlor. Quietly, not wanting to disturb any ghosts, she closed that door and went down the hall toward the back regions of the house in search of the kitchen.

Here the deathly order ceased abruptly. It was not a large kitchen. In fact, for the size of the house it was quite small, but even so every available horizontal space had collected a formidable amount of clutter. Saucepans, frying pans, casseroles were all piled on the draining board; the sink was stacked with dirty dishes, and the table in the middle of the room bore witness to a snatched meal—not a very appetizing one at that, unless one happened to enjoy cornflakes, fried eggs, and fruit-cake all at the same time. The final touch was the half-empty bottle of whisky which stood in the middle of the table. For some reason it loaded the sad disorder of the scene with potential disaster.

The refrigerator was in a corner by the cooker. Flora started towards it, tripped over the torn corner of a rug, and almost fell flat on her face. Inspecting the rug, she saw that the floor was dirty. It didn't look as though it had been swept for a week, let alone scrubbed.

She opened the fridge and quickly stowed away the pie before more horrors should offend her eye. Shutting the door, she turned and leaned against it, surveying the shambles as a number of thoughts ran through her mind. The most obvious was that Jessie McKenzie was a dirty slut and the sooner Hugh got rid of her the better. No man, however, feckless, could have got a kitchen into such a mess in a matter of days.

She looked at it hopelessly and her heart ached for him, and at the same time she knew that he would be mortified beyond words if he found out that Flora had seen it all. With this in mind, her instinct was to tiptoe tactfully away and let him think it was Watty who had delivered the pie.

Besides, she had to fetch Jason from school. Flora looked at her watch and discovered that it was only a quarter to three. She had an hour before she was due at the school. What could she do with the time? Walk around the harbor? Have a cup of coffee in Sandy's Snack Bar? But of course she would do none of these things, because even while she was considering them, she pulled off her gloves, unbuttoned her coat, hung it on the peg behind the door, and rolled up her sleeves. *You fool,* she told herself and searched for an apron. She found one slung by the sink, a blue butcher's apron, designed for a man and much too large for her. She tied it twice about her waist, found a dishcloth and turned on the hot tap. The water was boiling, and she told herself that this was the one good thing that happened since she walked into this benighted house.

In a cupboard below the sink she found, somewhat unexpectedly, a sturdy scrubbing brush, quantities of soap powder and a packet of steel wool. (It seemed that Jessie McKenzie had good intentions, even if she didn't carry them through.) These she made lavish use of. When it came to putting things away, Flora simply piled the clean dishes out of sight, hung cups and jugs on hooks, then turned her attention to the pile of saucepans. By the time she had finished they were not only clean but also shining, and when she had placed them nearly ordered as to size, on the shelf over the cooker, they looked not only businesslike but attractive. Once she had achieved a clean and empty sink, the transformation of Hugh Kyle's kitchen took a surprisingly short time. She cleared the table, threw away the stale fruit cake, placed the whisky bottle tactfully out of sight, and shook the crumbs from the tablecloth. She wiped the table and various counters with a damp cloth. Everything shone. There is nothing in life so satisfying as rendering a very dirty room totally clean. Flora by now was enjoying herself. There remained only the floor. She checked the time and as it was only twenty past three, she took up the torn rug, bundled it out of the back door, and searched for a broom. That and a dustpan came to light in a dank cupboard which smelled of boot polish and mice. She swept the floor free of what appeared to be months of dirt, filled a bucket with boiling water and suds, and got down to work.

Three buckets and half a packet of soap powder later, she had just about finished. The linoleum shone wet, smelt clean, and revealed a pattern of brown and blue tiles, unexpectedly fresh and pretty. Only a dark cavern beneath the draining board remained, and into this Flora plunged head-first, by now so enthusiastic that she didn't even quail at the thought of mousedroppings or cobwebs or possible scuttling spiders. As her scrubbing brush scraped and banged against the wainscoting, the small enclosed space grew thick with steam. At last she laid down the brush, wrung out the cloth, and wiped away the last of the suds.

It was finished. Flora backed out from under the draining board and was just about to get to her feet when she noticed, through the legs of the kitchen table, planted fair and square in the middle of her clean floor, another pair of feet; brown leather shoes with rubber soles; the bottoms of tweed trousers. Sitting back on her heels, her gaze traveled slowly upward until it finally came to rest on Hugh Kyle's astonished face.

It was hard to say which of them was the more surprised. Then abruptly, Flora said, "Oh, damn."

"What's that for?"

"I hoped you wouldn't come back."

He did not comment on this, simply stared about him, completely bewildered. "What the hell are you doing?"

She was annoyed at being found out, not because of the lowly nature of her task, but because Hugh would be stupidly offended by her interference, and doubtless turn stuffy and dour. "What do you think I'm doing? I'm scrubbing the floor."

"But you shouldn't be doing that."

"Why not? It was dirty."

He looked about him, taking in the sparkling shelves and counters, the shining sink, the squared-off order of saucepans and crockery. His eyes came back to her face. He still looked bewildered. He put up a hand to rub the back of his neck, the very picture of a man at a loss for words.

"I must say, that's extraordinarily kind of you, Rose. Thank you very much."

She did not want him to feel too grateful. She said, lightly, "It's a pleasure."

"But I still don't understand. Why are you here?"

"Mrs. Watty cooked a pie for you and she asked me to deliver it. It's in the fridge." A thought occurred to her. "I never heard you come in."

"The front door was open."

"Oh, heavens, I forgot to shut it."

Her hair had fallen across her face. She pushed it back with her wrist and stood up. The huge apron drooped damply around her legs. She picked up the bucket, emptied it down the drain, wrung out the cloth, and slung the lot into the cupboard beneath the sink. She shut the door and turned to face him, rolling down her sleeves.

"You have a useless housekeeper," she told him, bluntly. "You should get someone else to look after you."

"Jessie does her best. It's just that she's been away. She had to go to Portree to see her mother."

"When is she coming back?"

"I don't know. Tomorrow or maybe the next day."

"Well, you should give her notice and find somebody else."
She felt brutal, but she was annoyed with him, because no man
had the right to look so tired. "It's ridiculous. You're the doctor in this town. There must be somebody who'd help you.
What about your nurse, the one who works in the surgery?"

"She's a married woman with three children to look after.
She has more than enough to do."

"But wouldn't she know somebody who could come and
work for you?"

Hugh shook his head. "I don't know," he said.

She had seen that he was tired, but now she realized that
at this moment he not only didn't know, he didn't care,
whether anybody could find him a new housekeeper or not. She
began to regret having attacked him, nagging at him like some
discontented wife.

She said, more gently, "You know, you surprised me just
as much as I must have surprised you. Where did you suddenly
appear from?"

He looked around for something to sit on, saw the chairs
which Flora had piled in a corner, and went to pick one up and
set it by the side of the table.

"Lochgarry," he told her, settling back with his legs
crossed and his hands in his pockets. "I've been to the hospital.
I've been to see Angus McKay."

"Is that the old man you told me about who lived up Loch
Fhada? The one who fell down the stairs?"

Hugh nodded.

"He finally agreed to go to the hospital then?"

"Yes. He finally agreed. Or should I say, he was finally
persuaded."

"By you?"

"Yes. By me. The ambulance went out to Boturich and
collected him this morning. I went over to see him this afternoon. He's in a ward with five other old men, all staring at the
opposite wall and waiting for death, and he doesn't even know

what's hit him. I dispensed the usual dose of hearty good cheer, but he just lay there and looked at me. Like an old dog. I felt like a murderer."

"But you mustn't feel like that. It's not your fault. You said yourself that his daughter-in-law was at the end of her tether having to take care of him. And so far out in the country and everything. And he might have fallen downstairs again, or had some even worse accident. Anything could have happened."

He let her say all this without interrupting. When she finished speaking, he was silent for a little, watching her from beneath his heavy brows. Then he said, "He's old, Rose. He's frail and confused and now we've uprooted him. That's a monstrous thing to do to any man. He was born at Boturich, his father farmed Boturich before him, and his grandfather. Angus brought his wife back to Boturich, and his children were born there. And now, at the end of the day, when we have no more use for him, we cart him off and stow him away, out of sight and out of mind, and leave him to be cared for by strangers."

Flora was astonished that he, a doctor, should allow himself to become so emotionally involved. "But that's the way things are. You can't change things like that. You can't stop people's growing old."

"But you see, Angus isn't people. Angus is part of me, part of my growing up. My father was a busy doctor, and he didn't manage to find much time to spend with a small boy, so on fine Saturdays I used to bicycle fifteen miles each way up Loch Fhada to Boturich to see Angus McKay. He was a tall, rangy man, strong as an ox, and I thought he knew everything. He did too, about birds and foxes and hares, and where to find the fattest trout, and how to tie a fly that not the wiliest salmon could resist. I thought he was the wisest being in the world. All powerful. Like God. And we'd go fishing together, or up the hill with a spyglass, and he'd show me where the golden eagles were nesting."

Flora smiled, liking the picture of the old man and the boy together. "How old were you then?"

"About ten. A little bit older than Jason."

Jason. Flora had forgotten Jason. She looked at her watch, and then, in a panic, began to untie the strings of the apron. "I must fly. I'm meant to be fetching Jason from school. He'll think he's been forgotten."

"I was rather hoping you'd make me a cup of tea."

"I haven't got time. I'm meant to be there at a quarter to four and it's twenty to now."

"Supposing I call the headmaster and tell him to hang on to Jason for a bit."

Such a reaction on his part was unexpected. *Why*, thought Flora, *he's really trying to be nice to me*. She laid down the apron. "Won't Jason mind?"

"He won't mind." Hugh got to his feet. "They've a train set up at the school and if the boys are good, they're allowed to play with it. He'll jump at the chance of getting it to himself." He went out into the hall, leaving the door open. Flora stood where she was, staring after him. She had discovered that it is disconcerting when someone whom you think you have neatly pigeonholed starts acting out of character. She heard him dialing the school. She turned to fill the kettle, and put it on to boil. Hugh's voice came down the hall.

"Hello, Mr. Fraser? Dr. Kyle speaking. Have you got young Jason Armstrong there? Would you be so kind as to hold on to him for another fifteen minutes or so. Antony's young lady's on her way to fetch him and take him back to Fernrigg, but she's going to be held up. Well, if you want the truth, she's just about to make me a cup of tea. Yes, she's here. Well, that would be very civil of you. Thank you. We'll be here when he comes. Tell him not to bother to ring the bell, but just walk in. We'll be in the kitchen. Very well. I'm obliged to you. Goodbye, Mr. Fraser."

She heard him put down the receiver, and the next moment he appeared back in the kitchen.

"That's all settled. One of the junior masters is going to bring Jason down in his car and drop him off at the gate."

"Does that mean he won't get to play with the train set?"

Hugh went to fetch a second chair from the corner. "I wouldn't know."

Flora had found a teapot with a broken spout, a jug of milk in the fridge, and a couple of old, pretty Wedgwood mugs.

"I don't know where the sugar is, or the tea."

He delved into some cupboard and produced them. The tea was kept in a very old tin with a picture of George V on the side. It was bent and most of the paint had gone. Flora said, "This looks as if it's been around for some time."

"Yes, like everything in this house. Including me."

"Have you lived here all your life?"

"Most of it. My father lived here for forty years, and it would be an understatement to say that he didn't believe in change for its own sake. When I came back to take over from him it was like stepping back into the past. At first I thought I'd make all sorts of alterations and bring the whole place up-to-date, but before long the famous West Coast rot had set in, and it took me all my time and effort just to get the surgery built. Once that was up, I forgot about the house. Or perhaps I just forgot to notice it."

Flora felt relieved. At least he hadn't gone out and chosen the dining room furniture for himself. The kettle boiled. She filled the teapot and put it on the table. She said, politely, "It's a good solid house," and it sounded like telling a proud mother that her baby looks healthy when you can't think of another thing to say about the wretched infant.

"Tuppy thinks it's dreadful," said Hugh placidly. "A mausoleum she calls it. And I'm prepared to believe her."

"There's nothing wrong with it." She met his skeptical eye. "I mean," she floundered on, "it has possibilities." She sat down at the table and poured the tea. The atmosphere had become pleasantly domestic. Encouraged by this, she went on. "There's no house that can't be made very nice if you give it a little thought. All it needs is . . ." She searched for inspiration. "A coat of paint."

He looked amazed. "Is that all it needs?"

"Well, it would be a start. A coat of paint can do wonders."

"I'll have to try it." He helped himself to milk and a generous amount of sugar, stirring the lot into a real workman's brew. He drank it, apparently without scalding his throat, and at once poured a second cup. "A coat of paint." He set down the teapot. "And perhaps the blinds pulled up to let some sunshine in. And the smell of new polish. And flowers. And books and music. And a fire burning in the grate when you come back from work at the end of a long winter's day."

Without thinking, Flora said, "You don't need a new housekeeper, you need a new wife," and was instantly on the receiving end of a glance so sharp that she wished she had not spoken at all. "I'm sorry," she said quickly.

But he did not seem to be offended. He put more milk and sugar into his tea and stirred it. He said, "You know I've been married." It was a statement of fact, not an accusation.

"Yes. Tuppy told me."

"What else did she tell you?"

"That your wife was killed in a car accident."

"Nothing else?"

"No." She felt impelled to stand up for Tuppy. "She only told me because she's so fond of you. She doesn't like to think of you living on your own."

"After I got engaged to Diana I brought her back to Tarbole. The visit wasn't what you'd call a success. Did Tuppy say anything about that?"

"Not really." Flora was beginning to feel uncomfortable.

"I can tell by your face that she did. Tuppy didn't take to Diana. Like everybody else, she thought I was making a terrible mistake."

"And was it a mistake?"

"Yes. Right from the very beginning, but I was so blinded by my feelings I wouldn't admit it even to myself. I met her in London. I was at St. Thomas's working for my F.R.C.S. I had a friend there, John Rushmoore—I'd know him at Edinburgh University. We used to play rugger together. Then he got a job in the City, and I met up with him again when I went south. It was through him that I first met Diana. She and John belonged to a world that I had never known, and like any country bumpkin, I was bedazzled by it. And by her. When I wanted to marry her, everybody told me that I was mad. Her father had no opinion of me at all. From the beginning he had me pegged as a hairy-heeled Scotsman after his daughter's money. My professor was equally unenthusiastic. I had another two years to go before I had a hope of getting my F.R.C.S., and he believed that I should put my career before my matrimonial aspirations. And of course my father agreed with him.

"It may sound strange to you, but my father's good opinion was the one that mattered most to me. I felt that if I had that, then the rest of them could go to hell. So I brought Diana home to meet him, and to show her off. It took some persuading to get her here. She'd only been to Scotland once before, on some grouse-shooting houseparty or other, and she didn't relish the idea of Tarbole. But I finally talked her into it, naïvely, imagining that my father and the friends I'd known all my life would be as besotted by her as I was.

"But it didn't work out. In fact, it was a disaster. It rained the entire time, Diana hated Tarbole, she hated this house, and she hated the country. All right, she was spoiled. And like so many spoiled women, she could be wholly charming and engaging, but only with people who amused or stimulated her. There wasn't anybody here who fitted that bill. She rendered my father speechless, and he wasn't what you'd call a talkative man at the best of times. He was immensely courteous and she was a guest in his house, but by the end of the third day we'd all had enough. My father brought it all to a head. He topped himself up with whisky, took me into his surgery, and told me he thought I'd gone out of my mind. He told me a lot of other things as well, but most of them are unrepeatable. And then I lost my temper and I said a lot of unrepeatable things. And by the time that session was over, there was nothing for me to do but bundle Diana back into my car and drive back to London.

We were married a week later. You could say because of parental opposition rather than in spite of it."

"Did it work?"

"No. At first it was all right. We were infatuated with each other. I suppose, if you were romantically minded, you'd say we were much in love. But our two worlds were too far apart and we had nothing in common with which to build any sort of a bridge. When we first met, I think Diana imagined herself as the social wife of a brilliant surgeon, but instead she found herself married to a struggling student who spent most of his waking hours at the hospital. It wasn't much of a marriage, but the fault was just as much mine as hers."

Flora wrapped her hands, for warmth, around her mug of tea. She said, "Perhaps if circumstances had been different . . ."

"But they weren't different. We had to make the best of what we had."

"When was she killed?"

"Nearly two years after we married. By then we were hardly ever together, and I thought nothing of it when Diana told me that she was going away for the weekend to stay with an old schoolfriend who lived in Wales. But when she was killed, she was in John Rushmoore's car, and he was driving. And they weren't going to Wales, they were going to Yorkshire."

Flora stared at him. "You don't mean . . . your friend?"

"Yes. My friend. They'd been having an affair for months and I'd never even suspected. Afterward, when it was all over, it all came out. Everyone had known, it seemed, but no one had had the heart to enlighten me. It's a shattering thing to lose your wife and your friend in one fell swoop. It's even more shattering when you lose your pride as well."

"Was John Rushmoore killed too?"

"No." Hugh was casual. "He's still around."

"Is that why you threw over your F.R.C.S. and came back to Tarbole?"

"I came because my father was ill."

"You never thought of going back to London?"

"No."

"Couldn't you still become a surgeon?"

"No. It's too late. I belong here now. Perhaps this is where I've always belonged. I'm not sure if I could have lived my life in a city, away from clean air and the smell of the sea."

"You're just like . . ." Flora began, and then stopped herself just in time. She had been about to say *You're just like my father.* Listening to Hugh, she had forgotten that she was meant to be Rose. Now she found herself consumed by an entirely natural compulsion to exchange confidence for confidence, memory for memory. Hugh had opened a door, which had previously been shut and barred in her face, and she wanted very much to go through it.

But she couldn't because, as Rose, she had nothing to offer him in return. As Rose, she could share no memories, offer no comfort. The frustration of this was suddenly more than she could bear, and for a moment she actually considered spilling out the truth. In his present mood, she knew that he would understand. She had given her promise to Antony, but Hugh was, after all, a doctor. Wasn't telling a doctor a secret rather like confessing to a priest? Did it really count?

From the very beginning, all Flora's finer instincts had reacted against the lie that she and Antony had embarked upon, simply because it was bound to affect and involve other and innocent people. But now it seemed that the lie had turned, and Flora herself was caught up in its tangled coils—bound hand and foot, shackled by it, and unable to move.

Hugh waited for her to finish her sentence. When she did not, he prompted her. "Who am I like?"

"Oh . . ." *I promise,* she had said to Antony, only yesterday on the beach. ". . . Nobody. Just someone I once knew who felt the way you do."

The moment was over. The temptation past. She was still Rose, and she did not know whether she was glad or sorry. The kitchen was warm and quiet. The only sounds came from outside. A lorry changed gears, grinding up the hill past the gate.

A dog barked; a woman, climbing up from the ships with her laden basket, called across the road to her friend. The sky was filled with the scream of gulls.

The peace was terminated abruptly by the arrival of Jason. The front door opened and slammed shut with a force that shook the house. It took them by surprise, and Flora jumped and looked at Hugh and saw her own blank expression mirrored on his face. They had forgotten about Jason. Jason's high voice pierced the air.

"Rose!"

"She's here!" Hugh called back. "In the kitchen."

Footsteps raced down the passage, the door was flung wide, and Jason burst in.

"Hello. Mr. Thomson brought me in his car and there's a great big boat in the harbor and he says it's come from Germany. Hello, Hugh."

"Hello, old boy."

"Hello, Rose." He came around to her side of the table and put his arms around her neck to give her an absent-minded kiss. "Hugh, I've drawn a special picture for Tuppy. I did it this afternoon."

"Let's see it."

Jason struggled with the buckle of his satchel and hauled out the drawing. "Oh, bother, it's all crumpled."

"That's all right," said Hugh. "Bring it here."

Jason did so, leaning against Hugh's knee. Hugh took the drawing and unfolded it carefully, smoothing out the creases on the top of the kitchen table. Once before, Flora had noticed his hands. Now, for some reason watching them deal so deftly with Jason's smudged and garish painting did something peculiar to the pit of her stomach. She heard him say, "That's a fine picture. What is it?"

"Oh, Hugh, you are stupid."

"Elucidate."

"I don't know what that means."

"Explain it to me."

"Well, look. It's an airplane and a man in a parachute.

And then there's this man, and he's landed already, and he's waiting for the other man, and he's sitting under a tree."

"I see. It's very good. Tuppy will like it. No, don't fold it again. Leave it flat. Rose will carry it for you and then it won't get creased again. Won't you, Rose?"

She was taken unawares. "What?" She looked up from the table and met the startling blue of his eyes.

"I said you'd look after the picture."

"Yes, of course I will."

"Are you having tea?" asked Jason. "Is there anything to eat?" He looked about him hopefully.

Flora remembered the ditched fruitcake. "I don't know. We just had a cup of tea."

Hugh said, "If you look in that red tin on the dresser there might be a biscuit."

Jason fetched the tin, put it on the table and wrestled it open. He produced from it a large chocolate biscuit, wrapped in silver paper.

"Can I have this?"

"If you want to risk it. I've no idea how long it's been there."

Jason removed the paper and took an experimental mouthful. "It's all right. A bit soggy, but it's all right." Munching, he stared from High's face to Flora's. "Why didn't you come for me, Rose?"

"I was making Hugh a cup of tea. You didn't mind, did you?"

"No, I didn't mind." He came to lean against her. She put her arm around him and pressed her chin against the top of his head. "I played with the train set," he told her in a voice of the deepest satisfaction. Flora began to laugh. She glanced across at Hugh, expecting to have him share her amusement, but he did not seem to have heard Jason. His expression was abstracted and withdrawn, and he was watching the two of them with the total absorption of a man on the verge of making some marvelous discovery.

* * *

Jason was in bed, Tuppy safely tucked away upstairs, and Rose had departed—looking very charming—to be given dinner by Brian Stoddart. Isobel sat alone by the fire, doing her knitting and listening to Mozart. To be on her own was for her a rare pleasure; to listen to Mozart instead of the nine o'clock news on television, an even rarer one. It caused Isobel a slight pang of guilt, because Tuppy always listened to the nine o'clock news, and the reason Isobel didn't have to was because Tuppy was ill. But the guilt was not enough to be troublesome. And she had had a busy day. After all that telephoning, she felt exhausted. Squelching her conscience, Isobel knitted on, reveling in the novelty of self-indulgence.

The telephone rang. She sighed, glanced at the clock, drove her needles through the ball of wool, and went out into the hall to answer it. It was Hugh Kyle. "Yes, Hugh."

"Isobel, I'm sorry to disturb you, but is Rose there?"

"No, I'm sorry, she's not."

"Oh. Well, never mind."

"Can I give her a message?"

"It's just that . . . she was here this afternoon delivering a splendid pie Mrs. Watty made, and she's left her gloves behind. At least, I think they must be hers. And I didn't want her to think she'd lost them."

"I'll tell her. I won't see her again this evening, but I'll tell her in the morning."

"Has she gone out?"

"Yes." Isobel smiled, because it was so pleasant for Rose, bereft of Antony's company, to be having some fun. "Brian Stoddart's taken her out for dinner."

There was a long silence, and then Hugh said, faintly, "What?"

"Brian Stoddart's taken her out for dinner. Anna's away so they're keeping each other company."

"Where have they gone?"

"I think to Lochgarry. Brian said something about the Fishers' Arms. He had a drink here before they went."

"I see."

"I'll tell Rose about the gloves."

"What?" He sounded as though he had forgotten about the gloves. "Oh, yes. Any time. It doesn't matter. Goodnight, Isobel."

Even for Hugh, that was fairly abrupt. "Goodnight," said Isobel. She put down the receiver and stood for a moment, wondering if something was wrong. But nothing occurred to her. Just her imagination. She turned off the light and went back to the music.

Lochgarry lay some fifteen miles to the south of Fernrigg, at the head of a sea loch and on the junction of the main roads from Fort William, from Tarbole, and from Morven and Ardnamuchan to the south. Long ago, it had been simply a small community of fisherfolk, with a modest inn to serve the needs of infrequent travelers. But then the railways had come, bringing in their wake wealthy sportsmen from England, and after that nothing was the same again. The Lochgarry Castle Hotel was built to accommodate not only the sportsmen, but their retinues of families, friends, and servants, and in August and September the surrounding hills echoed to the crack of guns.

After the Second World War, things changed again. Industry arrived, in the shape of a huge sawmill and lumberyards. More houses went up, as did a new school to take the place of the old single-room schoolhouse, and a little cottage hospital. The roads were widened and improved, and summer traffic swelled over the years to a flood. The seafields which sloped down to the water were transformed into caravan sites, and an area of rough pasture banked with clumps of whin and gorse had been landscaped into a nine-hole golf course.

The Fishers' Arms, the little inn which had stood facing out over the loch for as long as anybody could remember, bore witness to all that change. Over the years it had been many times enlarged, improved with bow windows, decorated with porches, painted white and trellised with creepers. Inside, up

crooked stairs and down sloping passages, were not only bedrooms, but bathrooms as well. One owner built a bar. Another
built a restaurant. A third bulldozed the garden into a car park.
By the time Flora set eyes on it, its original modest form was
lost forever.

The car park, when they reached it, seemed full. Brian
parked his car and they stepped out into the blowy dusk. The
air smelt of seaweed, and random lights of cottages were reflected in the dark waters of the loch. From inside the inn came
sounds of clashing crockery, the smell of good food cooking.

"It seems to be very popular," Flora observed.

"It is. But don't worry, I booked a table." He tucked his
hand beneath her arm, and they crossed the car park and went
up the steps and through the main door. Inside were bright
lights and tartan carpeting and plastic flower arrangements. A
notice pointed up the stairs to the ladies', and Flora detached
herself gently from Brian, and said that she would go upstairs
and shed her coat.

"You do that. You'll find me in the bar."

A white-coated waiter appeared. "Good evening, Mr.
Stoddart. It's a long time since we've seen you."

"Hello, John. I hope you've got a good dinner for us tonight."

In the meantime, Flora made her way upstairs and found a
ladies' that was a marvel of floral wallpaper and mauve flounc-
ing. She took off her coat, hung it up, and went to the mirror to
comb her hair. For the occasion she had put on her turquoise
wool skirt (inevitable, as she had no other) and a long-sleeved
black sweater. But she had dressed without enthusiasm, not
really wanting to keep this date with Brian, but knowing that
she had no excuse for getting out of it. Because of that, she had
taken little trouble with her appearance, yet it seemed to be one
of those times when everything looked right. Her hair shone
like a fall of silk, her skin bloomed, her dark eyes were bright.

"You look so pretty," Isobel had said.

"You're glittering like something off a Christmas tree,"
Brian had told her as he packed her into his car, a shining

maroon 3.5-liter Mercedes. Flora had found time to wonder whether Brian had paid for it, or his wife. The drive from Fernrigg had been immensely fast, though otherwise without incident, and they had talked of trivialities. Whether this had been Brian's intention or Flora's own, she was not entirely sure.

She went downstairs. The bar was crowded, but Brian had somehow managed to get the best table by the fire. When she appeared through the door he stood up and waited for her to join him. She was aware of being watched. Eyes followed her across the room as though the sight of a woman who was unfamiliar, young, and attractive, was something not to be missed.

He smiled, as much for the audience as for her.

"Come and sit by the fire. I've ordered you a drink." They sat down, and he reached in his pocket and took out a gold cigarette case and held it out to her. When she shook her head, he took one for himself and lit it with a gold lighter that had his initials engraved upon it. He already had a tumbler of whisky on the table before him, but now Flora's drink came, borne on a silver tray.

The glass was frosted with ice. "What is it?"

"It's a martini, of course. What else would it be?" Flora was about to tell him that she never drank martinis, but he went on, "And I ordered it specially dry, the way you like them."

As he had apparently gone to so much trouble, it seemed churlish to refuse the drink. Flora took it from the tray and the cold burned her fingers. Brian raised his whisky to her, and his eyes watched her across the rim of the tumbler.

"Slaintheva," he said.

"I don't speak the language."

"It means 'good health.' It's Gaelic. The only word of Gaelic I've learned since I've lived here."

"I'm sure it's a very useful word. I'm sure it gets you out of all sorts of awkward situations."

He smiled, and she took a mouthful of the martini and almost choked. It was like drinking cold fire, and took her breath away. Gasping, she set down the glass and he laughed at her. "What's wrong?"

"It's so strong."

"Rubbish, you ought to be used to them. You never used to drink anything else."

"I haven't had one . . . lately."

"Rose, you're not reforming, are you?" He sounded genuinely concerned. "I couldn't bear it. You used to drink martinis without batting an eyelid, and chain-smoke to boot."

"I did?"

"Yes, you did. Gauloises. You see, I haven't forgotten a single detail."

She tried easing out of this. "I do smoke still, but not very often."

"It must be the influence of a good man."

"I suppose you mean Antony?"

"Who else would I mean? I can't believe there have been that number of good men in your life."

"All right, so it's Antony."

Brian shook his head, a man bewildered. "What on earth induced you to get engaged to him?"

Having the conversation steered into such intimacy, so early in the evening, was a little like finding oneself skating on the thinnest possible ice. Flora became wary. "I should have thought there was every reason in the world."

"Give me one."

"I might, if it was your business."

"Of course it's my business. Everything you do is my business. But somehow it's wrong. You and Antony don't match. You're not a couple. When Anna told me you were going to marry him, I could scarcely believe it. Still can't, for that matter."

"Don't you like Antony?"

"Everybody likes Antony. That's his trouble. He's too damn nice."

"There's the reason you were asking for. He's nice."

"Oh, come off it, Rose." He set his drink down on the

table, and leaned toward her, his hands loosely clasped between his knees. He wore, this evening, a smoothly cut blazer, a pair of dark gray trousers very slightly flared, and Gucci slippers with the red and green trademark. His hair was very black, crinkling back from his forehead; his pale eyes, beneath the dark brows, were bright and watchful. In the closeness of the car she had been aware of the expensive smell of his aftershave. Now, she saw the gold gleam of his wristwatch, his cufflinks, his signet ring. It seemed that not one single detail had been neglected.

His scrutiny, and her reaction to it, were dangerous. She searched for some safer topic. "Did Anna tell you about Tuppy's dance?"

For an instant, annoyance clouded his bright gaze, and then was gone. He leaned back in his chair, reaching for his whisky as he did so.

"Yes, she told me something, just before she went off."

"You've been invited."

"Doubtless."

"Are you going to come?"

"I expect so."

"You don't sound very enthusiastic."

"I know Tuppy Armstrong's parties of old. All the same people, wearing the same clothes, saying the same things. But then, as I told you the other night, there are many penalties attached to living out here, in the back of beyond."

He did not look a man who suffered too many penalties.

"That's not a very gracious reaction to an invitation."

He smiled, once more all charm. "No, it isn't, is it, and if you're going to be there, looking as seductive as you always do, then wild horses wouldn't keep me away."

Despite herself, Flora laughed. "I won't be looking particularly seductive. In fact, I shall probably look singularly odd."

"Odd? Why odd?"

She told him that morning's drama of the dress, making it as good a story as she could. When she had finished, Brian was incredulous. "Rose, you can't. You can't go to any sort of a party in some old rag out of the Fernrigg attic."

"What else can I do?"

"I'll drive you to Glasgow and you can buy a dress there. I'll drive you to Edinburgh. Or London. Better still, I'll fly you to Paris. We'll stay for the weekend and go shopping at Dior."

"What pretty ideas you have."

"I'm glad you think they're pretty. I think they're irresistible. Come on, when shall we go? Tomorrow. You used to enjoy living dangerously."

"I am not going shopping with you," Flora told him firmly. "Absolutely, flatly, no."

"Well, don't blame me if everybody laughs his head off when you appear in something out of the dressing-up box. But one thing's for sure, if anybody can get away with it, then you can. Come on, drink up, John's semaphoring from the other side of the room, and that means our table's ready."

The dining room was very warm and dim with candlelight, with soft piped music. Most of the tables were already occupied, but theirs waited for them in the curve of the bow window, made snug by the drawn curtains. It looked very intimate. They sat down. Another round of drinks appeared. Flora, who was just beginning to feel the impact of the first martini, looked in some dismay at the second.

"I really don't want another drink."

"For heaven's sake Rose, stop being so boring. This is a night out. Enjoy it. You're not driving."

She looked at his dark whisky. "No, but you are."

"Not to worry. I know the road like the back of my hand. And I know the police force too, such as it is." He opened a menu as big as a newspaper. "Now what are we going to eat?"

There was scampi on the menu but also oysters. Flora loved scampi, but she loved oysters even more, and she hadn't had them for ages. Brian was complaisant. "All right, you can have oysters, but I'm going to have scampi. And then shall we share a steak? And perhaps a green salad? What else? Mushrooms? Tomatoes?"

Painstakingly, their meal was finally ordered. The waiter produced the wine list, but Brian waved it aside and asked him to bring a bottle of Chateau Margaux 1964. The waiter looked respectful, gathered up the menus, and went away.

"Unless," said Brian, "you'd rather have champagne?"

"Why should I want champagne?"

"Isn't champagne the suitable drink for romantic celebrations, for reunions?"

"Is that what this is?"

"It's certainly a reunion. And one that I wouldn't have missed for the world. As for the other, well, I suppose that's up to you, Rose. Or is it too early in the evening to expect you to make such a world-shattering decision?"

She knew a sensation of panic. The thin ice was beginning to crack and the conversation, unless Flora was very careful, was going to slip out of her control. She eyed him across the starched white tablecloth, the red candles, the wine glasses shining like soap bubbles. He was waiting for her to reply, and to give herself time to think she took a mouthful of the second martini. It tasted, if possible, even stronger than the first, but all at once everything became immensely clear and perfectly simple. All she had to do was to be very careful.

She said, "Yes. Just a little early."

He began to laugh. "Rose."

"What's so funny?"

"You. You're funny. Pretending to be so cool and prissy and hard-to-get. O.K., so you're engaged to that upstanding young man Antony Armstrong, but you're still Rose. And you don't have to pretend with me."

"Don't I, Brian?"

"Do you?"

"Perhaps I've changed."

"You haven't changed."

He said it with such assurance that she was prepared to believe him. Up to this evening everything that she had gleaned of Rose's character had been based on conjecture and guess-work. Now, unexpectedly faced with a man who obviously knew the truth, Flora found herself reluctant to be told it. Illusions were perhaps childish but they could be comforting too, and Rose was, after all, her sister. For an instant something like family loyalty battled with curiosity, but only for an instant. Flora's finer feelings were not as strong as her curiosity, and stimulated by the punch of the drinks she had already consumed, she became reckless.

She put her arms on the table, and leaned across it, towards Brian. "How do you know I haven't changed?" she asked him.

"Oh, Rose . . ."

"Tell me how I was."

His face brightened. "Like you are at this moment. You've reverted to type already. You can't help it. You could never help it. You could never resist the smallest opportunity to talk about yourself."

"Tell me how I was."

"All right." His hands moved out to his tumbler of whisky and as he talked he turned it, but his excited eyes never left Flora's. "You were beautiful. Long-legged and marvelously young. Like a colt. You were sulky and you could be selfish. You were certainly self-centered. and you were sexy. God, you were sexy.and I found you utterly fascinating. Now. Is that what you wanted to hear?"

She could feel the heat of the candles, burning her face. The neck of her sweater was too tight, and she put up a finger to pull it loose. "All that," she said faintly, "at seventeen?"

"All that. It was a strange thing, Rose, but after you'd gone, I couldn't get you out of my mind. That had never happened to me before. I even went down to the Beach House once or twice, but it was shuttered and closed up and there was no trace of you anywhere. Like the tide, coming in and washing the sand clean."

"Perhaps that was just as well."

"You were special. There was never anyone quite like you."

"You speak from experience."

He grinned as though filled with modest pride. "The best thing about you was that I never had to pretend."

"You mean I always knew that I was just one of a long line."

"Exactly."

"And Anna?"

He took a drink from his glass before answering this one. "Anna," he said slowly, "is an ostrich. What she doesn't see doesn't worry her. And as far as her husband is concerned, she takes some pains to see nothing."

"You're very sure of her."

"Do you know what it's like to be loved to distraction? It's like being buried in a feather bed."

"Did you never love anyone to distraction?"

"No. Not even you. What I felt for you can only be described by one of those old-fashioned words that you find in the Bible. Lust. It's a wonderful word. You can really get your tongue around it."

With marvelous inappropriateness, their first course arrived. As disembodied hands set down plates and straightened knives and forks, Flora sat staring at the candle flames and trying to collect her scattered wits. Somebody took away her glass, and she realized that at some time she had finished her second drink. Now there was a glass of wine, shining like a great red jewel. The sweater she had put on had been a mistake. It was far too thick, the collar choked her, she was far too hot. Pulling again at the neck, she found herself looking down at a plateful of oysters. The waiter had gone. From across the table Brian asked her, "Don't you want them after all?"

"What?"

"You have an uncertain expression on your face. Don't they look good?"

She pulled herself together. "They look delicious." She took a slice of lemon and squeezed it. The juice was sticky on her fingers. Across the table, Brian was tucking into his scampi with the appetite of a man with a pristine conscience. Flora picked up her fork and then laid it down again. The question stuck in her throat, but with an immense effort, she made herself ask it.

"Brian, did anybody ever find out . . . I mean, did anybody ever know about you and me?"

"No, of course they didn't. What do you think I am? An amateur?" She started to breathe a sigh of relief. "Only Hugh," he finished casually.

"Hugh?"

"Don't sound so horrified. Of course he knew. Oh, don't sit there gaping like a fool, Rose. He found us!" He grinned boyishly, as though recalling some youthful prank. "What a scene that was! He's never really forgiven me, but to be honest with you, I've always put that down to jealousy. I always suspected that he fancied you himself."

"That's not true!"

Her vehemence took him by surprise. He stared at her. "Why do you suddenly say that?"

"Because it isn't true." She cast about for some way to prove her point. "Antony said it wasn't true."

Brian seemed amused. "So you've already discussed it with Antony, have you. That's very interesting."

"Antony said he wasn't . . ."

"Antony would," Brian interrupted bluntly. "All his life Hugh's been a sort of father-figure to Antony. You know, the rugger-playing hero. Every boy should have one. Hugh pretends to be such a high-minded bastard, but his wife had been dead for three years by then, and at heart I suspect he's just as carnal as the rest of us."

She felt defeated. The possibility that Hugh had been in love with Rose had always been at the back of Flora's mind, ever since that first disconcerting encounter on the beach. It had bothered her a little, but it had not really mattered.

But now it did matter.

It was hard to know when it had started to matter. Perhaps that day when she and Hugh had stood at the foot of the stairs at Fernrigg and he had told her about Angus McKay, and the sun had come out and filled the house with a sudden, golden light. Perhaps this afternoon, when he had taken Jason's picture and spread it out on the table to smooth out the folds. Perhaps when she had looked up, over Jason's head, and caught Hugh's look of wonderment.

She was hot no longer. Not cold. She was simply nothing. Numb. She wished passionately that she had never asked about Rose, had never found out about her; but now it was too late. The pieces of the jigsaw clicked relentlessly into place and the finished picture was repellent. Rose at seventeen, naked, tumbled on some bed, seducing—or being seduced by—Brian Stoddart.

But harder still to accept was the idea of Hugh ever having been in love with anyone as vile as Rose.

Somehow the nightmarish meal progressed. Brian, perhaps mellowed by whisky and wine, had stopped talking about himself and was describing at some length the new boat he was planning to build. He was well into this when John, the waiter, came across the room to tell him that he was wanted on the telephone.

Brian looked blank and unbelieving. "Are you sure?"

"Yes, sir, the girl on the exchange asked me to give you the message."

"Who is it?"

"I've no idea."

Brian turned to Flora. "I'm sorry. God knows who it is." He laid down his napkin. "Will you excuse me?"

"Yes, of course."

"I shan't be a moment."

He left her, weaving his way between the tables, and disappeared through a door at the back of the dining room. To be left alone was something of a reprieve. Flora pushed her plate away from her and tried to think intelligently, but the dining room was stuffy, her head ached, and she had drunk far too much. She stared at the candle flames, but they had started behaving strangely, and refused to stay in focus. She looked around, caught the eye of a waiter, and asked for a jug of water. When it came she filled a tumbler and drank it in one long draft. She set down the glass and was aware that someone had come to stand across the table from her, his hands resting on the back of Brian's chair.

She recognized the hands. For the second time that day, she looked up and found herself face to face with Hugh Kyle.

Her first reaction on seeing him was a surge of pure pleasure: instinctive, so great that it took all words, all breath away.

He said, "Good evening."

He looked, if possible, larger and more overpowering than ever. He wore a bulky overcoat over his suit, and that caught Flora's attention, becuuse he did not look like a man come out to dinner.

"But what are you doing here?" The joy sounded in her voice and it didn't matter.

"I've come to take you home."

Flora looked around her. "But where's Brian?"

"Brian has already gone home."

"He's gone home?" She was being stupid. She knew she was being stupid. "But there was a telephone call."

"There was no telephone call. Or if you like, I was the telephone call. It was the only way I could think of to get Brian out of the place." His eyes were hard as blue glass. "And if you are thinking of going after him, he is now in his car and on his way back to Ardmore."

His voice was even, and very cold. Flora's pleasure was gone, dissolved to nothing, leaving a sinking sensation, like drowning, in her stomach. She realized that his coolness belied a scarcely suppressed inner rage, but she was too fuddled to try and discover what it was all about.

"He's gone without me?"

"Yes, without you. Come along, I'll take you home."

His high-handedness made Flora feel she should raise some objection. "I . . . I haven't finished my dinner."

"From the way you were behaving when I found you, it doesn't appear to be very appetizing."

His voice was cutting. She became angry, and afraid, too. She said, "I don't want to come with you."

"No? I suppose you intend walking. It's fifteen miles and a hard road."

"I could get a taxi."

"There are no taxis. Where's your coat?"

It took some remembering. "It's upstairs, in the ladies'. But I'm not coming with you."

He called one of the young waiters over and told him to go upstairs and find the coat. "It's navy blue. It has a tartan lining." The boy departed and he turned back to Flora. "Come along, now."

"Why did Brian go?"

"We'll talk about it in the car."

"Did you make him go?"

"Rose, people are beginning to be curious. Don't let's have a scene."

He was right. The hum of conversation in the rest of the room had dropped. From various tables, faces were turned towards them. The thought of any sort of a scene was anathema to Flora. Without another word, very carefully, she got to her feet. Her legs felt rubbery and peculiar. Concentrating, not looking at anybody, she walked out of the room.

The waiter had found her coat. Hugh tipped him and helped her into it. She began painstakingly to do up the buttons, but her fingers were so clumsy that she had only done up two before he lost patience, took her by the elbow and propelled her ahead of him across the hall and out of the door.

Outside it was dark and drizzling, with a chill wind blowing up out of the west across the water. After the heat of the restaurant, the wine, and the rich food, the piercing cold struck at Flora like a solid thing, and she felt she had been pole-axed. The darkness swung around her. She shut her eyes and put her hand to her head, but Hugh grasped her other wrist and jerked her forward across the puddled car park to where his car waited. She stumbled and would have fallen had he not been holding her, and one of her shoes came off. He waited impatiently while she retrieved it and struggled it on again, and then she dropped her bag. She heard him swear as he picked it up and stuffed it into the pocket of his overcoat.

The shape of the car loomed up. He opened the door and bundled her in and slammed the door behind her. He walked around the front of the car and got in behind the wheel. The second door slammed shut. She felt suffocated by the hugeness of his presence. Her coat was rumpled up around her, her feet were wet, her hair was tumbled and blown all over her face. She slumped down into the seat and jammed her hands into her pockets and told herself that if she started to cry, now, she would never forgive herself.

He turned toward her. "Do you want to talk, or are you too drunk to talk?"

"I'm not drunk."

He made no effort to turn on the car lights. She stared into the darkness and said, through teeth clenched tight with the effort of not crying, "Where's Brian?"

"I told you. He's gone back to Ardmore."

"How did you make him go?"

"That's no concern of yours."

"How did you know where I was?"

"Isobel told me. You left your gloves at my house and I rang Fernrigg to tell you. Isobel told me that Brian had taken you out for dinner."

"That's not a crime."

"In my book it is."

He always pretends to be such a high-minded bastard.

"Because of Antony? Or because of Brian?"

"Because of Anna."

"Anna knew all about it. Anna was in the room when Brian asked me out to dinner."

"That's not the point."

"Why isn't it the point?"

He said, wearily, "You know bloody well."

She turned to look at him. Her eyes, by now, had become accustomed to the darkness, and the pale shape of his face loomed before her.

His wife had been dead for three years, and at heart I suspect he's just as carnal as the rest of us.

Hugh had been in love with Rose. She had not wanted it to be true, but his sudden appearance, his resentment, made it true. In love with Rose. For this she felt she could have killed him.

"Yes I know," she told him coldly. "You're jealous." She did not know if it was Rose who spoke, or the wine she had drunk, or her own miserable disappointment. She only knew that she wanted to hurt him. "Brian has things that you don't have. A wife and a home. You can't bear that." It wasn't any good fighting the tears. They were brimming over, streaming down her face, and this was his fault too. And something else had happened, because she was no longer Flora. She was Rose, totally Rose. Rose thinking up the cruelest and most wounding thing she could say. Rose, saying it. "Your wife destroyed you by dying the way she did."

The last word hung in the silence between them. There was a short, considered pause, and then Hugh slapped her face.

It was not a very hard blow. If it had been, Hugh being the size he was, would probably have knocked her unconscious. But Flora had never been hit, by anybody, in all her life. Extraordinarily, it stopped her crying. Silenced by pain and humiliation, she simply sat there, her head ringing and her mouth slack with shock.

He reached out to switch on the lights of the car and she covered her face with her hands.

"Are you all right?" he asked.

Blindly, Flora nodded.

He took her wrists and pulled her hands away from her face. The effort of making herself look at him was almost beyond her, but she did it.

"Why do you want so much, Rose?" he asked. "Why do you want everything for yourself?"

I'm not Rose. I am not Rose.

Reaction set in. She had begun to shiver. "I want to go home," she told him.

9

FLORA

A thirst woke Flora in the night—a raging thirst as bad as some terrible form of torture. Her mouth felt dry and her head ached, and as soon as she woke, the horror of the previous evening broke over her, and she lay for a little in a welter of remorse, too overcome by misery even to be able to get up and fetch herself a glass of water.

Her eiderdown had slipped off the bed and she was cold. In the darkness she leaned down to pull it back into position again, and as she did this, she felt a stab of pain so intense that it took her breath away, and left her gasping and clammy with sweat. After a little the pain faded, but not entirely. She lay cautious, very still, eyeing the pain from a distance, waiting to see what it was going to do next. She was still thirsty. Carefully, she reached for the bedside light, but as she eased herself up into a sitting position, she was gripped by nausea, shot out of bed, and reached the bathroom in time to be violently sick.

* * *

By the time the gruesome session was over, Flora—racked by retching, and with her stomach emptied of everything except pain—was in a state of collapse. She found herself on the bathroom floor, dressed only in her thin nightdress, and with her thudding head supported by the mahogany rim of the tub. Sweating, she closed her eyes and waited for death.

After a little, when it had not arrived, she opened her eyes again. The bathroom, from that worm's-eye view, appeared enormous, distorted out of all proportion. Through the open door the passage stretched into infinity. The sanctuary of her bedroom seemed a world away. Presently, painfully, she pulled herself to her feet and, cautiously keeping close to the wall, made her way back to her bed. She fell across it exhausted and lay shuddering, without even the strength to curl herself up under the covers.

She thought, I am very ill. She was freezing cold. The window was open and the night air poured in over her and it was like being sluiced with buckets of icy water. She knew that if she hadn't died in the bathroom, she was going to die here, of pneumonia. With an enormous effort she slid under the blankets. Her hot-water bottle had gone cold and her teeth were chattering.

She did not sleep again, and the night seemed to last forever. Her pillows became hot and lumpy, her bedclothes tangled and soaked in sweat. She prayed for the morning—for a day that would bring people and comfort and clean sheets and something to stop her head aching. But there were still many hours to endure before the dawn slid palely into the sky, and by then she had fallen into a sleep of sheer exhaustion.

It was Isobel who finally rescued her. Isobel, concerned because Flora had not appeared at breakfast, came upstairs to investigate. ". . . You're probably just having a lie-in, but I thought I'd better . . ." She stopped when she saw the chaos of Flora's room: clothes from the previous night still littering the floor, left to lie where Flora had dropped them; the tumbled bed; the blankets askew; a sheet trailing on the carpet.

"Rose!" She crossed to the bed and found Flora white as a ghost and with a fringe of dark hair stuck damply to her forehead.

"I'm really all right," Flora told her in a desperate sort of a way. "I was sick in the night, that's all."

"My poor child. Why didn't you wake me?"

"I didn't want to disturb anybody."

Isobel laid a hand on her forehead. "You're raging hot."

"I had such a pain . . ."

". . . and you're all untidy and uncomfortable." Isobel twitched at the bedclothes in an effort to square them up, and then decided against it. "I'll go and get Nurse McLeod and we'll have you cozy in no time." She made for the door. "Now don't move, Rose. Don't even think of trying to get up."

When they came, bustling and busy, it was just the way she had dreamed. Concerned faces and gentle hands, clean linen, two hot-water bottles in woolen covers. A fresh nightdress, her face and hands sponged, the smell of eau de cologne, a bedjacket.

"Whose bedjacket is that?" asked Flora as they put it on her. She didn't have a bedjacket of her own.

"It's mine," said Isobel.

It was shell pink, very lacy, with wide, loose sleeves.

"It's pretty."

"Tuppy gave it to me."

Tuppy. Flora felt so guilty she could have wept. "Oh, Isobel, you've got Tuppy in bed and now me and the dance and everything." She did weep, the helpless tears gathering in her eyes and spilling down her cheeks. "I can't bear being such a nuisance."

"You're not a nuisance. Don't even think such silly things. And Nurse is here to take care of Tuppy and she'll help me take care of you too, won't you Nurse?"

Nurse was bundling up the dirty bedclothes. "Oh, we'll have her right as rain in no time. No nonsense about that." She went from the room, heavy-footed, headed for the washing machine.

Isobel wiped Flora's tears away with a tissue. "And when Hugh comes to see Tuppy," she went on, "we'll tell him . . ."

"No," said Flora, so loudly and clearly that Isobel looked quite put out.

"No?" she questioned gently.

"I don't want Hugh. I don't want to see a doctor." She took hold of Isobel's hand, meaning to hold her there until Isobel was persuaded. "There's nothing wrong with me. I've been sick, but I'll get better now. It's nothing." She was filled with panic. Isobel was gazing at her as though she had gone mad. "I don't like doctors," she improvised wildly. "I've always been like this, ever since I was little . . ."

Isobel, with the expression on her face of one pacifying a dangerous lunatic, said soothingly, "Well, we'll see. If that's how you feel . . ."

Flora slowly let go of her hand. "Promise, Isobel?"

Isobel withdrew out of reach and instantly became more firm. "Now, I never make promises unless I know I'm going to be able to keep them."

"Please."

Isobel had reached the safety of the door. "You have a little sleep and then you'll feel better."

She slept and was deviled by dreams. She was on a beach and the sand was black and full of spiders. Rose was there, too, in a bikini, walking along the edge of an oily sea with a long queue of men following her. But all at once the men saw Flora and Flora had no clothes on whatsoever. And Rose started laughing. Flora tried to run away, but her feet wouldn't move and the black sand had turned to mud. And there was a man behind her, he had caught her, he was hitting her face. He was going to kill her . . .

She awoke in a cold sweat to Nurse McLeod's gentle shaking. She looked up at Nurse's bespectacled, horsey face, Nurse's crisp white hair. "There now," said Nurse. "Time to wake up. Dr. Kyle's here to see you."

"But I'm not going to see him," Flora told her clearly. She was still trembling from the nightmare.

"That's too bad." Hugh loomed up at the end of the bed, a hulk of a man, scarcely focused. "Because he's going to see you."

The dream faded into oblivion. Flora blinked, and his image resolved into detail. She stared at him glumly, feeling betrayed.

"I *told* Isobel not to tell you."

"Like the rest of us, Isobel doesn't always do what she's told."

"But she promised . . ."

"Now, then," said Nurse, "you know Miss Armstrong never did anything of the sort. If you'll excuse me, Doctor, I'll leave you for a moment, and go back and see to Mrs. Armstrong."

"That's all right, Nurse."

Nurse left them, with a rustle of her starched apron. Hugh, gently, closed the door behind her, and came back to Flora's side. He sat, unprofessionally, on the edge of her bed.

"Isobel says you were sick."

"Yes."

"What time did it start?"

"In the middle of the night. I don't know what time. I didn't look at the time."

"Well, let's have a look at you." He pushed back her hair to feel her clammy forehead. His touch was cool and professional. She thought, *last night he slapped my face.* The memory was so impossible to believe that it could have belonged to another nightmare. She prayed that it did, and knew that it didn't.

"Did you have a lot of pain?"

"Yes."

"Where?"

"Everywhere. My tummy, I suppose."

"Show me exactly." She showed him. "How's your appendix?"

"I haven't got one. I had it out four years ago."

"Well, that's one possibility eliminated. Are you allergic to anything? Any food?"

"No."

"What have you been eating? What did you have for lunch yesterday?"

The effort of remembering was exhausting. "Cold lamb and baked potatoes."

"And dinner last night?"

She closed her eyes. "I had a steak. And some salad."

"And before that?"

"Oysters."

"Oysters," he repeated, as though approving her choice. And then, again, "Oysters?"

"I like oysters."

"I like them too, but they have to be fresh."

"You mean I ate a bad oyster?"

"It would appear so. Did you taste it? They're usually unmistakable."

"I . . . I can't remember."

"I've had trouble with the Fishers' Arms and their oysters before. I see I'll need to go and have a word with the proprietor before he kills off the entire population of Arisaig."

He stood up, produced from some pocket a silver case containing a thermometer. "It's funny," he mused. "I haven't had a call yet from Ardmore." He picked up her wrist to take her pulse.

"Brian had scampi."

"Pity," murmured Hugh, and stopped up her mouth with the thermometer.

She was, it seemed, trapped, prostrate, at the mercy of his cutting tongue. To escape from him Flora turned away her face and stared bleakly out of the window. Slow morning clouds rolled across the sky. A seagull was screaming. She waited for him to be finished, to take the thermometer out of her mouth, to go away and leave her to die.

But the moments passed, and he did none of these things. The room seemed to have been invaded by a curious stillness as though everything it contained had been frozen or petrified. After a little, mildly curious, Flora turned back to look at him. He had not moved. He stood by her bed, holding her wrist, his eyes downcast and his expression thoughtful. The loose sleeve of Isobel's bedjacket had fallen back and from folds of shell pink wool, Flora's arm emerged looking, she thought, as thin as a stick. She wondered if she were suffering from some wasting disease, and he was trying to summon up the courage to tell her she was doomed.

She was rescued from this impasse by the arrival of Isobel, edging her head gingerly around the door before she entered, as though she were afraid that Flora might spring from the bed and start strangling her.

"How's the invalid?" she asked brightly.

Hugh dropped Flora's wrist and took the thermometer out of her mouth.

"We think she had food poisoning," he told Isobel. He put on his spectacles in order to read the thermometer.

"Food poisoning?"

"It's all right, don't sound so alarmed. You're not going to have an epidemic. She ate a bad oyster at the Fishers' Arms last night."

"Oh, Rose."

Isobel sounded so reproachful that Flora felt guilty all over again.

"I couldn't help it. And I like oysters."

"But what about the dance? You'll be in bed for the dance."

"Not necessarily," Hugh told her. "If she does what she's told, she should be up and about in good time for the dance. Just starve her for a couple of days and keep her in bed." He picked up his bag and stood, resting one hand on the brass knob at the foot of the bed. He said to Flora, "You'll probably feel very depressed and a bit weepy for the next day or so. It's one of the nastier symptoms of food poisoning. Try not to let it worry you too much." The moment he mentioned the word *weepy* Flora knew that she was going to cry again. Perhaps he realized this, because at once, ushering Isobel firmly before him, he made for the door. As he went out, he looked back over his shoulder gave her one of his rare smiles, and said, "Goodbye, Rose."

Flora, bawling, reached for the box of face tissues.

He was right about the depression. Flora spent most of the first day sleeping, but on the next was overwhelmed by gloom. The weather outside did not help. It was gray, it rained, and there was nothing to be seen from the window save scudding black clouds and an occasional wet, wheeling gull. The tide was in. The waves breaking on the shingle beach below the house made a deeply melancholy sound, and the darkness invaded the house so early that lights had to be turned on at three o'clock.

Flora's thoughts, inward-turning, self-pitying, churned incessantly but, like someone treading a mill, got nowhere. Lying there in the strange bed in the strange house, she suffered once more from a dismaying loss of identity. And she could not believe that she had ever embarked on the mad charade with so much hopeful confidence, which, on hindsight, looked more like sheer stupidity.

"Identical twins are meant to be two halves of the same person, and separating them is like cutting that person in half."

Rose herself had said that in London, but at the time Flora had not thought it important. But now it was important because Rose was vile, without principles or morals. Did that mean that the seeds of the same vileness lay latent in Flora?

If their mother had taken Flora and their father had chosen Rose, would Flora have grown up into a person who, at seventeen, would cheerfully jump into bed with a married man? Would Flora have ditched Antony just when he most needed her, and flown to Spetsai with a rich young Greek? Would Flora have been sufficiently unscrupulous to use Rose as Rose had used Flora? At first all this had seemed beyond the bounds of possibility, but after that terrible scene with Hugh in his car, Flora was no longer so sure of herself. *Your wife destroyed you by dying the way she did.* Those were Rose's words. But it was

Flora who had spoken them. The dreadful sentence seared across her conscience. She shut her eyes and turned her face into the pillow, but that did no good, because she still couldn't get away from the inside of her own head.

And if this weren't enough, there were other anxieties, other uncertainties, which seemed to be heaped on top of her, like some deadening weight. How, when the time came, she was going to bear saying goodbye to the Armstrongs? And when she went, where would she go? She couldn't return to Cornwall. She had only just left, and Marcia and her father surely deserved a little time on their own. London then? It would have to be London with all its attendant problems. Where would she live? Where would she work? What would she do? She saw herself waiting for buses, queueing in the rain, shopping in the lunch hour, paying the rent, hoping to make new friends, trying to find old ones.

And finally, there was the specter of Hugh. But she couldn't let herself think about Hugh, because every time she did, she found herself once more dissolved into pointless floods of tears.

If you were Rose, you wouldn't care what the Armstrongs thought of you. You'd just say goodbye, and go and never look back.

I'm not Rose.

If you were Rose you wouldn't need to find a job and queue for buses. You could take taxis for the rest of your life.

But I'm not Rose.

If you were Rose, you would know how to make Hugh love you.

There didn't seem to be any answer to that one.

Everybody was extraordinarily kind. Isobel brought messages from Antony, whom she had telephoned in Edinburgh to let him know that Rose was ill. There was a clumsy bunch of flowers which Jason had picked, and a deep pink azalea from Anna Stoddart.

I am sorry you are under the weather, and hope you'll be up and about by Friday. Brian and I send our love.

Anna

"It's out of the Ardmore greenhouse," Isobel told her. "They have the most beautiful greenhouses over there, the envy of my heart. Rose . . . Rose, you're crying again."

"I can't help it."

Isobel sighed, and patiently reached for the tissues.

There were also sessions with Nurse McLeod, who, once she dropped her professional manner and stopped talking about draw sheets, became quite cozy, bringing up her sewing to let Flora see how her "ballgown," as it was now designated, was getting along. "You see, I'm attaching the lining to the dress. It gives it much more body, and I thought I'd make a wee belt. Mrs. Watty has a pearl buckle in her button box that she can spare."

There was a get-well card from Mrs. Watty, and from Tuppy a bunch of the last of her precious roses, which she had directed Watty to cut for her. Tuppy had arranged them herself, standing the vase on her bedside table, and snipping the wet stalks all over the eiderdown. Isobel had carried them down the passage. "From one old crock to another," she told Flora, and put them on Flora's dressing table.

"Does Hugh come every day to see Tuppy?" Flora asked Isobel.

"Not every day. Not any more. He just drops in when he happens to be passing. Why?" There was a smile in her voice. "Did you want to see him?"

"No," said Flora.

Thursday morning dawned a beautiful day. Flora awoke to a morning bright as a new coin. There was sunlight, blue sky, and now the screaming of the gulls reminded her of summer.

"What a day!" Nurse McLeod crowed, bouncing in to draw back the curtains, retrieve Flora's cold hot-water bottle, and tidy the bed, which meant tucking in the sheets so tight that Flora could scarcely move her legs.

"I shall get up," said Flora, bored with her invalid existence.

"You'll do no such thing. Not until Dr. Kyle says you may."

Flora's spirits sank immediately. She wished that Nurse had not mentioned his name. Despite the cheerful weather, she was still miserable, although the miserableness now had nothing to do with being ill. It was just the usual routine stuff, and it was centered, pinpointed, on that unforgiveable thing she had said to Hugh. It hung over her like a great sword, and would continue to hang there, she knew, until somehow, she had made herself apologize to him.

The very idea made her feel ill all over again. She slid down under the covers, and Nurse cocked a professional eye at her. "Are you not feeling better yet?"

"Yes, I'm all right," Flora told her dully.

"How about something to eat? Are you hungry? I'll maybe ask Mrs. Watty to make a little semolina."

"If you bring me semolina," Flora told her coldly, "I shall throw it out of the window."

Nurse tut-tutted and went down to the kitchen with the news that one of her patients, at least, was well on the road to recovery.

Isobel appeared later on with a breakfast tray—not a very lavish one, to be sure, but there was toast on it, and some marmalade jelly and a pot of China tea. "And some mail for you," said Isobel. She took a postcard out of her cardigan pocket and laid it, picture side up, on the tray. Flora saw bright blue sky, bright green chestnut trees, and the Eiffel Tower. Paris?

Puzzled, she turned it over. It was addressed, in an untidy and unformed hand, to Miss Rose Schuster, Fernrigg House, Tarbole, Arisaig, Argyll, Écosse. Bewildered, Flora read the message, which had been written extremely small in order to accommodate it on the space allowed.

I said I'd be in touch. It was super finding you. Decided to stop off here for a couple of days on my way to Spetsai. Am sending this to you at Fernrigg, because I have a strong suspicion that by now you're there, in the bosom of the family and, who knows, perhaps married to Antony. Give him my love.

It was undated, unsigned.

"Is it from a friend?" Isobel asked.

"Yes. From a friend."

Cunning Rose. Isobel would never read another person's postcard, but even if she had, this one would have told her nothing. It felt, to Flora's fingers, dirty. She made a face and dropped it over the side of the bed into the wastepaper basket.

Isobel, watching her, was concerned. "You're not feeling ill again, are you?"

"No," Flora assured her. She smothered toast with marmalade and bit off a hungry mouthful.

When the meager breakfast had been consumed, Isobel departed bearing the tray, and Flora was alone once more. Despite herself, the message from Rose had both upset and angered her. As well, she was hating herself. She longed for the reassurance of a loving spirit. She needed a little fussing-over, a little caring. There was only one person who was capable of providing this, and Flora wanted her now. Deviantly, not waiting for anybody to say that she could, Flora got out of bed and went in search of clothes. She would go and talk to Tuppy.

Jessie McKenzie was back from Portree. Her old mother, who had taken to her bed after what was euphemistically known as "a turn," had decided, after all, that she wasn't going to die.

This sudden recovery had been brought about, not by the timely arrival of her dutiful daughter, but because a neighbor, calling to cheer the invalid, had left the news that Katy Meldrum, already the mother of a cross-eyed child called Gary, was once more in the family way. Katy was a shameless girl

and had always been so, impervious to both pointing fingers
and the gentle remonstrances of her sorely tried priest. Now,
with her belly swelling larger each day, she was walking the
town scornful and amused, and speculation as to the identity of
the father was rife. Most folk had their money on young Robby
McCrae, the constable's brother, but there was talk of a
deckhand off one of the boats from Kinlochbervie, and him a
married man with a family of his own.

It was too good to miss. To die before the mystery was
solved, thus missing all the fun, was unthinkable. The old lady
heaved herself up on the pillows, walloped the wall with her
stick and, when her startled daughter appeared at the door,
demanded sustenance. In two days she was up and about again,
gleaning gossip and adding her own opinion to those of others.

Jessie decided she might as well go home.

Home was one of the old fisher cottages, tucked down in
the back streets of Tarbole, where she kept house for her
brother, who worked as porter in one of the smokehouses.
Early each morning Jessie climbed the hill to the doctor's
house, where she answered the telephone, took messages, chatted to visiting tradesmen, gossiped with the neighbors, and
drank tea. In between these diverting occupations, she banged
cheerfully about the house, creating more dirt than she dis-
posed of, did the doctor's laundry, and prepared his evening
meal.

As often as not, since he was so busy, she was away home
before he appeared to eat the fish pie, or the shepherd's pie, or
the two fried chops (her culinary imagination was not exten-
sive) which she would leave for him, hardening in the oven
between two plates. Sometimes when she returned the next
morning the dried-up meal would still be there, untouched.
And Jessie would shake her head, scrape it all into the garbage
can, and find someone to tell that if the doctor did not take
more care of himself, he would be well on the way to a break-
down, or worse.

Being the doctor's housekeeper gave her a certain importance, a standing, in the town. What would he do without you?

folks asked. Jessie would shake her head, modest but proud. And what would they all do without her, she asked herself, answering the telephone the way she did, day in, day out, taking messages and leaving notes. She was indispensable. It was a rare sensation.

She therefore received something of a shock when she let herself into the kitchen that Thursday morning after her return from Portree. It was a beautiful day, and she had climbed the hill in the cold sunshine, filled with grim relish at the thought of the chaos she was bound to find. After all, she had been away for four days, and all the world knew that Dr. Kyle was a handless creature when it came to doing for himself.

Instead, she found sparkling order: a clean floor, a polished sink, saucepans neatly ranged above the cooker, and scarcely a dirty dish to be seen.

The shock was like a blow to her heart. Slowly, she realized what must have happened. He had found somebody else to take her place. He had let somebody else into Jessie's kitchen. Her mind made a quick catalogue of the Tarbole women as she tried to think who it could have been. Mrs. Murdoch? The very idea was chilling. If it had been Mrs. Murdoch, then the whole town would know by now that Jessie had been deposed. They would all be talking about her, probably laughing behind her back. She wondered if she was going to faint.

But her panic was calmed by familiar sounds from upstairs. The doctor was out of bed and getting dressed. She could hear him moving to and fro in his bedroom. She stood, gazing upwards. She thought, *Well, he's there and I'm here. And here I'm staying.* Possession was nine tenths of the law. (Or something. Jessie was vague on this point.) She only knew that if she was going to leave this house, she would have to be forcibly ejected. No high-stepping Tarbole female was going to take her place.

Thus emboldened, she took off her coat, hung it on the back of the door, and went to fill the kettle. By the time Dr. Kyle came downstairs, his breakfast was waiting. She had found a clean tablecloth. The bacon was done just the way he liked it, and the egg was well-cooked with none of those nasty jelly bits on the top.

He had stopped by the front door to pick up his mail. Now, as he came down the hall, he called out, "Jessie," and she replied, in a cheerful voice, "Good morning, Doctor!" and turned to greet him as he came through the door.

It was a little disappointing to see him looking so fit and pleased with himself, but at least he was not wearing the hangdog expression of a man about to sack his housekeeper.

"How are you, Jessie? How did everything go?"

"Oh, not so bad, Doctor."

"How's your mother?"

"She has great spirit, Doctor. She's made a miraculous recovery."

"Splendid. I am glad." He sat at the table and took up a knife to slit open the first letter. It was typewritten. A long white envelope with a Glasgow postmark. Jessie took time to notice this as she laid the bacon and eggs, with a little flourish, on the table in front of him.

She poured his tea, and set that down as well. The cup steamed invitingly. The toast was crisp. It was a lovely breakfast. She stepped back to eye him. He read to the bottom of the page, and then turned the letter over to finish it. She saw a flourishing signature.

She cleared her throat. "And how did you manage, Doctor?"

"Um?" He looked up, but he had not heard her. She decided that the letter must be of some importance.

"I said, How did you manage while I was away?"

He gave her one of his rare smiles. She had not seen him in such a good humor for years.

"I missed you, Jessie, as a son misses his mother."

"Get away."

"No, it's true. The place was a midden." He caught sight of the bacon and eggs. "Now, that looks good." He laid the letter aside and started to eat, it seemed to her, like a man who hasn't seen good food for a month.

"But . . . it doesna look like a midden now."

"No, I know. A good fairy came and cleaned it up for me, and since then Nurse has been keeping an eye on things."

Jessie didn't mind Nurse. Nurse ran the surgery. She was one of the family, as it were. Not an outsider. But the good fairy? If it was that interfering Murdoch woman . . . Once more Jessie felt faint, but she had to know.

"And who might the good fairy have been, if I'm allowed to ask?"

"Certainly you can ask. It was Antony Armstrong's young lady. She's staying at Fernrigg. She dropped by one afternoon and stayed to do the scrubbing."

Antony Armstrong's young lady. Relief swept through Jessie. It wasn't Mrs. Murdoch. So Jessie's reputation was safe, her standing in Tarbole unimpaired, her job secure.

Her job. What was she doing, standing here, wasting time, with all the house to be seen to? With an enthusiasm she hadn't shown in years, she collected dustpans, dusters, brushes, and brooms, and by the time Hugh departed for his morning rounds she was already halfway down the staircase, on her knees, noisily attacking dust and cobwebs. The air was rich with the smell of new polish, and Jessie was singing.

"We'll meet again, I don't know where, don't know when . . ."

At the front door he paused. "Jessie, if anybody calls, tell them I'll be in the surgery at ten. And if its urgent, they'll probably reach me at Fernrigg. I want to drop in and see Mrs. Armstrong." He opened the door, and then hesitated and turned back. "And Jessie, it's a marvelous morning. Pull all the blinds up and open the windows and let the sunshine in."

In normal circumstances, Jessie would have been hotly opposed to such outlandish ideas. But this morning she only said, "Righty ho." She did not even turn from her task as she said it, and his last sight of her was her round pinafored rump, a pair of straining nylons, and the legs of her apple green locknit bloomers.

* * *

He opened the door and said, "Good morning."

Tuppy was still eating her breakfast. She looked up at him over her spectacles because she had been reading her mail at the same time.

"Hugh."

He came in and shut the door. "And it's a perfect morning. You can see forever."

Tuppy did not comment on this. To be truthful, she was a little put out at being caught, even by Hugh, with her breakfast tray on her lap and her bed not yet straightened. She took off her spectacles and eyed him suspiciously, detecting a certain self-satisfaction in his manner.

"What are you doing here at this hour of the day?"

"I've got an early surgery this morning, so I thought I'd make a few calls first, and you're one of them."

"Well, you're far too early, and I don't know where Nurse is and I'm not ready for you."

"Nurse is on her way up. She'll be here in a moment or two."

"And you," she told him, "look like a cat that's been at the cream."

He came to his usual resting place, leaning on the rail at the foot of her bed. "Jessie McKenzie has returned from Portree. The air is full of song and the house is getting a good clean-through. Like cascara."

"That's very gratifying, but it doesn't explain your smug expression."

"No, not entirely. I have got something to tell you."

"Is it something I'm going to enjoy hearing?"

"I hope so." Characteristically, he came straight to the point. "I had a letter this morning from a young man called David Stephenson. He qualified from Edinburgh three years ago, and since then he's been working at the Victoria Hospital in Glasgow. He has excellent qualifications and he's been strongly recommended to me. He's about thirty, with a young wife, who used to be a nurse, and two small children. They've had enough of city life, and they want to come to Tarbole."

"A partner?"

"A partner."

Tuppy found herself without words. She leaned back on her pillows, closed her eyes, counted ten, and then opened them again. He was waiting for her comment. "I wanted to tell you before anyone else," he said. "What do you think?"

"I think," she told him, "that you are without doubt one of the most infuriating men I've ever known."

"I know. Infuriating. Because I didn't tell you before."

"Here we've all been, trying to get you to take on a partner for months. And all you've done is evade the issue and procrastinate like an idiot."

He knew her very well. "But you're pleased?"

"Of course I'm pleased," she told him, crossly. "Nothing you could have told me could make me more pleased. But I wish I'd known you'd got this up your sleeve. Instead of going on at you all the time, I'd have saved my breath to cool my porridge."

"Tuppy, sometimes I think you forget I am no longer Jason's age."

"What you mean is, you are perfectly capable of engaging a partner for yourself without any interference from an old busybody like me."

"I never said that."

"No, but that was what you meant, just the same." But she could not go on being indignant and pretending to be cross. Her pleasure and satisfaction were very real. Now she allowed herself to smile. "You'll be able to ease up a little," she told him. "Have time to do some of the things you enjoy."

"It's not fixed up yet. He's coming to see me next Wednesday, to have a look at the place, get the feel of things."

Tuppy became practical. "Where will they live?"

"That's one of the problems. There isn't a house."

This was right up Tuppy's street. "We must all cast about and ask questions and see if we can find one."

"Well, don't start casting about until the deal's fixed. Until then it's still on the secret list."

"All right, I won't breathe a word. Dr. Stephenson." She said the name aloud and it sounded good and dependable. "Dr. Kyle's partner. Just think of that."

Having imparted his news. Hugh became practical. "How are you feeling this morning?"

"Better than I felt yesterday, but not as well as I'll feel tomorrow. I'm beginning to get restless, Hugh. I warn, you, I'm not going to sit here like an old crock for much longer."

"Perhaps next week you can get up for an hour or two."

"And Rose. How is poor little Rose?"

"I haven't seen poor little Rose yet."

"Well you must go and see her, make quite sure she's going to be all right. Really, that horrible oyster. People should be more careful. It would spoil tomorrow evening for all of us if she couldn't be there. The whole point of having the dance was for everybody to meet Rose."

As she spoke, he had wandered away from her bedside to the window, as though the lure of the radiant morning was more than he could resist. Watching him, wondering if he was listening to a word she was saying, Tuppy was visited by a strong sense of *déjà vu*.

She said, "You know, you were standing there, in the window, just where you are now, the day I felt so ill and I told you that I wanted to see Antony and Rose. And somehow you arranged it. You and dear Isobel, of course. I'm very grateful to you, Hugh. It's all turned out so well. I'm really a very lucky person."

She regarded his back view affectionately across the room, waiting for his reply. He turned from the window, but before he could say anything, there was a knock at Tuppy's door. Thinking it was Nurse come to fetch her breakfast tray, Tuppy called, "Come in."

The door opened and Rose came into the room. The first person she saw was Hugh, framed in the window. She paused for perhaps a fraction of a second, and then without a word did a swift about turn and walked out again. Tuppy was left dumbfounded, with only a fleeting impression of Rose's long legs in dark stockings and the swirl of a short pleated skirt like a child's kilt.

Hugh recovered from the shock of this extraordinary performance before Tuppy did.

"You come back here!" he called after Rose in, Tuppy thought, a not very kind voice.

They waited. Slowly, Rose appeared again, hanging onto the door knob as though poised for a second quick getaway. She looked, thought Tuppy, about fifteen. Hugh was glowering at her across the room in the most uncharitable way. It was really a funny situation. In the normal way, Tuppy knew, Rose's sense of humor would have got the better of her, and she would have been overcome by giggles in which Tuppy was perfectly prepared to join her. But now Rose looked more like crying than laughing. Tuppy hoped that she wasn't going to.

The outraged silence lengthened, and at last Hugh said, "Who told you to get up?"

Rose looked more uncomfortable than ever. "Well, actually, nobody."

"Didn't Nurse tell you to stay in bed?"

"Yes, she did. It wasn't her fault."

"Why did you get up, then?"

"I thought I'd come and see Tuppy. I didn't realize you'd be here."

"That's fairly obvious."

Tuppy could not bear any more. "Hugh, stop hectoring Rose. She's not a baby. She can get out of bed if she wants to. Rose, come and get this tray off my lap, and then I can have a good look at you."

Rose, appearing grateful for an ally, closed the door and came to remove the tray and put it down on the floor. Tuppy took her hands and drew her down on the bed beside her.

"But you're so thin! Your wrists have gone like little twigs. You must have had a horrid time." She began to have second thoughts about Rose's getting up, for indeed, Rose did look awful. "Perhaps you should still be in bed. And you must be all right for the party tomorrow. Just think of all the preparations wasted, if you aren't there." She was diverted by a happy thought. "One thing, you won't have to bother too much with the flowers, because Anna's coming over with all the pot plants out of her greenhouse. She's going to fill the Land Rover with them, the dear girl. And I thought perhaps a few big branches of beech leaves, they always look. . . ."

Her voice died away. Rose was not responding. She simply sat there, looking down, her face quite plain, all bones and without a scrap of makeup. Her hair had lost its luster and her usually sweet-natured mouth had a droop to it which caused Tuppy a definite pang of anxiety. And she remembered the young Rose of five years ago, and the sulks into which she had lapsed from time to time, apparently for no good reason at all. Then, Tuppy had ignored them, telling herself that all seventeen-year-olds were apt to be sulky. But she had never expected to catch that miserable expression on Rose's face again.

On Antony's account, she felt concerned. *Oh, dear, I do hope she's not going to be moody.* Moodiness was, in Tuppy's book, an unforgiveable sin, evidence of the worst sort of self-indulgence.

Her thoughts darted about, trying to imagine what could be at the root of this. Of course she had been ill, but . . . had she had a quarrel with Antony? But Antony wasn't here. Isobel, perhaps? Impossible. Isobel had never quarreled with anybody in her life.

"Rose." She became a little impatient. "Rose, my dear child, what's the matter?"

Before Rose could reply, could say anything, Hugh replied for her. "There's nothing wrong with the dear child except that she's had food poisoning and she's got out of bed too soon." He came back to Tuppy's bedside, taking professional charge of the situation, and at the sound of his voice Rose appeared to make some effort to pull herself together. Tuppy, as always, felt grateful to him.

"Now how are you feeling?" he asked Rose. "Truthfully."

"I'm all right. Just a bit wobbly about the legs."

"Did you eat some breakfast?"

"Yes."

"And you didn't feel sick again?"

Rose looked embarrassed. "No."

"In that case, the best thing you can do is to get out of doors for a little and get some fresh air." Rose appeared to be unenthusiastic. "Now. While the sun's shining."

Tuppy patted Rose's hand in an encouraging fashion. "There. Why not do that? It's such a lovely morning. It'll do you good."

"All right." Reluctantly, Rose got off the bed and made for the door, but as she did this, Tuppy's housekeeperly instincts rose to the surface. "Rose, dear, if you're going down, take my tray, and that'll save Nurse a trip. And if you see Nurse, tell her to come up. And," she added as Rose, burdened by the tray, made her way through the door, "if you are going out, have a word with Mrs. Watty before you do. She may want you to pick some beans."

As far as domestic arrangements were concerned, Tuppy seemed to have a sixth sense. Mrs. Watty, after exclaiming in surprise at Flora's appearance, agreed that, yes, she would like some beans, and produced a large basket which Flora was expected to fill.

"Does Nurse know you're up and about?"

"Yes. I've just seen her. She's got a face on."

"You'd better keep out of her way."

"I will."

Carrying the basket, she went back to the hall. She didn't want to pick beans. She didn't really want to go out at all. She had planned to cozy up on Tuppy's bed and be cherished, but those schemes had been thwarted by Hugh. How could Flora have possibly known that he would have already started his calls at nine o'clock in the morning?

She could not be bothered to go upstairs again for her coat, so she borrowed from the cloakroom one of the many aged ones which hung there. It was a bulky tweed, lined in rabbit fur, and she was buttoning herself into it when Hugh appeared down the staircase, one hand in his pocket, and his bag bumping against the side of his leg.

"I've had a word with Nurse," he told her, "and she has accepted the inevitable. Are you just going out?"

"Yes. To pick beans," she added resignedly.

His eyes crinkled in amusement. He put out a hand to open the door and hold it for her. She went out in front of him. The dazzle of sunshine was blinding. Through the trees the blue waters of Fhada spread bright as sapphire silk, in all the extravagance of a flood tide. The air was like wine, the sky full of wheeling gulls.

Hugh looked up. "They're flying inland. That means stormy weather."

"Today?"

"Or tomorrow." They went down the steps side by side. "It's a good thing there's to be no marquee tomorrow night, or it would doubtless end up in the top of a tree."

They reached the gravel. Flora stopped. "Hugh."

He paused, looking down at her.

Now. Say it Now.

"I'm terribly sorry I said what I said the other night. I mean, about your wife. I had no right to say such a dreadful thing. It was unforgivable. I . . . I don't expect you to forget it, but I wanted you to know I was sorry."

It was said. It was done. The relief of having it over made Flora feel quite tearful again. But Hugh did not appear to be as impressed by Flora's self-abasement as she was.

"Perhaps I have an apology to make, too," he said. She waited. "But mine will doubtless keep."

She frowned, not understanding, but he did not choose to explain. "Don't worry about it. Take care of yourself. And don't pick too many beans." He started to walk away from her and then remembered something. "When is Antony coming?"

"Tomorrow afternoon."

"That's good. I'll see you tomorrow evening, then."

"You're coming to the party?"

"If I can. Don't you want me to come?"

"Yes, I do." She amended this by adding, "I only know about three people, and if you don't come I'll only know two."

He looked amused. "You'll be all right," he told her. And with that sparse comfort he got into his car and drove away, through the gates and out of sight. Flora watched him go, still miserable, only slightly comforted, and now very confused. *My apology will keep.* What was he going to apologize for? And why did it have to keep? She wrestled with those problems for a moment or two, and then, because any mental exertion was still beyond her, abandoned the struggle and headed for the vegetable garden.

It was Friday.

Isobel awoke, listening for the rain. It had rained all yesterday afternoon and most of the night. From time to time she had awakened, shaken out of sleep by gusts of wind or the rattle of a squall of raindrops, hard as flung pebbles against her windowpane. She was haunted by visions of wet footprints and mud being tracked through the house as Watty came in and out, the caterers unloaded their cases of china and glass, and people trod to and fro carrying trays of glasses, branches of beech leaves, and large, dripping peat-filled pots containing the Ardmore pelargoniums.

But at seven o'clock in the morning, it seemed to have stopped. Isobel got out of bed (when she got back into it again, it would all be over), went to her window, drew back the curtains, and saw a pearly grayness—mist lying on the face of the sea, a thread of watery pink reflected from the first ragged rays of the early sun. The islands were lost, and the still water scarcely moved against the rocks beyond the garden.

There was still rain about, but the wind had died. She stood there, reluctant to start a day which would probably not end for another twenty hours. After breakfast coffee, though, she knew that she would feel stronger. And this afternoon Antony would be arriving from Edinburgh. The thought of Antony arriving cheered her up. She went to run her morning bath.

Jason did not want to go to school. "I want to stay here and help. If I've got to come to the party, I don't see why I shouldn't stay here and help."

"You haven't got to come to the party," Aunt Isobel told him placidly. "Nobody's making you come to the party."

"You could write Mr. Fraser a note and say I'm needed at home. That's what the other mothers do."

"Yes, I could, but I'm not going to. Now, eat up your egg."

Jason lapsed into silence. He was uncertain about the dance because he was going to have to wear the kilt and the doublet that his grandfather had worn when he was Jason's age. The kilt was all right, but the doublet was velvet and Jason thought perhaps it was sissy. He was not going to tell his friend Doogie Miller about the velvet doublet. Doogie Miller was a year older than Jason and a good head taller. His father owned his own boat, and when he was old enough Doogie was going out with him as deckhand. Doogie's good opinion mattered a great deal to Jason.

He finished his egg and drank his milk. He looked at Aunt Isobel across the table, and decided to have a last try, for he was not a child to be easily diverted.

"I could carry things for you. I could help Watty."

Isobel reached across the table to rumple his hair. "Yes, I know you could, and you'd do it beautifully, but you have to go to school. And Antony's coming back this afternoon, so he'll be here to help Watty."

Jason had forgotten about Antony. "He's coming back this afternoon?" Aunt Isobel nodded. Jason said no more, but he sighed deeply, with satisfaction. His aunt smiled at him lovingly, not realizing that he was already deep into schemes to get Antony to put some feathers on the arrows he had made last weekend.

* * *

Later in the morning Anna Stoddart turned the Ardmore Land Rover in at the gates of Fernrigg, bumped along the potholed drive (when was somebody going to get those holes filled in?), and drew up on the gravel, alongside a blue van which she recognized as that belonging to Mr. Anderson of the Tarbole Station Hotel. The front door of the house stood open. Anna got out of the Land Rover and, with her hands in the pockets of her sheepskin coat, went up the steps.

Already the hall had been stripped of furniture and rugs, with those pieces of furniture too heavy to be moved pushed to the walls. Mrs. Watty, driving an old-fashioned polisher that made a sound like a jet engine, was engaged in buffing up the parquet. Isobel was coming downstairs with a pile of clean white tablecloths in her arms, and Watty was making his way down the kitchen passage with huge baskets of logs to be stacked by the open fireplaces. They all saw her, greeted her with smiles or nods, and continued on their way. Isobel did say, over the top of the pile of linen, "Anna, how lovely to see you," but she said it an absent sort of way, and when she reached the foot of the stairs did not stop but continued straight on, heading for the dining room. Anna, not knowing what else to do, followed her.

The big table had been drawn to one side of the room, and was already spread with red felt pads. Onto these Isobel now dumped her burden. "Heavens, they're heavy. Thank goodness we don't use them every day."

"But Isobel, you've done so much already. You must all have been so busy."

"Yes, I suppose we have . . ." Isobel took the top table-cloth and shook it out of its folds with an expert flick of her long narrow wrists. "Have you brought the pot plants?"

"Yes, the Land Rover's stacked with them, but I'll need someone to help me carry them."

"Watty can help you." Isobel smoothed out the folds of the tablecloth, and then abandoned it to go in search of Watty. Anna trailed behind her. "Watty! Mrs. Watty, where's Watty?"

"He's around somewhere." Mrs. Watty raised her voice over the sound of the polisher, but was obviously not going to switch it off, or do anything bout finding her husband.

"Watty! Oh, there you are. Can you help Mrs. Stoddart get some things out of the Land Rover? Oh, you're doing the logs. I forgot. Well, where's Rose? Mrs. Watty, where's Rose?"

"I've no idea." Mrs. Watty steered the polisher into a dark corner behind the curtains.

"Oh." Isobel pushed her hair out of her face. She was beginning to get flustered, and no wonder, thought Anna. "I'll find Rose," Anna told her. "Don't worry. You go back to your tablecloths."

"She's probably in the drawing room. Watty brought in some beech branches, and Rose said she'd arrange them, though she didn't sound very confident. Perhaps you could help her."

Mr. Anderson of the Tarbole Hotel, important in his new role of caterer, now appeared from the direction of the kitchen and asked Miss Armstrong if she could spare a minute. Isobel started back to her tablecloths, thought better of it, went after Mr. Anderson, then remembered Anna.

"I'm sorry, I must go. Can you manage?"

"Don't worry," said Anna. "I'll find Rose."

It was always like this. Anna remembered Fernrigg parties from childhood and they always followed the same pattern. Drinks and sitting out in the drawing room, supper in the dining room, dancing in the hall. Brian said that he found Tuppy's parties tedious. He complained of the same people, in the same clothes, making the same conversation. But Anna liked things that way. She didn't like things to change or be different.

Even the preparations, the apparent chaos, filled her with satisfaction, because she knew that by eight o'clock everything would be just the way it always was, ready and waiting for the guests to arrive, with nothing overlooked and no detail forgotten. Only this evening it would not be quite the same because Tuppy wouldn't be there. But still she *was* there, Anna told herself, even if she wasn't able to stand at the foot of the stairs in her antique blue velvet and the inherited diamonds. She would be upstairs, listening to the music, perhaps drinking a little champagne, remembering . . .

Mrs. Watty said, "Do you mind moving, Mrs. Stoddart? I'm just about to polish that bit of floor." Anna apologized and got out of the way and went to look for Rose.

She found her in the drawing room, kneeling on the floor by the grand piano, trying to sort out the long twigs of beech which she had spread on an old sheet. There was a large pot beside her, patterned in roses, and some scraps of crumpled chicken wire. Rose's expression, as she looked up and saw Anna, was distraught.

"Hello," said Anna.

"Anna, thank heavens you've come. Everybody seems to take it for granted that I can do the most wonderful arrangements, and they won't believe me when I tell them that I can't even stick six daffodils into a jug without their collapsing."

Anna took off her coat, laid it on a chair, and went to help. "You have to cut the stems different lengths, otherwise they stick up like a broom head. Where are the secateurs? Look, like this. And then . . ."

Rose watched admiringly as the arrangement took shape. "You are clever. How can you be so clever? How do you know what to do? Did somebody teach you?"

It was marvelous to be told she was clever. Anna said no, nobody had taught her. It was just a thing she loved to do, so maybe that was why she was good at it. "Aren't there some chrysanthemums we can put with them? They could use a bit of color."

"Isobel asked Watty to bring some in, but she also asked him to do about a dozen other things as well and the poor man's nearly out of his mind."

"It's always like this," Anna told her. "It seems to be disorganized, but it's always all right in the end. And we can get some berries, or something, later. Where is this vase meant to be going?"

"Isobel thought on the piano."

Rose stooped to lift the bowl and put it in its place. Anna watched her with admiration. She saw the long, slender legs, the tiny waist, the shine of dark hair, artlessly casual. It was just the way Anna had always longed to look, and yet she was without envy. Was this one of the better symptoms of pregnancy, or was it because she liked Rose so much?

She had never thought she could like Rose. Before, when Rose was younger and Brian had brought her and her mother to the Yacht Club for a drink, Anna had been paralyzed by shyness of Rose, even a little afraid of her disparaging eyes and her thoughtlessly rude remarks. She had dreaded meeting her again.

But Rose had changed. Perhaps, thought Anna, that had something to do with Antony. She couldn't be sure of it; she only knew that Rose was a different person. Why, Anna hadn't even minded when Brian had asked her out for dinner. In fact, it made Anna feel pleasantly worldly to be going off on her shopping spree, knowing that her husband was to be so charmingly diverted while she was away. That was real sophistication —something that Anna had yearned for, all her married life.

Perhaps she was really growing up at last. Perhaps she was learning to accept things.

"What do you think of that?" Rose asked her, stepping back from the piano.

Anna, still kneeling on the floor, said, "That's just right. Rose, I want to tell you—Brian enjoyed his evening with you so much and he was so sorry about the oyster. He was really furious, and he rang up the Fishers' Arms and gave the manager the most terrible telling off."

"That wasn't his fault." Busy with broken branches and a few wet scraps of leaves, Rose knelt beside her. Her hair fell forward and Anna could not see her face. "And I've never thanked you for the azalea. You didn't need to send it."

"But of course I sent it. I felt responsible, in a way."

"How is Brian?"

"He's very well." Anna amended this. "Except, of course, for his eye."

"His eye?"

"Yes, poor man, he walked into a door. I don't know how, but he gave himself the most terrible bang and he got quite a black eye." She smiled, because Brian had looked funny, like a man in a farce. "But it's all right now, and fading fast."

Rose said, "How horrid for him." And then, "Do you think we should go and pick berries now, or bring in the pot plants?"

"We'll have to get Watty to help us do that." Anna felt a little shy. "The thing is . . . well, nobody knows yet, but I'm not allowed to carry heavy things. Hugh told me not to. You see, I'm having a baby."

"You *are*?"

Anna nodded. It was wonderful to have a confidante, another woman you could tell.

"Yes. In the spring."

"I am pleased. And the spring's the best time to have a baby. Like lambs and calves . . ." Rose became a little confused. "I mean, you've got all the summer in front of you."

"I wondered . . ." Anna hesitated. The idea had been in the back of her mind for some time, but now she was sure. "I wondered if you'd be a godmother. I haven't said anything to Brian yet, and of course I'd have to tell him, but I thought I'd ask you first. Anyway *I* want you to be a godmother. If you'd like to." Rose was looking uncertain. "If you would," she finished faintly.

"Yes, of course," said Rose. "I'd love to. I'm very flattered. The only thing is, well, I won't be here much, and . . ."

"It doesn't matter if you're here or not. You'll be somewhere. And one should always pick special friends for godparents." The emotion of the situation became too much for Anna. She shied away from it, reverting to a safer subject where she felt on firmer ground. "Now, if we had some dahlias we could do a sort of sunburst on top of the bureau. Tuppy's got lots of dahlias in her border. Let's go out and pick the lot. Poor Watty, it'll break his heart."

By the middle of the afternoon, everything had come to a full stop. Because there was nowhere else to sit everybody had gathered in Mrs. Watty's welcoming kitchen. Mrs. Watty, indefatigable, was making a batch of scones. Her husband, before getting into the fishmonger's van and driving to Tarbole to collect Jason from school, sat at the kitchen table with a face like an undertaker, and drank tea. (The massacre of the dahlias had been the final straw.) Nurse was ironing, and Isobel, visibly wilting on her long legs, pushed her hair out of her face and announced that she was going to her room to put up her toes. She waited for comments but nobody argued with her. Her eyes lighted on Flora.

"You too, Rose. You've been busy as a bee all day. Go and have a rest."

But Flora didn't want a rest. Instead she felt a deep need to be out of doors, away from the house, on her own.

"I thought I might take Plummer for a walk."

Isobel brightened. "Oh, could you bear to? He's been following me around all day with such reproachful eyes, and I haven't the energy to take him myself." Flora glanced at the clock. "When do you think Antony will be here?"

"Any moment now. He said he was leaving Edinburgh at lunchtime." Isobel stretched her lanky length. "I'm going to bed before I fall down."

She departed. Watty noisily sipped his tea. Flora went to get a coat.

She found Plummer in the hall, looking defeated by its unfamiliar appearance. He hated change the way he hated suitcases stacked by the front door. Ignored and forgotten, he had taken refuge in his basket, which had been hidden away beneath the stairs.

When Flora called him he gazed at her, hurt and dejected. When he finally realized that she was going to take him for a walk, his joy knew no bounds. He leapt from his basket, his

paws skidding on the polished floor, his old tail wagging like a
piston. Delighted noises came from the back of his throat. Outside, he dashed to find something to carry and came prancing
back to Flora with a stick in his mouth so long that it trailed on
the ground behind him. Thus burdened, Flora and Plummer set
out.

It was cool, gray, very still. The sun had not broken
through all day and the road was still wet from the previous
day's rain. They went out of the gate and turned down the road
which led to Tarbole. After a mile or so the road dipped and
ran alongside the water for a hundred yards or so. A small
beach lay revealed, which Plummer instantly went to investigate, but Flora, bundled in her coat against the chill, settled
herself on the low sea-wall to wait for Antony.

There were few cars. As each one appeared over the top of
the hill she looked up to see if it was Antony. She sat there for
half an hour and was beginning to get cold before he finally
appeared. She recognized his car at once, got off the wall, and
stood in the middle of the road, windmilling frantically with
her arms to make him stop. He saw her, slowed down, and
pulled the car over to the side of the road.

"Flora." He was out of the car, and they met in the middle
of the road and hugged. She could not remember when she had
been so pleased or so relieved to see anybody.

"I've been waiting for you. I wanted to see you before
anyone else did."

"How long have you been here?"

"It feels like ages, but I don't suppose it was very long."

"You look cold. Come on, get into the car."

She started to do so then remembered Plummer, who was
finally sighted at the farthest end of the little beach, pursuing
some apparently fascinating odor. Flora called, but he took no
notice. Antony whistled and Plummer's ears pricked up. He
turned, gazing expectantly in their direction. Antony whistled
again and that did it. Plummer galloped back, scrambled handily up the rocks, leapt the wall like a puppy, and flung himself
at Antony. It took some time to persuade him to get onto the

back seat of the car, along with a suitcase, a crate of beer, and a stack of gramophone records.

"What are the records for?" Flora asked as she settled herself beside Antony.

"They're for tonight, when the band goes off to eat buns and drink whisky. The party falls to bits if the music stops, and Tuppy's records are practically prewar, so I thought I'd bring a few of my own. But first things first. . . ." He turned toward her. "Are you all right?"

"Yes."

"You are a ninny. The minute I turn my back you start eating bad oysters. Isobel rang me up in a panic. I think she thought you were going to die on her. Were you having dinner with Brian?"

"Yes."

"I thought that's what she said." He seemed amused by this, but also unperturbed. "That'll teach you to go gallivanting with the Casanova of Arisaig. And what about the party tonight? Has Isobel collapsed yet?"

"Just about. I left her heading for her bed and a little nap. And Anna Stoddart and I cut all Tuppy's dahlias and Watty won't speak to us."

"It happens every time. And how's Tuppy?"

"Looking forward to seeing you. She says she's getting better every day. And she may be allowed up next week, just for an hour or two every day."

"Isn't that great?" Without warning he leaned forward and kissed her. "You feel thin. Your face is all bones."

"I'm all right."

"You've hated it, haven't you, Flora? The whole bloody business."

"No." She had to be truthful. "No, I haven't hated it. I've just hated myself. I feel mean and small and every day it's worse, because I get fonder and fonder of them all. One minute I'm Rose and I'm going to marry you and I'm not lying. And the next minute I'm Flora again, and I am. I don't know which is worse. Antony, that promise I made—I've kept it. And you'll keep yours, won't you? You'll tell Tuppy the truth?"

He sat back, turning his profile to her, and stared dejectedly ahead, his hands on the driving wheel. He said at last, "Yes," and Flora felt sorry for him.

"It's awful, I know. In a way, I wish we could go back and you could tell her now and get it over, but with the party and everything . . ."

"I'll tell her tomorrow." That was final. He did not want to talk about it any more. "And now for God's sake, let's get home. I'm hungry and I want tea."

"Mrs. Watty's made scones."

"And let's put tomorrow out of our minds. Don't let's talk about it any more."

With that ostrich-like remark, he reached for the ignition key, but Flora stopped him.

"There is just one more thing." She put her hand into her pocket. "This."

"What's this?"

"It's a postcard."

"Pretty crummy-looking postcard."

"I know. I threw it in the wastepaper basket, and then I thought perhaps you'd better see it, so I took it out again. That's why it's all bent."

He took it from her cautiously. "Paris?" He turned it over, instantly recognized the writing, and read it through in silence. When he had finished there was a long silence. Then he said, "What a bitch."

"That's why I dropped it into the wastepaper basket."

He read it again, and his sense of humor got the better of him. "You know, in a way, Rose is quite a bright girl. She set this whole thing up, and you and I fell for it, like a couple of suckers. Or I did. The joke is definitely on me. And if one can remain detached, I suppose it's quite a good one. 'Decided to stop off for a couple of days.' Do you suppose she ever got to Spetsai?"

"Perhaps she met another man on the plane. Perhaps she's

in Gstaad or Monaco or . . ." Flora cast about for the most unlikely place she could think of and came up with, "Acapulco?"

"I wouldn't know." He gave Flora back the postcard. "Throw it in the fire when we get back to Fernrigg." He started up the car. "And that will be the end of Rose. Wherever she is, she's gone."

Flora did not reply. She knew that Rose hadn't gone. And she wouldn't go until Antony told Tuppy the truth.

10

HUGH

The band arrived just as Antony was on his way upstairs to change. They came in a small battered car belonging to and driven by Mr. Cooper, the postmistress's husband, and players and instruments were packed in so tightly that it took some time and thought to get them finally extricated.

That achieved, Antony led them into the house and showed them to their assigned space in a corner of the hall. There they established themselves—Mr. Cooper with his accordion; the fiddler (a retired roadman, some relation of Mrs. Cooper); and the drummer, a long-haired lad in high boots whom Antony recognized as a Tarbole boy, deckhand on his uncle's fishing boat. The three had decked themselves out in a sort of spurious uniform—blue shirts and tartan bow-ties—thus presenting a brave show.

Antony gave them all a nip of whisky, and at once they got down to business and started to warm up—the old man tuning

his fiddle and Mr. Cooper playing long, trilling arpeggios on
the keyboard of the accordion.

Time was running short. Antony left them and ran upstairs to search out his evening clothes, which he was much
relieved to find ready and waiting, laid out on his bed: shoes,
stockings, garters, skean dhu; shirt, tie, waistcoat and doublet,
kilt and sporran. The shoe buckles, silver buttons and skean
dhu had all been polished, and his gold studs and cuff links
arranged on the top of his chest of drawers. Somebody, probably Mrs. Watty, had been busy, and he blessed her heart, because as usual he had left everything to the last minute, and
had resigned himself to a frantic search for the mislaid pieces of
equipment.

Ten minutes later, the very picture of a well-dressed Highland gentleman, he was downstairs again. By now the caterers
had arrived. Mr. Anderson, in a starched white jacket, was
setting out smoked salmon on the buffet table, assisted by Mrs.
Watty. Mrs. Anderson, a stately lady with a formidable reputation for good behavior, had taken up her position behind the
bar and was engaged in giving the glasses a final polish, holding
each one up to the light to check for possible smudges.

There did not seem to be anything more for Antony to do.
He glanced at his watch, and decided there was time to pour
himself a whisky and soda and take it upstairs to say goodnight
to Tuppy. This he was just on the point of doing, when he was
diverted by the sound of a car coming up the drive and grinding
to a halt on the gravel outside the house.

"Who on earth can that be?"

"Whoever it is," said Mrs. Anderson, sedately plying her
teacloth, "they're fifteen minutes early."

Antony frowned. This was the west of Scotland, and nobody was ever fifteen minutes early. More likely an hour and
three quarters late. He waited apprehensively, with visions of
himself spending the next half hour trying to make polite conversation into Mrs. Clanwilliam's hearing aid. A car door
slammed, footsteps crunched on the gravel, and the next moment the front door opened and Hugh Kyle appeared. He wore

a dinner suit and looked, thought Antony, immensely distinguished.

"Hello, Antony."

Antony let out a sigh of relief. "Thank God it's only you. You're early."

"Yes, I know." Hugh shut the door behind him and came forward, his hands in his pockets, his eyes taking in the festive scene. "This is very splendid. Just like old times."

"I know. Everybody's been working like a beaver. You're just in time for a dram. I was going to pour myself one and then go up to see Tuppy, but as you're here . . ." He poured two whiskies, topped them up with water, handed one to Hugh. "Slaintheva, old friend."

He raised his glass. But Hugh did not appear to be in a health-drinking mood. He stood there holding the drink and watching Antony, and his blue eyes were somber. For some reason Antony was instantly apprehensive. He lowered his glass, without having tasted the whisky. He asked, "Is something wrong?"

"Yes," Hugh told him bluntly. "And I think we'd better talk about it. Is there somewhere we could go, where we wouldn't be disturbed?"

Flora sat at the dressing table, wrapped in the shabby blue bathrobe she had had since she was at school, and applied mascara to her long, bristly lashes. Her reflection, the woman in the mirror who leaned toward her, seemed to have nothing to do with Flora Waring. The elaborate makeup, the carefully arranged fall of shining hair, were as formal and unfamiliar as a photograph in a magazine. Even the bedroom behind her was alien. She saw the glow of the electric fire, the drawn curtains, the ghost-like form of her dress hanging on the outside of the wardrobe door where Nurse McLeod, with some pride, had ceremoniously arranged it.

Her pride was justifiable, for it now bore no resemblance to the dim garment which Mrs. Watty had produced from the trunk in the attic. Bleached, starched, stitched, it waited for

Flora, crisp and cold as newly-fallen snow. The blue lining
showed in bands between insets of lawn and lace, and a line of
tiny pearl buttons ran from waist to throat.

Its presence was disturbing. Silent and reproachful, it
seemed to be watching Flora and, like a disapproving onlooker,
was quite unsettling. She knew that she did not want to put it
on. All this time she had been putting off the moment when she
had to come to terms with it, but now there seemed no further
excuse to delay. She laid down the mascara brush and sprayed
herself recklessly with the last of Marcia's scent. She stood up
and reluctantly slipped out of the familiar comfort of the old
blue dressing gown. For an instant her reflection stood before
her: tall, slender, her body still brown from the summer's sun,
the tan emphasized by the white lace bikini of bra and briefs.
The room was warm, but she shivered. She turned from the
mirror and went to take the dress from the hanger, step carefully into it, ease her arms into the long tight sleeves, and finally edge it up over her shoulders. It felt resistant and cold,
like a dress made of paper.

She did up the tiny buttons. That took some time because
the buttonholes were glued shut with starch and had to be
worked open and each button coaxed into place. The high collar was agony—hard as cardboard, it cut into her neck below
her jawline.

But finally, everything was done, the little belt buckled,
the cuff buttons fastened. She moved cautiously to inspect herself and saw a girl stiff as a sugar bride on the top of a wedding
cake. *I'm afraid,* she told herself, but the girl in the mirror
offered no comfort. She simply stared back at Flora dispassion-
ately, as though she didn't particularly like her. Flora sighed,
stooped cautiously to turn off the electric fire, switched off the
lights, and left her room. She went down the passage to show
herself off and say goodnight to Tuppy as she had promised to
do.

She heard the faint beat of jigging music. The house felt
very warm (Watty had been bidden to turn up the heat) and
smelt of log fires and chrysanthemums. Cheerful voices floated

up from the kitchen, creating an atmosphere of suppressed excitement—like the day before Christmas, or the moment of opening some mysterious tinsel-wrapped parcel.

Tuppy's door stood ajar. From within came the companionable murmur of voices. Flora tapped at the door and went in, and saw Tuppy plumped up against fresh pillows and wearing a white bedjacket tied with satin bows; and beside her, looking like a child out of an old portrait, her great-grandson, Jason.

"Rose!" Tuppy flung out her arms, a typical Tuppy gesture, gay, loving, rather dashing. "My dear child. Come and let us look at you. No, walk up and down so that we can really see." Rigid with starch, Flora obliged. "What a clever creature Nurse is! To think that dress has been in the attic all these years, and now it looks as though it's just been created. Come and give me a kiss. How good you smell. Now sit, just here, on the edge of the bed. Carefully, though, you mustn't crush the skirt."

Flora arranged herself cautiously. She said, "With this collar, I feel like a giraffe-necked woman."

"What's a giraffe-necked woman?" asked Jason.

"They come from Burma," Tuppy told him, "and they put gold rings on their necks and their necks go on forever."

"Was it really your tennis dress, Tuppy?" He gazed at Flora, scarcely recognizing her for the everyday person he had come to know, familiar in her jeans and sweaters. He felt rather shy of this new person.

"Yes, it really was. When I was a girl."

"How you played tennis in this, I can't imagine," Flora said.

Tuppy considered this problem. "Well, it wasn't very good tennis." They all laughed. She took Flora's hand and gave it one of her proprietary little pats. Her eyes were very bright, her color high, but whether it was due to excitement or to the brimming glass of champagne which stood on her bedside table, it was impossible to say. "I've been sitting here listening to the music, and my feet have been dancing away under the sheets, having a little party all to themselves. And then Jason came to see me, looking the image of his grandfather, and I've been telling him all about the party we had when his grandfather was twenty-one, when we lit the bonfire up on the hill behind the house, and all the country people came, and there was an ox roasting on a spit and barrels of beer. What a party that one was!"

"Tell Rose about my grandfather and his boat."

"Rose won't want to hear about that."

"Yes, I will. Tell me," Flora urged.

Tuppy did not need any more encouragement. "Well, Jason's grandfather was called Bruce, and what a wild boy he was! He spent all his days with the farm children, and at the end of the holidays I could scarcely cram his feet into shoes. But he was the child who always had a passion for the sea. He was never afraid of it, and he could swim really quite strongly by the time he was five. And when he was only a little older than Jason, he got his first dinghy. Tammy Todd—he works at Ardmore—well, it was his old father who built it for Bruce. And every year, in the summer, the Ardmore Yacht Club used to have a regatta, and there was a race for the children and . . . what was it called, Jason?"

"It was called the Tinker's Race, because all the sails were patched!"

Flora frowned. "Patched?"

"He means that all the sails were home-made," Tuppy explained, "all in marvelous colors, sewn together like patchwork. All the mothers worked for months, and the child with the gayest sails won the prize. And Bruce won it that first year, and I don't think any prize ever meant so much to him as that one did."

"But he won more races, didn't he, Tuppy?"

"Oh, yes. Lots and lots of races. And not just at Ardmore. He used to go down to the Clyde and sail with the Royal Northern, and then when he left school, he crewed for an ocean race, and went over to America. He always had a boat. It was the greatest pleasure in his life."

"And then the war came, and he joined the navy," Jason prompted, not wanting the story to end.

"Yes, he went to sea. And he was in a destroyer with the Atlantic convoys, and sometimes they'd come into the Gairloch or the Kyles of Lochalsh, and he'd get home for a weekend's leave, and as likely as not spend the whole time either working on his boat, or sailing one of the dinghys."

"And my grandmother was in the navy, too, wasn't she?"

Tuppy smiled indulgently at Jason's enthusiasm. "Yes, she was in the Wrens. They were married very soon after the beginning of the war. And what a funny wedding it was. It kept being put off because Bruce was always at sea, but finally they got married in London on a weekend leave, and Isobel and I had such a time getting there—all the trains full of soldiers and everybody sharing sandwiches and sitting on each other's knees. We did have fun."

"Tell us more stories," said Jason. But Tuppy threw up her hands.

"You didn't come here for stories. You came to say goodnight and then go down to the party. Just think, it's your very first dance. And you'll always remember wearing your grandfather's kilt and his velvet doublet."

Jason, reluctantly, got off the bed. He went towards the door. He said to Flora, "Will you dance with me? I can only do 'Strip the Willow' and an 'Eightsome Reel' if everybody else knows how to do it."

"I can't do either, but if you can teach me, I'd love to dance with you."

"I could probably teach you 'Strip the Willow.'" He opened the door. "Goodnight, Tuppy."

"Goodnight, my love."

He left them. The door closed behind him. Tuppy leaned back on her pillows, looking tired but peaceful.

"It's very strange," she said, and her voice, too, seemed tired, as though the day had been too long for her. "This evening I seem to have lost all track of the years. Hearing the music, and knowing just how everything is looking downstairs,

and all the fuss and the commotion; and then Jason coming in.
And for a moment I really thought it was Bruce. Such a strange
feeling. But a nice one, too. I think it has something to do with
this house. This house and I know each other very well. You
know, Rose, I've lived here all my life. I was born here. I
wonder if you knew that?"

"No, I didn't know."

"Yes, I was born here and I grew up here. And so did my
two little brothers."

"I didn't know you had brothers, either."

"Oh, dear me, yes. James and Robbie. They were much
younger than I was, and my mother died when I was twelve, so
in a way they were my children. And such dear, wicked little
boys. I can't tell you how naughty they were, and the dreadful
things they used to get up to. Once they built a raft and tried to
launch it off the beach, but they got swept out to sea by the ebb
tide, and the lifeboat had to go out after them. And another
time they lit a campfire in the summer house and the whole
place went up in smoke and they were lucky not to be roasted
alive. It was the only time I ever remembered seeing my father
really angry. And then they went away to school, and I missed
them so much. And they grew into young men, so tall and
handsome, but still as wicked as ever. I was married by then
and living in Edinburgh, but oh, the stories I used to hear! The
escapades and the parties! They were so attractive they must
have broken the heart of every girl in Scotland, but so charming that no female had the heart to stay angry for long, and
they were always forgiven."

"What happened to them?"

Tuppy's gay and valiant voice cracked a little. "They were
killed. Both of them. In the First World War. First Robbie and
then James. It was such a terrible war. All those fine young
men. The carnage and the casualty lists. You know, even someone of Isobel's generation cannot begin to imagine the horror of
those casualty lists. And then, so near the end of the war, my
own husband was killed. And when that happened I felt that I

had nothing left to live for." The blue eyes shone with sudden tears.

"Oh, Tuppy."

But Tuppy shook her head, denying sentiment and self-pity. "But you see, I had. I had my children, Isobel and Bruce. But I'm afraid I wasn't a very maternal person. I think I'd used up all my mothering on my little brothers, and by the time Bruce and Isobel turned up I wasn't nearly as pleased as I should have been. We were living in the south, and they were so pale and quiet, poor little souls, and somehow I couldn't make myself get enthusiastic about them, and that made me feel guilty and sorrier than ever for myself. It was a sort of vicious circle."

"What happened?"

"Well, my father wrote to me. The war was over at last, and he asked me to bring the children home to Fernrigg for Christmas. So we got into a train and we came, and he met us at Tarbole on a dark winter's morning. It was very cold and it was raining, and what a miserable little party we were, all dressed in inky black, gray in the face and sooty from the train. He had brought a wagonette and we got up behind the horses and drove back to Fernrigg just as the dawn was beginning to light the sky. And on the road we met an old farmer my father knew, and he stopped the horses and introduced the old man to the children. I remember them now, shaking hands so solemnly.

"I thought it was just for Christmas I'd come home. But we stayed over the New Year, and the weeks turned into months, and the next thing I knew, it was spring again. And I realized that the children were at home, they belonged to Fernrigg. And now they were rosy and noisy, and out of doors most of the time, just the way children should be. And I began to be interested in the garden. I made a rosebed and I planted shrubs and a fuchsia hedge, and gradually I began to realize that however tragic the past had been, there still had to be a future. This is a very comforting house, you know. It doesn't seem to change very much, and if things don't change, they can be very comforting."

She fell silent. From downstairs now came the sounds of cars arriving, the swell of gathering voices rising above the jig of the music. The party had started. Tuppy reached out for her glass of champagne and had a little drink. She laid down her glass and took Flora's hand again.

"Torquil and Antony were born here. Their mother had a difficult time when Torquil was born and the doctors told her that she really shouldn't have a second child, but she was determined to take the risk. Bruce was naturally very anxious about her, and so we arranged that she should come to Fernrigg for her pregnancy and to have the baby. And I think everything might have gone well, but Bruce's ship was torpedoed just a month before Antony was born, and after that I think she lost all will to live. There was no fight in her. And the worst bit of it was that I understood. I knew how she felt." She gave a wry smile. "So there we are, Isobel and I, right back where we'd started, with two more little boys to bring up. Always little boys at Fernrigg. The house is crawling with them. Sometimes I hear them running in from the garden, calling up the stairs, making such a racket. I think, because they died, that's why they've never grown old. And as long as I am here to remember them, then they are never really gone."

Once again, she fell silent. Flora said, at last, "I wish so much you'd told me this before. I wish I'd known."

"It's sometimes better not to talk about the past. It's an indulgence which should be kept for very old people."

"But Fernrigg is such a happy house. You feel it the moment you walk into it."

"I'm glad you felt that. I sometimes think it's like a tree, gnarled and old, the trunk twisted and deformed by the wind. Some of the branches have gone, torn away by the storms, and at times you think the tree is dying—it can't survive the elements any longer. And then the spring comes again, and the tree opens out into thousands of young, green leaves. Like a miracle. You're one of the little leaves, Rose. And Antony. And

Jason. It makes everything worthwhile to know that there are young people around again. To know you're here." Flora could think of nothing to say, and with a characteristic change of mood, Tuppy became brisk. "What am I doing, keeping you here, talking a lot of rubbish, when everybody is downstairs waiting to meet you! Are you feeling nervous?"

"A little."

"You mustn't be nervous. You're looking beautiful and everyone—not just Antony—will be in love with you. Now, give me a kiss and run along. And tomorrow you can come and tell me all about it. Every tiny detail, because I shall be waiting to hear."

Flora got off the bed. She bent and kissed Tuppy and went to the door. As she opened it Tuppy said, "Rose," and Flora looked back. "Have fun," Tuppy told her.

That was all. She went out of the room, and shut the door behind her.

It was no time to be emotional. It was simply childish to become sentimental, to get upset because an old lady had had a glass of champagne and started to remember. Flora was not a child. She had learned long ago to control her feelings. She had only to stand very still, and press her hands to her face and close her eyes, and in a moment the lump in her throat would stop growing like a great balloon and the foolish tears would recede and never be shed.

She had been a long time with Tuppy. From the hall the swelling sounds of the party, already well under way, rose to taunt her. She had to go down. She couldn't start crying now, because she had to go down, and meet everybody. And Antony was waiting, and she had promised him . . .

What had she promised him? What madness had impelled her to make that promise? And how could they ever have imagined that they would get away with their deception without destroying both themselves and everyone else involved?

The desperate questions had no answer. The dress she wore, starched and relentlessly uncomfortable, had become a physical embodiment of her own shame and self-loathing. Wearing it was torture. Her arms were forced into sleeves that were too narrow; her throat constricted by the high, tight collar, until she felt she couldn't breathe.

Rose. Have fun.

But I'm not Rose. And I can't pretend to be Rose any longer.

She pressed her fist to her mouth, but it wasn't any good, because by now she was crying—for Tuppy, for the little boys, for herself. Blinding, salty tears filled her eyes and streamed down her cheeks. She imagined herself, blotchy and with her mascara running, but that was of no importance because she had come to the end of the charade. She could go to no party, face nobody. Instinctively, she had started back toward the sanctuary of her own room, and now she was running, like a person trying to escape—down the long passage, till she had reached her door and was inside, shut away. She was safe.

Now the music and the laughter were deadened to a faint murmur and there was only the ugly sound of her own weeping. The room felt icy. She began, clumsily, to undo all the tiny awkward buttons of the dress. The collar lay loose and she could breathe again. Then the bodice and the narrow cuffs. She wrenched the dress from her shoulders and it slid with a whisper to the floor, and she stepped out of it and left it there, like the discarded wrappings of some parcel. Shivering with cold, she snatched up her old familiar dressing gown, and without bothering to do up the buttons or tie the sash bundled herself into it, flung herself across the bed, and was abandoned, at last, to the inevitable storm of weeping.

Time was lost. Flora had no idea how long she had lain there before she heard the sound of her door open, and gently, close again. She was not even sure whether or not someone had actually come into the room until she felt the pressure on the edge of her bed as someone sat beside her. A warm presence, solid and comforting. She turned her head on the pillow, and a hand reached out and smoothed her hair back off her face. She looked through swimming eyes, and the dark blur with the white shirt front gradually resolved itself into Hugh Kyle.

She had expected perhaps Isobel or Antony. Certainly not Hugh. She made an enormous effort to stop crying, and as the tears did recede a little, she wiped them away with the heel of her hand, and looked at him again. Hugh's image sharpened, and she saw a man she had never seen before—not simply because he was dressed differently, but because it was unusual for him to be so patient, sitting there as though he had all the time in the world, not saying anything and apparently prepared to let Flora cry herself to a standstill.

She made an effort to speak. To say something, even if it was only, "Go away." But Hugh—Hugh, of all people, opened his arms to her, and this she found impossible to resist. Without a second thought, Flora pulled herself up off her pillows, and cast herself into the waiting comfort of his massive embrace.

He seemed impervious to the damage she was probably wreaking on his crisp white shirt front. His arms were warm and strong about her shaking shoulders. He smelt of clean linen and aftershave. She felt his chin against the top of her head, and when, after a little, he said, gently, "What's wrong?" the words came, incoherent and disjointed, but still they came—a torrent of words, a flood.

"I've been with Tuppy . . . and she was telling me . . . the little boys . . . and I never knew. And I couldn't bear it. And she said . . . a leaf on the tree . . . and I couldn't bear it . . ." Telling him all this was not helped by the fact of her face being pressed so closely to his shirt front. "I . . . could hear everybody and the music, and I knew . . . I couldn't come down. . . ."

He let her cry. When she had calmed down a little, she heard him say, "Isobel wondered what had happened to you. She sent me to find out, and to bring you down."

Flora shook her head as vehemently as possible under the constricted circumstances. "I'm not coming."

"Of course you're coming. Everybody's waiting to meet you. You can't spoil it for them."

"I can't. I'm not going to. You'll have to say I'm sick again, or something . . . anything . . ."

His arms tightened. "Now come along, Flora, pull yourself together."

The room became very still. Out of the silence random sounds impinged on Flora's conscious mind: faint strains of music from the other end of the house, the wind rising, nudging the window, the distant murmur of the sea; and so close that it was felt rather than heard, the regular thud of Hugh's heartbeat.

Cautiously, she drew away from him. "What did you call me?"

"Flora. It's a good name. Much better than Rose."

Her face ached from crying. Undried tears still lay on her cheeks, and she tried to wipe them away with her fingers. Her nose was running and she could not find a handkerchief and had to sniff, enormously. He reached into his pocket and produced his own handkerchief. Not the beautiful silk one which showed from the top of his breast pocket, but a comfortable everyday one, the cotton soft from washing.

She accepted it gratefully. "I don't seem to be able to stop crying. I don't usually cry, ever." She blew her nose. "You won't believe that, but it's true. These last few days I don't seem to have done anything but cry."

"No, but you've been under a considerable strain."

"Yes." She looked down at the handkerchief and saw it covered with dark smudges. "My mascara's run."

"You look like a panda."

"I suppose I do." She took a deep breath. "How did you know? About me being Flora?"

"Antony told me. I mean, he told me your name was Flora, but I've known for some time that you weren't Rose."

"When did you know?"

"The day you were ill, I knew for sure." He added, "But I've had my suspicions for some time."

"But how did you know?"

"When Rose was here, that summer five years ago, she had an accident on the beach. She was sunbathing, or occupied in some other relatively harmless way, and she cut her arm on a broken bottle that some joker had buried in the sand. Just here." He reached out and took Flora's hand, pushed up the sleeve of her dressing gown, and drew with his finger a line perhaps two inches long on the outside of her forearm. "It wasn't very serious, but it had to be stitched up. I pride myself on being fairly adroit when it comes to sewing people up, but even I couldn't do a job that left no trace of a scar."

"I see. But why didn't you say anything?"

"I wanted to speak to Antony first."

"And have you?"

"Yes."

"Did he tell you everything? About me and Rose and our parents?"

"Yes, everything. It's quite a story."

"He . . . he's going to tell Tuppy tomorrow."

Hugh corrected her. "He's telling Tuppy now."

"You mean, this very moment?"

"This very moment."

"So . . ." She was almost afraid to say it. "So Tuppy knows I'm not Rose."

"By now she does." He watched her face. "Is that why you were crying?"

"Yes, I think so. I seemed to be crying for so many things."

"But an uneasy conscience was one of them."

Flora nodded—a miserable confession.

"You didn't like lying to Tuppy?"

"I felt like a murderer."

"Well, now you don't need to feel like a murderer any longer." He sounded, all at once, much more like his usual dry self. "So perhaps you'll get off that bed, and get into your dress and come downstairs."

"But my face is all dirty and swollen."

"You can wash it."

"And my dress is all crumpled."

He looked for the dress, spied it where she had abandoned it on the floor. "No wonder it's crumpled." He stood up and went to retrieve it, shaking it out of its creases and laying it across the foot of the bed. Flora wrapped her arms around her knees and watched him.

"Are you cold?" he asked her.

"A little." Without comment, he went to turn on the electric fire, pressing down the switch with the toe of his shoe, and then moved to the dressing table. Flora saw the green gleam of a champagne bottle and a couple of wineglasses.

"Did you bring those up with you?"

"Yes. I had an idea some sort of a stimulant might be useful." He commenced, neatly, to deal with the gold wire and the foil. "It seems I was right."

There was a pop as the cork flew out, an explosion of golden bubbles which he caught expertly, first in one glass and then the other. He set down the bottle and brought Flora over a brimming glass, and then he said, "Slaintheva," and they drank, and the wine was dry and nose-tickling and tasted of weddings and the best sort of celebrations.

The bars of the fire reddened. The room grew bright and warm. Flora took a second courage-bolstering mouthful, and said, abruptly, "I do know about Rose."

Hugh did not reply at once to this. Instead, he retrieved the champagne bottle and came to settle himself at the foot of the bed, his wide shoulders propped against the brass rail. He set the bottle handily on the floor at his side. He said, "What do you know about her?"

"I know that she had an affair with Brian Stoddart. But I didn't know that before he took me out for dinner. Otherwise, I promise you, I would never have gone."

"I imagine he reminisced in some detail."

"I couldn't stop him."

"Were you shocked, or were you surprised?"

She tried to remember. "I don't know. You see, I didn't

have time to get to know Rose. We just met in London for an evening, and then she flew off to Greece the next day. But she looked like me, and so I imagined that she *was* like me. Except that she was rich and she had all sorts of things that I could never hope to have. But that didn't seem to be basically important. I just thought of us as two halves of the same whole. We'd been separated all our lives, but basically we were still the one person. And then Rose went, and Antony arrived and told me what had happened, and that was the beginning of wondering about Rose. She knew Antony needed her, but she'd still gone off to Greece. That was one of the reasons I came to Fernrigg. I suppose to try and make up for what Rose had done." It was all too difficult and Flora gave up. "It doesn't make any sense at all, does it?"

"I think it makes a lot of sense."

"You see . . ."

But he interrupted her. "Flora, that first day I spoke to you on the sands by the Beach House, you must have thought I was some sort of a maniac."

"No."

"Out of interest, what did you think?"

"I . . . I thought you were perhaps a man who'd been hurt by Rose."

"You mean, that I'd been in love with her?"

"Yes, I suppose so."

"I never really knew Rose. She was certainly never concerned about me. And I don't think she even looked twice at Antony. But Brian was a different kettle of fish."

"Then you weren't in love with her?"

"Good God, no." Flora could not keep herself from smiling. "And what's that Cheshire Cat grin for?"

"I thought you must have been. And I couldn't bear it."

"Why not?"

"Because she was so vile. And I suppose," she added with the air of one determined to make a clean breast of the whole thing, "because I liked you so much."

"You liked *me*?"

"That was why I was so horrible to you that night you brought me home from Lochgarry."

"Are you always horrible to people you like?"

"Only when I think they're jealous."

"I wish I'd known. I thought you hated me. I also thought you were drunk."

"Perhaps I was, a little. But at least I didn't slap your face."

"Poor Flora." But he did not look particularly repentant.

"But if you weren't angry because of jealousy . . ." It took some working out. "Hugh. Why were you angry?"

"Because of Anna."

Anna. It was Anna. Flora sighed. "You'll have to explain. Otherwise I shall never understand."

He said, heavily, "Yes." He had finished his glass, and now reached down to where the bottle stood on the floor, and refilled both their glasses. It was becoming as cozy, thought Flora, as a midnight feast.

He said, "I don't know how much you know about the Stoddarts."

"I know about them, because Tuppy told me."

"Good. That'll save a lot of time. Well, where shall we start? Five years ago, Rose and her mother came to stay at the Beach House, that you know. Looking back, I've never been able to work out why they came to Fernrigg at all. It was the most unlikely place for a couple of jet-setters like the Schusters, but perhaps they'd seen Tuppy's advertisement in the *Times,* or they thought it would be novel to get back to the simple life. Anyway, they came, and Tuppy is always very conscientious about her tenants. She feels responsible for them, as if they were houseguests. She invites them up to Fernrigg, introduces them to her friends, and I think that is how Rose and her mother met the Stoddarts.

"Anna was expecting a baby that summer. Her first. And Brian, perhaps frustrated by potential fatherhood, was amusing himself with the barmaid at the Yacht Club. She was a Glasgow girl who'd come up to Ardmore for the summer just to do this job, and I think she and Brian probably suited each other down to the ground."

"Did everybody know about this?"

"Tarbole is a small community. Everybody knows everybody else's business, only in this case nobody ever talks about it, out of loyalty to Anna."

"And she ignores what Brian does?"

"She appears to. But Anna, beneath that diffident exterior, is a very passionate and high-strung woman. Very much in love, and possessive of her husband."

"Brian described her as an ostrich, only seeing what she wanted to."

"How charming of him. And of course, most of the time she is, but in some women pregnancy unleashes a number of very violent emotions."

"Like jealousy."

"Exactly. This time, Anna didn't bury her head. She suspected he was carrying on with this girl, and she worked herself up into a highly nervous state. What she didn't realize, and thank God she never did, was that Rose had now appeared on the scene. The only reason I found out was through Tammy Todd who works at the Ardmore Yacht Club. Tammy and I were at school together long ago when we were both small, and I think he felt that perhaps I ought to know what was going on.

"One morning I had a phone call from Anna, very early. She was incoherent with anxiety because Brian had been out all night. He'd never come home. I tried to reassure her, and then I went searching for him and I found him at the Yacht Club. He said there'd been a party, and rather than disturb Anna, he'd decided to sleep the night there. I told him to go home and he said that he would.

"But later in the day I got another message to ring Anna. By now I was away out in the country, a two-hour drive from Tarbole, visiting the young son of a sheep farmer. The mother suspected appendicitis, but mercifully, as it turned out, she was wrong. Anyway, Anna told me she was hemorrhaging. I told her I'd get back as soon as I could, but that Brian was to call the hospital and get an ambulance. She told me that she was still alone. Brian had never come back. So I rang the ambulance myself and the hospital at Lochgarry, and I drove like the hammers of hell back to Tarbole, and when I got to the surgery I rang the hospital again, but it was too late. Sister told me that Anna had arrived, but she'd lost the child. She said that Anna was asking for her husband, but that nobody knew where to find him. I said that I would find him, and I put down the telephone and got into the car and went to the Beach House, and walked in and found Rose and Brian in bed together."

"But didn't her mother know what was going on?"

"I honestly don't know. She certainly wasn't in the house at the time. As far as I can remember, she'd gone over to Lochgarry for a round of golf."

"Hugh, what *did* you do?"

He put up a hand to rub his eyes. "Oh, the usual things. Lost my temper, flung my weight around. But of course it was too late to start being indignant, because Anna's baby was already dead."

"And now she's having another one." Hugh nodded. "And you weren't going to stand by and let it happen all over again."

"No."

"Were . . . were there any repercussions?"

"No. By the time Anna came out of hospital, Rose and her mother had gone."

"Tuppy never knew? Nor Isobel?"

"No."

"Nor Antony?"

"Antony was working in Edinburgh. He only met Rose fleetingly when he happened to be home for a weekend."

"What did you think when you heard Antony was going to marry Rose?"

"I was appalled. But I told myself that all this had happened five years ago. Rose had probably grown up. I prayed that she had."

"And Anna? Anna never found out?"

"Brian and I made a deal. The only one we're ever likely to make. The truth would have destroyed Anna. Thinking that Brian was running around with a little whore from Glasgow was one thing. Knowing that he was sleeping with Rose was another. It would have been disastrous, and inevitably it would have involved the Armstrongs."

"And what did Brian get out of the deal?"

"Brian, despite his tomcat tendencies, had a hard head. Materially, financially, Brian had more than anyone else to lose. He still has for that matter."

"You really hate him, don't you?"

"It's mutual. But this is a small place, a tight community. So when we have to, we endure each other's company."

"He couldn't have been very pleased to see you that evening at Lochgarry."

"No, I don't think he was."

"Anna says he's got a black eye."

Hugh looked amazed. "No? Really?"

"You didn't hit him, did you?"

"Only a little," said Hugh.

"What will happen to that marriage?"

"Nothing will happen to it. Brian will probably continue to sow his wild oats, if the words apply to a man of his age, and Anna will continue to ignore his peccadilloes. And the marriage will survive."

"Will the child help?"

"It'll help Anna."

"It seems very unfair."

"Life is unfair, Flora. Surely you've found that out by now."

"Yes." She sighed deeply. It was all very troubling. "I wish Rose had been nicer. I wish she hadn't become like that. Amoral and ruthless. Hurting everybody. She and I are identical twins. We were born under Gemini. Why is she like that?"

"Environment?"

"You mean, if I'd been brought up by my mother instead of my father, I'd have been like Rose?"

"No. I can't imagine that you would."

"Besides, I envied Rose her environment. I envied her mink coat and her flat in London, and the way she had so much money she could go anywhere and do anything she wanted. And now I'm only sorry for her. It's a horrible feeling." She rested her chin on her knees and looked thoughtfully at Hugh. "Now, I wouldn't want to be Rose."

"I wouldn't want you to be Rose, either. But for a bit you had me very confused. For years people have been telling me I work too hard, I must get a partner, I'm going to crack up. And I've simply laughed at them. But all at once I began to wonder if I was going out of my mind. First I found you cleaning my kitchen, which was so un-Rose-like and out of character that it was positively unnerving. And then I found myself telling you about Angus McKay, and the next thing I knew I was blurting out the story of my marriage. And that, if you can believe it, was even more out of character than Rose scrubbing the floor. I hadn't talked about Diana in years. I've certainly never told a living soul the things I told you."

"I'm glad you told me."

"And then just when I was beginning to think that perhaps Rose wasn't so bad after all, there she was, off on the razzle with Brian Stoddart again. And Dr. Kyle, the lumbering old fool, was left standing there with egg all over his face."

"No wonder you were so angry."

From far away came the strains of a waltz. One two three. One two three.

. . . carry the lad that's born to be king,
Over the sea to Skye.

He said, "If we don't go now, the party's going to be over by the time we get there."

"Do I have to go on being Rose?"

"I think you have to." He got off the bed, collected the

empty champagne bottle, and stood it, like an ornament, in front of Flora's mirror. "For one more evening. For Antony and for Isobel and to save about sixty people a lot of embarrassment." He went over to the basin, turned on the hot tap, and wrung Flora's washcloth out under the scalding water. "Now get out of bed," he told her, "and come and wash your face."

She was ready, creamed and combed and wearing a minimum of makeup. She had climbed back into the dress and done up most of the buttons, while Hugh had dealt with the tricky ones at the neck. It was still as uncomfortable as ever, but now, emboldened by champagne, Flora decided that it was nothing that could not be endured. *Pour être belle il faut souffrir.* She did up the belt and faced him.

"I don't look blotchy, do I?"

"No." That was all she expected, but he added, "You look quite enchanting."

"You look enchanting too. Successful and distinguished. Except that some reckless female has smudged mascara onto your shirt front and knocked your tie crooked into the bargain."

He glanced into the mirror to check this, and appeared to be astonished. "How long has my tie been like that?"

"For the last ten minutes."

"Why didn't you put it straight for me?"

"I don't know. It's so corny."

"Why should it be corny to straighten a man's tie?"

"Oh, you know, those old movies you see on television. The couple are all dressed up, and the woman in love with the man, but he hasn't realized it. And then she tells him that his tie is crooked, and she straightens it for him, and the whole thing becomes terribly meaningful and tender, and they gaze into each other's eyes."

"What happens then?" asked Hugh, sounding as though he really wanted to know.

"Well, then he usually kisses her, and a heavenly choir starts singing, 'I'll Be Seeing You,' or something, and they put their arms around each other, and walk away from the camera with *The End* written on their backs." She ended inconsequently, "I told you it was corny."

He seemed to be considering the pros and cons of the situation. He said at last, "Well, one thing's certain. I can't go downstairs with my tie standing on its head."

Flora laughed, and carefully, meticulously, put it straight for him. Without fuss, he stooped and kissed her. It was the most satisfactory sensation. So satisfactory that when it was over, she put her arms up and around his neck, and pulled down his head and kissed him back.

But his response was baffling. She drew back and frowned up at him.

"Don't you like to be kissed?"

"Yes, very much. But perhaps I'm a little out of practice. It hasn't happened to me for such a long time."

"Oh, Hugh. You can't live without love. You can't go on living without loving somebody."

"I thought I could."

"You're not that sort of person. You're not meant to be lonely and self-sufficient. You should have a wife, and children running round that house of yours."

"You forget, I tried it once and made the most abysmal failure of it."

"That wasn't your fault. And there are such things as second chances."

"Flora, do you know how old I am? Thirty-six. I shall be thirty-seven in a couple of months. I'll never make a fortune. I'm a middle-aged country doctor with little ambition to be anything else. I'll probably spend the rest of my days in Tarbole, and end up as set in my ways as my old father. I never seem to have any time to myself, and if I do, then I go fishing. That's a dull future to ask any woman to share."

"It needn't be dull," said Flora, stubbornly. "It can never be dull to be needed and to be important to people."

"It's different for me. It's my life."

"If somebody loved you, it would be her life, too."

"You make it sound easy. Almost facile."

"I don't mean to."

He said abruptly, "What will you do when all this is over? I mean, this time with the Armstrongs."

"I'll go away." It was hard not to be hurt by his sudden change of subject.

"Where?"

Flora shrugged. "To London. To do what I was trying to do when I met Rose. Find a job. Find somewhere to live. Why?"

"I suppose I'm just beginning to realize what a void you're going to leave in all our lives. A darkness. Like a light going out." He smiled, perhaps at himself. Shying from sentiment, he became practical. "We must go." He reached out and opened the door. "We must go *now.*"

She saw the long passage stretching ahead; she heard once more the voices and the music. Her courage faltered.

"You won't abandon me?"

"Antony will be there."

"Will you dance with me?"

"Everyone will want to dance with you."

"But . . ." She could not bear to let go of this tenuous thread of friendship which at last lay between them.

"I'll tell you what. We'll have supper together. How would that be?"

"You promise?"

"I promise. Now let's go."

Afterward, when it was all over and a thing of the past, Flora's memory of Tuppy's party for Antony and Rose was reduced to a number of brief and totally unrelated incidents—blurred impression without order or priority.

It was coming down the stairs into the hall with Hugh beside her, like a couple of deep sea divers descending into a world of light and noise, with a multitude of upturned faces waiting to welcome her. Each way she turned there was someone waiting to introduce herself or himself, perhaps to kiss or congratulate her, or shake her hand. But if she remembered a single name, she was quite incapable of fitting it to a face.

It was a number of large young men in kilts and small old men, similarly attired.

It was being ceremoniously led into the drawing room to be presented to Mrs. Clanwilliam. Mrs. Clanwilliam's hair was either a wig or a bird's net, crowned by a tiara of antique diamonds, and she sat by the fire with her stick by her side and a strong whisky in her hand. She was not in the best of tempers and had been in two minds about coming to Tuppy's party. There wasn't much point, she told Flora, in coming to a party if you couldn't dance, and had to sit by the fire like an old crock. The reason, she added in the hooting voice of a very deaf person, that she was unable to dance was because she had broken her hip falling off a stepladder while attempting to paint her bathroom ceiling. She was, she added as a casual afterthought, eighty-seven next birthday.

It was the Crowthers, dancing together in the middle on an "Eightsome Reel." Mr. Crowther uttering cries which sounded as if he were calling odds, and Mrs. Crowther whirling the skirts of her tartan silk dress, and disclosing shoes designed for highland dancing, with ties that came up over her ankles.

It was champagne. It was a very old man with a face the color of loganberries telling someone that Tuppy was a splendid little woman, and if he'd had any sense he'd have married her years ago.

It was dancing "Strip the Willow" with Jason, who swung and turned Flora down a long line of partners. The room spun like a top around her. Disembodied arms appeared from nowhere to catch her. Silver cuff buttons dug into her arms. She was held and turned again and delivered back to Jason.

It was Anna Stoddart in a surprisingly becoming dress, sitting on a sofa with Isobel, and looking as pretty as Flora had ever seen her.

It was turning from the bar and finding herself face to face with Brian Stoddart. She instantly searched for evidence of his black eye.

He frowned. "What's that piercing glance for?"

"Anna told me you'd walked into a door."

"Dr. Kyle should learn to keep his nose out of other people's business and his hands in his pockets."

"So it *was* Hugh."

"Don't put on that innocent face, Rose, you know bloody well it was. It's just the sort of thing he'd enjoy boasting about. Interfering sod." He looked about him morosely. "I'd ask you to come and dance, but jumping up and down isn't my idea of dancing and the band doesn't seem to be able to play anything else."

"I know," said Flora sympathetically. "It's tedious, isn't it? The same faces, and the same clothes, and the same conversation."

He gave her a wary glance. "Rose, do I detect a note of sarcasm in your voice?"

"Perhaps. Just a very small one."

"You used to be able to do much better than that. You're losing your touch."

"That's no bad thing."

"You sound like a girl who's been brainwashed."

"I'm not the same girl you knew, Brian. I never was."

"Unhappily, I was beginning to suspect that." He stubbed out his cigarette. "It breaks my heart, Rose, but I fear you've reformed."

"You could try it yourself."

He looked at her, his pale eyes hard and bright as a bird's. "Rose, spare me that."

"Don't you ever think of Anna?"

"Almost all the time."

"Then why don't you get a glass of champagne and go and sit beside her and tell her she's looking beautiful?"

"Because it wouldn't be true."

"You could make it true. And," she added sweetly, "it wouldn't cost you a single penny."

* * *

Antony had been nearby all evening, and she had danced with him, but there had been no opportunity to talk to him. She knew that before the evening was very much older, it was essential that she get him to herself. She found him at last in the dining room, standing at the buffet table, loading a plate with smoked salmon and potato salad.

"Who's that for?"

"Anna Stoddart. She's not going to stay till the end of the party, and Isobel insists that she has something to eat."

"I want to talk to you."

"I want to talk to you, too, but there hasn't been a chance."

"How about now?"

He looked around him. Nobody seemed at that moment to be either needing or demanding his attention. He said, "All right."

"Where can we go?"

"You know the old pantry, where Mrs. Watty and Isobel clean the silver?"

"Yes."

"Well, gather up some champagne and a couple of glasses, and try to look as if you're going to the kitchen on urgent business. I'll meet you there."

"Won't we be missed?"

"Not for ten minutes. And even if we are, everyone will think we're indulging in a little snogging and will politely look the other way. See you."

He left her, bearing Anna's supper in his hand. Flora collected two glasses and an opened bottle of wine. Looking casual, she headed down the kitchen passage. The pantry led off the passage before one actually reached the kitchen, so nobody saw Flora go in, or even knew she was there.

It was a narrow room, with a window at one end, and long cupboards down each wall. There was just room in the middle of the floor for a small oilclothed table, and it all smelt of polish and scrubbed wood, and the stuff Isobel used to get the tarnish off Tuppy's best forks.

She sat on the table and waited for Antony to join her. When he did, it was with the air of a conspirator. He shut the door gently behind him, and leaned against it, like a beleaguered heroine in a bad film. He grinned at her.

"Alone at last." They surveyed each other across the room and his grin became rueful. "I'm not sure if I've ever before endured an experience like this evening. I just pray I never have to go through it again."

"Well, perhaps it'll teach you a lesson. Not to get engaged to girls like Rose."

"Don't you be so sanctimonious. You're in this up to your neck, just like I am."

"Antony, I want to know what Tuppy said."

His smile died. He came forward, reached for the champagne bottle and filled the two glasses which Flora had brought. He picked one up and gave it to her.

"She was very angry."

"Really angry?"

"Really angry. Tuppy can be quite a formidable person." He hitched himself up onto the table beside her. "I've never had such a rollicking in my life. You know the sort of thing. Never lied to me in your life, and now just because you think I'm in the last stages of senility, et cetera, et cetera."

"Is she still angry?"

"No, of course not. Never let the sun go down on a quarrel. Kiss and make friends. I've been forgiven, but I'm still feeling about three inches high."

"Is she angry with me, too?"

"No, she's sorry for you. I told her the blame was entirely mine, which it was, and that you had simply been coerced into a situation which was right over the top of your head. You knew I'd told Tuppy?"

"Yes. Hugh said that he said you had to."

"He's known for some time that you weren't Rose."

"I didn't have a scar on my arm."

"It's like something out of the Arabian Nights. The lad
with the starred scimitar on his left buttock is the rightful
prince. How was I to know Rose had a scar on her arm, silly
bitch." He took some champagne and sat gazing dolefully
down into the glass. "Hugh arrived early this evening. I
couldn't think what the hell he was doing until he fixed me
with a cold eye and said that he wanted to talk to me. It was
like being sent for by the headmaster. We came in here because
there wasn't anywhere else to go, and I told him the whole
long, complicated story. About you and Rose, and your parents
separating, and about Rose going off to Greece, and you being
in the flat when I came to London. And he said I had to tell
Tuppy. Now. This evening. No more delay. He said that if I
didn't, he would."

"If you hadn't told her, I couldn't have gone through with
it tonight."

Antony frowned. "What do you mean?"

"I don't know. I suppose you can only lie for so long. At
least, to somebody who trusts you. Somebody you love. And
although I seem to have done nothing but lie for the past seven
days, I'm not actually very good at it."

"I should never have asked you to come."

"I should never have said that I would."

"Well, having decided that, let's have some more champagne."

But Flora got off the table. "I have had quite enough." She
smoothed down her dress, and Antony laid down his glass and
reached out to take hold of her shoulders and pull her toward
him. He said, "You know, Miss Flora Waring, you are looking
quite exceptionally pretty tonight."

"It's Tuppy's tennis dress."

"It's nothing to do with Tuppy's tennis dress, charming
though it is. It's you. All bright-eyed and radiant. Sensational."

"Champagne, perhaps."

"No. Not champagne. If I didn't know you better I'd say you were in love. Or loved."

"That's a pretty thought."

"I still haven't worked out why the hell it isn't me."

"We decided that ages ago. It's something to do with chemistry."

He pulled her into his arms and gave her a resounding kiss. "I shall have to go to night classes. Learn all about it."

"Yes, you do that."

They smiled. He said, "I've probably told you before, but you are the most super girl."

In love. Or loved.

Antony was no fool. All evening Flora had been aware of Hugh. He stood, head and shoulders above the rest of Tuppy's guests, his presence refusing to be either missed or ignored. But since they had made their entrance down the stairs together, they had neither looked nor spoken to each other, although his had been among the masculine arms which had swung her through the dance she had done with Jason.

It was as if they had an unspoken pact. As if he too had recognized that their relationship had become all at once so precious a thing, so delicate, that a clumsy word or a proprietary glance would be enough to snap it. The small, shared understanding was enough to fill Flora's heart with hope. Those reflections, which would have done credit to a daydreaming fifteen-year-old, surprised her. She was, after all, twenty-two, and her grownup past lay littered with friendships and affairs and half-hearted infatuations. She thought of London: coming out of a restaurant to satin-wet streets and the dazzle of neon signs with her hand in some man's hand, deep in his overcoat pocket. And that summer in Greece. She remembered a clifftop carpeted in wild anemones and her companion with his sun-browned body and thatch of sun-bleached hair. It was as though over the last few years she had given away small pieces of herself—had perhaps, broken a few hearts, and in return had her own heart chipped once or twice.

But it had never been love, just looking for love. Having
been brought up by a single parent had made the search more
confusing for Flora, because she had no example to follow, no
idea of what she had really been looking for. But now, in the
course of this incredible week, she had come upon it. Or rather,
it had come upon Flora like some sudden explosion of light,
taking her so unprepared that it had rendered her incapable of
any sensible sort of reaction.

And it was different. Hugh was older. He had been married before. He was a hard-working doctor, tending to the
needs of a remote, rural community. He would never be rich,
and his future held no surprises. But with piercing certainty,
Flora knew that he was the only man who could fill her life
with the things that she really wanted: love, security, comfort,
and laughter. She had found them all in his arms. And she
wanted to be able to return to those arms whenever she felt the
need. She wanted him beside her. She wanted to live with him
—yes, in that terrible house—and stay in Tarbole for the rest of
her days.

It had certainly never been like this before.

At midnight the members of the band, sweating with exhaustion after two encores of "The Duke of Perth," laid down
their instruments, mopped their brows with large handker-
chiefs, and filed out in the direction of the kitchen, where Mrs.
Watty waited to serve them supper and large tankards of export. As soon as that happened Antony and Jason, well-versed
in procedure, produced the Fernrigg record player and the pile
of records which Antony had brought with him from Edinburgh on the back seat of his car.

Most of the guests, even more exhausted than the band
after the energetic dance, gravitated towards the dining room in
search of sustenance and cool drinks. But Flora found herself
sitting on the stairs with a young man who had driven all the
way to Fernrigg from the far reaches of Ardnamurchan, where
he ran a small salmon fishery.

He was in the middle of describing this venture to her when he realized that nearly everyone else had gone to eat supper.

"I'm sorry. Would you like something to eat? Would you like it here? I'll fetch you something if you like."

"It's so kind of you, but in fact, I said I'd have supper with Hugh Kyle."

"Hugh?" The young man looked about him. "Where is he?"

"I've no idea, but he'll turn up."

"I'll go and look for him for you." The young man stood up, dusting down the pleats of his kilt. "He's probably stuck in some dark corner with an old fishing crony, exchanging unlikely yarns."

"Don't worry about me. Go and get some supper for yourself . . ."

"I'll do that at the same time. I'd better hurry or all the cold turkey will have gone."

He left her. The record player had started up. A different music filled the air and after the jig of the accordion and the scrape of the fiddle, it sounded strangely alien and sophisticated, and reminded Flora of a life that seemed to have finished a long time ago.

Dance in the old-fashioned way,
Won't you stay in my arms.

Antony was dancing with a girl in a blue dress; Brian Stoddart, with the most elegant woman in the room, all black crepe and dangling earrings.

Just melt against my skin
And let me feel your heart.

She knew that Hugh would come and find her because he had promised. But after a little she began to feel ridiculous sitting on the stairs waiting to be claimed, and slightly anxious, like a young girl afraid of being stood up on her first date. The young man from Ardnamurchan did not return and Flora wondered if he had joined in the fishing discussion. Finally, unable to contain her impatience, she got up and went to search for Hugh herself. She went from one room to another, casually at first, and then less casually, and finally without shame, asking anybody she happened to find herself standing next to.

"Have you see Hugh Kyle? You haven't seen Hugh anywhere, have you?"

But nobody had seen him. She never found him. And it was not until later that she learned that there had been a telephone call, that a premature baby was on its way, and Hugh had already gone.

The storm blew up during the course of the evening, and by the early hours of the morning had reached full force. For Tuppy's guests, putting on cloaks and coats preparatory to departure, it came as something of a shock. They had arrived on a calm evening, and now they had to leave in this. The opening and shutting of the front door caused gusts of cold air to sweep into the house. Smoke billowed from the hall fire and the long curtains bellied in the draught. Outside, the garden shone with black rain, the gravel was puddled, and the air filled with flying leaves and small branches and twigs newly torn from trees.

At last, running down the streaming steps, hunched into coats and scarves, heads bent against the wind, the last couple left. Antony shut the front door and, with some ceremony, locked and bolted it. The household trailed exhaustedly up to bed.

But there was too much noise for sleep. The seaward side of the house took the brunt of the storm's fury. The squalls came in great gusts, shaking the very structure of the solid old walls, and the voice of the wind rose to something very like a scream. And beyond all this, distant but menacing, was the surging boom of long rollers driven inshore by the swell of the turbulent ocean to smash themselves into clouds of white spume on the margins of Fhada sands.

Flora curled up for comfort, wide-eyed, dry-eyed, and listened to it. She had finished the evening with a mug of black coffee, and the thud of her own heart was as disturbing as a clock which chimes through the dark hours of the night. Her head was filled with jigging music, with random images, with voices. She had never lain so wide awake.

The first gray rays of dawn were beginning to seep into the sky before she finally fell into a restless and dream-haunted sleep, peopled by strangers. When she awoke, it was day once more, still dark and gray to be sure, but the endless night was behind her. She opened her eyes, grateful for the cold light, and saw Antony standing by her bed.

He looked weary and unshaven and slightly bleary-eyed, his copper head tousled as though he had not taken the time to comb it. He wore a tweedy turtleneck sweater and an old pair of corduroys, and he carried two steaming nursery mugs and he said, "Good morning."

Flora dragged herself out of sleep. Automatically she reached for her watch, but, "It's half past ten," he told her. "I brought you some coffee. I thought you might need it."

"Oh, how kind." She stretched, tried to blink the sleep out of her eyes, pulled herself up on the pillows. He handed her the mug and she wrapped her hands around it and sat holding it, yawning.

He found her dressing gown and put it round her shoulders, turned on the electric fire, and came to sit beside her on the edge of the bed.

"How are you feeling?"

"Ghastly," she told him.

"Drink some coffee and you'll feel better."

She did so, and it was scalding and strong. After a little she asked, "Is everybody up?"

"They're gradually surfacing. Jason's still asleep, I shouldn't think he'll appear till lunchtime. Isobel's been up for

an hour, and I doubt whether Mrs. Watty and Watty went to
bed at all. Anyway, they've been beavering away since eight
o'clock this morning, and by the time you put in an appearance, I doubt if you'd realize that there's been a party at all."

"I should have got up and come to help."

"I'd have let you sleep, only this arrived by the morning
post." He put his hand into his back trouser pocket and produced an envelope. "I thought perhaps you'd want to see it."

She took it from him. She saw her father's handwriting,
the Cornwall postmark. It was addressed to Miss Rose
Schuster.

Flora laid down the mug of coffee. She said, "It's from my
father."

"I thought it might be. You wrote to him?"

"Yes. Last Sunday. After you'd gone back to Edinburgh."
She looked at him in apology and went on feeling guilty, trying
to explain. "I had to tell somebody, Antony, and you'd made
me promise not to tell anyone here. But I figured my father
didn't count. So I wrote to him."

"I hadn't realized the need to confess was so strong. Did
you tell him everything?"

"Yes."

"I wouldn't think he'd be very impressed."

"No," Flora agreed miserably. She began to slit the envelope.

"Do you want me to go away and let you read it in
peace?"

"No, I'd much rather you stayed." Cautiously, she unfolded the letter. She saw, "My dearest Flora."

"Well, I'm still his dearest Flora so perhaps he isn't too
upset."

"Did you think he would be?"

"I don't know. I don't think I thought about it."

With the comforting presence of Antony beside her, she
read the letter:

Seal Cottage
Lanyon
Lands End
Cornwall

My dearest Flora,

I have already addressed the envelope of this letter as
instructed by you. It is on the desk beside me now, proof
that a lie, however well-meant, can never be contained or
controlled but spreads like a disease, inevitably involving
more and more people.

I was glad that you wrote to me at such length. Your
letter took some reading and as you seem anxious for some
sort of response, I shall try to deal with your problems in a
fairly abbreviated way.

Firstly, Rose. The coincidence of your meeting like
that was something that I always hoped would never happen. But it did, and so I owe you an explanation.

Your mother and I decided to separate within a year
of getting married. We would have parted then and there,
only she was eight months pregnant, and all the arrangements for the baby's birth had been made locally, so we
continued to live together for that last month. During that
time, we agreed that she should have the custody of the
child, and bring it up by herself. She was going back to
make a home with her parents, and she seemed quite
happy to do this.

But of course, it wasn't a baby, it was twins. When
Pamela was told, she became quite hysterical, and by the
time I was allowed to see her, had made up her mind that
she could not possibly cope with two babies. She would
take one. And I would take the other.

The prospect, I don't mind admitting, appalled me.
But Pamela, with that announcement off her chest, dried
her eyes, and the babies, in two bassinets, were trundled
into the room.

It was the first time either of us had seen you. Rose

lay like a little flower, sleeping, with silky dark hair and seashell fists curled up under her chin. You, on the other hand, were bawling your head off and seemed to be covered with spots. Your mother was no fool. She reached out for Rose, Sister put the sleeping baby into her arms, and the choice had been made.

But I made a choice too. I couldn't bear you crying. You sounded heartbroken. I picked you up out of your crib, and held you up and you gave a great burp and stopped crying. You opened your eyes and we looked at each other. I'd never held a child before that was so tiny and so new, and I was completely unprepared for the effect it would have on me. I found myself filled with pride, fiercely possessive. You were my baby. Nothing and nobody was going to take you away from me.

So that is how it all came about. Should I have told you? I never knew the answer. Probably I should. But you were such a happy child, so complete and self-contained, it seemed insane to introduce unnecessary questions and possible insecurities into your young life. Pamela had gone, taking Rose with her. The divorce went through and I never saw either of them again.

Heredity and environment are puzzling factors. Rose sounds as though she were turning into a very passable replica of her mother. And yet I cannot allow myself to believe that under different circumstances, you would have turned into someone selfish, thoughtless, or dishonest.

Which is why your present situation leaves me so concerned. Not just for yourself and the young man, but for the Armstrongs. They sound the sort of people who deserve more than an empty deception. I advise you both to tell them the truth as soon as you can. The consequences may be unhappy, but you have no one to blame but yourselves.

When you have done this, I want you to come home. This—as I used to say when you were small—is not an asking, but a telling. There are many things we need to talk about, and you can take a little time to lick your wounds and recover from what has obviously been a traumatic episode.

Marcia sends her love with mine. You are my own child, and I am your loving

Father

She came to the end and wondered if she was going to cry. Antony waited. Flora looked up into his sympathetic face.

She said, "I've got to go home."

"To Cornwall?"

"Yes."

"When?"

"Right away."

She handed him the letter to read. While he did this, she finished her coffee and got out of bed, pulling on her dressing gown and tying the cord. She went to the window and saw the low scud of black clouds. The tide had reached the flood, and cold gray water broke and streamed over the rocks beyond the garden. A few tattered gulls braved the weather, their wings banked to the wind. The lawn below the window was littered with leaves and the remains of broken slate which had blown from some roof.

Antony said, "That's a nice letter."

"He's a nice man."

"I feel I should come with you. Take the brunt of the storm."

Flora was touched. She turned from the window to reassure him. "There's no need. Besides, you have enough problems of your own to sort out. Right here."

"Do you want to go today?"

"Yes. Perhaps I can get a train from Tarbole."

"The London train leaves at one o'clock."

"Would you drive me to Tarbole?"

"I'd drive you to the ends of the earth if it would help."

"Tarbole will do very nicely. And now I must get dressed. I must go and see Tuppy."

"I'll leave you." He laid down the letter, picked up the two empty mugs, and made for the door.

"Antony," she said. He stopped and turned back. She took off the engagement ring. It was a little tight, and it took some effort to get it over her knuckle, but it was off at last. She went to lay it in his hand, and then reached up to kiss his cheek.

"You'd better put it somewhere safe. One day, you're going to need it again."

"I don't know. I can't help feeling that it's not very lucky."

Flora said encouragingly, "You're just a superstitious Highlander. Where's your thrifty streak? Just think how much it cost."

He grinned, and put it into his pocket. "I'll be downstairs when you want me," he told her.

She dressed and tidied her room, as though to leave it neat were the only thing that mattered. She picked up the letter from her father, and went out of the room and down the passage to where, she knew, Tuppy was waiting for her.

She knocked on the door. Tuppy called "Yes?" and Flora went in. Tuppy was reading the morning paper, but now she laid it down and took off her spectacles. Across the room, their eyes met, and she looked so grave that Flora's heart sank, and perhaps this showed in her face, for Tuppy smiled, and said lovingly, "Flora!" and the relief of not being called "Rose" any longer was so great that Flora simply shut the door and went across the room like a homing pigeon, straight into Tuppy's arms.

"I don't know what to say. I don't know how to say I'm sorry. I don't know how to ask you to forgive me."

"I don't want you to start apologizing. What you and Antony did was very naughty, but I've had the night to think it over, and I realize now that you did it with the best intentions in the world. But then, the road to hell is paved with good intentions, and I was so angry with Antony last night, I really could have slapped him."

"Yes, he told me."

"I suppose he thought I was on my last gasp, and ready to accept anything, even a lie. And as for Rose, thank goodness he's not going to marry her. Any girl who could treat Antony the way she did—running away with another man—without even having the good manners to explain. I think it was very thoughtless and cruel."

"That was one of the reasons I came to Fernrigg. Because I wanted to help Antony."

"I know. I understand. And I think it was very sweet of you. And how you've carried on all this week, being Rose, is beyond my comprehension. And being ill in the middle of it. You really have had a wretched time."

"But you forgive me?"

Tuppy kissed her soundly. "My dear, I could never do anything else. Flora, or Rose, you are yourself. You've brought us all so much pleasure, so much happiness. My only sadness is that you and Antony don't seem to want to fall in love and get married. That's much more disappointing than having you tell me all those dreadful lies. But then, I know, falling in love isn't anything you can manipulate. Thank heavens. How boring life would become if it were. And now don't let's talk about it any more. I want to hear all about last night, and . . ."

"Tuppy."

"Yes?" Tuppy's blue eyes were suddenly watchful.

"This morning I had a letter from my father. Antony may have told you, he's a schoolmaster, he lives in Cornwall. I wrote to him at the beginning of the week, because I felt I had to tell someone what was happening, and of course I couldn't tell any of you."

"And what does your father say?"

"I thought you'd better read it."

In silence, Tuppy put on her spectacles, and took the letter from Flora. She read it through, from beginning to end. When she had finished, "What an extraordinary story," she murmured. "But what a very nice man he must be."

"Yes, he is."

"Are you going to go home?"

"Yes, I have to. Today. There's a train at one. Antony says he'll drive me to Tarbole."

Tuppy's face became all at once drawn and old, her mouth bunched, her eyes shadowed. "I can't bear you to leave us."

"I don't want to go."

"But you'll come back. Promise me that you'll come back. Come back and see us all, whenever you want. Fernrigg will be waiting for you. You only have to say the word."

"You still want me?"

"We want you because we love you. It's as simple as that." Having made this clear, she reverted to her usual practical manner. "And your father's right. I think you must go home for a little."

"I always hate saying goodbye. And I feel so badly about Jason and Isobel and the Wattys and Nurse. They've been so kind, and I can't imagine how I'm going to tell them . . ."

"I don't see why you should have to tell them anything. Just say a letter has come for you, and you have to leave. And when Antony comes back from the station, he can explain it to them all. He got you into this situation and that, for certain, is the very least he can do."

"But all the people at the party last night?"

"The news will filter through the grapevine that the engagement is off. It will be a nine-day wonder, that's all."

"But they'll have to know, sooner or later, that I was never Rose. They'll have to know sometime."

"That bit of information will doubtless filter through too, and they'll wonder a little and then forget about it. After all, it isn't really that important. Nobody's been hurt. Nobody's heart has been broken."

"You make it sound so simple."

"The truth always simplifies everything. And we have Hugh to thank for that. If it hadn't been for Hugh, taking charge, goodness knows how long this stupid farce would have gone on. We owe him everything. We always seem to be in his debt, if not on one score, then another. He's very fond of you,

Flora. I wonder if you realize that? You probably don't because he's naturally shy of showing his emotions, but . . ."

The words died away. Flora sat intensely still, staring down at her own clasped hands. The knuckles showed white and her dark lashes made smudges against the sudden pallor of her face.

With a perception sharpened by years of dealing with young people, Tuppy caught her distress. It chilled the air, and stemmed from some emotion far deeper than a natural reluctance to say goodbye. Much concerned, Tuppy laid her own hand over Flora's and found it icy cold.

Flora did not look up. "It's all right," she said, sounding as if she were trying to reassure Tuppy about some unbearable pain she was suffering.

"My dear child, you must tell me. Has someone upset you? Is it Antony?"

"No, of course not . . ."

Tuppy cast her mind back, searching for clues. They had been talking about Hugh, and . . . Hugh. Hugh? As though Flora had spoken the name aloud, Tuppy knew.

"It's Hugh."

"Oh, Tuppy, don't talk about it."

"But of course we must talk about it. I can't bear you to be so unhappy. Are . . . are you in love with him?"

Flora looked up, her eyes dark as bruises. "I think I must be," she said, sounding completely uncertain.

Tuppy was astounded. Not because Flora had fallen in love with Hugh, which Tuppy found totally understandable. But because it had happened without Tuppy knowing all about it.

"But I can't imagine, when . . ."

"No," said Flora, suddenly blunt. "Neither can I. I can't imagine when it happened, or why, or how. I only know that it can't have any future."

"Why can it have no future?"

"Because Hugh's the man he is. He's been hurt once and he doesn't intend getting hurt again. He's made a life for himself, he doesn't want to share it, and he doesn't need another wife. He won't let himself need one. And even if he did, he doesn't seem to think he has enough to offer her . . . I mean material things."

"You appear to have talked it over in some detail."

"Not really. It was just last night, before the party. I'd been drinking champagne, and somehow that made it easier to talk."

"Does he realize how you feel?"

"Tuppy, I have a little pride left. Short of flinging myself at his head, I seem to have reached the end of the road."

"Did he talk about Diana?"

"Not last night, but he has told me about her."

"He would never have done that unless he felt very close to you."

"You can be close to a person, but that doesn't mean you're in love with them."

"Hugh is stubborn and very proud," Tuppy warned her.

"You don't have to tell me that." Flora smiled, but there wasn't much joy behind it. "Last night, we were going to have supper together. He said he wasn't going to dance with me because everybody else would want to dance with me, but we'd have supper together. So stupid to let it be so important . . . but it was important, Tuppy. And I thought perhaps it was important to him, too. But when the time came, he'd gone. There was a phone call, a baby coming. I don't know. But he'd simply gone."

"My dear, he's a doctor."

"Couldn't he have told me? Couldn't he have said good-bye?"

"Perhaps he couldn't find you. Perhaps he couldn't take time to find you."

"I shouldn't mind, should I? But it did matter, terribly."

"Will you be able to go away, and forget him?"

"I don't know. I don't seem to know the answer to anything. I must be out of my mind."

"On the contrary, I think you are exceptionally wise.

Hugh is a very special person, but he keeps his qualities well hidden beneath that manner, that sharply honed tongue of his. It takes a person of considerable perception to realize that the qualities are really there."

"What am I going to do?" Flora spoke quietly, but it sounded to Tuppy like a cry from the heart.

"What you were always going to do. Go home to your father. Pack your clothes and find Antony and say goodbye and drive to the station. It's as easy as that."

"Easy?"

"Life is so complicated that sometimes it's the only thing left to do. Now give me a kiss and run along. Forget everything that's happened. And when you come back to Fernrigg, we'll start all over again, with new beginnings."

"I can never thank you properly." They kissed. "I don't know the right sort of words."

"The best way to thank me is to come back. That's all I want."

They were disturbed by small sounds from the end of the bed. Sukey had decided to wake up. Her claws scratched the silk of the eiderdown as she made her way cautiously up the length of the bed, apparently with the sole intention of clambering onto Flora's knee and reaching up to lick her face.

"Sukey! That's the first time you've been nice to me." Flora gathered the little dog up into her arms and pressed a kiss on the top of Sukey's head. "Why is she suddenly being so nice?"

"Sukey takes notions," said Tuppy, as though that explained everything. "Perhaps she realizes that you're not Rose after all. Or perhaps she just wanted to say goodbye to you. Is that what you wanted, my darling?"

Sukey, thus addressed, forgot about Flora and went to curl up in the crook of Tuppy's arm.

Flora said, "I must go."

"Yes. You mustn't keep Antony waiting."

"Goodbye, Tuppy."

"It's not goodbye. It's au revoir."

For the last time, Flora got up off the bed, and went to the door. But as she opened it, Tuppy spoke again.

"Flora."

Flora looked back. "Yes?"

"I never thought of pride as a sin. To me it's always seemed rather an admirable quality. But two proud people, misunderstanding, can make for a tragedy."

"Yes," said Flora. There did not seem to be anything else to say. She went out of the room and shut the door.

It took so little time to pack, so little time to clear her room of all traces of her presence. When she had finished it appeared impersonal, stripped—ready and waiting for the next person who should come to Fernrigg to stay. She left the white dress that she had worn the night before hanging on the outside of the wardrobe door. It was creased now, molded to Flora's shape, grubby around the hem, and stained where someone had spilled champagne down the front of the skirt. She opened the cupboard and took out her coat. With this over her arm, and carrying her suitcase, she went downstairs.

Everything was back to normal. The hall looked as it always did, furniture back in place, the fire smoldering, Plummer sitting beside its warmth, waiting for someone to take him for a walk. From the drawing room came the sound of voices. Flora set down her case and her coat, and went in and found Isobel and Antony standing by the fire deep in conversation. This ceased instantly as Flora appeared, and they stood there, with their faces turned towards her.

Antony said, "I've told Aunt Isobel."

"I'm glad you know," said Flora, and meant it.

Isobel appeared to be stunned by confusion. It had taken her some time to understand what Antony had spent the last fifteen minutes trying to explain to her. She was tired and suffering from lack of sleep, and in no condition to listen to, let alone comprehend, the long and involved story.

But one fact was sadly clear. Rose—no, Flora—was leaving. Going. Today. Now. Just like that. Antony was going to drive her to Tarbole to catch the London train. It was all so sudden and unexpected that Isobel felt quite faint. Now, seeing Flora so pale and composed, it began to be real.

"There's no need to go," Isobel told her, knowing it was hopeless but still wanting to try to persuade her to stay. "It doesn't matter *who* you are. We don't want you to go."

"That's very sweet of you. But I must."

"The letter from your father. Antony told me."

Flora said to Antony, "What about the others?"

"I've told them you're leaving, but I haven't told them you're not Rose. I thought that could wait till later. It might make things a little easier for you." She smiled her thanks. "And Mrs. Watty's packing you a box lunch. She has no faith in restaurant cars."

"I'm ready when you are."

"I'll tell them," said Antony. "They want to say goodbye." He went out of the room.

Flora went over to Isobel's side. "You'll come back, won't you?" said Isobel.

"Tuppy's invited me."

"I wish you were going to marry Antony."

"I wish I was too, just to belong to such a marvelous family. But it can't work out that way."

Isobel sighed. "Things never seem to work out the way you want them to. You think they're all beautifully arranged, and then in front of your eyes, they all fall to pieces."

Like my flower arrangements, thought Flora. She heard the voices of the others, coming down the passage from the kitchen. "Goodbye, Isobel." They kissed with great affection, Isobel still not quite clear how this unsatisfactory situation had come about.

"You will come back?'

"Of course I will"

Somehow, the last of the farewells were accomplished. They all stood in the hall with sad faces and said what a shame it was she had to leave, but of course, she would be back. Nobody seemed to notice that she was no longer wearing Antony's engagement ring, and if they did, they made no com-

ment. Flora found herself kissing Nurse, and then Mrs. Watty,
who pressed a bag containing plum cake and apples into the
pocket of Flora's coat. Finally Jason. She knelt to his height
and they hugged, his arms so tight around her neck that she
thought he would never let her go.

"I want to come to the station with you."

"No," said Antony.

"But I want . . ."

"I don't want you to come," Flora told him quickly. "I
hate saying goodbye at stations, and I always cry and that
would be dreadful for both of us. And thank you for teaching
me how to do 'Strip the Willow.' It was the best dance of the
whole evening."

"You won't forget how to do it?"

"I shall remember for the rest of my life."

Behind her, Antony opened the front door, and the cold
wind flowed in like a sluice of icy water. Carrying her case he
went down the steps to the car, and she ran down after him, her
head bent against the rain. He flung her suitcase into the back
of the car, and helped her in and slammed the door behind her.

Braving the weather, they had all come out into the open
to see her off in style, with Plummer standing at the front of the
little group, looking as though he expected to have his photograph taken. The wind tore at Nurse's apron, blew Isobel's hair
into confusion, but still they stayed there, waving as the car
came around in a circle and sped away from the house down
the spine-jolting, potholed drive. Flora twisted around in her
seat and waved through the back window until the car turned
into the road and the house and its occupants were lost from
sight.

It was over. Flora turned and slumped in her seat, her
hands deep in her pockets. Her fingers closed over Mrs. Watty's
"box lunch." She felt the shape of the slice of cake, the round
firmness of an apple. She stared ahead, through the streaming
windscreen.

But there was nothing to be seen. The rain closed in on
them. Antony drove with the side lights on, and every now and

then a large wet sheep materialized out of the gloom, or they passed the side lights of another small car, going in the opposite direction. The wind was as strong as ever.

"What a horrible day to be leaving," said Antony.

She thought of the day they had climbed the hill; of the islands, looking magical, floating on the summer sea; of the crystal air and the snow-capped peaks of the Cuillins. She said, "I'd rather it was like this. It makes it easier to go."

They came down the hill into Tarbole and saw the harbor full of boats, stormbound by the weather.

"What time is it, Antony?"

"A quarter past twelve. We're far too early, but perhaps it doesn't matter. We can go and drink coffee with Sandy, just the way we did that first morning when we arrived from Edinburgh."

"It seems so long ago. A lifetime."

"Tuppy meant it when she asked you to come back."

"You'll take care of her, won't you, Antony? You won't let anything happen to her?"

"I'll keep her safe for you," he promised. "She can't forgive me, poor Tuppy, for not cutting my losses and marrying you, and bearing you back to Fernrigg as my bride."

"She knows it could never happen."

"Yes." He sighed. "She knows."

They were into the town now, running alongside the harbor. Waves broke over the low stone wall and the road was awash with salt water, the gutters choked with dirty foam. There was the familiar smell of fish and diesel oil, and the scream of air brakes tore the air as a huge lorry came grinding down the hill from Fort William.

They came to the crossroads, and then by the bank where Flora had once illicitly parked the van. The little station, gray stone, soot-stained, waited for them. The lines of the railway curved away beyond the platform, out of sight. Antony switched off the engine. They got out of the car and went into the ticket office, Antony carrying Flora's suitcase. Despite her protestations, he bought her a ticket back to Cornwall.

"But it's so expensive, and I can pay for it myself."

"Oh, don't talk balls," he said rudely, because he was feeling emotional and didn't want to show it.

Making out the ticket took some time. They stood and waited. A small fire burned, but the office smelt musty. Peeling posters exhorted them to go to Scottish resorts for their holidays; to take boat trips down the Clyde; to spend weeks at Glorious Rothsay. Neither of them spoke for the simple reason that there didn't seem to be anything left to say.

The ticket was at last ready. Antony took it and gave it to Flora. "To do the thing properly I should have bought a return, and then we'd be sure of your coming back."

"I'll come back." She put the ticket into her bag. "Antony, I don't want you to wait."

"But I must put you onto the train."

"I don't want to wait. I hate goodbyes and I hate railway stations. Like I said to Jason, I always make a fool of myself and cry. I'd hate to do that."

"But you've got forty minutes to wait till it leaves."

"I'll be all right. Please go now."

"All right." But he sounded unconvinced. "If that's what you want."

Leaving her case in the ticket office, they went out into the station yard. By his car, he said, "This is it, then?"

"Tuppy said au revoir."

"You'll write? You'll keep in touch?"

"Of course."

They kissed. "You know something?" said Antony.

She smiled. "Yes, I know. I'm a super woman."

He got into his car and drove away, very fast, and almost instantly seemed to have disappeared around the corner by the bank. Flora was alone. The rain was thin, but steady and very wetting. Above her, the wind banged about at chimney pots and television aerials.

There came a moment of hesitation.

Two proud people, misunderstanding, can make for tragedy.

She began to walk.

The hill, black with rain, seemed steep as the side of a roof.
The gutters ran like waterfalls. As she climbed up out of the
shelter of the town the force of the wind struck like a solid
thing, causing Flora to lose her breath and her balance. The air
was filled with blown spume and she could feel its salt on her
cheeks and taste it on her mouth. When she finally reached the
house at the top of the hill, she stopped at the gate to get her
breath. Looking back, she saw the gray and turbulent sea,
empty of boats. She saw the tall columns of spray rearing up
beyond the far harbor wall.

She opened the gate and closed it behind her and went up
the sloping path to the front door. Inside the porch, she rang
the bell and waited. Her shoes were sodden and the hem of her
coat dripped onto the tiled floor. She rang the bell again.

She heard someone call, "I'm just on my way . . ." and
the next instant the door was flung open and she was faced by a
woman of indeterminate age, spectacled and flustered. She
wore a flowered pinafore and bedroom slippers that looked like
dead rabbits, and with the certainty of someone who has just
been formally introduced, Flora knew that this was Jessie Mc-
Kenzie.

"Yes?"

"Is Dr. Kyle in?"

"He's still in surgery."

"Oh. When will he be finished?"

"I couldn't say for sure. We're all at sixes and sevens this
morning. Surgery's usually at ten o'clock, but this morning,
because of the accident, the doctor wasn't able to get started
'till half past eleven . . ."

"Accident?" said Flora faintly.

"Did you not hear?" Jessie was agog with the horrific
news. "Dr. Kyle had not even started on his breakfast when the
telephone rang, and it was the harbormaster, and seemingly,
there'd been an accident on one of the fishing boats; a derrick
cable snapped and a muckle load of fish boxes fell to the deck,

right on top of one of the young laddies working there. It crushed his leg. Seemingly, it was a mangled mess . . ."

She was unstoppable, settled down to a good gossip, with her arms folded across her pinafored breasts. Jessie was not fat, but her unsupported body appeared to be slipping in all directions. She was obviously a woman who put comfort before beauty and yet, Flora knew instinctively, should there be a whist drive or a church soiree in the offing, Jessie would be the first to lace herself into a formidable all-in-one, in the same way that some people only wear their teeth when company is expected.

". . . Dr. Kyle was there first thing, but they had to get the ambulance to take the poor laddie to Lochgarry . . . and Dr. Kyle went too . . . an operation, of course. He wasn't home till the back of eleven."

It became necessary to interrupt.

"Would it be possible to see him?"

"Well, I couldn't say for sure. Mind, I saw Nurse on her way home, so maybe surgery's finished. And the doctor's not had a bite to eat all morning. I've a pot of soup on the store, and I'm expecting him any moment . . ." She peered at Flora, her eyes, behind their round spectacles, bright with curiosity. "Are you a patient?" She probably thought Flora was pregnant. "Is it urgent?"

"Yes, it is urgent, but I'm not a patient. I have to catch a train." The moments were slipping by and Flora began to be desperate. "Perhaps I could go and see if he's still busy."

"Yes." Jessie thought this over. "Maybe you could."

"How do I get to the surgery?"

"Just follow the wee path round the house."

Flora began to back away. "Thank you. I . . ."

"It's a terrible morning," Jessie observed, conversationally.

"Yes. Terrible." And with this, she made her escape out into the rain.

The concrete path led around the side of the house and beneath a covered way to the surgery door. Flora went in and found it empty, but muddy footmarks all over the polished linoleum, chairs standing around the walls, and a few disarranged magazines on a table bore witness to the queues which had tramped through during the course of the morning. There was a smell of disinfectant and wet mackintoshes. At the far end of the room, a small office had been formed by means of glass partitions, and inside was a desk and filing cabinets and boxes of card indexes.

The door with his name on it stood at the far end of the long room, and Flora went toward it, her wet shoes leaving a fresh track of damp footprints behind her. She found it in her heart to be sorry for whomever had to clean the floor at the end of the day.

With a conscious gathering of courage, she knocked at the door. There did not seem to be any reply, so she knocked again, and from within his voice bellowed, "I said, *Come in!*" It was not a good start. Flora went in.

He did not even look up from his desk. She could only see the top of his head, and that he was busy writing something.

"Yes?"

Flora shut the door behind her with a small slam. He looked up. For a moment he appeared to be transfixed, and then he took off his spectacles and sat back in his chair the better to stare at her.

"What are you doing here?"

"I've come to say goodbye."

She was already wishing she had not come. His office was impersonal and unnerving. It offered neither encouragement nor comfort. His desk was enormous, the walls were the color of margarine, the linoleum brown. She caught sight of a case of sinister-looking instruments and hastily averted her glance.

"But where are you going?"

"I'm going back to Cornwall. To my father."

"When did you come to this decision?"

"I had a letter from him this morning. I . . . I wrote to him at the beginning of the week to tell him what was happening. Where I was. What I was doing."

"And what did he have to say to that?"

"He said I had to go home."

A glimmer of amusement crossed Hugh's face. "Are you in for a hiding?"

"No of course not. He's not angry. He's just being very kind. I told Tuppy, and she said that she thought I should go. And I've said goodbye to everybody at Fernrigg and Antony brought me to Tarbole in his car. I've got my ticket and my suitcase is at the station, but the train doesn't leave till one, so I thought I'd come and say goodbye to you."

In silence, Hugh laid down his pen, and stood up. All at once he seemed as enormous as his ponderous desk, in proportion to it. He came around to where Flora stood, and sat on the edge of the desk, bringing their eyes to the same level. She thought he looked very tired, but, unlike Antony, he had apparently found time to shave. She wondered if, between the premature baby and the young boy with the crushed leg, he had had any sleep at all.

He said, "I'm sorry about last night. Did you wonder what had happened to me?"

"I thought you'd forgotten about having supper with me. And then someone told me about the phone call."

"I did forget," Hugh confessed. "When the call came through, I forgot about everything else. I always do. It wasn't until I was halfway there that I remembered our date, and then, of course, it was too late."

She said, "It didn't matter," but it didn't sound, even to Flora, very convincing.

"Believe it or not, it mattered to me."

"Was the baby all right?"

"Yes, a little girl. Very small, but she'll make it."

"And the boy, this morning, on the fishing boat?"

"How did you know about that?"

"I've been talking to your housekeeper. She told me."

"Yes, she would," said Hugh dryly. "We won't know about the boy for a day or two."

"You mean, he may die?"

"No, he's not going to die. But he may lose his leg."

"I am sorry."

Hugh folded his arms. "How long are you going to stay with your father?"

"I don't know."

"What will you do then?"

"Like I told you last night, I suppose. Go back to London. Look for a job. Look for somewhere to live."

"Will you come back to Fernrigg?"

"Tuppy's asked me."

"But will you?"

"I don't know. It depends."

"On what?"

She looked him straight in the eye. "On you, I suppose," she told him.

"Oh, Flora . . ."

"Hugh, don't push me away. We've been so close. We can surely talk."

"How old are you?"

"Twenty-two. And don't say you're old enough to be my father, because you're not."

"I wasn't going to say that. But I am old enough to recognize the fact that you have everything in front of you, and I'm not going to be the man who takes it away from you. You're young and you're beautiful and very special. You may imagine that you're marvelously mature, but in truth, your life is only just beginning. Somewhere, some time, you'll find a young man waiting for you. Someone who hasn't been married before, and has more to offer you than second best—who one day will be able to afford to give you all the good things of life that you truly deserve."

"Perhaps I don't want them."

"Mine would be no sort of a life for you." He was trying to be very kind. "I tried to make you see that last night."

"And I told you that if somebody loved you, that would make it the right sort of life."

"I already made that mistake."

"But I'm not Diana. I'm me. And that terrible thing I once said to you was absolutely true. By dying the way she did, Diana destroyed you. She's destroyed your trust in people, and your confidence in yourself. And she's made you so that to stop yourself from being hurt, you're prepared to hurt other people. I think that's a horrible way to be."

"Flora, I don't want to hurt you. Can't you understand? Supposing I did love you? Supposing I loved you too much to let you destroy yourself?"

Bleakly Flora stared at him. It seemed an extraordinary time to start talking about love, right in the middle of a quarrel. For they were quarreling, momentously, their voices raised to a pitch where, if Jessie McKenzie were sufficiently curious to put an ear to the wall, she would be able to hear every word. For Hugh's sake, Flora hoped that that was not happening.

She said at last, "I don't destroy that easily. If I've survived this last week, I can survive anything."

"You said that Tuppy had asked you back to Fernrigg."

"Yes."

"Will you come?"

"I told you, it depends . . ."

"That was a ridiculous thing to say. Now, when you do come . . ."

Flora lost her temper. There seemed to be no way of breaking down his stubborn pride without actually going to the lengths of telling him that he was behaving like a fool. "Hugh, I'm either coming back to you, or I'm never coming back at all."

The silence that followed that outburst was fraught with the astonishment of both of them. Then Flora stumbled on, with the hopeless despair of one who knows that she has burnt her boats behind her. "Though why I should bother, I can't imagine. I don't think you even like me very much." She glared at him crossly. "And your tie's coming undone," she added, as if this were the last straw.

It was, too. Perhaps he had dressed quickly and carelessly. Perhaps, during the course of the morning, it had simply slipped of its own accord, the way her father's so often did, and . . .

Her reflections came to a dead halt as she suddenly realized the significance of what she had so thoughtlessly said. She stared at the wretched tie, waiting for Hugh to pig-headedly straighten it for himself. She decided that if he did this, she would walk out of this room, and down the hill, and she would catch the train and go away, and never think about him again.

But he made no move to do anything about the offending necktie. His arms remained rigidly folded across his chest. He said at last, "Well, why don't you remedy the situation?"

Carefully, slowly, Flora did so. She pulled up the knot, set it neatly in place, dead in the center of his collar. It was done. She stood back. He still didn't move. It took more determination than she would have believed possible, just to look up and meet his eyes. She saw him, for the first time disarmed and defenseless as a very young man. He said her name and held out his arms, and the next instant, with a sound that was halfway between a sob and a shout of triumph, Flora was in them.

She said, "I love you."

"You impossible child."

"I love you."

"What am I going to do with you?"

"You could marry me. I'll make a marvelous doctor's wife. Just think of it."

"I've been thinking of nothing else for the past three days."

"I love you."

"I thought I could let you go, but I can't."

"You're going to have to let me go, because I've got a train to catch."

"But you'll come back?"

"To you."

"How soon?"

"Three days, four days."

"Too long."

"No longer."

"I shall ring you up every night at your father's house."

"He'll be impressed."

"And when you do come, I'll be on the station platform, with a bunch of roses and an engagement ring."

"Oh, Hugh, not an engagement ring. I'm sorry, but I've had enough of engagement rings. You couldn't make it a wedding ring?"

He began to laugh. "You're not only impossible, you're intolerable."

"Yes, I know. Isn't it awful?"

He said it at last. "I love you."

Jessie was anxious about the pot of soup. If the doctor delayed a moment longer, it was going to be boiled to nothing. She was already partaking of her own midday meal: leftover potatoes, a leg of cold chicken, and a tin of baked beans. Her favorite. For afters she was going to eat up the tinned plums and custard and then make a strong and restoring cup of tea.

She was about to pick up the chicken leg in her fingers (it didn't count, provided you were on your own) when she heard voices, and footsteps running up the path from the surgery. Before she had time to dispose of the chicken leg the back door was thrown open, and Dr. Kyle stood before her, holding by the hand the woman in the navy blue coat who had come asking for him.

The woman was smiling, her hair blown by the wind all over her face. And Dr. Kyle's face was a picture. Jessie was at a loss. By rights he should be exhausted, weighed down by troubles and hard work, treading heavily up from the surgery for his bowl of soup, the sustaining broth that she, Jessie, had concocted for him.

Instead, here he was, all smiles and bouncing good spirits and looking as though he were good for another forty-eight hours without a wink of sleep.

"Jessie!"

She dropped the chicken bone, but he didn't seem to have noticed, anyway.

"Jessie, I'm going down to the railway station, I'll be back in ten minutes."

"Righty ho, Dr. Kyle."

It was still raining but, although he wore no raincoat, it didn't seem to bother him. Out he went again with the woman still in tow, leaving the back door standing open and a wind like a knife pouring into Jessie's kitchen.

"How about your soup?" she called after him, but it was too late. He had gone. She got up to shut the door. Then she went through to the front of the house, and, cautiously, not wishing to be observed, opened the front door. She saw them going away from her down the path. They had their arms around each other and they were both laughing, oblivious of the wind and the rain. She watched them go through the gate and start down the hill towards the town. Their heads disappeared below the top of the wall, first the woman's and then Dr. Kyle's.

They were gone.

She closed the door. She thought, Well! But she knew that sooner or later, she would find someone to tell.